I Want To Write Something Funny But I'm Too Sad

Lucille Field

Also by
Lucille Field

On the Way To Wonderland

In Memory Of My Mentors

Rose Walter

David Hollander

Bea Coleman

Frieda Azark

Dorothy Klotzman

And a special remembrance for my dearest friend
Bea Kreloff

Foreword

I loved *I Want to Write Something Funny But I'm Too Sad* because I felt like I was listening in on conversations with friends I would like to have. Lucille Field's great gift is her ability to create vivid portraits of women who are aging gloriously. Her characters are smart, witty, thoughtful, and still sexy in their senior years, even though they know their days may be limited. Field often focuses on older lesbians, bringing to life a group that is almost completely invisible in the mainstream media, and even in feminist literature. It is such a rare treat to read a book that is so completely centered on women's relationships with each other, whether they are family members, mentors, lovers, or friends. This book is a treasure.

Martha Richards
Founder and Executive Director of WomenArts, who writes and lectures frequently on arts and cultural policy issues.

oooooooooooooooooooooooooooooo

Lucille Field's *I Want to Write Something Funny But I'm Too Sad* is a moving collection, full of tough stories of women making hard choices—joyfully freeing, and at other times, meeting the forces of sexism, and homophobia, not always winning. She offers complex viewpoints within the evolution of a love of music, a love of women, and a growing lesbian feminist politics of the day.

These fine narratives are stories of loyal devotion, crucial friendships, and the magnificent, transforming role of music. Field has a lean, direct voice that catches detail and dialogue on the run, and the range of lives insists on triumphant stories, full of delight in fun, food, sex, art, music, nature and lesbianism lived in community or in coupledom. Field shows political consequences experienced by many as gender oppression—violating and destructive. It's a stark picture of the dangers and the limitations of what's possible for the women, and she details complex and rebellious lives among chosen and blood family.

The novella, "The Story of Rachel," is an important witnessing of the full tragedy of this particular woman's life, told in clear-eyed and urgent sharp outline. There is a wonderful motion through all of the different experiences. The stories speak to facing the future without making death the centerpiece, and add some hilarity and a streak of wonderful ridiculousness. We can appreciate the plain good fun and gritty reality.

The title story is a refreshing take with trademark arch humor, and commentary on aging, death, and how to live as older lesbians through the end of one's life. Everything comes up here, and there is no easy answer.

In "A Match Made in Heaven," lesbian and gay friendship, and devotion to music and art gets a full hearing, literally. Ending with the words, "Hear the music, listen..." Field seems to be saying, bring it on and let the full song sing.

Beatrix Gates
Author of *Dos* and *In the Open*

Acknowledgements

I have been writing these stories for several years, most of them in the writing workshop shepherded by Karen Braziller, in Orient, New York. My splendid copy editor, Lily Sacharow, did her copy editing magic on the thirteen stories, and the fine copy editor, Amy Schroeder, did hers on the novella, "The Story of Rachel." My right arm, the poet Beatrix Gates, has helped me find my way through my writing for decades, and I am very grateful for her wisdom and skills.

My sister workshop writers in the years we were together were Jane Llewellyn Smith, who published the memoir of her teaching years at City and Country School in New York City, "Through the Passageway," before her death a few months later. The poet LB Thompson, collaborating with the artist, Ellen Wiener, created *Poems in the Suit of Diamonds,* a boxed set printed as playing cards, the poems and paintings sharing imagery and symbolism. Also in the group, was Fredrica Wachsberger, author of "In Her Own Name", the story of a nineteenth-century wife and her pursuit of financial independence.

Amei Wallach, another member of the workshop who completed a memoir of her German family and her quest to find out who they were and who she is. Added to these four books is my volume of short stories and a novella, *I Want To Write Something Funny But I'm Too Sad,* and you have poetry, two memoirs, and a book of family searches, a rich harvest of literary produce.

Joan Tennant, the MacMaven, has made the formatting of my book possible. Her expertise and judgment has been invaluable.

My daughter, Carol Elizabeth Goodman, is a wonderful writer and reader, and an insightful photographer, as you can see from the beautiful covers of both my books. And she also catches so many of my glitches, I cannot thank her enough. My family is generous with their praise and I am grateful for their support. My grandchildren, Leo and Mikey, (the poet, Mikael Berg,) are proud of their grandma, and I like that a lot.

My partner of thirty-eight years, Patsy Rogers, is steadfast in her loyalty and love, and I am so happy to be able to offer the same to her.

Author's Note

The stories and the novella in *I Want To Write Something Funny But I'm Too Sad* are fiction. The characters are fictitious, imagined, and have been created by the author.

Once again I quote the words of the great short story writer Grace Paley "...for those who write short stories...You begin by stealing people, sometimes yourself, sometimes your best friend, sometimes someone you had a delicious argument with, sometimes someone you slept with, sometimes someone you didn't care for at all. You steal that person, and then you let them talk..."

From: "The Debt She Paid," Contemporary Women's Writing 3.2 (2009, December) Special Issue: <u>Grace Paley Writing The World</u>.

Contents

ooo

The Story Of Rachel
A Novella

The Couple

One of the women who lived in the old farmhouse overlooking the bay named every tree she planted on the property. At first she gave them operatic names, for women characters suggested by the shapes of the trees. She called her weeping birch Desdemona, her weeping cherry CioCio San, and the nearby upright Japanese cherry Suzuki. The flowering plum tree was Barbarina, and the weeping blue Atlas cedar in front of the house, Sappho.

Every time there were visitors, she would take them on a tree identifying tour explaining her choices of names with a capsule description of the characters. "Desdemona," she would say, pronouncing the name in Italian, "is from Verdi's Otello, and CioCio San and Suzuki are the two women in Puccini's Madama Butterfly. CioCio San wept for the U.S. Navy lieutenant who had abandoned her while Suzuki stood by her like a rock." She would pat each tree as she spoke of it with a familiar caress. "The flower girl in Mozart's Le Nozze di Figaro is Barbarina, a pretty little girl with a sweet voice," she said fondly, patting the plum tree's trunk. "And of course, this eloquent tree," her arms outspread as if reciting, "blue as the sea around Lesbos, has to be Sappho, in Donizetti's opera."

At last count, she had named fourteen trees, having added Tosca, Rosina, Aida, Carmen, Elvira, Zerlina, Isolde, Susanna, and Turandot to the list. Running out of space, she would now buy only one tree a year, sometimes a living tree at Christmas, which she would name and plant, or a special tree, like the weeping pussy willow she just had to have. This last one she gave her own name and would shyly tell it when prodded. "This is Mimi. *Mi chiamano Mimi*," she would sing, from Puccini's La Boheme, "*ma'il mio nome é Lucia*. They call me Mimi but my name is Lucy," she translated.

When her mother died, Mimi decided to plant a tree in her memory, a white Kousa dogwood she named Bianca, her mother's name. She planted it in a corner of the property facing the water where her mother had loved to sit and watch the sailboats and windsurfers. It was the perfect spot for the white tree, so like her mother who had become, in her old age, very white—hair, skin, even her facial expression.

After her beloved piano teacher Ernesto committed suicide when he could no longer live with AIDS, she spent a very long time at several tree nurseries, searching for the right one to plant for him. When she discovered a weeping hemlock, its angular branches drooping in despair, she recognized it immediately. It became a dramatic presence in her blue garden.

Mimi was a retired public school music teacher who still gave piano lessons in the music studio she had converted from a guest bedroom. She lived with Peggy, the same partner she'd been with for thirty years. They were a lesbian couple, married in every way except legally. Their families were comfortable with the relationship, though their backgrounds were quite different: Mimi's was Italian-American and Peggy's was Irish-American. The two families mingled and interacted happily at frequent family events, Catholicism being the binding force. Holidays were worked out on a hers and hers basis, and like every couple together for a long time, they had long since ironed out most of the wrinkles.

Peggy did not much participate in Mimi's tree naming, although she was happy to go tree hunting with Mimi and to voice a generally supportive opinion. She had a secret world all her own. She knew with deep certainty that people she had loved returned to her as birds.

Living on a bluff at the bay was perfect for Peggy. She was mostly a painter of waters and landscapes, and spent many hours daily sketching a marsh, a lake, the ocean, or the bay.

Peggy never tired of the sounds and scenery when painting in her studio near the beach and watching the many shore birds and others in the area. Mimi and Peggy had bird feeders and birdbaths scattered all around the house and property, and they were rewarded with a great variety of birds year round. Because of the different bodies of water—the tidal saltwater marsh, bays and inlets, plus the many beaches—shore birds, plovers, sandpipers, and others were plentiful. Peggy loved her birds the way Mimi loved her trees—personally and intimately.

There was no preconceived plan that Peggy had about the birds, it had just happened early one fall morning. She was deeply saddened by the recent death of one of her closest friends and had been at the memorial service the day before. She was sitting on a railing at the marsh, trying to sketch her friend's face from memory. She was not an expert portrait painter, but she could do a recognizable picture if she applied herself.

Something was wrong, she could feel it. As she penciled the face, it kept changing in subtle, unexpected ways. Just when she thought she had it, a line here and there would change, a shadow would fall in an odd spot, and the shape of a feature would alter. Finally, she gave up and put the drawing aside and sat looking at the marsh grasses and eddying water. After a while, she got ready to leave. It was still very early in the morning and she wanted a pot of strong tea. She picked up her sketchpad and idly glanced at the top sheet. She blinked hard and looked again at the page—she had drawn a great blue heron's head, not her dear friend's face.

How could she have done that, she thought, *without intending to?* She shook her head in wonder and started to stand, taking a last look at the marsh and its changing light. Right there on the closest bank, stood a great blue heron, motionless, staring at her. "Oh my," she said aloud, "are you Marge? You must be Marge?" They looked at one another for a very long time until the big bird raised its wings and flew off. Peggy was sure her friend had returned to her as the heron. Every day, Peggy would walk to a different waterfront, and the great blue was nearly always there. She was absolutely sure it was the same heron. She just knew it.

As time passed, a few more close friends died. Cancer and age were taking their toll. It became easier for Peggy to recognize which bird had the personality and look of each of them. Just as Marge had been powerful and elusive like the great blue heron, Audrey, the lovely and graceful dancer came back as a long-necked white egret. When feisty, fierce Ginger died, the osprey that built a nest on a platform by the bay was surely she. It made perfect sense to Peggy.

She was secretive about her birds. She supposed people might think her quite crazy if they knew of the long conversations she had with them. She did all the talking of course, but the birds heard her, she was sure of that.

She sketched her birds in many settings. The red-winged blackbird that took up residence in the woods behind the house after Barbara, a well-known African American playwright died suddenly of a heart attack. Barbara was an obvious match for the redwing: beautiful, black, and talkative. The soft-colored female cardinal, seemingly mateless, came to the ground under the feeder morning and night the day after Sue succumbed to breast cancer. Soft, sweet, shy Sue was certainly that lady cardinal. She even held her head the same way Sue did, sideways, eyes not quite meeting yours.

One wintry day, Mimi came to the studio bringing a steaming hot pot of fish chowder and biscuits for their lunch. She hadn't been there for ages and looked around at the paintings and the sketches push-pinned to the cork walls. "Heavens," she exclaimed, "are you going into competition with Audubon? What's with the birds?"

Peggy put her spoon down, looked at Mimi for a stretched-out moment, and stood in front of a large painting of the great blue heron. "This is Marge, and this," she pointed to a sketch of the osprey in flight, a fish in its talons, "is Ginger." She smiled tentatively and stopped before a watercolor of the female cardinal on the ground beneath a bird feeder.

"Can you guess who this is?" Peggy asked shyly.

Mimi considered for a bit and then said "Sue...is it Sue?"

Peggy moved to Mimi and enclosed her in her arms. "I should have known you'd get it. You always do." The women walked arm in arm to sit on the porch glider, and then kissed with deep affection that turned into passion as the embrace continued. They stretched out on the pillows, kissing and stroking with more and more urgency until finally they moved indoors to lie on the thick rug in front of the fire. Their lovemaking was slow and sure. They knew each other's bodies and intimate desires well after so many years. They were still in love, still lovers.

"Who says sex isn't fun after sixty?" growled Mimi playfully.

"Not I," caroled Peggy, "not we." They sang together in close harmony.

A peaceful time followed; months with no deaths, no disasters. No trees to name, no birds to name. Mimi gave music lessons and recitals, and accompanied other musicians from time to time. Peggy painted seascapes at different times of the day, enjoying the changes in light, never tiring of the different bodies of water in the area, happily painting the variety of views.

The couple was preparing for a trip to Santa Fe in the summer: Peggy's recent bird and sea paintings were to be shown in a small gallery on Canyon Road. Mimi was excited about seeing opera and hearing chamber music. They had several close friends there and would be staying with another couple, both artists, women in their eighties, who had been together for fifty years.

They would be gone for a month, so a house sitter had to be arranged for, someone to take care of the garden and trees, feed the birds even though it would be summer. There was some criticism of their feeding the birds in summer when there was plenty of food around for them. It was wrong according to some friends. But these birds were their family and they would be fed. And the trees, also family, would be watered. It would be hot, and rain might be scarce.

Two weeks before their departure, they kept the annual appointments with their doctor: mammograms, gynecological exams, cardiograms, blood tests. "The works," Peggy complained, "not an orifice overlooked."

Three days later, their doctor phoned to say that Mimi's pap smear was suspicious and more testing was needed. "We're leaving for Santa Fe in ten days," wailed Mimi to Peggy. "Your show opening, we can't miss that. I don't care, we're going, no matter what."

The next days brought x-rays and a scan followed by a visit to a gynecology oncologist who explained that Mimi had uterine cancer. The other specialist Mimi had seen for a second opinion agreed that a complete hysterectomy was necessary, with further treatment to be recommended after the surgery. The eagerly anticipated vacation was out of the question. Peggy would fly out for the gallery opening and return in two days. Mimi would have the surgery as soon as Peggy returned. Arrangements were made and the women returned home with heavy hearts, sad and frightened.

Peggy was leaving the next afternoon and the lovers welcomed the twenty-four hours they could be alone with one another. They had dinner in front of the fire, sitting at small tray tables. Jan DeGaetani, their favorite mezzo-soprano, was singing one of their favorite songs from the final recording the singer had made before her death, the last of the five Rückert *lieder* of Mahler.

> *Ich bin der Welt abhanden gekommen*
> *I have become lost to the world*
> *On which I wasted so much time.*
> *So long has it known nothing of me,*
> *It may well think I am dead!*
> *It matters nought to me*
> *If it takes me for dead.*
> *Nor can I even deny it,*
> *For truly am I dead to the world.*
> *I am dead to the world's clamor,*
> *At peace in a quiet realm.*
> *I live apart, in my own heaven,*
> *In my love, in my song.*
> *In meinem Lieben, in meinem Lied.*

At the last line they held each other close and wept and wept. "I'm not going to leave you, not even for a day," cried Peggy.

"I want you to go, you must go. I can't bear for you to miss the opening. My fault, it's all my fault," Mimi sobbed.

Peggy opened her arms and looked at Mimi with brimming eyes. "Oh, sweetheart, it's not your fault. Why do you say that? What do you mean?"

Mimi took a shaky breath and explained that she had been "spotting" for a long time, but had thought it was the estrogens she was taking. Other women had that problem; it was even written on the druggist's fact sheet that came with the pills. She didn't want to give them up, as she had felt really good taking them and they protected her against heart disease and osteoporosis.

Peggy shook her head slowly. "Why didn't you ask our doctor about the bleeding? Why didn't you tell me?"

"Because I was waiting for my annual check-up—I thought it would go away. I didn't want to think about it. See, I told you it was all my fault." Now she cried uncontrollably.

Peggy did not leave Mimi to go to Santa Fe. The women spent every moment together until it was time to go to the hospital for the operation. The surgery was followed by six weeks of recuperation. Some lymph nodes were positive, which was ominous news, but radiation "seeds" and chemotherapy were, they hoped, going to successfully deal with further cancer.

A year passed before new symptoms appeared, followed by more surgery for colon cancer, then radiation and chemo for the liver. The women held onto each other closely, afraid to let go, afraid to lose each other, afraid.

In the spring, Mimi brightened. First crocus and forsythia, then daffodils, soon tulips colored the ground. They sat in the garden and listened to music. They read poetry to each other. The fear had left with the winter. Now it was spring and every day was a treasure. They were happy.

"I want to plant two new trees," Mimi announced one morning. She was too weak to go to the nursery, but Jenny and Sara, the couple who owned a nearby nursery, came that day with a book of trees, ready to answer questions. Two hours later, Mimi and Peggy had each chosen a tree: a weeping white pine for Peggy and a Camperdown elm for Mimi.

The trees were planted the next day, very near each other. "The birds will love these trees," whispered Mimi, "I know they will." She took Peggy's hand. The women spent hours each day at the new trees, Mimi lying on a chaise longue, Peggy sitting alongside her, holding her hand. They talked quietly, reminiscing, remembering precious moments with laughter and with tears. Peggy read favorite poems and stories aloud, and the portable CD player she had rigged up to an outside speaker played their favorite music. Peggy's birds were there, too, and the women used their binoculars to watch them enjoy the trees.

The following week, Mimi was too weak to come outdoors, but a bed was set up for her at the window where she could look at the trees. Peggy continued to play their favorite music and read aloud, while birds perched on the sill to visit the feeders and Mimi. Hospice nurses, tender and unobtrusive, kept her comfortable. "This is a beautiful dying," Mimi murmured, her hand in Peggy's, hearing her sweetheart's soft voice saying how she loved her, how she would miss her.

Mimi died gently, smiling.

Peggy painted all the time now. She barely saw or spoke to her friends, although they tried hard to engage her. She would walk down to the water and stare across to the horizon, watching the shore birds swoop and swirl. Watering the two new trees was a labor of love, and she was pleased to see them doing so well. She drank innumerable cups of tea and barely ate more than toast and the marmalade she and Mimi had made last summer.

Before Mimi died they had named their trees together. Peggy had painted portraits of each of the trees. She had named the weeping pine Alceste, after Gluck's faithful heroine. Mimi had named the graceful and majestic elm Leonora, after the devoted heroine in Beethoven's Fidelio, surely the bravest and most loyal wife in opera.

One day in early summer, a few months after Mimi's death, Peggy was sitting in the garden near Leonora and Alceste, a book of poetry open in her lap, a soft breeze making the young leaves dance and the bay waves ripple, when a songbird began to sing. Peggy looked around for the singer of the unfamiliar song. In the elm tree, on a low branch, sat a northern oriole singing its lilting melody. Peggy watched it for a long time, listening to it singing, until it flew away.

The next day it was back in the same place and Peggy was ready with her sketchpad and colored pencils. The lovely singing bird posed gracefully. The drawing became a painting, her last. In the left corner, she inscribed Mimi.

Peggy died in her sleep soon after. Stroke or heart attack, there was no autopsy to tell.

The house had been left to the local lesbian community as a residence for infirm or elderly members of their group. It was supported by generous endowments from the members, and yearly fundraising kept it going.

It was known as *The Bird and Tree Residence*. The only conditions were that the birds be fed and the trees cared for year round in perpetuity. In the center of a beautiful garden facing the water were two trees, the Camperdown elm and the weeping white pine: plaques gave their names, Leonora and Alceste. Year after year, an oriole would perch in the elm, singing and singing. A mockingbird would echo the oriole's song from the pine tree where she sat.

The women living in the house were delighted.

When I Grow Too Old To Dream

One by one the years pass, and old friends that Vita means to call, but does not, die. She feels a bit guilty, but removes the feeling like a book she might put back on a library shelf.

What is the matter with me, she asks herself one morning, when she reads the obituary in *The New York Times* of a colleague she has been meaning to call for over a year—or is it two—and just hasn't gotten around to doing?

This has been a bad week for losing people she really cares about. She herself is no spring chicken. When she looks in the mirror with her glasses on, she is somewhat shocked at the reflection of a middle-aged woman—or can a woman of almost seventy-two call herself middle-aged? *Never mind*, she thinks, *I don't look that old, even with the pronounced grey streak in my dark hair, and lines beginning to be deeply etched from my nose to my mouth.* Her teeth seem to be shifting in her mouth, with some new spaces and crookedness she doesn't remember. And they are looking a bit yellow; *they used to be so white*, she scowls at the mirrored face. *This teaches me not to wear glasses when I look in the mirror*, she reprimands herself, looking again and smiling. "At least I still have a nice sweet smile," she says aloud to no one, and looks away.

Last week she had to fill a prescription for glasses to wear full time. It seems she has outgrown the drugstore reading glasses she has worn for several years. *What was astigmatism anyway?* She would Google it and find out. She gives up on this line of thought and makes a cup of tea and some toast with marmalade.

After her shower, she can't resist checking herself in the full-length mirror. *Are those laugh-lines or wrinkles,* she wonders, *and what about those sagging breasts, and the sagging flesh just about everywhere?* Maybe it's a good thing no one gets to see her naked anymore.

She thinks again that this has really been a sad week for her, losing people she loves. Her favorite aunt died at the age of ninety-two, a good age; but she had been on life support in a nursing home for over two years, and her end had been a grisly one. Vita is relieved when she hears of the death.

She is not relieved about the second death, her best girlhood friend, Nora, with whom she spent her teenage years—they'd lived across the street from each other. Nora has not sent her a Christmas card for the first time since she moved to Florida with her husband and grownup kids. The holidays have come and gone, and finally, in the early spring, Vita calls Nora. Her husband Hank answers the phone.

"Oh, hello Vita, how are you?" He sounds somewhat confused and distant, as if he is not quite sure who she is.

"I'm calling because I never heard from Nora like I usually do; not for Christmas and not for my birthday. How is she, is she home?" She is met with what seems to be a full minute of silence. Too long, it's taking too long. She can hardly breathe.

Finally, Hank speaks, "Nora died Thanksgiving." More silence.

Vita cannot believe what she hears. "Died? I didn't even know she was sick. What happened? What was it? Why didn't anyone let me know?" She stops speaking and waits.

"Nora died of pancreatic cancer. It was very fast, six weeks. The kids are still in shock. I can't believe she's gone. I'm sorry we didn't let you know; I didn't know you and Nora were still in touch."

They say goodbye and hang up. She knows they will never speak again. She and Nora had once been so close, they told each other everything. Nora told Vita about her heavy petting with Hank, the son of the man who owned the antiques shop around the corner. Vita told Nora when she had gotten nits in her hair from the little girl she gave piano lessons to in the apartment house down the street. Vita told Nora many things, but never the special feelings she felt. How excited she was every time she had a sleepover with Nora and they shared the 3/4-size bed, which meant they would almost touch, and how Vita would wait for Nora to fall asleep so she could get close enough for their bodies to touch, and how she got so excited that it would happen. Nora never knew.

Nora and Hank got married in Nora's parents' home soon after her father found Nora and Hank making love in his car in the driveway one night. Vita was her maid of honor, had played the piano and sang Grieg's *Ich liebe dich* for the ceremony. Nora was seventeen and Vita sixteen. Nora had left college during her first year to get married, and Vita had felt abandoned, discarded.

The familiar sadness and guilt—Vita's frequent companion lately—is hard for her to bear. She finds herself singing an old song her father used to sing to her until it becomes an earworm, going round and round. She sings it softly to herself.

> *When I grow too old to dream,*
> *I'll have you to remember.*
> *And when I grow too old to dream,*
> *Our love will live in my heart.*
> *So kiss me my dear,*
> *And then let us part,*
> *And when I grow too old to dream,*
> *That kiss will live in my heart.*

Did she sing that song at Nora's wedding? Of course not, it was much too sad, not a song for young people with their whole lives ahead of them. Vita spends the next few days looking through photo albums, trying to find pictures of Nora, finally unearthing a few. "My goodness," she says to the image of her friend, "you really did look like the Hollywood star Linda Darnell," and begins to cry.

Vita is just starting to come out of the dark space she has been living in, when Zerlina, her lawyer, calls to remind her that she has not made an appointment to draft a new will.

"You're not getting any younger, Vita. It's been four years since you made your last will, and your finances have changed. I sent you some paperwork last month to review, and you said you wanted to write your obituary for me to keep with the will." They make a date for the following week. Vita does not remember getting the papers, or where to look for them. She calls the office and they resend the material.

She has a few days to read through the documents, write the obituary, get a haircut, and organize herself. She thinks she will bring nice things for the office help and Zerlina's legal assistants. Flowers for the grim office, Zerlina decides, and a box of Godiva chocolates for the staff. *If I bring presents for Zerlina's sons, and something for her, I won't have to send any Christmas presents.* Vita spends the next days buying the gifts, and she is quite pleased with herself, but does not tackle the legal tasks that await her.

The lawyers' conference room, notable for its attempt to look as strong as possible, does appear quite masculine, although all of the lawyers and clerks are women. The room has dark wood walls and furniture, and tall upright chairs, stiff and backbreaking. Instead of looking impressive, it is unfriendly and uncomfortable.

Zerlina is just about five feet tall, with a shock of wild black hair and the reddest lipstick possible. She owes her name to her father, a famed tenor, who adored Mozart heroines both as characters and as wished-for lovers. Zerlina is bedecked in jewelry, real and costume, wherever possible to be worn: ears, neck, arms, hands, fingers, even in her hair. She glitters and gleams, shakes and shimmers, clinks and clangs as she moves, never staying in one place, even as she sits in a chair, atop several cushions, which envelop her like a throne.

Zerlina goes through estate information with Vita. It seems Vita will not have enough money to leave generous gifts to her family and charities as she has planned. A combination of the recession, some very aggressive investments, and poor choices in the stock market has left Vita's worth seriously diminished. Those gifts will have to be changed. Her lawyer suggests she consider leaving money to a few of her closest loved ones, and her jewelry, art, and remaining precious things to others.

"And you said you were going to write your own obituary," Zerlina again reminds her client, a hint of irritation in her voice, "That was four years ago and you've never done it, so you should do it for this new will, if that ever gets done."

"Did I say that I would do that? I don't remember. Why did I want to write my own obit?" Vita sits bewildered, thinking. *Maybe that was a good idea. At least I myself would get it right.*

"Okay, I'll do it, but it will take a while." She makes a hurried exit; she cannot spend another minute in this office having this discussion. The contemplation of her demise is getting too close for comfort.

Life, she muses, sitting in her office, what irony. I have to sit here and list all my precious possessions and figure out whom I want to leave what to. When I'm not Vita anymore, I'll be Mortis. What a name change. She sets about making lists: one of family and friends, another of possessions, and then plays a matching game of lists A and B.

When she gets irritated and bored with that exercise, she shifts to writing her obituary. This activity proves even more aggravating, morbid, depressing. She gives up. *What the hell,* she smiles. *I'm not planning to die yet. It can wait. It's too much like that O. Henry story: when the last leaf falls, comes death. It will be more fun to plan to whom I will leave my jewelry.*

The first decision is easy. Vita had been left a lovely lapis lazuli necklace by Marta, her gynecologist, a close friend and former lover. Her younger sister had also been Marta's patient for years, and was devastated when Marta had died of ovarian cancer, an ironic death for a gynecologist. Yes, Vita decides, that will be a perfect choice; her sister will be thrilled to have something of Marta's, especially a beautiful piece of jewelry.

She takes all her jewelry boxes and her leather jewelry travelcase, empties her drawers of every jewel she can find—costume, semi-precious, precious—and dumps everything on her bed. It makes quite a mound of glitter, and half the things don't even look familiar. She begins to unloosen the tangles, sorting the heap into piles of rings, brooches and pins, necklaces, and bracelets while she sings, *Baubles, Bangles, and Beads*. Vita then subdivides them into real and fake. The bedspread is almost half covered, and she makes one more miscellaneous pile of odds and ends.

Vita organizes the list of friends, relatives, and colleagues, and leaves the papers spread on the other half of the bed. *I'm tired, but now I can't get into my own bed, I've cluttered it up so much. Well, tomorrow is another day,* she muses, using her favorite expression for when she wants to stop doing a difficult task. She decides to sleep in the guest room, turns off the lights, and leaves.

More than two weeks go by before she even looks at the bed again. Her clothes, undergarments, shoes, and other necessities are all in her large walk-in closet so she does not need access to her bedroom. But a call from her lawyer reminding her to read her new will, sitting unopened on her desk since its arrival, gives her the nudge to get to work, to do something. She thinks she will start on her obit: if she can at least write the first sentence, the rest will follow more easily, and then she can read the damned will. She sits at her desk and opens the envelope. On top is an index of the contents of the papers her lawyer has sent, with little yellow tabs indicating where she is to sign when she is at the office. She has to read the material, and soon. She decides to make a cup of tea and then she will get to it, absolutely.

Some hours later, Vita has read the list of the will's contents and skimmed through the document. It is boring, the language so legal and the bequests so predictable that she decides she will go through it next week with Zerlina, to see if there need be any changes or errors corrected. It is too stultifying to deal with now.

Vita has made a good start on her obituary. She has her first line, with her imagined date of death at one hundred years of age:

Vita Elizabeth Pientowska, 1942-2042

She looks at the sentence she has typed into her computer, admires her work, reads it aloud, changes her chosen font several times, then looks at her watch and sees it is 6 PM— time for her evening martini. She saves her obit effort and hightails it for the kitchen. Hendrick's Gin and a whiff of dry vermouth, and she is ready. She turns on the TV news, sits in her recliner chair, and clinks the glass in her left hand to the ring on her right.

Here's to one hundred, Vita. You can do it. She drinks half her drink in one long swallow. When she has finished the other half, she heads back to the kitchen to heat up yesterday's leftover Thai dinner. She will definitely keep going on her obit tomorrow.

But tomorrow suddenly turns into today, the day she has to see her lawyer and sign her new will. How did last week disappear, what had she accomplished? She had been staying in the guest room, she remembers, read all of Alice Munro's short stories, and gone to the memorial tribute for Susan Paul, or *"Let's Celebrate Susan's Life"* as her colleague's partner had called the event. It was a party where people talked about their funny memories of Susan, and there was lots of laughter, as if everyone was afraid to grieve. Vita was very sad because she had not been in touch with Susan for a long time, and now dear Susan, her idol, mentor, and colleague was dead. That dark, heavy feeling of guilt kept her from even smiling at the memorial, or celebration, or whatever it was.

Vita had done other things she can't remember, and the week—or was it weeks—had passed. Now she was back in her bedroom. She changes the bed linens, opens the windows to air out the room, and feels pleased with herself. She is ready to pick up the work at her computer in her office. Oh, shit, she remembers, she has not read the will and has to leave for Zerlina's office soon. "Never mind, Vita," she says softly, "I think I said I would go through it with Zerlina. I'll try my obit again," and brings it up on her computer screen:

Vita Elizabeth Pientowska 1942-2042

Maybe she should put the dates under the name.
She tries it:

Vita Elizabeth Pientowska
1942-2042

Vita can't decide which looks better, or which is correct. They all look crazy. Will *The New York Times* print an obituary from their files, or will it just be the paid one she is trying to write? *Why would the Times have an obit? I'm not really famous or notable, unless they have the reviews of my books about famous women in history, or records of my teaching at Purchase at State University of New York. I don't know if either the reviews or records are possible, so I had better keep writing my own obit and leave it for my lawyer to deal with,* she decides.

> Vita Elizabeth Pientowska died at 100 years of age on December 31, 2042, of natural causes. Emerita Professor of History at Purchase College of the State University of New York, she taught for thirty years until she retired in June 2012. Dr. Pientowska received undergraduate and graduate degrees at Barnard College, and her doctorate in American History at Columbia University. Her seven book series of American Women in History includes feminists and suffragists Mary McLeod Bethune, Alice Paul, Jeanette Rankin, Eleanor Roosevelt, Bella Abzug, Gloria Steinem, and Hillary Clinton.

Not bad, she thinks, *for a first generation American, daughter of uneducated Polish immigrants. I might be worth a* Times *obit after all.*

She glances at her watch and realizes she has to leave. The ten lines she has written so far had taken much longer than she realized. She has to look up the women she's written books about. She only remembers the living women, and has to search her shelves for the other five books. She will have to read them some day—writing them was not like reading them.

She saved what she had written so far, shut the computer, and left for her appointment feeling good about what she had finally managed to accomplish.

The office gifts finally distributed—Vita had forgotten them her last visit—the two women are seated in the conference room, Zerlina looking at her watch and shaking her head with displeasure.

"Are we ready to sign, Vita?" Without waiting for a reply, she continues, "then I'll call in the witnesses so we can make it all legal." Zerlina, with her hand on the intercom, is ready to proceed.

"I'm sorry, Zerlina. I just didn't have the time to read it all, and I need you to go through it with me, page by page, in case I have questions." Vita dares not look at her lawyer, but stares down at the papers in her hands.

Zerlina is exasperated. Vita has done this every time, no matter what the task is. "Oh well," she sighs, "let's get to it." And they do, as quickly as they can. Vita has no pertinent questions, only superficial points she raises just to show she is listening. They finish, Vita signs, the witnesses sign, and Zerlina takes a deep breath.

"Okay, good," Zerlina says hopefully, "do you have the lists of valuables you are leaving and to whom, and how about that obituary?"

"I've got all my jewelry arranged and ready to put into envelopes for various people, and I gave something away to my sister last week," Vita says as if she had just climbed Everest.

"And here is the first part of my obit. I'll finish it in a day or so." Another puff up of her meager chest, this time accompanied by an I-told-you-so lift of the chin, and Vita makes ready to leave.

"Vita, you must give me the list of whom you are leaving which valuables to. We need to attach it to the will." Zerlina raises her eyebrows expectantly.

"I'm not dying yet, Zerlina, don't be in such a rush. I won't be leaving until 2042 so you'll get the lists when they are done and when I am ready and when I have done them to my satisfaction," she speaks hurriedly without taking a breath. Vita stands and removes her car keys from her bag. It's as if she had said *this meeting is over*. And it was.

The jewelry is on the bed, the obit is in her computer, and Vita is making a list of friends she wants to call, the friends and relatives she wants to get in touch with. They come to mind as people to whom she might leave some bauble or other. "Actually," she says, "what I really want to do next is clean up my office—my desktop and files—before I do all those other things."

She sweeps her jewelry off the bed into its canvas bag, again saves what she has written for her obit, just to make sure, and puts the list of calls under the phone. Vita looks at her watch, smiles, and leaves for the kitchen to make her evening martini.

This night, she thinks, *she will have more than two drinks*. She feels determined, full of energy, alive. Halfway through her second martini, she brings the bag of jewelry into the living room and sits with it in her lap. "I know what I'll do," she says, "I'll play grab bag; I'll stick my hand in the bag and whichever piece I pull, I'll decide who gets it." She finishes her second drink and rummages around in the bag, taking out a heavy gold flower pin with rubies and diamonds set in it. "Where did I get you?" she asks. She gets out her magnifying glass to examine the back of the brooch. "Tiffany, 18 carat," she reads aloud. She puts the canvas bag on the side table and spins the piece round and round in her hand, making the diamonds sparkle with reflected light, then sets it down and goes to fix a third drink. Feeling lightheaded, she makes her way to the bedroom and lies down. The room spins as she giggles, "I must be drunk," and drinking more of her third martini, gets the hiccups and eventually falls asleep.

In the morning she feels awful, but a cup of coffee helps her headache. She examines the gold flower on the seat of her chair and remembers the woman who gave her the jewel. Nora, her dearest friend, whom she loved; Nora who is dead, and she never said goodbye; Nora who gave her this gorgeous brooch for her fiftieth birthday and told Vita she loved her, that Vita was her best friend. How can she give this precious jewel away to anyone, how can she part with it? How can she part with any of her precious things, how can she be sure that the people she leaves the jewelry to will care for them the way she does? She puts the pin back in its case and into the canvas bag, ties it up securely, and stuffs it into her hiding place in the shoe bag in her closet.

"I will not think about the next will, the obituary, the jewelry and precious things, until I am old enough to do so," she resolves.

Vita looks into her mirror like the Marschallin, the princess in her favorite opera, *Der Rosenkavalier*. She sings to her reflection in her own dressing table mirror, contemplating her own looks and age. Vita hums the melody of *When I Grow Too*

Old To Dream, points a finger and shakes it, as if making an important point while lecturing to one of her classes.

I will try not to be so lonely, so alone, I will call my friends, see my friends, and most of all—she raises her right hand, and she and her image laugh at one another—I will definitely drink only one martini every night, Vita promises the woman in the mirror.

Mother Love

Lizanne sat slumped in her wheelchair, white hair pulled back from her forehead in a tight ponytail. The once bright blue of her eyes had washed out to an almost colorless hue, and they squinted out at her daughter from under heavy lids. "When can I go home? I don't like it here." She sniffed and blew her nose into the tissue her daughter handed her.

"What don't you like here, Mommy?" She wiped her mother's rheumy eyes with a clean tissue. She waited for the usual recitation of complaints.

Lizanne raised her head so she could look into her daughter's eyes. As she glared at Vicki, the color almost returned to the old woman's angry face.

"Victoria, why do you talk so much and say so little? And you don't remember anything I say." She crumpled the tissue and threw it at her daughter.

Her daughter picked it up and tossed it into a nearby trash can along with the other one she was holding.

"Tell me again, Mommy. Please," she encouraged.

"Victoria, it's not clean, the food has no taste, the people are rude, and everybody is old or sick or sick and old." She slapped her hand on the tray table for emphasis.

Vicki—her mother was the only person who still called her Victoria—could have repeated the litany word for word. She had heard it many times during the last five years but repeatedly asked, hoping her mother would one day face reality. The fact was her mother had no home, except for the nursing home she now lived in. The little one–bedroom apartment Lizanne owned at Leisure World in southern California had been sold in order to pay for the Golden Years Nursing Home. Now Medicaid took care of her.

"And it smells bad, and my clothes and the money you leave me get stolen—other things too," the old woman continued, her voice trembling with the effort. "I want to go back to my own home. Today. Now." *Slap* went her hand, twice.

Slap goes her mother's hand, twice, first on one cheek and then on the other. The little girl cries out and tries to get away from the furious woman, but she is held in her mother's tight grip.

"What did I do, Mommy, what did I do?" she pleads. "I was good today. I was really good." The five- year old rubs the tears in her eyes with her fists.

"Wait until I tell your father, Victoria, I'll tell him what a bad girl you are. I'll tell him everything." She pauses and rubs her palms together. "If he comes home tonight."

Without warning, the tears come. Lizanne's sobs frighten the child. Her mother holds out her arms to Vicki, who warily allows the embrace.

Poor baby, poor child, poor me. I had no Daddy. I had nothing, no one." The tears stop, and she releases the child to light a cigarette. Vicki picks up her book from the floor and goes quietly to her room.

Vicki visited Lizanne several times every week. Often there was a call from Golden Years complaining about her mother's behavior or attitude. Lizanne had hit an attendant, she threw her food, she was rude, demanding, unpleasant. It seemed to Vicki that "unpleasant" was the understatement of the year.

Vicki was a tall, big-boned, athletic-looking woman in her early forties—she thought she resembled her father, although she barely remembered him. Her mother had burned all the photos of him after tearing them to shreds one Christmas night when Vicki was in first grade. There had been no presents, no tree, no Santa, no Daddy.

No presents, no Daddy. Go to bed, Victoria. Stop hanging around me. You're no better than he is. Don't look at me with his big, soft eyes. I have nothing to give you… just like he gave me nothing… nothing except you, and a fat lot of good you do me. Get out of my sight. Now!

"Some merry Christmas," Vicki remembered.

Lizanne was approaching seventy but she acted and looked much older. No one at Golden Years knew why she didn't walk. She just stopped one day and refused to take another step. She ate heartily even as she complained how vile the food was. She shared a room with a sweet, friendly woman of eighty, who had tried to make friends but was rebuffed so often she finally gave up.

Smoking was allowed only on the outside terrace, and patients had to get themselves out there, even if they were in wheelchairs. Lizanne was a heavy smoker and constantly cajoled attendants or visitors to wheel her outside. Motorized chairs were not permitted, and she said it was too hard for her to wheel herself. Vicki tried to get her mother to give up smoking. She bought her Nicorette, the nurses tried the patch, and even had her see a hypnotist, which Lizanne had agreed to out of curiosity. But her mother did not want to stop—she said it was her only pleasure. She was glad when her daughter visited because she had someone to take her outside so she could smoke to her heart's content. She would light up as soon as Vicki wheeled her to the terrace.

Her mother lights another cigarette with the one she just finished. "I suppose you're hungry," she sneers. "You're always hungry. Well, make us something to eat."

"What should I make, Mommy? I can't reach the sink to get water for spaghetti. Can you do it?" The little girl looks at her mother with hopeful eyes. "Or I could make hot dogs. There's two in the fridge." She takes them out and examines them carefully. "Ooh, they smell funny—they smell bad."

Lizanne doesn't answer the child. She inhales deeply and fiercely blows out the smoke. She grabs a frankfurter from Vicki's hand and starts to stuff it into her daughter's mouth. "You're hungry, so eat— eat this. Little bastard, always wanting something from me. Just like your father, wanting, wanting, wanting."

She screams each word louder and louder, shaking Vicki hard. "I can still hear him with his whining voice. Can't you clean this house? Can't you do the laundry? Can't you cook dinner? Can't you, can't you?" She shoves the sobbing girl away and lights another cigarette.

Vicki and her lover Marcia played tennis at the nearby public courts near their home, twice a week. The only other exercise they got was walking together for an hour early each morning. That was their best time together: they talked, planned, and shared their hopes and dreams as they walked.

"I'll be late tonight," Vicki said one morning during their walk through the park. "I have to spend some extra time with my mother. They called to tell me she's not very well." She sighed and apologized with her eyes. "There are scallops for dinner, they won't take very long to cook. You can do the other stuff before I get home; okay?" Marcia nodded. She was used to this. There was frequently some problem with Lizanne or with Vicki's work.

Work at Vicki's public relations company was demanding. "Marcia, we know these musicians are difficult and temperamental." Marcia thought about Vicki's years of enduring a mother who was difficult and temperamental—she had gotten plenty of practice. "But you know I love what I do, and don't we enjoy the talented people I work with? All those fabulous concerts?"

Marcia nodded. "You bet I do," she agreed. Marcia was a family psychotherapist and saw patients in an office not far from their apartment. Vicki's company was located nearby. They tried to have dinner together as often as possible; Vicki did the main course and Marcia did the appetizer, salad, and vegetables. They listened to music or watched the news while they cooked, and shared a bottle of wine. They were lucky if they could do this once a week; they had lived with each other for eighteen years and treasured their time together.

Often the phone rang during dinner or early in the morning with a complaint call from Golden Years about Lizanne. Vicki worried that they would want to transfer her mother to another nursing home, or even insist that she take her mother to live with her. She had nightmares about that awful possibility.

That night, Vicki woke up screaming. A bad dream, the same one she has had before.

Her mother takes her to a wake. She doesn't want to be there. Her mother drags her toward a white coffin in the church. "Look at her," her mother insists. Vicki's eyes are shut tight. "You have to look at her," she says again through clenched teeth. Vicki opens her eyes when her mother shakes her violently. The little girl in the coffin is wearing her white confirmation dress and a veil. She sits up in the coffin and takes off the veil. It is Vicki. Vicki screams and screams until she wakes up.

Vicki stood at her mother's bedside and watched her labored breathing. She turned to the doctor, who motioned her outside.

"Your mother has pneumonia," he said. "Her lungs are in poor condition and she's having difficulty breathing, as you can see. We should send her to the hospital where they could put her on a respirator, but we can try to care for her here as best we can."

Vicki thanked the doctor and accepted the second option as graciously as she could. She thought moving her mother was a bad idea.

That night, Vicki and Marcia prepared their "quick, quicker dinner," as they had named it years ago. They had first met on a public tennis court when Vicki was twenty-five and Marcia was twenty-eight. Marcia invited her to play a set after their eyes had met knowingly when looking for a player, or perhaps a partner. The women had found both, and if there was such a thing as love at first sight, that had been it.

They had played many games together and cooked many meals together. A package of linguini and a can of Progresso white clam sauce were always at home. That evening, Vicki added some white wine to the sauce, dished up some salad—*et voila*—fifteen minutes later dinner. They made a substantial dent in the rest of the wine while Vicki shared the details of her mother's illness and the meeting with the doctor.

Marcia listened quietly and asked, "Vicki, honey, what will you do? What's best for your mother, or what's best for yourself?" She gently pushed Vicki into a chair and poured some more wine for them both. There was no answer to her question. She took two bowls from the shelf and filled them with the pasta and sauce, sprinkled some freshly ground asiago cheese over the top, filled the smaller bowls with portions of salad, and sat. "Vicki?" she asked, "what do you want to do about Lizanne?"

When there still was no reply, Marcia tried a different tack. "Vicki, I'm going to ask you something I have tried to ask for a long time." She took a sip of wine. "Ever since we met, all I know about your mother is what I've seen for myself, and that has not endeared her to me." Vicki raised her head and looked questioningly at Marcia. "And yet, my darling, you are so caring of Lizanne, so kind and loving. How can you treat her so kindly and caring when she has been so cruel and unloving to you?"

Marcia waited, the silence pulsating heavily in the room until Vicki said in a monotone, "she wasn't always that way. She loved me when I was little, before my father went away."

"But you were a small child, and from what little you've told me, she was abusive. She didn't take care of you, feed you, nurture you. What kind of mother is that?"

"The only mother I had," Vicki answered. "She told me her story bit by bit as I was growing up. She got less horrible as I got older. I guess she felt weaker as she got older and needed me to take care of her."

"And you have, up to this very moment. Must you take care of her this way forever? Marcia asked.

After a long pause, Vicki continued. She had never told much of Lizanne's story to Marcia before, but she knew that this was the moment she needed to tell it. "When Mom was a child, her father was killed in an accident. She never knew him. She never even saw a picture of him. Her mother—my grandma—worked nights in a factory. My mom slept on a cot at night in a neighbor's apartment. The kind lady, Mrs. Magid, was modestly paid to watch my mother. Grandma had to sleep during the day, and my mother kept quiet in their apartment." Vicki shook her head from side to side, sad with the memories. "She was a freshman in high school when she was called to the principal's office and told her mother had died. She never learned how. Mrs. Magid took her in as a foster child."

"My Momma told me that when she was in secretarial school, she was sent on a temporary job with an advertising agency. She was very good-looking—she showed me pictures—only eighteen years old, and she had never dated in high school. One of the men she was working for invited her out to lunch several times. He sometimes kept her working late, and then took her to dinner afterward. Momma was so impressed; he was sophisticated, handsome, and very attentive to her."

"Momma told me she had been swept off her feet. When the affair began, it was almost like Professor Higgins and Eliza Doolittle. "He was in charge and she was in love.""

When Vicki paused, Marcia went to the teacart that served as their bar and chose a bottle of brandy and two snifters. She poured small drinks for them, and kissed Vicki gently on the lips before handing a glass to her. "This is quite a story, Vicki darling. Are you okay?"

"I'm fine, Marcia. It feels so good to finally tell you everything. I need your help deciding what to do."

They were silent for a while, carefully swirling and drinking, and then Vicki continued. "They didn't live together. She lived in a studio he found for her on the West Side, and he could come and go as he pleased. And then, Momma told me, she got pregnant. She said it to me like she'd caught a cold."

Vicki got up and walked to the window and stood looking out for a moment before she sat down again, this time across from Marcia on a club chair, so she could face her lover.

"My momma told me she was still eighteen when he made her give up her job at his company. All she had for support was my father." She stared down at her unsteady hands, and clasped them tightly. "According to Momma, he was attentive. She thought he loved her, that he was pleased there would be a child. He would love their child, she was sure. And then they would get married and everything would be all right, a happy ending to her fairy tale. But my mother never got to be the princess in the story."

The glass she picked up began to shake more in Vicki's hand. "Neither, I guess, was I," she said, almost to herself.

Marcia was worried about Vicki's overly intense, almost frantic telling of the story.

"Take a deep breath, Vicki. Slow down, have some brandy." Marcia tried to calm her, but Vicki seemingly could not be eased.

"When I was little, she was my loving Mommy. She made beautiful clothes for me, she took me to wonderful places, she read to me, sang to me, danced with me. I adored her."

Vicki took the last little sip of her drink and carefully put the glass down. "That's the mother I would try to remember when she was mean to me—the good mother. That would push the bad mother away."

Was this the Lizanne Marcia knew? The brutal woman she had grown to despise, the woman Vicki was describing? She waited.

"When my father was with us he was fun. He played games with me, we went to children's theater, visited playgrounds. At Christmastime, we saw The Nutcracker." Vicki smiled with pleasure at the recollection. "Then he moved from his apartment, he didn't come upstairs for me. Now he met me downstairs in the lobby when he came to see me. I think he didn't want to see Mommy any more." Marcia became aware that Vicki had reverted to calling her mother "Mommy." which she did when she was with the old woman.

She began to understand that when Vicki used the childhood name, she was remembering from the days when her mother was a loving mother—her Mommy.

"Eventually, I didn't see my father at all. I guess he didn't love us anymore. Mommy cried all the time. She was different, always angry; sometimes really mean to me, other times holding me, and saying she was sorry. I never knew which mother I would get, so I mostly stayed out of her way. When my father stopped sending checks, we were in trouble. Mommy got a job as a girl Friday at a publishing company. It was a hard job—she had to do everything—including buying presents for her boss's girlfriend, and then for his wife. That made her mad. I ate school lunches and stayed late after school, until my mother could pick me up after work. She wasn't the same as she had been, but I loved her anyway. She was my Mommy."

Now it was clear to Marcia that Vicki had been protecting herself then, and still did now, from the sadistic mother by holding on to the kind Mommy. Vicki was looking pale and depleted. Marcia decided this was enough.

"Vicki, sweet, listen to me. I am going to Golden Years with you tomorrow. I want to be there when you speak to the doctor about the next step. I want to help. This is clearly very hard for you, and I'm your honey, and a honey is supposed to help you. Okay?"

Vicki nodded yes. "Thank you, honey darling." They went to bed arms entwined.

The meeting took place in the Golden Years' conference room at 4 PM the next day. Lizanne's condition had improved:

she was responding well to the wide spectrum antibiotic, her temperature was normal, and her breathing was not labored. The doctor no longer thought it necessary to consider moving her to the hospital.

"Your mother has made a remarkable improvement, but she is an awfully difficult woman. Has she always been so...?" The doctor struggled to find the right word.

"Nasty, bitchy, mean," Marcia filled in the blanks.

He smiled sympathetically at the women and Marcia ran with the ball. "Is there any kind of medication you could prescribe that would... smooth out the edges?"

"My mother was a different woman when I was young. It was as though she changed in front of my eyes," Vicki interjected, not allowing the doctor to answer Marcia.

Uh oh, thought Marcia, *here comes the good Mommy again.*

After giving her information some thought, the doctor responded to Vicki. "What would you say to having our geriatric psychotherapist, Dr. Langer, speak with Lizanne? I could ask him to get in touch with you first, Vicki, to get some background."

Marcia hugged Vicki in encouragement. Vicki reached out in response and offered her hand to the doctor, who took it with a gentle squeeze. The arrangements were made, and Vicki went to visit with her mother while Marcia went to read in the lounge.

"Am I dead, Victoria?" Her mother's voice was hoarse and weak. Her hair was combed back into a bun and someone had tied a festive-looking-lavender ribbon around it. Lizanne's face was softer, as if she couldn't make the effort to be as nasty to her daughter as usual, as if that was too much trouble for her.

"Did I almost die?" she asked with a sardonic smile.

"No, Mommy, but you were pretty sick."

"Too bad, that would have solved things for you. You'd have been dancing down the hallway." Again, that smile.

"Why do you always say such awful things, Mommy? You're my mother and I love you."

"That's the way I am, Victoria. You should be used to me after all these years. When have I ever been any different?"

"You were, when I was little you were sweet and you loved me." Vicki smoothed her mother's hair back.

"You must be dreaming, thinking of someone else. Those words don't apply to me." Lizanne closed her eyes and shut her daughter out.

"Goodnight, Mommy. I'll see you tomorrow. Sleep well." There was no reply. Vicki went to find Marcia.

"I'm taking you out for dinner at Shun Lee," Marcia said. "You can stuff yourself full of elegant Chinese food. We won't talk about Lizanne or politics or war."

"So what's left to talk about?" Vicki asked.

"Sex, darling, and love, and what wonderful trips we can take. Living in Paris, perhaps, that's what we can talk about."

The two didn't know whether the food or the conversation acted as an aphrodisiac. But whichever it was, it was welcome.

But that night she dreamed a new dream. *Her father has come to see her and her mother at the nursing home. He is a young psychiatrist, she is a child. He takes her outside to a playground. He pushes her on the swing faster and faster, and then the swing goes slower and slower, then stops. She looks around and he is gone. She is alone. She tries to swing herself but the swing won't move. There is no one in the playground. She calls, "Daddy, Daddy," but no one answers. When she reaches the nursing home, her mother is also gone.*

Vicki woke late: her dream had left her unsettled and sad. She would have to rush to her office for a meeting with some potential new clients, a string quartet called Artemis that she had been trying to sign with her agency for several years. She shifted into high gear. Marcia had already left for her 8 AM appointment, but had left a cup of tea for her on the warmer in the kitchen. Propped against the cup was a note:

"Hey babe, you are one hot lover. My head is still spinning. No more Chinese food for you for a while, at least for a day... well, maybe just a few hours. See you later. I love you madly. Marcia."

Vicki swallowed some tea, took a big bite of a croissant, and left, heart soaring. The sour aftertaste from the dream was gone. She was on time and ready for Artemis. Later that morning, she received a call from Dr. Langer. She returned his call as soon as she could, and decided to take charge of the exchange. "Have you seen my mother yet?" She spoke quickly, cutting off any opportunity for small talk.

"Yes, we spoke about her seeing me to talk about Golden Years, her health, any other matters she wanted to discuss."

"And she turned you down, right Dr. Langer?"

"Oh, no, she was very receptive to the idea. We set an hour's appointment for tomorrow."

Was that reproach she heard in his voice? Vicki gentled her own tone.

"Well, that's encouraging, Dr. Langer. I'm very glad to hear it." She waited for a reply, but he wasn't forthcoming. "If you need to speak with me or meet, just ask." Vicki tried to match his cooperative words.

"Thank you, Ms. Beganowski," he said, and they said goodbye and disconnected.

That was brief and to the point, she thought, but she was left feeling oddly unsettled.

The nurse helped Lizanne get ready for her appointment with Dr. Langer. She made her comfortable in the recliner chair by the window, then brushed Lizanne's hair so it hung loosely around her angular face, stepped back and looked appraisingly, then added flowery barrettes to each side. Lizanne had been moved to a private room after her illness, and Vicki had requested that she be kept there for as long as Dr. Langer would be seeing her.

"You want to look pretty for Dr. Langer," the nurse cooed in a syrupy voice.

"Huh," Lizanne vocalized, waving the nurse away. She looked out at the traffic, her eyes finally settling on a tree across the street. It had no leaves but the shape of the limbs and trunk pleased her, and she pulled her robe closed and waited.

"Mrs. Beganowski, is this a good time for us to talk?" Dr. Langer questioned softly from the doorway. Lizanne did not turn to look at him and said nothing.

He came close and pulled up a chair. "I'm Dr. Langer. I'd like to call you Lizanne, if you will call me Stephan. Is that okay?" No reply, just a slight nod.

Lizanne continued looking at the tree. The doctor made himself comfortable, not trying to meet her eyes. Perhaps he felt safer that way, he smiled, amused by his thought. He decided to tell her about himself.

"I'm Stephan Langer. I'm thirty-nine years old, like Jack Benny." He waited to see if she would laugh, but it did not come. "I have a Ph.D. in psychology, trained at the William Alanson White Institute, and I specialize in geriatric counseling. I am the therapist who is available to you, here at Golden Years, if you wish to continue meeting. Do you have any questions?"

Lizanne gave an almost imperceptible shake of her head.

Langer decided to break the ice with a challenging question, as he realized this might be a hard nut to crack.

"Lizanne, they tell me you are unhappy at Golden Years, that you don't like anything about it—the food, the personnel, the other patients, the cleanliness. Is that true?" He received no answer, not even a nod.

"Lizanne, you agreed yesterday that you wanted to talk to me. It's hard to have a conversation when I'm the only one talking. If you are not feeling well, or feel that you need some medical attention, I don't want to further upset you. I'd be happy to have the nurse come in." The doctor was again met with stony silence. "Okay, I see this is a bad day. I will come back again day after tomorrow, after lunch, and see if we can have a conversation then. Here is my card with my phone number on it. If you want to get in touch with me, you can ask the nurse to call the number for you."

"Don't be a fool," came the fierce voice from the chair, "I know how to dial a number if I want to." And she turned completely away from him, hiding her face in angry dismissal.

At least she spoke, Langer consoled himself, smiling wryly, and he left Lizanne alone.

Lizanne kept her eyes on the tree while she spoke to herself, barely moving her lips, making sure no one could see her. She spoke softly, crafting her plan, pleasing herself.

"You can't trust them, not any of them. Sure, he seems like a nice guy, but those are the ones you have to watch out for, the nice guys. I tried to teach that to my Victoria, not to trust, not to give herself to any man. They get it, she and Marcia, you don't find them tied up to any man. Why bother, they have each other—for companionship, friendship, sharing expenses."

"I'll charm that doctor when I'm ready, and I'll tell him whatever I feel like telling him. But he is a man, you can't change that. I can tell him a good story. I'll make it up and see if he falls for it. No, I'll make up stuff that'll shake him up— that I was abused, beaten, raped—that'll give him something to work on."

Satisfied with her plan, Lizanne closed her eyes and soon fell asleep. When the nurse came in to check on her, she was pleased to see the old lady resting. *She's an angel when she's sleeping,* the nurse thought, *but it won't last.*

Marcia and Vicki decided to go for a walk before starting dinner. They had not had their customary outing that morning, and the day had been busy for both of them. They needed to be outdoors, and they needed each other.

"I wonder if I should call Dr. Langer, see how it went with my mother today." Vicki was gathering pinecones for their fireplace. She felt that bending and stretching was the additional exercise she needed after sitting at her desk most of the day.

"Why don't you wait until after they've met a few times before you call him," Marcia, always the practical and wise one of the couple, always the even-handed psychotherapist.

Maybe I can see him when I'm there on Friday. That will give them some time," Vicki said, glad to find a way to postpone hearing what she anticipated would not be good news. She changed the subject. "What's for dinner?"

Marcia had done the shopping today. "Pheasant under glass, baby artichoke prepared Jewish style, and risotto puttanesca. How's that for a menu?" Marcia pulled Vicki close and hugged her, planting a kiss on her nose.

"So what's it really going to be, franks and beans?"

Marcia kissed her, this time lightly on the lips, not caring a whit for the people around them. "A little better than that: We're having rice and beans, tofu, onions, garlic and mushrooms, and a salad chock full of all those Asian greens you love."

Vicki smiled ruefully. "Well it's healthy, I'll admit it, but I liked that first menu better."

They picked up their pace and made for home, holding hands and swinging them while they hopped up on every sixth step. Passers-by smiled when they saw the two grown women.

Dr. Langer knocked on Lizanne's door and entered the room. She was sitting in the same chair, which had been turned to face him. "Good afternoon, Lizanne. It's Stephan Langer. How are you?" He spoke in a conversational tone as if he was a friend coming to visit. "I'm hoping that we can talk to each other more easily today. I asked if you would be comfortable meeting with me so we could discuss how things are going for you here. Remember?"

Lizanne looked at him as though she'd never met him before. She scowled, "I remember everything."

"Good. What would you like to talk about?" He waited. She shrugged.

"I've enjoyed talking to your daughter. Vicki is anxious for me to help you feel more happy in your home."

"Happy," Lizanne said in a voice that belied the word. "I would be happy to go home."

"Do you mean back to your California condo? That would make Vicki very unhappy, to be so far from you."

"Then I'd have to live here in New York with her, because she sold that condo." She laughed derisively. "She wouldn't have me." She turned as far away from him as she could and froze. Stephan could almost feel the ice encasing his patient. That's all he would get for now, but it was more than the first time. He decided to see her in his office from now on and get her away from the hospital atmosphere to his plants, books, paintings, and flowers.

Vicki did not get in touch with Dr. Langer before Friday, to give the process some time, as Marcia had advised. She asked the receptionist to let him know she would be coming in to visit her mother on Friday, and would like to meet with him before. For some reason, the whole thing made her uneasy. She was almost afraid to meet with the psychiatrist; she was not anxious to hear what he would say. Why did she always feel guilty when she was trying to help her, to understand her, to do things for her? She didn't even *like* her mother, but in some strange way, she loved her, or was it that she hated her? Would she ever solve the answer to that question?

"It's so hard when it's about my mother," she told Marcia on their morning walk. "I'm a wreck about seeing the doctor later."

"Would you like me to be with you at the meeting?" Marcia offered.

"Oh yes, I think so. Yes, I would," She hugged Marcia. She began to shake, and they had to sit at the nearest bench.

"I'm scared, Marcia, and I don't know why. It's like I'm a child again. Isn't that ridiculous?"

"There's a lot going on in your relationship. Maybe this will be good for you, not just for Lizanne. Maybe we can clear this cloud hanging over you and you can let more light into your feelings. I'm with you all the way. But I confess, I could do with less Lizanne in my life, and lots more Vicki."

Lizanne was wheeled into the doctor's office, her face set in fury. "Hello, Lizanne," said Stephan, "you look very nice." There was no ribbon in her hair today, no softness anywhere, and no response to his compliment. He tried another route.

"Welcome to my office, Lizanne. I try to make it as attractive as I can for my patients and for myself—I do spend most of my time here. Can I make you a cup of tea? I have some oatmeal raisin cookies I baked early this morning."

Her demeanor did not improve. Instead, she tightened her lips and said, "I want to make a complaint. I am here against my will." She drew herself up as tall as she could in the wheelchair "Do you mean at Golden Years, or here in my office?" He handed her a glass of water, hoping it wouldn't land in his face.

The question gave Lizanne pause. "Both," she said, sipping the water.

The answer was perfect. It gave him some room to maneuver. "In what way do you feel confined to Golden Years?" He did not ask who was responsible, but thought he knew what her answer would be.

She set the glass down heavily on the table near her wheelchair, and replied through a clenched jaw. "My darling daughter, she keeps me here. I have no choice." She sneered at her accusation and squinted her eyes at the doctor, trying to be as menacing as she could.

He refrained from smiling, keeping his expression serious and kind. "Let's talk about that. When we met last time, you knew you would not go back to your condo that had been sold, but you felt you could not live with Vicki. Is that right?"

Lizanne shrugged.

"Tell me where you would want to live, and how you might do it, Lizanne."

She tried to wheel the chair away from where she was, but the brakes were set. She gave up and looked around the room, and then moving her eyes to a large painting of a choir and orchestra comprised of elderly performers.

Stephan waited. Lizanne kept looking at the painting and finally asked, why it was in his office.

Stephan was pleased at her interest. "It is an expression of older people finding joy in making music. The painting is by Darcy Muth, a ninety-seven-year-old artist who lives in a residence very much like Golden Years in Santa Fe, New Mexico, called Rainbow Vision. I find the picture to be filled with color, pleasure, and life. Do you like it?"

"It's okay," Lizanne answered grudgingly, but the stern look on her face had softened, the freeze melting.

"Are you interested in art, Lizanne? What do *you* like about this piece? Would you like me to wheel you closer to it?" Stephan asked his questions while wheeling her nearer the painting.

Lizanne looked at it carefully as she drew nearer. "Everyone in the painting is old, even the conductor. How come?"

"This is a real scene the artist painted of a concert that took place at Rainbow Vision," Stephan explained. "The residents there who loved to sing formed a choir. Several others who played instruments began an ensemble and it grew into an orchestra. The chorus and orchestra worked on the same repertoire, joining forces for concerts. Darcy loved the scene so much, that she painted it."

Lizanne contemplated what he had said. "It is a metaphor for optimism, I suppose."

"Yes, that's probably why I love the painting so much. Thank you for pointing that out, Lizanne. This painting is actually something that led me to work in geriatric counseling." He felt the warm satisfaction of knowing they were on their way. The nurse entered; Lizanne was ready.

Vicki felt jumpy, unsettled: she had been sleeping poorly and was trying to keep Marcia from noticing. After several miserable nights and with no inkling as to the exact reason she was having so much trouble, she sat drinking a cup of chamomile tea with honey and bourbon before going up to bed. Marcia was sleeping peacefully and Vicki slid into her side of the bed as quietly as she could.

Vicki falls deeply into her familiar dream: *She is at a wake, but does not know who has died. She is not a child, but she is not an adult either. No one is with her, but someone is holding her hand. An organ is playing circus music and she is afraid as she is led up to the coffin. She looks in and sees her mother wearing sexy black shorts and a low cut cleavage-showing shirt covered in purple sequins. Lizanne gives a little wave, like the Queen of England greeting her subjects. Vicki waves back and starts to do a happy jig alongside the coffin. Lizanne smiles provocatively, which turns into a leer.*

Vicki is happy her mother is dead. She will throw a big party and everyone can celebrate. At the party, there is a giant cake. It breaks open and Lizanne bursts out of the cake, covered in whipped cream.

Vicki woke up crying and trembling. Marcia held her in her arms. "Did you have a bad dream, sweetheart? Come downstairs and I'll make you a cup of tea." They went to the kitchen and waited for the kettle to boil, the water poured into the mugs as Vicki told Marcia about the dream.

"I was so happy she was dead, Marcia. I thought she was going to die when she had pneumonia, and I was so disappointed when she didn't." The sobs turned into hiccups and she tried to sip her tea between spasms.

There was a little light outside the windows as though Aurora was trying to lighten the scene. "Here's what I think, Vicki. I think you, Lizanne, and Dr. Langer, should have a few meetings, sessions, whatever, together, and talk this out. Believe me, you weren't the only one who felt the way you did when Lizanne recovered—the nurses were not too pleased— nor was I."

Vicki thought for a while, and finally nodded agreement. "Yes, thanks honey. I'll call Dr Langer later to confirm today's appointment."

The day of the meeting, Vicki, was jumping out of her skin. "Something awful could happen," she told Marcia. "Anything could happen, I feel it." Marcia had never seen Vicki so upended.

Eventually, they gathered in the doctor's office and waited as he greeted the three women. "Are you comfortable, Lizanne?" Stephan asked after a moment of silence. "Can I get you anything? Would anyone care for some hot tea or cold water? I have both ready right here." Marcia and Vicki shook their heads *no thanks*, and Lizanne sat again in ominous silence.

Lizanne was slouched in her wheelchair, having refused to be helped into the more comfortable patient recliner by the doctor and nurse. Dr. Langer suspected Lizanne had set the stage for this moment, perhaps even had prepared a scenario in her mind. To Stephan, she had made the wheelchair seem a necessary prop to exhibit her vulnerability, her role as a reluctant participant, so she could use this moment to be at her most dramatic. Lizanne proved his suspicions right with her next statement. The old woman sat up in her chair, nodding her head in agreement with herself and what she had to say.

"You see, doctor, this is what I mean. Here I am again, against my will, at my daughter Victoria's request. It's always for her, her way, her needs." She clasped her hands in her lap and once again turned into a glacier.

Vicki folded into herself, unsure of what she should say or do. She had lost the courage to say what she had rehearsed in her mind over and over in the past week.

"Victoria–Vicki," the therapist corrected himself quickly, remembering that using Victoria was Lizanne's territory, and he did not want to cross into it. "Vicki, your mother has often expressed those feelings to me during our sessions. Can you respond to them?"

Vicki shook her head no. She helped herself to a glass of water, just to fill the silence.

"See, doctor, Victoria knows I speak the truth," Lizanne said as she came to life from her pose and pointed her finger accusingly at her daughter. "I am her victim," she shouted, emphasizing the pronouns, "I have to do what she says, go where she says, be what she says. I have no freedom to run my own life, make my own decisions and choices." Lizanne raised her head contemptuously and dismissed her daughter with a wave of her hand.

Marcia took Vicki's hand and held it firmly to show her support.

Dr. Langer looked at Vicki with sympathy and concern. "Do you have anything to say to your mother? You appear to me to be a caring daughter: you visit her regularly and you make decisions not only *for* her but *with* her. Surely you have feelings about what your mother is saying."

Vicki flung open her hands in a what can I do motion, and, seeming to give up, closed them. Moisture filled her eyes, but she did not cry. She had started to stand when the doctor put a hand on hers, urging her to stay.

"See," interjected Lizanne, "now she'll do her poor little girl act, like I'm being cruel to her, to get sympathy from you. I tried to teach her to be strong like I am, to stand up for herself like I do, to gain the upper hand and not let anyone take advantage of her. Yet, what is she? A weakling, a sniveling fool, not fit to get a man so she sleeps with another woman." Marcia and Vicki raised their eyebrows at this contradiction of Lizanne's usual teachings.

"I tried to make her powerful, like me. Tough like me. A winner, like me, like me, like *me!*" Lizanne half stands in the wheelchair, holding herself up on its arms, shrieking the last words like a Valkyrie, then sinking back down into the chair.

Marcia started to speak, but only squeezed Vicki's hand again, holding it close to her breast. Sensing that something vital was happening, she released Vicki's hand, and Vicki stood up. She stood in front of her mother without saying a word for a few seconds. She stared at her until their eyes met and Lizanne looked away quickly.

Vicki held a steady hand in front of the old woman as if stopping traffic. She pulled herself to her full height, and stiffened her back. She raised her head and spoke the words she had held inside for many years.

"You are a cruel, sadistic, ungrateful woman. You are not a mother. You are filled with feelings of bitterness, hatred, and viciousness. You are without love and affection. You tortured me, neglected me, abused me."

Lizanne dropped her head and covered her ears as Vicki continued. "I remember every slap, every unkind, unloving word. I was hungry for food, but I was even more hungry for a sign, a word of love from you."

At that, Lizanne uncovered her ears, met her daughter's eyes, and started to speak, "but, but I–" and with an angry grimace, again looked away and dismissed her daughter with a wave.

"Now I have no feelings for you at all," Vicki said quietly. "Not even hatred, not even pity." She turned, took Marcia's hand, and together, they walked to the door without looking back.

Dr. Langer, standing at the door, stepped out with the two women. "Don't worry about anything, Vicki. Golden Years will take care of Lizanne. I think that I will be able to help your mother from here on. She's ready, and so am I." Marcia smiled and nodded approvingly at the doctor. "The financials are all arranged, and we will be in touch if there is anything wrong. You know you can call me anytime you like."

"Thank you, Dr. Langer." Vicki said, her voice strong and sure. "I'm very grateful for your help." She shook his hand, as did Marcia, and he turned to walk back to Lizanne, who sat, once again, like an ice statue.

That night, Vicki and Marcia took a long walk along Madison Avenue to a quiet French restaurant they loved. The Bradford pear trees were just starting to turn green, and the air was soft and sweet. They sat in French wicker chairs at a table covered with a checked tablecloth. Candles burned in small holders and flickered on the women's faces, illuminating their beauty. Over a bottle of a velvety red table wine, they talked about the future, not sure where the conversation would lead.

"Let's make a list of what we would *like* to do, not what we have to do—that can come later," Marcia said in her lover's voice, taking her little pad and pen from her bag.

"I feel like I'm in that sweet Left Bank restaurant in Paris that we ate in every night the last time we were there," Vicki said, almost to herself. She finished her first glass of wine and speared a buttery snail from its shell. She chewed thoughtfully while Marcia poured a second glass for each of them.

"Would you believe it if I said I want to be in Paris with you, having this wine and eating escargot, with more wine than garlic?" Vicki said and raised her glass to Marcia, as if for a toast. The women laughed and clinked their glasses.

"To Paris," Marcia said thoughtfully, as she printed à Paris, putting her pen and pad back in her bag. "Is that so impossible? Just the other night, you were on the phone with a client. I heard you speaking French and I think you said you couldn't come to his concert because of your mother. Am I right?"

Vicki emptied her last shell and washed the contents down with her wine. *"Oui, c'est vrai, chérie."* She watched as the waiter swept away their empty dishes and returned in a moment with *ris de veau* for her and *boeuf bourgignon* for Marcia. Vicki thought for an instant, and then said, "Yes, I was speaking with my pianist. He is playing a recital of French Impressionists in two months at *l'Opéra Comique*. I would love to be there." She looked at Marcia, her eyebrows forming a question mark.

"So let's go," Marcia urged. "I am available, and so are you, if you want to be." The women sat quietly, eating wearily, the silence heavy with uncertainly, with possibility.

It was swiftly broken by Vicki's sudden explosion of "Yes, yes, yes! I can go, I want to go, oh *mon Dieu*, how I *need* to go." Her words ended as abruptly as they had begun, and she started stuffing her mouth with sweetbreads, as if she hadn't eaten for days—or was it years? *So this is happy*, she thought, and swallowed.

Safe Harbor

"My pee smells like popcorn," she says to no one, "how very odd. I must add this to my list." At her computer, she opens CHANGES and adds the new discovery, "pee smells like popcorn." She scrolls up to read the other entries: left hand index and middle fingers gnarled, bent, misshapen; lower lip thinning; left foot big bunion with toes going west; broken capillaries on both cheeks making permanent high color; Varilux glasses; bottom teeth crooked, piling up on each other; circles of black and blue marks up and down each arm. "Shit," she hisses, pushing away from the desk, "this is stupid."

Madeline Karr is forty-eight years old—tall, slim, and bald. Two long diagonal scars are where her breasts had been. She stands in front of the full-length mirror behind the bathroom door and looks at herself with cool, impersonal eyes. "What a mess," she says to no one, barely moving her lips. When the phone rings, she doesn't move to answer but lets the machine pick it up. "Maddy, honey, it's Val. Pick up if you're there. I need to talk to you. Please." Val, is her devoted agent and best friend. Maddy stays still. When the machine clicks off, she looks in the mirror again, her eyes lingering on her chest. "I remember when you started to grow tits," she says to no one, and heads for the shower.

From the Personal Journal of Maddy Karr

My breasts have started to grow bigger than buds. I don't like them so I press them close to my chest into a too tight athletic bra I bought with my allowance. I haven't gotten "the curse" yet and I'm glad. Maybe I'll never get it and that would be just fine with me. All I really want to do is play handball every afternoon after school with my best friend Bobbie, ride my bike, and read. I can do some of these things if I avoid Mom as much as possible.

Fridays, my parents go off to their bridge game and leave me to take care of Donny, my seven-year-old brother. Bobbie usually comes over to keep me company. Bobbie is really cool. She plays great handball and can really keep a secret. We tell each other everything: how much we hate our parents, our bodies, our younger brothers, and our smelly math teacher, Mr. DePiero. Seventh grade is hard, but changing from being a girl to a "young lady" is a real drag.

Maddy smiles as she puts down the raggedy journal she has found in a drawer she's been looking through. She reads a bit more, choosing pages at random, remembering the girl she was.

From the Personal Journal of Maddy Karr

Bobbie and I got our periods today, the same day, after gym. We know all about it from hygiene class and have the necessary stuff in our lockers. We decided not to tell our mothers.

Tonight, Mom found me washing bloodstains from my underpants when she barged through the unlocked bathroom door. She removed the locks "for safety's sake" when I was little.

Here's the scene: "What's taking you so long in here?" she demanded—when she saw the stains, she pulled and spun

me away from the sink and slapped me hard, first on one cheek and then on the other.
"Now you can have babies and be a slut and a whore," she wailed, sitting down hard on the toilet seat. I turned to finish my washing. Scene over.

Maddy says to no one, "Every cloud has a silver lining. No more periods ever again, chemo has taken care of those." She adds to her list.

She takes a green sleeveless dress from the closet, looks at the top ands hangs it back. She removes a pair of white pants from a hanger, slips them on over white cotton underpants, then rummages in a drawer for a t-shirt, choosing the blue one with breaching whales printed on it that she bought in Baja years ago. "Faded, like me," she says to no one. "I guess I'd better add 'faded, very faded,'" she amends, "to that damned list."

In the kitchen, she drops a Red Rose tea bag into a cup and pours boiling water over it, adds some almond milk, and stops to stare at a Stevia packet for a moment, shrugs, and with a dry laugh pours the Stevia into her cup. She is halfway through her tea when the phone rings; the machine picks up and her agent's voice, usually warm and cheerful, though somewhat hard-edged this morning, says, "Madeline, call me the minute you get this. There's big trouble with your manuscript and I need to see you ASAP or the contract will fall through. Friday, nine-oh-five AM. Call me. Love you."

Maddy sighs, finishing her tea and pouring a new cup. She walks to the tall window of her ninth-floor West Village apartment facing the river, and raises her cup to the Lady. She thinks about Dara, with whom she had taken this apartment six years ago because of its view of the Statue of

Liberty and the Twin Towers. When Dara left two years ago, after Maddy's second breast surgery, Maddy had kept the apartment even though the rent was high for her alone. Now, after some real success with her third novel, she can pay the rent more easily.

"I can pay the rent, I can drink tea, the towers are gone, but I can see you, Lady, I can let the phone ring," she says to the statue. But I can't, I can't, I can't keeps repeating inside her head, stuck like a defective CD. She goes back to the mirror, takes off her shirt, and examines the chemo shunt implanted in her right shoulder.

"I should add this to my list, I suppose. 'My shunt runneth over'." She makes a clown face for the mirror, something she did in college when she needed to amuse her roommate, a very serious young woman who had a hard time keeping up with her assignments. She couldn't remember her name. Maybe it's in my journal, she wonders.

From the Personal Journal of Maddy Karr

I chose this college not only because it's a great school, but it's as far from home as possible. It took me no time at all to decide when I got the acceptance for early decision. I knew my family would never visit. It's so great to feel safe from their probing and intrusion. Free at last, free at last! I've got a good scholarship and a waitress job, so I'm okay. I won't have to take anything from them ever again. I feel like a woman, my girlhood behind—how sweet it is.
Bobbie will be at a state university near home, halfway across the country from me. Last night before leaving for our schools, we lay on her bed, arms and legs tightly entwined. Both of us were crying, and we promised to write, call, and visit each other. Bobbie promised to come to New York, since I swore never to return to Chicago. I wiped tears from her face. We knew this was really goodbye. It will be a

long time before we can hold each other again, and then it might be only as close friends. Now we have to go our separate ways, and we're scared to leave one another, but excited, too. Bobbie and I held on tight, but let each other go in the end.

Maddy smiles at the long ago memories, and speaks to the Lady, who listens as she always does. "I'll never forget our senior year of high school. That's when Bobbie and I became lovers—can you imagine what our classmates, our teachers, our mothers would have said if they knew what we were up to?"

Did the statue nod? Maddy shrugged and continued. "It began during a school trip to Washington, D.C., our first time away from home. After staring at the two beds in our hotel room, without saying a word, we decided to share one. Later that night, we explored each other's bodies as we lay together, no explanations required for suspicious mothers. For the first time, we weren't ruled by shame or suspicion. We even forgave our hated mothers for a moment, amazed that we got permission to go on the trip, after all that wheedling and all those promises."

Maddy moves to the other window for a different angle. "Every day we had to invent believable reasons to be together—schoolwork, research, library, papers—anything we could make up. Bobbie and I lied to our mothers all the time: where we were, where we were going, what we were doing, and why we were doing whatever we were lying about. We were experts at making excuses, backing each other up. We laughed like crazy at our lies and at our mothers for believing us. And all that time we had our life of fun and naughty pleasure right in front of our gullible moms. How lucky we were to have had that year." She could swear that the statue was smiling back at her.

Maddy sits at the computer and opens a new document. She decides on a letter format, starts with To whom it may concern, deletes, and types Dear friends. She stares at the screen for a long time. "Who are my friends?" she asks no one. Bobbie never comes to New York. She lives in Oakland with Jen, another phys ed major. They had fallen in love in college, and have been inseparable for thirty years. Bobbie and Maddy speak rarely: when they do, Bobbie tells Maddy everything, Maddy doesn't say much. *Today,* Maddy thinks, *I don't really know her anymore.*

"I can't call Dara a friend, either," she muses out loud. "Are ex-lovers friends? When she walks away—make that runs—when your breasts get cut off, when you're throwing up like crazy, when you're bald, disfigured, ugly, ugly, ugly?" The last three words are screamed. She deletes *Dear friends,* also.

She starts again, Dear Val, I'm sorry not to answer your calls. I'm trying to think things through. I'm not going for any more chemo and I can't put you, my best and most devoted, most loyal buddy, through my horrible illness any more. You are so kind and loving, you deserve more than what I can give you now. I think my writing days are over, sweetie.

"I can't give you anything but cancer, baby. That's the only thing I've plenty of baby," she sings to the computer, furiously wiping away tears. "Shit, piss, fuck," she whispers hoarsely, then deletes all she typed. "Some writer I am" she says to no one, and picks up the journal, starting to read where it opens. It's a perfect place—the story of meeting Peg, the love of her life, and their early years together.

From the Personal Journal of Maddy Karr

I am majoring in English at Barnard, with a concentration in creative writing. I write in every genre and style I can, as my courses require, and I am starting to find my voice. I have been getting published in school publications: poetry, short stories, articles for the school newspaper. I'll try anything and everything. My professors are encouraging and classmates seeming to be getting to know me through my writing. My confidence is growing with each piece I write and my feet barely hit the ground, I'm so high! Whenever I have time, I go to literary events and lectures at school and in the city. Late this afternoon, I drifted into the lounge where a talk about "Virginia and Vita" was being held. The letters of Vita Sackville–West and Virginia Woolf have just been published, and the room is filled with devotees, one of them named Peg, who sat down next to me.

Peg majors in music, she's a composer of mostly vocal works. She is working on her doctorate at Columbia and is completely smitten with the two Vs, as she calls them. "I want to write an opera based on the letters," she tells me, her eyes shining with anticipation. Later, we found ourselves at a local Broadway pub almost without knowing how we got there. By midnight we reached Peg's studio apartment on West 101 Street.

The large room is in a five-story walk-up brownstone off West End Avenue. A small upright piano stands against the wall between two tall windows that face the street. A studio couch covered with an Indian paisley spread is in a corner, and a small round table and four chairs are near a wicker screen that is shielding the galley kitchen near the entrance. A large, old-fashioned black and white-tiled bathroom is off a short hallway dressing room with two closets and a chest of drawers. What amazes me are the walls: every inch of space is covered by sheets of poetry all written by women, protected in plastic and hung as close to one another as possible. The two Vs, Edna St. Vincent Millay, Elizabeth Barrett Browning, Emily Dickinson, Audre Lorde, Adrienne Rich, Robin Becker, Marilyn Hacker, Jewelle Gomez, and some poets I've never heard of.

"These are poems that I love," Peg explained. "I'm going to set all of them eventually. Some are already composed. That's what the lavender stars in the corner of some pages mean—those are 'sing me' songs."

I moved around the room, slowly investigating, stopping to read more carefully from time to time. "Oh my god," I gasped, "here's one of mine from the school poetry journal. What's it doing here?"

"I love that poem. I haven't set it yet...I wanted to meet you first. Now I will."

I was suspicious. I carefully asked if she knew whom I was when she sat next to me?

"Sure, I'm no fool, you were pointed out to me by a friend at the lecture on women's journal writing last week. I've been dying to meet you ever since I read this poem, Peg said, pointing at the wall. "When you turned out to be a red-haired, jade green-eyed, willowy six-footer, I knew you were the girl for me."

At this effrontery, I laughed and sat on the couch, grinning broadly at my new friend. "I took one look at you, that's all I meant to do and then my heart stood still," I sang with my sweet, pure soprano. "How tall are you anyway, Ms. Blue Eyes?"

Peg, stood on her toes and pulled herself up to her full height, raised her chin, and sang loudly, "Five foot two, eyes of blue, but oh what those five feet can do," then fell on the couch giggling wildly, and before we knew it, we were in each other's arms.

That first night was a miracle. Peg was the only lover I'd been with since Bobbie, and I was very shy at first, but not for long. Bobbie and I had made sex up as we went along, having fun, thinking we were inventing everything we did. Mostly we kissed, rolled around on top of each other, eventually touching enough to bring one another to orgasm.

Peg was a flame and she ignited me like a July Fourth rocket. In spite of our different heights we fit together like petals on a tulip. Our bodies quickly became familiar to one another and our lovemaking was bold. It felt brilliant to us, how we could intuitively find secret places of pleasure, and were able to tell each other what and where and how, without reserve. "No holds barred," Peg had giggled.

Maddy has to stop reading. She walks to the window and finds the statue. She says hello to the Lady, takes some deep breaths, and after a few minutes tells her more of the story.

"We were with each other most of the time, spending every night together, showing up unexpectedly after classes or at the library or music studio. We could hardly bear to be apart, and soon I left the dorm to move in with Peg. Around campus we were known as 'big and little,' arms linked everywhere we went, heads bent together as we sat on our private bench or in the library, having endless discussions about our work and our plans. We talked and talked until it became clear what we wanted to do."

Maddy feels light-headed telling these memories, and goes to the kitchen to have tea and Lorna Doones, Peg's favorite cookies. Feeling better, she picks up the journal and continues to read.

From the Personal Journal of Maddy Karr

I am writing the libretto for the opera Peg is composing. No surprise, it is based on the letters of the two Vs. We applied for a grant from Open Horizons, who had expressed interest in the project. Their generous contribution has enabled us to work together every possible moment, I at the computer and Peg at the piano. An opera will certainly be born.

Next year I'll be a senior and Peg will be completing the opera, which is her doctoral project. Busy, busy, busy.

Busy was the operative word, Maddy remembers. How hard they worked, loving every minute. Peg's doctoral advisor was more than approving of the opera, and the whole department was enchanted with the two Vs. With a sigh of pleasure, she reads on.

Peg was doing final revisions on the opera, completing her doctoral thesis, and. my libretto has been accepted as my senior year project. Columbia and Barnard are going to co-sponsor the first performance of Vita and Virginia at the International Festival for Women in Music, with funding from the Saint Cecilia Foundation! We were ecstatic, working side by side in a fever of excitement, eating only when we were famished, making love at odd hours, sleeping when our eyes closed. I had two short stories published, one in Ms. and one in the New Yorker. I was supporting us with work tutoring and advising students on research for their papers. Peg and I were consumed with the two Vs and with one another.

Putting the journal aside, Maddy turns to read aloud from a stack of poetry books, poems her long-ago lover would have set to music, had she lived. Adrienne Rich is in her lap and she is going back through the places she had once marked with slips of colored paper. "Stripped, I'm beginning to float free…" Next, Audre Lorde, "I dream of a place between your breasts…" Marilyn Hacker, then Robin Becker. She goes on reciting until her throat is dry and her voice fails. She sips water carefully. *Must add 'vocal chords dried out' to the list*, she thinks, but doesn't go to the computer.

She stops reading and sings, "Peg o' my heart, I love you, we'll never part, I need you. Dear little girl, my little girl." She croaks the song until she begins to sob. "Oh Peg o' my heart, my sweetheart," she wails, "how do I do this, tell me how to do this?"

She walks slowly to a shelf and takes down a bound music score. *Vita and Virginia, an opera in three acts*, music by Margaret Rosen, libretto by Madeline Karr, based on the letters of Vita Sackville West and Virginia Woolf. Maddy sits down suddenly; the volume is too heavy. She is very tired, very weary. She puts her head back and instantly falls asleep.

When she awakens hours later, it is barely morning and she is not refreshed or stronger. She feels light-headed, dizzy, weak, nauseated.

"Should I try to eat something?" she asks herself, then has a little water and goes back to the computer.

"Dearest Peg o' my broken heart," she starts a new letter. "I really did try to go on to live a life, after, after…the opera was presented, Dr. Rosen, and beautifully performed. Oh, Peg, my sweet, you would have loved it. Tatiyana sang Vita and Arlene sang Virginia, your two favorites. Could you hear them? Audiences loved it, and reviews were quite good—*The New York Times* said, 'it was very strong for a work by a woman composer and a woman librettist.' Imagine! In the 1980's!

Some reviewers said *Vita and Virginia* was a woman's subject, a feminist theme: 'powerful music for women to write.' Really! One said there was a 'cloistered atmosphere in the audience.' I guess all those women, strong women and lesbians who were in the theater unnerved the male reviewers. Never mind Peg darling, not that the 'L' word ever came up, either about the two Vs or women in the audience. Since it was 'cloistered' perhaps they were nuns."

Maddy looked at the view for a moment, smiled, and went on with her letter. "Never mind Peg darling, the two Vs is still often performed at conferences, festivals, and small opera venues in Europe, Canada, and the U.S., in different cities. You would be proud. Only it's such a long time ago, such a long time since you've been gone, since I could touch you, hold you, nibble your eyelashes like Margaret Mead's Trobrianders do."

She picks up the photograph of Peg. "I really have tried, my Peg. I wrote and wrote, even a really successful novel that eventually got published and sold a respectable number of copies. And I had girlfriends. Well, I mean, I had sex. But those bodies felt wrong in my arms… bad fit, I guess. You know the song, 'They're either too short or too tall'... or is it 'They're either too young or too old?' Never mind. I was with a few women whom I liked quite a lot. I had some fun."

Maddy stands up stiffly, gets the watering can from under the kitchen sink, and fills it halfway. She begins to water the living room plants, and stops at the album of the their opera, with a large picture of Peg on the cover. She sets down the can and puts the album close to her heart.

"Why wasn't I with you that night? We always did everything together. We were never apart. Why *that* night of all nights," she asks the beloved face, "did I do that damned reading at The Women's Bookshop?"

"If I had been with you at the concert, we would have walked home, arm in arm, like we always did on late nights, and everything would have been different. You would be here now, safe in my arms." She gently sets the album back on the table, turns away, and throws the empty watering can to the floor with a crash.

Maddy looks at Peg again and mutters fiercely, "We could have fought him off together, kicked him in the balls, hit him across the throat." She shudders deeply, and after steadying herself, takes a pink tulip from a vase, strokes it, then brings it gently to her lips. "I should have been with you, my sweet love. We should have been together." She lays the tulip carefully in front of the picture, saying in an urgent voice, "Oh, Peg, how I need you. Now I am getting slowly slashed, burned and poisoned. Oh, *how* I need you."

The ring of the phone is jolting, the message coming as though from very far away. "Maddy, it's Dara. Just calling to see how you are. I know it's been a long time, but–" Maddy rips the machine's plug from the wall, grabs the journal from her desk, and moves closer to a lamp.

From the Personal Journal of Maddy Karr
Dara is too young for me. She is a bright lawyer who specializes in cases involving lesbians and their children. I tease her, saying she wants to be involved with an older woman so she won't have to deal with having children of her own. She says, "Shit, I could have them if I wanted to."

We'd lived together for more than two years when I had my first breast cancer operation. I had my second mastectomy a year later. Dara travels often for cases and lecturing, and is not home much. "Never mind," I tell her, "I can take care of myself. I prefer to."

Last night, Dara walked into my study as I was doing arm exercises. It was a soft summer night, and the Lady was lit against a dark sky. Dinner had been a disaster. Dara cooked highly–seasoned Thai food that I just couldn't handle and finally had to give up on.

Dara looked down at me with pitying eyes as I sat in my desk chair. I was wearing a scarf on my bald head, a white tank top, and shorts. I'm very thin except for my left arm, which is swollen with lymphodema. Without moving, I waited for her to speak.

"I can't do this anymore," Dara said tentatively. "I can hardly look at you anymore." Her voice got stronger. "I'm so sorry for you. I know I'm horrible. Some feminist, huh," she scoffed at herself. "I should be supportive and stick with you, but I can't, Maddy, I just can't do it. I'm leaving. I have to leave. I've made arrangements. I'm going tomorrow. I'm sorry, Maddy." Her voice softened with emotion.

I didn't move, I didn't blink—I barely breathed as I spoke calmly.

"Of course you have to go, Dara. I've said it to you many times. You've got to go and live your life. I'm grateful you stuck it out as long as you did. Thank you, my dear." I held my hand out to her, but she didn't seem to see it.

I turned back to my desk as Dara walked out the door. I sat, stone-faced, staring at the computer, and watched the tropical fish swim back and forth on the screen saver until the sky lightened.

Maddy puts the journal down and says to herself, "It was no tragedy when Dara left, nothing else could be tragic after Peg died. Actually, it was easier for me, no one to please or take care of, just me, my writing, my illness."

To the Lady she explains, *"I have stopped writing in my journal. I have nothing more to say."* She picks up the journal and writes those words, underlines them, closes it, and replaces it on her desk.

Maddy walks to the window for a closer look at the statue. She has a cup of herbal tea sweetened with honey and is taking small sips. It is just light enough now to see the water. She raises her cup to the towering figure. *"You've been my best girl, next to Peg, of course. You've listened, you've been faithful, accepted me the way I am."*

She walks slowly to her computer, sitting down to start a new paragraph. "You are here, Peg o' my heart, you are always with me. Listen, my sweetheart."

She moves to the CD player and puts on several discs, their opera and one collection of Peg's songs recorded by their favorite soprano, Victoria de los Angeles. Music fills the apartment, playing through speakers in every room.

Maddy continues the letter. "Peg, do you hear your precious, beautiful music? It gives me joy. It gives me courage. It gives me you. Thank you, my darling, for your love, for your music, for us. Forever, your Maddy."

She prints out the letter and places it on her desk near a photograph of Peg and herself, taken at the workshop performance of their opera. She empties her cup into the sink, rinses it, and puts it in the dish drying rack. She changes to a pair of jeans and her favorite sweatshirt, the cozy black one she had given to Peg many years ago, with shiny gold letters reading, "Happiness is Music."

Maddy walks to the window and opens it wide, removes her headscarf, and throws a kiss to the Lady. In the empty apartment, the soprano sings to no one.

Choices

Probably everyone remembers where s/he was when President Kennedy was shot. She certainly did. She had been lying on her dining room table, legs akimbo, having a "kitchen table" abortion. She had taken the day off from work and was ready. The man, still wearing his hospital scrubs, had come midday and insisted that the radio be turned up high to cover any sounds she might make. He was there through an arrangement by a mutual friend who was a nurse, who had assured her that the abortionist was also a nurse. A small man, he fit easily between her spread legs, a bucket on the floor and a stack of towels nearby. There had been no anesthesia or painkillers, and she grit her teeth and gripped her hands tightly against the pain, determined not to make a sound. The radio in her kitchen sounded very far away and it took a while before she realized what was being reported.

"Did he say that President Kennedy has been shot?" she asked tentatively. The little man grunted, "I'm not listening. I'm busy." A dry laugh followed.

She concentrated on the radio announcer's voice. She pushed away the pain. She moved out of her body. Yes, John F. Kennedy had been shot. As soon as the abortion was over and the man had cleaned up and left, she turned on the TV. President Kennedy was dead. Lyndon Johnson was President.

She had been raped by her hairdresser almost eight weeks ago. He was a charming, attractive man who had come from Bari, Italy, almost a year before. He worked in a classy salon on Madison Avenue where she had been getting her hair done for several years. "A Cut Above" was close to her agent's office and convenient for music rehearsals. She became his client when her regular hairdresser left. She had assumed he was gay. Weren't all male hairdressers gay? When he invited her to dinner to talk about her hairstyle for the television program she was to appear on, she thought he was looking to make a connection into her circle of performers and felt comfortable with that. He was cultured and interesting, and she was bored that week—her lover was away on a business trip. She had enjoyed the excellent meal at the small Italian restaurant he had taken her to, so when he asked her to come to his apartment to test out a new style he had in mind for her, she went.

It didn't matter whether he was gay or not, he was violent and kinky. He tied her hands, raped her, went down on her, urinated on her—she would love "golden showers," he assured—and explained smugly that he was making love to her while continuing to humiliate her. He said the most loving things in Italian, while he violated her repeatedly. Eventually, he untied her, helped her dress, and offered to drive her home in his Ferrari. She left as fast as she could, got a cab, and waited until she was home before starting to tremble uncontrollably. She closed her bedroom door tightly and began to wail with fury.

Now she was here, the abortion over and John F. Kennedy killed. She had not reported the rape. *Those fucking cops would say she had it coming, going up to his apartment,* she thought. What did she expect, a permanent wave? Too much trouble, too hard, too much responsibility.

And President Kennedy was dead. She didn't know why any more than she knew why for anything, for everything. All she knew was that she had missed her period, and the test had come back positive. She would have to have an abortion—it seemed the only solution.

The first abortion she'd had was in Philadelphia. She had been married at twenty and they had agreed not to have children. It was a terrible marriage. Her husband was a poor and infrequent lover, and she started having affairs a year after their wedding. Her husband worked nights at the Federal Reserve Bank and labored over his doctoral dissertation in his free time. They were rarely together, with her going to graduate school and taking violin lessons. The man she was seeing regularly, an FBI agent, also was married. She never saw a reason to leave her husband; her family knew nothing of her life, and she liked things the way they were. Then she became pregnant by her lover. Her diaphragm had failed her.

In the early 1950s, before the ruling on Roe v. Wade, it was nearly impossible to find a way to have a safe abortion. There were no clinics; doctors were unwilling to give any information or help, and she certainly could not let her husband or family know about her situation. Finally, a close friend gave her a number to call, and she eventually was steered to a doctor in Philadelphia.

The first time she went to the doctor's office to be interviewed, she had been relieved to be in a regular waiting room with, it seemed, patients for seemingly ordinary medical care. The doctor checked her blood pressure, examined her briefly, and asked a few questions about her health. He asked why she wanted to terminate the pregnancy. She told him the truth: she was married but pregnant by another man. Her husband deserved better.

The doctor described the procedure: her cervix would be dilated and packed to remain open, and eventually she would have a spontaneous miscarriage. They discussed payment—which had to be paid immediately, with cash, to his nurse—and made an appointment for the following week. She paid the then enormous amount of five hundred dollars, plus an additional hundred for the medications (she had been forewarned about the cash and had it with her). There would be no paperwork or phone calls when she left the doctor's office.

After the procedure, she was to stay overnight in a local hotel in case there were complications. She would let the nurse know the details of her reservation when she came back the following week for the procedure. The doctor would check on her in the hotel room the next morning, and then she could return home. She was instructed to come with a friend who could drive her back to Manhattan. The nurse told her there might be severe cramps and bleeding. She would be given medications to deal with all the possibilities.

She drove alone to Philadelphia the following week. She did not want anyone with her. She did not want to check into a hotel. She could handle it by herself. She told the nurse she was staying with the friend who had recommended the doctor. Could she have the medications and instructions now so she could familiarize herself with them? The nurse agreed and went through them with her.

She had the abortion quickly and painfully, rested in the office for an hour, then left and drove home, stopping along the way when the cramps got bad. She sat on the towels she brought in case of heavy bleeding. She didn't dare take the pain pills, in order to stay alert for driving. She never contacted the doctor again.

Her husband never knew, though she was miserable for ten days until the process had finally run its course. He never questioned, though she spent a good deal of time on the living room couch. They barely saw one another and there was no intimacy between them, only everyday matters.

Her lover did know what was happening. She hadn't told him initially, but he had suspected he was responsible for her pregnancy. She spoke to him about it the night before the abortion, when they had gone to see the movie The Quiet Man. He was very grateful she was taking care of things, as he said, and apologized for not being able to go with her. He came to see her a couple of times when it was safe, while she waited for the "happening." When he was sure her husband would not be there, he brought her some chocolates. She would have appreciated an offering of money but was too proud to ask, and he did not offer.

She swore over and over she would never get pregnant again, would never have another abortion. She hoped the procedure would keep her from having children. It would destroy her cervix or her uterus, or there would be punishment for what she had done. A lapsed Catholic, she knew she would be punished somehow, someday, though since she had never wanted a child, she consoled herself with that thought.

But she did get pregnant again a couple of years later: the same FBI lover; the same situation, except she and her husband had divorced. "Why was this happening?" she had whined to her best friend and neighbor. "I've always been careful, I always used my diaphragm, with jelly," her finger poked the air for emphasis. "This is crazy," she'd cried, "I should be a lesbian. They don't get knocked up. Now what do I do?" She cried harder "I can't call the doctor in Philadelphia again after what I pulled." She again started to call around to see if there were any other possibilities, but weeks went by and she was stymied. So much trouble, responsibility, too hard.

Weeks went by and it seemed hopeless. Nobody knew anybody; every lead was a dead end. By the time she decided she would tough it out and have the baby, she had started running a very high fever and soon developed viral pneumonia, which kept her in bed for three weeks. The night she had tickets for a play, The Bad Seed, she had what was ironically called, a "spontaneous abortion." It happened all by itself—not fun, and certainly not expected. She had supposed her reproductive parts wouldn't work right because of her first abortion but she knew she hadn't heard the end of that adventure. *There's no question about it,* she thought, she would stop having sex with men. But she got fitted for a new diaphragm at the Margaret Sanger Institute and made her lover use a condom as well. Better safe than sorry, she decided, and the affair went on.

She continued to make sex, not love, as it suited her, with appealing men she met on her concert tours and travels. But she was very careful. Getting caught once is an accident, twice is careless, thrice is suicidal. Never again, she promised herself.

When she married a second time some years later, it was to her accompanist, a gay man. He was a marvelous pianist, handsome and interesting. They had an understanding: they would each continue to have relationships, she now with women, he with men. He needed his parents to be ignorant of his private life, so he would be sure to inherit their considerable wealth.

Their agreement was that they would eventually have a child. He was adopted, and adored by his parents, who had no knowledge of his sexuality. In their late seventies, all they cared about was their son and daughter-in-law having a child. They wanted a grandchild, they wanted an heir, and they wanted their son and his child to inherit their money. His mother longed to teach a granddaughter to play the piano. She, herself, played a different Beethoven sonata every day. His father wanted a grandson to take to ballgames.

She and her husband decided it was time to try to have a biological child of their own. In time, she became pregnant; getting stoned on good weed helped them over the hump of their sexual preferences. There would be no abortion this time. Her husband would prove to his parents that he was a real man, and they would finally be grandparents. She would hire a nursemaid for the baby and go on with her life as a violinist. She hoped she and her husband would eventually learn to love their child.

Eight weeks later, after an arduous visit to the 1964 World's Fair, she had a miscarriage. She went to Mount Sinai Hospital, and he took off for Fire Island. He stopped by to see her for a few minutes, bringing her the coral satin nightgown and robe she had asked for out of her closet, and then left without a parting glance.

Of course, she fumed, it's the Philadelphia story where she screwed herself with that first abortion, ruined all her insides and now she could never have a baby even if she wanted one. She knew it. Serves me right, she berated herself. She alternately cried and raged all weekend.

When she got pregnant again after a night of drinking martinis, her husband had fallen madly in love with some new man he had met at the baths. He wanted out of the marriage, out of fatherhood, out of the pseudo-straight life he was leading. To hell with his parents, he'd said, they would just have to live without a grandchild. He had to live his life.

What would she do with his baby? She not too gently inquired of her husband. She was not having it to please his parents, and she was not willing to be a single mother.

He looked at her coldly, making it clear that he was out of there. That she would not be having that baby, even if he'd have to rip it out of her belly with his own two hands. He would find a way to get rid of it.

She remembered how frightened of him she felt at that moment. He was murderous. He loathed her. He probably loathed all women. What had happened to the handsome marvelous musician she had married? Was he a Jekyll and Hyde character?

She found her courage and let him know she would not have a back alley or kitchen table procedure. She would only have it done by a qualified doctor, and she wanted the abortion in a proper medical facility. She would not allow it any other way.

He arranged for the abortion at a hospital in Mexico City. She went down alone and had it done without anyone else knowing. A real doctor in a real hospital, clean, nice, and pain-free. The only problem was that her uterus had been perforated during the procedure. Just a little tear, the doctor had said. It would take a long time for the wound to heal; she wasn't sure the torn place ever would.

When she got back to New York, she was wobbly for weeks. Her husband had packed all her belongings while she was recovering at a friend's apartment, and helped himself to many of her books and recordings and some art she cherished. She came back to an empty apartment, except for the packed boxes stacked in the living room and a note on top of one saying she had to be out of the apartment by the end of the week. It had been rented and the new tenants were coming in the first of the month. She quickly moved to a new apartment on the Upper West Side. She was through with the East Side.

The months went by and she practiced relentlessly, getting a new concert program ready. She had decided that a celibate life suited her just fine, for now.

A year later, on that fateful night of the dinner with her hairdresser, she felt uncertain about his intentions. She told him she was a lesbian and had been with her lover for three years. This was not completely true—she had only just begun an affair with a violist—but she thought it would keep him in line. He laughed and said in Italian that she simply had not met the right man yet; that she should have an Italian male lover, a real man who would stop her silliness with women.

She told him that she was completely happy with her lifestyle. Her radar should have crackled when he made his big speech about "the Italian man's view of love and sex". Sex you can do with anyone, even a dog, he'd said, but love is a gift that only a real lover can bestow on a woman. Of course, he insisted, only an Italian man could be a real lover.

But because he seemed generally good-natured and respectful, she made her terrible misjudgment of him.

She had not had sex with a man for a long time. She and her second husband had only been intimate those few times when they were trying to have a child. They'd smoke a joint, drink a Negroni, make sex—it hadn't been so bad. In the beginning, she and her gay husband had some fun. Then the fun stopped. He seemed different, cold and removed.

The encounter with the hairdresser taught her that rape is the nightmare one never wakes up from. It was always there for her—the terror, the fright, the humiliation and pain. A part of her got taken, stolen, and she feared she'd never get it back. So hard, too much trouble in her life.

She thought pregnancy resulting from rape was especially toxic. She hoped and wished this pregnancy would not hold. Another abortion, a miscarriage, a perforated uterus, sheer will, would all combine to make it fail. But what if it didn't? The irony of it was frightening; that this might be the time it would work. She could not take that chance.

Could she tell her current lover, who would surely ask how she could have gone to his apartment, if she was looking for trouble. And maybe that was right, blaming the victim. No, she'd better keep this to herself. She would make inquiries, find someone, do *something* to end this hateful pregnancy. Now she had money and an understanding doctor—a lesbian gynecologist—what could be better? She'd help her find a way. It was getting close to December 13, 1971, when Roe v. Wade would be argued at the Supreme Court, but she could not wait for such a miracle.

She had been pregnant five times. She could have had five children. Instead, she had four planned abortions and one from Mother Nature. Now she was middle-aged, too old to think about children. Her latest partner had become cool, and spoke of taking a break and living separately.

She did not want to be alone, but she did not want a new relationship. It didn't seem to be worth the trouble anymore. Besides, she was tired of telling her life story, or a version of it to some new woman. *A tale too oft told*, she thought wryly. Perhaps she'd like being alone, might even prefer it. When her dog, Vita Sackville Pest died last Thanksgiving, she decided to have no more dogs. It was too much responsibility, too much trouble, too hard. That applied to lovers as well, men or women—too much responsibility, too much trouble, too hard.

She might accept the teaching position she had been offered at the local college. She would try to do more concerts.

Perhaps a new agent, she mused to herself. Maybe call a friend about dinner. There was a good concert she might go to. She had eggs in the fridge and a can of vegetarian baked beans, but she wasn't hungry. She'd have a scotch instead, a double. She really should get up and do something. Too much trouble, too hard.

I Want To Write Something Funny
But I'm Too Sad

There are three, maybe four possibilities for me and my partner Blaine: I could die first—after all, I am twelve years older; Blaine could die first, which does not seem fair; or we could die together, at the same time, which is too tragic for words. I suppose there's no chance that we could both just go on living, even with all the new meds and treatments that keep people going on and on. But I don't think that's really feasible.

So the discussion—or should I say the argument—will keep going on. It starts our day with breakfast and ends with our goodnight kiss. Take this morning:

Blaine, as she makes her coffee, says, "If we sell the house, seeing as the real estate market is up now, we could afford..."

I interrupt, as I often do, angry that my tea bag has just fallen apart because of my furious beating it with a spoon so that the tea will get dark sooner. "I know, I know, if we sell the house, we will have enough money to buy a cottage at the Never Say Die retirement joint, complete with meals, housekeeping, landscaping, and gossiping for the inmates."

Blaine, ever the rational woman, will ignore my words, soothe, and try to tempt: "and the dining room will be replete with gluten–free meals for your celiac, lactose–free foods for your dairy intolerance, low–fat for your cardiac flutters." She was cooing at me now, seeing my fury grow with each dietary suggestion.

"And it all tastes like old-mown hay—no seasoning, no color, no excitement. Have a heart, Blaine, I love the meals we cook right here in our own kitchen. Healthy for us both, tasty to the tongue and palate, and we don't have to be pleasant to a bunch of straight seniors we don't know, who can't hear anything we say so we have to shout."

"Don't be difficult, Willy"—that's short for Willow—"you would love it at Never Say Die. They have a Shakespeare Theatre Ensemble; a 'Nuts About Words' group; the 'Meditation Mull–Overs'; Massage and Exercise Enrichment; 'Swim and Swingers', and lots more activities. You'll never be bored."

"I'm bored to death just listening to this."

"Silly Willy, don't you dare say those words!"

"Bored or never?"

"You lose 'life credits' if you say the words death, dying, die, or died at Never Say Die."

"The damned place sounds like a concentration camp, not an old-age home. What the hell are 'life credits'?" I ask my lady, but she has gone to her meditation nook. She won't play the Blaine-game, and isn't listening to me any more.

We are discussing the invitation to lunch (and a sales pitch, I suppose) at the "Never Say Death Camp" for old folks, tomorrow afternoon. Blaine wants us to go. I'm singing Put the Blame on Blaine, Girls, until my girlfriend gets that Medusa look, and I get a sapphically brilliant idea.

"Did it ever occur to you, Blaine, my darling," I say in my best Katherine Hepburn voice, "that there are no lesbian ladies living at that playground for the aged? I checked—there are two couples of gay guys, and one pair of guys who sleep in separate bedrooms. What do you think of that! We'd be truly queer—oddities, preternaturals, food for fantasy. I will probably have to explain at the lunch table that we are lesbians, not Latvians. How would you like handling that, huh?"

"That's where you're wrong, Willy! There is a couple that belongs to the L Word Lovers League (the LWLLers), who signed up for a cottage just last week, and they are thinking of putting the deposit down. What do you think of that, O Wise Woman?"

"Ha!" I respond humorlessly. Thinking of putting down some bucks, are they? Let me know when some actual greenies leave their wallets. And who are these pioneers in the local lesbian world?"

"Two good women, Willow, whom you've met, and you've never been mean to, though you only met them once. Remember?"

"If I had a clue as to who these LWLLers are, then perhaps, even maybe, I might possibly be able to consider them as being a pair that I could approve of." I give Blaine my most winsome smile, which always looks like a leer to her.

"You have to guess who they are," she bats her eyelashes at me like a flapper girl and sits on my lap. Uh oh, now Blaine is being cute. That's always dangerous. I put a hand on each of her ample breasts. My adorable, just right, not–too–thin honey giggles.

"Well?" I query, playing Blaine's game. "Give me a clue." She plants a kiss on my nose.

"One of them is short and thin and the other is tall and thinner."

"That's no clue. All the LWLLers are under or over weight, no matter their height, except us, of course," I say smugly.

Blaine removes my hands from her bosom, stands up to her full 5'3", and shakes my shoulders lightly. "You're being mean and you don't even know who they are. She gives me a stronger shake and says, "It's Mei Lin Rosenthal and Flo Gentlee for your information."

"Wow." I clap my hands. "I guess they want to diversify Never Say Die, as they did with LWLLers. Great. An Asian Jew and an African American: two lesbian couples! Will wonders never cease?" I must confess, this has caught me by surprise. Interesting. I have spent years complaining about the homogeneous white LWLLers women. Hmm, they would certainly be an addition to the Never Say habitat. And I still don't know what 'life credits' are. I am starting to get curiouser and curiouser. So maybe we should go to the 'Don't Die' Lunch. We could sit at the same table as Mei Lin and Flo, if they'll be there. I'll put this in Blaine's hands, she's really good at matchmaking—friends, that is.

The place is beautifully landscaped and groomed outside, with dull dining rooms on the main floor, a cheerful café, a library and lounge outfitted with leather furniture, very male, and a huge stone fireplace that never seems to be burning. The art is stuffy and uninteresting, with some work by the residents for sale.

The Never Say Die Habitat (I call it The Last Resort) is a big property, filled with identical homes and streets named for flowers. There is some bad sculpture and a large pond that attracts Canada Geese who fertilize the grounds generously. The athletic facilities are in separate areas with glass walls. The facilities appear unused; no one is in the pools or gym.

Blaine has arranged a gluten–free meal for me, with unsweetened lemonade made with freshly squeezed fruit, her idea of a shot of vitamin C. The dining room is filled with wannabees and "why am I here" folks. The sales pitch is somewhat unctuous and patronizing—too much for my taste. But Mei Lin and Flo are at our table, and they interest me. They are both really attractive. One is tall, the other short, and both athletic–looking. In fact, Mei Lin is as tall as I am, 6'2". Flo is only 5'2", an inch shorter than Blaine, and the couple looks like they are amused all the time. Mei Lin and I tower over our sweeties like a couple of basketball players. We make an odd quartet.

The food is just short of awful. Mei Lin is eating fried chicken, Flo is having Pad Thai, expertly wielding her chopsticks. Blaine is pushing a mystery salad around her plate, and I am looking at a vegetable platter that appears to be mush. The old folks at the next table seem to be content with their overdone steaks and starchy pasta, things forbidden to me, but I do have my own teeth and could chew something more substantial than vegetables boiled to a puree.

There are lots of canes, walkers, and several wheelchairs for the many straight, white widows and widowers. What am I doing here? My legs work just fine.

The speaker at the microphone is smiling broadly, loudly welcoming us with outstretched arms. All around the room, hearing aids are whistling their discomfort.

There are graphs, financial information, costs, and schedules showing us on a screen how we can afford Never Say___, that dreadful word that will cost you life credits, so how come the name of the place is Never Say Die? Ah, Irony, how delicious thou art; Art, how artless your irony.

Flo and Mei Lin are at our home tonight having dinner, hoping we can get to know each other better, and to talk about you–know–what. In my court bouillon, that I have nursed along all year, I have poached a gorgeous striped bass from our local waters. Some seafood risotto and a salad are lovely accompaniments to the fish. We have been enjoying some Saint André with rice crackers and smoked trout. With the main course, we served ice cold Prosecco in our best champagne glasses. By the fifth glass we are all good friends.

"Do you really want to live or die at Never Say?" I ask, as Blaine softly pinches my arm to complain about my question.

Mei Lin laughs behind her hand and replies with a question, just like a Rosenthal should.

"Well, Willy, are you and Blaine signing up for the wait list?"

Not really having an answer, I pour some more bubbly, but play it safe with a mild response to avoid another pinch. "We need to get more information about it, and I want to see what the place feels like."

"Why?" Flo asks in her cultivated, warm voice. "You have this beautiful home, and by the aromas coming from your kitchen, I gather that the food chez vous is far superior to our recent lunch, so why are you considering Never Say Die Habitat? Ridiculous name that suits the problem in this country of older people not being able to face the fact that someday they will die."

"Now you will lose some life credits for saying that dirty word die. Naughty girl," I shake my finger at Flo. "Go stand in the corner," I command, acting as dominatrix.

"What the hell are 'life credits'?" Flo asks. Nobody answers or knows. We all laugh, eat and drink, and talk about where we went to school, what our professions are, and finally, when we came out. Flo asks, "How, when and where?"

"I picked Blaine up at Orchard Beach, in the Bronx near City Island, almost three decades ago. She was wearing short shorts, (hot pants I think they're called) a tee–shirt and a really butch hat. So I plopped down next to her and asked how the water was.

"I never go into the water, never go swimming. There are sharks out there." Blaine puffed on a cigarette, looked at me from stem to stern and smiled approvingly.

"I said to her, 'I'm Willow, call me Willy, and there are no sharks out there.'"

"Of course there are, there are sharks in all waters. I'm from Captiva, Florida, and I know that for a fact. Call me Blaine."

"What about in lakes and streams? And the bathtub?"

"Sharks. Everywhere. Would you like to have dinner with me on my boat?" Blaine asked.

"'Where's your boat? I don't have dinner with strange women who think there are sharks in lakes and their bathtub.'"

By this time, Flo and Mei Lin were doubled over with laughter as the story went on.

" 'My boat is parked in Eastchester Bay, and my dingy is right there.'" Blaine pointed aimlessly.

"And so it was—Blaine took me to her fabulous houseboat that she'd built herself—cooked me an odd dinner of cabbage, carrots, potatoes, and pork, and we've never been apart since."

"How about you two?" Blaine asks.

"We'll tell you later, it's somewhat bizarre. Let's go to our home, Mytilene, it's only six minutes from here. We have some beautiful brandy, we'll drink and talk," Flo says.

Eventually, dinner is over. We leave after Blaine's idea of dessert: mystery flavored gelato and cookies. I don't eat the gelato, (it tastes like chopped liver that might be served at Never Say), but I take the plate of cookies with me. I am relieved to have no more pinches, Blaine just smiles as a reward for my being a good girl.

We head for Mei Lin and Flo's brandy, where the topic of planning for the future comes up again. Blaine opens the discussion. "I am having an awful time with Willy. She just doesn't want to face the fact that we are getting older and need to plan how we will live our last years in a safe, comfortable environment." She leans away from me, expecting a pinch, but I give a little kick instead, it misses and I land on my own toes.

"I have the perfect plan for our waning years, and I am completely willing to share it, if you are interested?" I ask. Flo and Mei nod. Blaine rolls her eyes.

Mei Lin, with inquiring eyes says, "So, nu, tell us already, I'm all ears."

"Eyes," I contradict, and get a nasty poke for my stereotypic jest.

"It's a very simple, economical plan, and can be put to work quickly." I am puffed up with self-assurance. I take a sip of the really great brandy to heighten the moment. Too long—I almost forget what the plan is.

"Ah yes, the plan. We have a nice house, with a study for me and an office for Blaine. I can still walk the steps up to our bedroom, but when that becomes a problem, we'll get one of those nice seats that ride up and down. We have a bench in the shower and holding bars in the bathrooms, but we'll have to get raised seats for the toilets." Flo and Mei Lin seem amused, but polite. Blaine looked neither.

"To continue: we have Juan and his cousin to mow, trim, and pull the weeds; our Polish household technician who does laundry and some cleaning; in fall and spring we can get the cleaning company in to do the heavy stuff, and windows. There, that will take care of the house."

"What about cooking, shopping, driving, and medical stuff, like remembering when to take pills and exercise, do all the things old folks need to?" Flo asks, while the others nod their heads in agreement.

"Those things are the easiest of all to take care of—this is the genius of the Wiley Willy Plan of Action." I wait for Mei Lin to get another bottle of brandy, which I open, while the suspense, or perhaps the annoyance builds. Snifters poured, Mei Lin says xié xié (thank you) and Flo taps her fingers on her glass. I get the message and lay my plan on them.

"You have a guest bedroom, sitting room, and a bathroom available for a bright, capable young dyke to live with you," I say.

"You forgot to say gorgeous," Blaine insinuated. I ignore the inference and continue.

"She can cook, shop, drive, clean and tidy up. She pays no rent, and we pay her a nice amount of expense money, weekly. We all have Long Term Care insurance and can have a health aide, or nurse if necessary. We don't have to sell our house, buy a cottage, pay high maintenance monthly, play, swim, exercise, or talk to strangers, and give up our precious privacy. We will just wait to die at the camp for old people. Or..." I pause for an over dramatic moment, "we can continue to live the rest of our lives as we choose, the way we choose, and with whom we choose. That's my plan." I stand up, twirl around, and take a deep bow and wait for the applause.

Instead of applause I get something better—silence. They are thinking it over, I hope. It's taking too long. Now I don't like the silence. Finally, Flo says, "Well girl, you've got some good stuff there," in a new voice, resonant, with a Southern lilt. It feels like she's kissed me with honey on her lips, sweet and sweeter.

Mei Lin tilts her head to the side and gestures as if she is conducting a choir. "This is what my family in China does to a certain extent, and my Jewish family as well. In Beijing, my grandma, who was married at fourteen and had her first and only child at fifteen. She lived with my Mom and Dad, took care of all the children, and ruled like an empress over the household help, supervising the shopping and cooking. That balabusta was one tough fortune cookie, let me tell you, but the house ran like clockwork." She shows us a photo on her iPad. "That's my nainai," she says proudly. "Gone but not forgotten." She wipes away a tear.

"What about your Jewish family?" my shiksa sweetie asks.

"Oy vey, don't ask, you shouldn't know from it," Mei Lin looks downcast, but perks up in a second and sings My Yiddishe Bubbie (substituting for MaMa), until we all beg for mercy.

"It's like I told you: in China and in Boro Park, Brooklyn, it was pretty much the same. My widowed mother-in-law, who's younger than my nainai was, lives on her social security in a studio apartment, by herself. We go there for Shabbos dinner every Friday and obey her rules. My mother-in-law runs the show. Five days a week she walks a flight up to her daughter Shayna's apartment in the same building. My sister-in-law can only make tea. She's smart, but her coffee is bitter like bile, so first thing Mom does is make coffee for them. Then Shayna and her husband go to work while her sturdy mother cleans, shops, and cooks, and takes care of the baby. If it's Friday, she makes gefilte fish, the best anywhere. 'It's no big magillah,' my mother-in-law says, 'it's my job.'"

"And that's how the Rosenthal household works," Mei Lin chants as if she was reading from the Torah.

From her shaking shoulders, I can't tell if Flo is laughing or crying. Tears are running down her cheeks, and her whole body is in motion. Aha, it's both.

"Oh Lord, that's not much different from my home, where my Gran raised me and my five sisters and brother in Georgia, except that Gran was the attractive dyke living with us. Gran had our mama when she was a teenager, worked on a cruise ship, and wasn't home much."

"She did all the work—the shopping, the cooking, the cleaning. When each of us got old enough, out of diapers, we'd be assigned chores we'd have to do: making our beds; putting our dirty laundry in the basket; dusting and sweeping, and when we were fit for the job, vacuuming, washing dishes, and ironing. She was the boss: told us what to do, and then inspected everything to see if it was up to her standards."

"And what happened if it wasn't?" I inquire.

"We'd get a whuppin' and have to do it over again. It worked out fine, according to her requirements," Flo said, laughing. "We just made a game out of everything. We loved our Granny." She empties her glass with a major swallow and pours some more.

"And girls, could she cook! Her kitchen was the best in the South. Everything I know about cooking I learned from her. We'll never find a smart, capable young dyke to cook like she could. When one of her girlfriends came for an overnight visit, the fried chicken and apple pies she made were a treat. We'd do a square dance when one of those ladies showed up. Granny was somewhere in her forties then, but don't be misled, her bed used to shake the house when one of her sweeties was visiting, oh yeah," Flo croons. She is actually smacking her lips with the memories. Her sweet smile warms the room.

I remind her that we want to hear how she and Mei Lin got together. Mei Lin says she will tell us, after she has a bit more brandy. She had a good swallow and started.

"Well, this may sound bizarre, but Flo and I met in a Buddhist temple in Taiwan. She was praying and saying beads and stuff, and I was waiting for my previous girlfriend, who had left to go shopping, but didn't seem to be coming back." Mei Lin stops to take a breath and Flo jumps in.

"I saw this gorgeous gal looking around for someone, and I decided that someone was me. So I introduced myself. Her person never showed up, it seems they were on the verge of breaking up, and I got the prize: the beautiful, brilliant, abandoned (but not for long) Mei Lin. It was Mei Lin and me forever. And we're living happily ever after."

Blaine and I applaud the story that makes lots of sense to us, it's not bizarre at all. There was a little bit left in the bottle, enough for a small swallow each. We drank it and said goodnight.

We are back at Never Say, this time for an early dinner, to give the food another chance. There's a bottle of fancy local red wine on the table, and we start right on it. The kitchen has prepared a gluten-free dinner for me: broiled salmon with lemon and dill, basmati rice, and a big salad. It looks pretty good. Blaine is having seafood Jambalaya with rice, and Flo has steak frites, very rare.

They have made a big mistake with Mei Lin's meal. In front of her is a sectioned plate of Chinese foods, the combination kind you get at the buffet takeout places, no relation to authentic Chinese cuisine. The MSG forms a mushroom cloud over her plate. They have supplied wooden chopsticks tied together at the top, to help people who've never used them. She's a good sport and asks our waitperson if she might start with matzoh ball soup instead, as this is the Jewish New Year. Out comes a bowl of Wonton soup. Everyone in the dining room is keeping an eye on us. "Well, they tried," Mei Lin giggles behind her hands.

"Do they think we might steal the stainless steelware?" Flo asks. I am about to answer when a piercing alarm goes off. We stand, ready to leave, thinking it might be a fire alarm.

"Oh, don't bother," says our waitperson, "it's only Mrs. Parkerhurst falling out of her wheelchair again. That alarm goes off every time someone is about to fall off a scooter or wheelchair, or has an untied seat belt. It's awful screechy, isn't it?" She puts down dessert, little plastic containers of pudding, and leaves with a self-satisfied grin.

The tour we take after dinner is confusing because we feel lost immediately. All the houses look the same—how would we ever find our own? As the light fades, we are led inside to see an apartment, a small cottage, then a large cottage with a water view, which we have just enough light to see. They are like all model homes shown to prospective buyers, but more so, with white carpeting, and everything else white and metallic gold—an attempt for a thirties movie set look that came from a thrift shop.

Mei Lin tugs at Flo and says, "If I'd known we'd be in Hollywood I would've worn my sequins."

Our guide seems pleased with her remark. "I'm so glad you see how glamorous we are."

I am absolutely overcome with the white-straight-permed-powdered-hushed-polite-deadness. Uh oh, I've said the forbidden word.

"Let's have a drink at your house," Flo suggests. "Being the token black girl is exhausting. Two residents have already asked me if I do windows."

"Me too." Mei Lin says, "I feel like a novelty doll, but I don't know if it's for being Chinese or Jewish."

"Both, honey," Blaine informs in her best travel agent information voice.

At our house, we take off our shoes and stretch out on the couches. "How long do I have to wait for my drink? I want some chocolate milk," I demand like a three–year–old.

"No problem," answers Flo. "I keep a whole case of Yoo-hoo in our downstairs fridge. I'll go home and bring some. Mei Lin won't let me keep it where people might see. Matter of fact, I will just have one with you." We all end up slurping Yoo-hoos, then settle down for some serious talk about death, finances, and our next step.

"Let's just get to the issues," Flo imperiously commands. "Do we want to or don't we?"

And we clink our Yoo-hoos, which I can't drink any more of because it's so sweet I'm nauseated.

Blaine yawns noisily and comes up with this: "before we answer Flo's question, here's an assignment. Let's figure out how much it costs to run our homes—every detail from housekeeping, utilities, keeping the grounds manicured, food for all meals, and anything else you can think of—then list all the costs for an apartment or a cottage at the Never Say Die Habitat. And also, how much you might get for the home you own now. Don't forget the monthly maintenance, tips, Christmas presents, whatever. Use a bookkeeping ledger, and we can compare the costs penny for penny."

Flo grumbles, "That'll keep us busy for a while."

Mei Lin soothes, "don't worry, I'm available to help. You know we Asians are wizards with numbers."

"I thought it's Jewish people who are the money experts. You'll consult your father, no doubt," Flo says.

Blaine and I are too tired to even laugh, so we leave for home and our bed. "This is too much like work," I whine.

"That place is having a bad effect on all of us. I feel twenty years older." I take Blaine's hand and pull her into the bedroom. "The only antidote is making love."

"Yippee," says Blaine.

I always read the obituaries in *The New York Times*; I guess to make sure I'm not in them. Now I've decided to read them in the neighborhood daily, the *New Fork Evening Paper*, as well as the weekly Life and D—th News, published by Never Say you–know–the–rest. I'm happy to report that my name does not appear in obits in either of these rags. But here's a flash you won't read anywhere else: nary a week goes by without someone from our local Habitat passing on to his or her just rewards.

I call a gathering of "the Fizzy Four", my new name for our quartet.

We meet at the newest cool saloon in the area, The Petulant Imbiber—a strange name for a bar, but I like it.

The first complaint is from Flo: "We haven't had time to finish our financial stuff, Willy."

"That's because you haven't let me help with the numbers, you control freak," Mei Lin complains to Flo.

"Well, I'm okay with taking more time to finish," Blaine says arrogantly.

A tiny pinch comes from me, as a reward for her kindness. "You fraud, we haven't even started because you are never ready," Blaine accuses. It sounds like an ad for Viagra. I take a defensive route, "Well, that's because I'm doing a lot of research."

"Liar, liar, thong on fire," Blaine almost spits, "you are the control freak, not Flo, that's what you are."

"Hey, just a minute, Fizzy Four," Mei Lin holds up her hand, "this is getting rough. We're supposed to live together till death do us part, two couples in perfect harmony, each in our cozy cottage built for two."

"That's a bicycle, my little mushroom. You mean," and Flo begins to sing. Daisy, Daisy, give me your answer true...on a bicycle built for two." As usual Mei Lin starts the laughter, it's contagious and soon the four of us are laughing like hyenas.

Eventually, Blaine brings us to order. "Why are we here, Willy? What's up?"

I tell them about the newspaper stats I've put together on Never Say Die. "What do you think of the numbers? It looks to me that although you never say die, you just do. It gives me the Willies and spooks me out."

Before I can continue with my diatribe, Flo stops me. "Hey girl, you can say die if you need to, but spook is out of the question." Is she kidding? I'm not sure until she laughs so hard she knocks her drink over.

Blaine has her serious face on. "If it's a fact that at least one or more residents dies every week, thus possibly making room for new buyers, then maybe something suspicious is going on."

"Are you suggesting that the old folks are getting knocked off, Blaine?" Mei Lin asks.

"For heaven's sake, Blaine, these folks are old—nineties are nothing, and there are a number of Neverers who are in their hundreds," I remonstrate in my best shrink voice.

Blaine sends the ball back to my side of the court. "Even so, Willy, why are so many residents dying all the time?"

"Lordy, lordy, the plot sickens, I mean thickens," Flo almost sings.

"Well, actually," I clear my throat, "they are not dying all the time, it's the really old or sick ones that do, at expected intervals. I'm afraid I exaggerated. Sorry."

"But you must admit, the food is pretty poisonous," Mei Lin dishes up. "Maybe the chef is adding a bit of mischief." Our laughter sticks like a bone in our throats.

Flo offers a new possibility. "The geriatric specialist who is available for everyone who lives and works in Never, Never Land, what's his name? Oh yes, Dr. Livermore, he might be someone we could talk to." I listen to the silence. "We could meet with him as prospective buyers and ask about the health and death, no, about the health and well–being of the residents. I can't think how to sneak the D – word into the conversation."

"I'll write a script," our playwright Mei Lin offers. "That way we won't let the bad word in. I'm more scared of losing my 'life credits' than losing my life." She grins broadly.

We high-five all around, and make a date to do our finances and for me to speak to Dr. Livermore about life expectancy. We put off speaking about my revised Willy's Perfect Plan for Perfect Perpetuity.

Blaine and I are sick of talking about numbers. We are tired of struggling with the task of trying to determine the better financial choices. We are bored with the struggle of being bored, with the problem of what to do with the rest of our lives, starting with where we should live, and how. As the weeks pass, we stop going to the movies, we stop seeing our friends, we stop making love. We are at a standstill, up against a stone wall, unable to turn left or right.

This is awful. Blaine is actually crying. She is thoroughly miserable. We're not having a good time, no fun, how did this happen?" I have to do something. I wait for the moment of gestalt and wait, but all I get is heartburn, which I've been getting every night after dinner. And then it happens: I get a bright idea!

"Let's go to see our astrologer, she'll help us." I am met with a raised eyebrow and a sneer.

"We don't have an astrologer, you're thinking of Nancy Reagan," Blaine reminds me.

"Just kidding," I say with a toothy leer. "Let's go to see Sappho, our accountant, she's a genius with numbers."

The eyebrows raise and surround amazed dark brown eyes, and the sneer transforms into a gorgeous smile. "That's brilliant, Willy. Call her right now...but don't let her spout reams of poetry at you, get to the point ASAP," Blaine orders.

And I do. I explain the issue to Sappho and she tells us what to bring to a meeting in two days. She assures us that she has lots of our financial information from years of doing our tax returns. "This will be a piece of cake, girls, so much fun to do. I even have all the information about the costs, at Never Say Die Habitat. I got the numbers a couple of months ago when I was considering possibilities for myself." Blaine and I fall into each other's arms and do a quick Black Bottom, which we learned at our dance lessons last year.

I get on the phone with Mei Lin and Flo to tell them our plan. "How cool is that, darlings. I never did think of doing such a thing. My shrink brain is rusted out from all the crap we've been trying to deal with," Flo says, excited, her voice at least an octave higher since her dour hello. "I'm on it, girls, Ms. Numbers, here we come." We make a dinner date for the next day. It is 10:00 PM and the sun has just come out. We're singing "Happy Days Are Here Again."

I am sitting in Dr. Livermore's office with my skirt pulled down over my knees, legs crossed at the ankles, trying to look like a lady. I've been warned that the doctor is another Rush Limbaugh, whom the residents at Never Say like, even love, conservative as they are.

"What can I do for you, Mrs. Teary?"

I correct him gently. "My name is Dr. Willow Teary, Dr. Livermore."

"What are you a doctor of, Mrs. Teary?" he asks suspiciously. "And what kind of name is Wallow?" He continues the inquisition without my answers.

"I am a psychiatrist. The name is Willow, you know, like a willow tree. But please call me Dr. Teary."

"Yes, well, what can I do for you, are you having a medical problem?" I see that I am to remain nameless, and decide not to use his name either.

"Several of my friends and I are looking into the Never Say Die Habitat as a residence we might move into, and I have been asked by them to talk to you about the health and well-being of the residents."

"I don't discuss the health of my patients—because that is a privacy issue," he almost barks at me.

"Of course, but I am only speaking in general terms, I am not asking about specific patients and their medical issues. As a physician, I am perfectly aware and respectful of privacy regulations, and, as a psychiatrist, I am more than devoted to confidentiality." I smile without charm.

"I do not consider psychiatry a proper medical practice. Poking around in people's feelings is not medicine," he says and starts reading the mail on his desk.

I almost lose it, but I grit my teeth and swallow my fury. Give me Rush any day. "Before I even consider living here, I want to ask you, as the official physician at Never Say, why so many of the community here die at alarming rates? The number of fatalities at this retirement institution exceeds any other such facility in this state." I really have no proof that this is a fact, I'm just basing it on the obituaries I read. I think this may come back and bite me, so I shut up.

Livermore's face is livid; he is looking apoplectic. He stands and points to the door. "Out, out, out, out. Leave my office. Now!"

I have to get one more lick in before I scoot. "You should watch your blood pressure. The carotid artery in your neck is pulsating dangerously. You don't want to have a stroke, do you? You are way overweight, you have a tremor, and you don't look well to me at all. Good day, Mr. Livermore." I make a hasty exit. I may have gone too far.

I leave with head held high. As a matter of fact, I've never felt better, that is until I get home. When I think of the conversation with Livermore, how I manipulated the truth about the deaths at Never Say to make it look really bad, I have to stop and consider my maneuvering. My pushing Livermore to look as awful as possible only exacerbates my doubts about my own plans for the future. I am in a murky funk. I feel guilty, a fine thing for a psychiatrist.

When Blaine comes home I announce: "It's time for us to get out of here." She raises her eyebrows in question. "I mean someplace away from here and Never Say Die and death, death, death! There, I've lost a zillion life credits, whatever the fuck they are."

Blaine is the best travel agent in the world. She will know how to get us away from it all, my perfect person for performing travel miracles. And she always finds just the right place to ease on down the road to. These thoughts comfort me and I sigh with pleasure.

I am stretched out on a lounge chair under a sea grape tree, contemplating the intensely blue waters of Sun Beach Bay on the idyllic isle of—no, not Lesbos—but Vieques, Puerto Rico. I am thinking about what I will look like when I get really old—nineties, hundreds. I wonder what my place will be in the universe, and other little thoughts like that. I have no answers, only questions.

Blaine is lying in the sun sipping a rum concoction, listening to Mahler's Fifth. The other members of the Fizzy Four are coming down on the next flight from San Juan, arranged for by Blaine. These thoughts comfort me and I sigh with pleasure.

Flo and Mei Lin arrive in time for drinks called Cuba Libres. A team of horses couldn't have kept them from being with us here on Shangri–La, otherwise known as paradise. They are as fed up as Blaine and I with the machinations of the decision process we are embroiled with back home. Either we will go back home with answers or we will declare the situation insoluble. Or both. It doesn't take long for us to agree not to talk about it at all.

And so we swim and eat, play tennis and golf, go sightseeing, drink, and dance. Dance is the best. We dance and dance—with each other, with adorable Viequen guys, and with their gorgeous women—dance the calories away every night, and then consume some more. Every day is hedonistic in purpose and execution. We eat mangoes until we are sick, and are aghast to find out we have eaten endangered turtle steaks, so we swim away our guilt at midnight in the moonlight.

We are happy, not the least bit sad, and not one of us speaks the words Never Say Die. We make love with our sweethearts, we swim nude, we boat to Phosphorescent Bay and float in the magic phosphorescent water, turning our bodies gleaming with silver. We are supposed to leave for home tomorrow, but like proper hedonists—is that an oxymoron? We decide to stay a few days longer.

Back home, I have been secretly thinking about our plight, in private, not discussing it with anyone. I have an earworm going round and round in my head, but I can't grab it. I just can't come up with what's on the tip of my tongue, the edge of my mind, the solution to the problem of what to do with our last twenty-five years.

Should we just forget the whole thing? Blaine won't like that—she's pretty set on the ease of living at a good retirement facility. "Just think," she occasionally urges when we're alone, "no more lawn mowing, spring and fall house cleaning, home maintenance, or cooking unless we want to." She comes up for air. "It's all done for us, no worry, easy does it. What's wrong with that?"

I'm not convinced, but I say kindly, "I'm thinking about it, honey, I'm trying to come up with the right answer for us both, but somehow, living, and dying in such a place just gives me my Willies."

Blaine just shakes her head. "Well maybe this will help: didn't we have a fabulous time with Flo and Mei Lin on Vieques? Didn't we get along beautifully? Didn't they dance like angels?"

"I think you mean devils, but yes, that's all true. Why are you asking?" I prompt my honey, pretty sure that I know the answer.

"Listen to this, smart mouth. Our friends were so happy to be with us for ten days and nights—they had so much fun—they have decided that if we choose to go to Never Say, they'll be right there with us. How about that?"

That's no surprise to me, I've suspected as much for quite a while, but something kicks in my brain, which activates happily when Blaine asks her question. A voice keeps saying Val-Kill, Val-Kill in my head, and then I remember my hero's precious words:

'The greatest thing I have learned is how good it is to come home again.'

"Simple words spoken by Eleanor Roosevelt, when she'd come home to Val-Kill," I say to my girlfriends during our first get together after our paradisical island getaway. "Do you think we would say that when we'd come home to Never? No. In cold fact, we'd never be able to find our own homes in that morass of identical houses."

"So what are you getting at with Val-Kill and Eleanor?" Flo asks, although I think she's several steps ahead of me.

"We could create our own Val-Kill, just like Eleanor Roosevelt did with her special girlfriends. Those women created a little commune of their own away from woes that worried them. We can find the right spot with the perfect properties for a couple of small homes, build our own, or renovate, or whatever we would need to do. We'd have privacy, share our lives the way we choose, help each other, hire women we need as we age—health aides to live in or work part time." Three questioning pairs of women's eyes stare at me when I finish.

"And those women can't all be straight," Flo says hopefully. I add a crucial piece of information that I think will be a dealmaker. "Our accountant told me that my plan would likely be more economical than paying into an expensive facility and its high maintenance fees that will only grow with time." This is met with sounds of approval from my friends.

"And don't forget, we have each other," and Mei Lin starts us off in a chain of hugs.

The sales personnel at You–Know–Where, stay in touch with invitations to all kinds of special events, meals, films, concerts, and other goodies. We resist all, being fairly sure we are never moving to Never Say, until the invite to come to an exploration of "Life Credits and How They Add Up—or Go Down." Mei Lin and Blaine decide to see if they can find out what the damned things are. It isn't a life or death (oops) issue, but the four of us are still curious, so we all end up going to explore them.

The residents have little booklets with covers titled "Enjoy Your Life Credits." I sneak a look at the inside pages of the book the woman sitting next to me is writing in, and see lists of numbers arranged in a way I can't make out. The screen on the stage is lowered, and the cover flashes on it. One of the sales people is in place with his pointer. At last we are going to find out what life credits do, or what they mean.

The first slides we see on the screen have giant plus signs at the top. The background is bright white with all the punctuation in green—for Go, I suppose. Underneath are about twenty categories: attendance at activities, participating at the gym, finishing all the food on your plate, helping differently-abled residents, smiling at everyone. "What's next?" I whisper to Flo, "changing your underwear every day?" The Powerpoint continues.

The next pages are topped with minus signs, printed in an ominous red type. The background is gray and shadowy. The same arrangement of categories with listings below, are pointed out by the salesman who preaches the gospel of "beware these sins" in a foreboding voice. Mostly, the list of do–nots are the opposite of the do's, but additional warnings include: alarms going off for falling, arguing with personnel, complaining about the food, complaining about the weather, failing to applaud performers, yelling "louder, I can't hear you" at lectures, neglecting to keep your hearing aids from whistling, and many more. This is no laughing matter. We are sitting in the back of the room and make our hasty exit.

"Oh dear," says Mei Lin, "we still don't know what the prizes and punishments are for the life credits and debits. Do you think you get thrown out if the minuses go high enough?"

Flo interjects, "No, I think you just die sooner."

"Then if the plusses reach a certain number, maybe you live longer." Blaine nods her head with approval.

"Good thinking, but I don't need to know anymore. I'll take my chances on the vagaries of life," Mei Lin adds.

"Do we really need to know?" I ask dryly, sick to death of the whole thing.

"We probably never will know, and who the hell cares," Blaine adds, to my surprise.

"It looks like we four are finished with the Never Say Die Habitat and their life and death bullshit," I say. We gesture with thumbs up, except for me. I have my forefinger raised.

"Oh, what a relief it is," Flo quotes from the Alka Seltzer ad.

And so begins the Fizzy Four research quest for the right space for two one-story domiciles, or possibly a couple that already exist. We know we want to be near water, have a view of some mountains, a university nearby with all the cultural amenities to please us, and of course, a good hospital with well-trained practitioners. We will need a bus to get us to the city when we don't want to drive, a good neighborhood library, and fresh and healthy food shops.

We will seek out LGBTQ groups when deciding on a location. We will check the numbers for women of our own ages: for ethnic diversity, for political affiliation, and for compatibility in general.

"Let's start with location," Blaine advises. "I'll come up with some suggestions for places, and check with real estate people as well."

Mei Lin, our professor of art history and playwright, offers this: "I'll work with Blaine to get details on universities and colleges, and I think I can check for museums and performance spaces as well." We cheer our learned friend.

Flo, our master chef and lawyer, as expected, cooks up, "I'll do the restaurants and shopping facilities research, once I know from Blaine where to look."

I offer to see about medical support, hospitals and personnel. Blaine gives me a big fat kiss—beats pinches.

The Fizzy Four gets quiet, really quiet. "What's wrong with this," Mei Lin asks. "Something doesn't feel right," Blaine says. Don't ask me what; it's a gut feeling.

We meet at Flo and Mei Lin's where we drink some beautiful Jasmine tea. We clink our cups and wait for we don't know what.

"I think I know what's got us all singing the blues." Flo shakes her head and pops a spring roll into her mouth. Mei Lin wipes some tears that are slowly rolling down her cheeks.

We just sit gloomily in the living room. Flo can't stop eating, Mei Lin is still wiping tears, and Blaine is waiting for me to answer her unasked questions.

"Oh for God's sake, we must have been in La-La-Land. What we're planning is really not that much different from what we have right here."

"True, true," I agree. "Beautiful beaches are nearby, the scenery is gorgeous, a lesbian health group is here, many friends, wineries, so much good stuff is close by."

Flo drowns another spring roll in the soy sauce. "And the fish markets and farm stands are abundant with everything fresh and delicious." Flo pops the roll in between smiling lips.

"Caregivers and medical help is close by with a University Hospital less than an hour away. Music is everywhere including a concert hall, and how could we forget that New York City and all its culture is a bus, train, or car ride away?" Mei Lin adds, tears all dried up, and happy again.

"Say it, girl—tell it like it is." Flo chews a Swedish meatball. "Usually I eat when I'm not happy, but not tonight," and reaches for another pig-in-a-blanket. "But now I'm eating because I'm happy. Tell it, Willy."

I turn to look at each face. They look back at me and smile. "Our two houses are only a few minutes from each other, and our friendships are miraculously intact, in spite of all the *sturm und drang* we've gone through. We have everything we were searching for, right here. And," I add teasingly, "*we can all still drive.*"

My sister/friends are all applauding—I don't know whether to laugh or cry. "The Fizzy Four has what it wants, at least for now. Val-Kill is here, and we can grow old together in our own homes. We'll worry about later when it comes," I say, as we form a circle with our arms, hoping that "later" isn't too soon.

Wedding Fever

Linda opened the envelope that contained yet another wedding invitation. That made six "save the dates," five actual invitations written in the traditional language on fancy embossed heavy paper, and three casual email invites that were too cute for words. She supposed she would have to RSVP and attend them all—not an easy task, since she and her long time girlfriend Sara had recently broken up over the marriage issue. The complication of being asked to sing at some of these weddings was soured by the choices of music the couples were making, songs that were from decades past, bearing no relevance to the struggle LGBTQ couples had endured as they made their way up the mountain to reach the 2013 Supreme Court decision reversing the Defense of Marriage Act. Surely some savvy composer was at work creating songs more appropriate than "Love and Marriage" with words more inspiring than "go together like a horse and carriage," the selection a couple of guys asked her to sing.

One quite elderly couple, two women who had been together for forty-five years, had dropped by, music in hand, to ask her to sing the old wedding songs "Because" and "Oh Promise Me," and she had agreed with a rueful smile.

Linda did not want to get married; it was just copying what straight people did. Why did she and Sara need to do it anyway, after so many years together? Besides, she was sixty-three years old, and that was too old to get married. Sara was only forty-nine, so she had a different view.

"There's a big tax advantage, Linda," Sara had said, "we get all the goodies straight couples have had forever."

They had argued for hours, then days, and finally for months after the Supreme Court decision, and then decided to take a break from each other, which led to the parting of the ways. Sara stayed in the house they owned on the North Fork of Long Island, and Linda moved back into her Greenwich Village apartment in the city.

The invitations kept coming for both of them as a couple because they had not announced the breakup. Who knew what would happen in the future? They missed one another terribly.

Oh good goddess, Linda thought. *How am I going to sing those ancient songs?* "Because you come to me, with naught save love. And hold my hand and lift mine eyes above..."

And what about that old saw Oh promise me that someday you and I, will go together to some distant sky...

Oh well, she would do as she was asked, no fuss. She called her friend Christine, a lesbian minister, who was being asked to perform most of the ceremonies.

"So how should we arrange, program these ceremonies?" she asked Christine, at a breakfast meeting. "Have you met with the brides yet?"

"All these weddings will be different. Gabby and Trish want their ceremony on their deck overlooking the Sound; Blue and Fara are getting married in the UU Church; Sybil and

Sam want me to share the ceremony with the lesbian rabbi from the Village; and the others haven't said much yet." All 72 inches of Christine's big frame shook with laughter.

Linda took her lead. She would have to be seriously insouciant, if that was possible when here she was with a broken heart, planning other couple's happiness.

Linda made a date with Sara to meet at one of their favorite restaurants out on the island, near the house, so they could share all the wedding invitations that had come for them.

"You look great, Sara," Linda greeted her. And she did: Sara was just gorgeous. She had a new hairstyle, her red hair cut shoulder length, curling toward her face, and she was wearing makeup that emphasized her emerald green eyes.

"Thanks, Linda," Sara almost smiled. "You look nice, too."

And that was that, not very warm. Linda was going to have to work hard at this, if she could figure out what it was she was working at. She stood and handed Sara the packet she had carefully put together and tied with a bright purple moiré ribbon. She could have just handed the papers across the table, but she wanted Sara to see, in case she hadn't noticed before, that not only had she lost some weight, she was wearing a new outfit to show herself off.

Linda stood for a moment hoping for some words of praise. Sara looked Linda up and down but said nothing.

Linda sat with a disappointed plop. She fidgeted with her cutlery and napkin while her ex-honey looked through the mail. She drank water, examined her nails, and finally glanced at her cell phone—knowing full well how Sara hated her doing that at the table—waiting for what Sara would say.

"Well, Linda, it looks like you have some singing to do," was all she said.

"Sara, we're invited to these weddings as a couple. What do you want to do?" Linda asked.

"At this time, we're not a couple. We could go separately, or not go, or pretend we're still together." Sara tightened her lips, and licked them nervously.

Linda felt encouraged by her saying, "at this time." Did she mean that things could change? She reached for Sara's hand, but Sara pulled it away.

"Sara, let's talk, this is getting crazy. We can't go on this way. I'm miserable, aren't you?"

"Have you changed your mind about marriage?"

"Is this an either-or situation, Sara honey?" Linda sat up straighter, trying to look commanding. "Surely we can negotiate this, can't we try?"

"All our friends are getting married," Sara answered. "I want to be married, too. I've always wanted to be married, to have a wedding, to get dressed up, to do what straight people can do. It's political, it's feminist, it's activist, and it's financially practical." Sara got louder with each proclamation. People at nearby tables looked over at them, and two gay men wearing rainbow ties applauded.

Linda knew she had to make a move; she was older and wiser than Sara by fourteen years, so she thought it was up to her. She really didn't want to get married, for some of the very reasons Sara wanted to. She did not want to have a wedding or get dressed up, and certainly not to just do what straight people did. She was not straight, never had been, and did not intend to copy them in any way. But Linda had to do something to placate Sara.

"Okay, here's a plan: we meet with Jean and Bobbie, get all the facts, and then decide what we want to do. How about that?" Their lawyer and accountant had been a couple even longer than Linda and Sara, who relied on the two women for their expertise and friendship.

Sara tilted her head and looked at Linda more kindly. "You make the arrangements and I'll be there." She smiled and added, "You look really nice, Linda. You've lost some weight... and you're wearing something new, yes?" She took Linda's hand.

"Thank you, Sara, and," Linda began, as she felt on a roll, let's go to the weddings together, to share our friends' happiness. I'll sing better if you're with me."

"What should I wear," Sara replied with raised eyebrows and a warm smile.

They had a lovely dinner at The Fork in the Road, sharing Sara's favorite dish, The Fork's Delicious Fish and Seafood Stew, a beautiful green salad, and Sara's latest dessert passion: blood orange sorbet with Tate's ginger cookies.

Both feeling quite mellow, they walked to their house hand in hand. Was this going to work out eventually? Were they on the way to some kind of bliss, wedded or unwedded?

The women exchanged a long look and a lingering kiss at the front door, hugged hard, then went right to their bedroom and made love, lively, like it was when they were new. Linda decided she'd settle for this bliss for now.

The next week they had a date with Bobbie, their accountant, and Jean, their lawyer, in the women's shared offices in East Hampton. Bobbie and Jean had made all the financial and legal arrangements for Sara and Linda, so it would be relatively straightforward to talk about their situation. But Linda was a nervous wreck about the whole thing and didn't know why. Perhaps she should see a therapist and figure out why she was making such a big deal about the marriage thing. Was she just being stubborn, or scared, or did she have some premonition that something awful would happen if they got married? Could it be those maudlin wedding songs she had to sing that were making a travesty of love and marriage? She did not know. All she knew for sure was that she was more fearful of getting married than she was of losing federal income tax benefits.

They all sat at the long table in the conference room looking at the folders Jean and Bobbie had carefully prepared. Bobbie handed each of them a purple folder, then straightened her purple tie. She was wearing a perfectly tailored grey pinstripe suit, and today her resemblance to Katharine Hepburn was more striking than ever. She ran her fingers through her short, blond-streaked hair, and then adjusted her pant legs so the creases were prominent.

"Do you want us to read this stuff now?" Sara asked rudely, rolling her eyes with annoyance at Bobbie's fussing. They were off to a bad start, Linda worried, if her temporary ex was starting to challenge right off the bat.

"Actually," Bobbie waved the folder in the air, "you'll need more than a dictionary to make your way through all of this, so keep the bourbon nearby."

Sara ruffled through the pages with her thumb, too fast to read any, and haughtily said, "I know there are more than sixteen hundred federal tax advantages we gain with the removal of DOMA." She was met with silence. "Is that information here?" she asked, waving the pages in the air.

"Truth is, we don't know what it's all about yet. There are lots of details to be figured out. Some of it will be financially advantageous for married LGBTQs; the benefits straight couples have will be available to all married couples. Don't forget, now, this only applies to the states that recognize marriage equality. The other states have laws that don't recognize equality, but things are changing every day, and who knows what the IRS will come up with."

Linda interjected with a make–nice, "well, we'll go through all this material and gather as much information as we can."

Jean smiled gratefully. "We've accessed as much as we can for now, and we'll keep you posted as things get clearer." She looked across the table at Bobbie and shrugged. Bobbie stuck her tongue out at her, which was more venomous than cute. Linda wondered what was going on.

Sara stood and poured some water from the pitcher at the other end of the table. "I don't care about the details. I want to marry Linda, and Linda doesn't want to marry me. And that's what this is all about." She slammed her water glass on the table and sat down almost as hard.

"I didn't say I didn't want to," Linda sputtered, "I mean, I want, oh shit, I don't know what I mean." She was stuck with both feet planted firmly in midair. She felt like a jerk, but all she could do was laugh.

Much to her amazement, Bobbie and Jean joined Linda in what was starting to sound like hysteria. Sara glowered. "Not funny," she growled.

"I'll tell you what's funny," Bobbie said with a raised hand. "Jean and I are in the same fucking conundrum. I'm the money girl, I want to do what's financially smart. There are more than a thousand federal benefits we could have, just like heteros. But she's the legal brain who wants to get married because the Supremes said we could, legally. So we're paralyzed, we can't agree on the same reason we want to marry. Isn't that the most ridiculous thing you ever heard?"

"We've moved into separate bedrooms because all we do is fight about marriage," Jean shook her head mournfully.

"But at least you're together under one roof," Linda said, consolingly.

"Big deal," Jean whined, "she has a chair up against the door. Did you ever hear anything more ludicrous?"

They decided to go out to dinner locally and stop talking about marriage.

"I'll tell you what," Linda said after her second bourbon Manhattan, "let's all get engaged. Isn't there a Tiffany's in East Hampton?"

"What a great idea." Jean said, several sheets to the wind.

"Bobbie, beloved, will you be engaged to me?" Bobbie agreed so enthusiastically that she nearly fell off her chair.

"I always wanted a Tiffany engagement ring," Sara bubbled over her Prosecco. "Let's go there right now!" And she wobbled to the door.

Linda arranged with their waiter to hold their table—they had not ordered dinner yet—and the four women took off down the block, happily and somewhat unsteadily, to Tiffany's.

The salesman saw four extremely jolly women coming through the door. Or were they high, he wondered. He signaled the security guard, who was stationed in a room off the showroom, where he could watch the customers on video cameras.

"We want to get engaged," Sara demanded, "and we want diamond engagement rings for all of us," she said, as if she was ordering bagels at a deli. She perched on one of the high-backed stools in front of the rings.

"Certainly, Madam," the salesman started to respond, but Bobbie cut in.

"None of this 'Madam' stuff, we don't run a bordello. We are very serious women who want to get married to our sweethearts, now that we can get married, but we have to get engaged first, so we need to have rings." She took a deep breath and shook her fourth finger left hand at him.

A well-dressed handsome man probably in his twenties emerged from an adjoining room and waved at the salesman. He stood at the nearby counter.

"Hi," greeted Linda cheerfully, "are you Mr. Tiffany?"

The young man grinned. "No, I'm security. I've been listening to your conversation and I'm enchanted by you four women, so I came out to say hello."

"Hello," the four answered in unison. "We're getting engaged," Bobbie reached over to shake his hand in anticipation of his good wishes.

"Congratulations," the security guard approved. "My husband and I got married last week. We never got engaged, but it's not too late, is it?"

"Absolutely not! I'm a lawyer, and I'm telling you it's perfectly legal to get engaged after you get married," Jean lectured, handing him her card.

The salesman watching the interaction, was amused and charmed, but decided it was time he took control. "Do you want the same rings or different rings? May I show you what we have, or do you know what you want? At that, he unlocked the case and took out a tray and displayed it carefully. "And are you planning to buy rings today, or are you just browsing?"

"Oh no," Sara assured, "we are going to walk out of here thoroughly engaged women. I'm getting engaged to Linda, and she's getting engaged to me."

"And I'm getting engaged to Jean," Bobbie hugged her, "and she's getting engaged to me. And that's final!" And they all took out their credit cards to show they could pay for their rings.

They each tried on every ring in every tray, and the security guard modeled a few on his pinky because none fit on his engagement finger. They advised each other, asked prices, and were pleased that the ring each wanted fit perfectly. The men stood transfixed as each couple placed each ring on the finger of her fiancé, and lo and behold, they were engaged, affianced, betrothed, promised to one another, though none of them knew when, if ever, her marriage would take place.

An hour later, the four women, arms entwined, pranced out of Tiffany's, waving their left hands to passers by, boasting, "We're engaged! We're going to get married, and we have the rings to prove it." No one seemed shocked and several people called out "Mazel tov; way to go; best of luck;" and other congratulations to the betrothed women.

They almost danced back into the restaurant, showing off their rings in turn to the waitstaff, the maître d', the chef, and every customer in the place. Mr. Della Bella, the owner, had not only held their table, but had arranged for champagne to appear, and the resulting elevation sent the four women flying.

Linda and Sara applied themselves to reading all the information Bobbie and Jean had supplied. They read every article and essay they could find on the financials of same sex marriage, holding long discussions with friends and colleagues on the issue. What became clear was that there was more work to be done to make marriage equality national, to overturn prohibitive state laws by making new laws applicable to all fifty states, and for the IRS to clarify all the benefits possible to married couples, gay or straight. The more they learned, the more they realized that it was no myth—there would be financial benefits to many couples, but who and why was not yet clear.

Then, just when they were feeling overwhelmed, Bobbie called. "Just listen to this," she exalted. "It's in today's *Times*, have you read it yet?" Without waiting for an answer, she read, "As of the 2013 tax year, same-sex spouses who are legally married will not have to file federal tax returns as if either were single. Instead, they must file together as 'married filing jointly' or individually as 'married filing separately.' "What do you think of that? It's from this big article called 'Gay Marriages Get Recognition From the I.R.S.'" Sara and Linda were stunned, each unable to answer for her own reasons.

After a few minutes, Linda said dryly, "and what about divorce, I wonder?"

"Oh, Linda," Sara moaned, "you are always so damned practical."

Meanwhile, more invitations and announcements arrived, to which they dutifully responded. The rings sparkled on their left hands but they were no closer to tying the knot. Their families were mostly admiring of the engagement rings, but regularly asked, "Have you set a date yet? Why not?"

Each wedding they went to soured their engagement euphoria a little more, as it became clear that engagements were supposed to be temporary. Each ceremony, whether in temple, church, or mosque, backyard or living room or the local town hall, made their rings sparkle less, and hopes for their own wedding dwindle. Discussions between the two couples went back to what they had been before their pledges to marry.

Six months later, Jean called with the news that she and Bobbie had decided to marry in three months, and were making the arrangements.

"I'm tired of going in circles about it. Bobbie has worn me down and I want her to be happy," Jean said wearily. "I just don't want to fight anymore."

"Well, that's wonderful news," Linda responded, in a somewhat saccharine voice. "Where and when?"

"Here, talk to Bobbie, she'll give you the details," and Jean passed the phone to her bride-to-be.

By this time, Sara had overhead the conversation and she grabbed the phone from Linda, covered the receiver with her hand, and smirked most unattractively at her partner.

"Ha, I told you so! I told you they would do it. Everyone will be married before us." And she gave Linda her ringed finger for emphasis.

"Bobbie, sweetie, so you're going to the chapel, and you're gonna get married!" Sara sang happily off key. Linda put her fingers tightly in her ears. "Fabulous," Sara chirped cheerfully. "I'm so happy for you, you rotten women you. But I thought we were supposed to have a double wedding."

"No way," Bobbie said kindly. "You're making that up, Sara, all we were having was a double engagement. You'll have to have your own wedding."

Linda had put the call on speakerphone, as did Jean, and they all voiced their agreement with their girlfriends.

"But this is what I wanted to ask you,"—here Bobbie dramatically paused—Sara, I want you to be my lesbian–of–honor, and Jean wants Linda to be her lesbian–of–honor, and that way we can all be up at the altar together." Sara broke into sobs.

"I hope those are tears of happiness, not misery." Jean broke in, trying to lighten the moment.

"We accept the honor of being your lesbians–in–waiting or honor or whatever. It will be a great pleasure," Linda soothed, taking Sara in her arms.

"What should I wear," Sara interjected, recovered from her weeping, "I have some great ideas."

"Let's get together tomorrow and make plans," Bobbie said happily.

"You bet she has plans," Jean broke in, "she's been making them for years."

The wedding was quite sedate, all things considered. Bobbie and Jean had spent hours talking about what they and their attendants would wear, and then days finding the shop that could make their vision come true.

Bobbie had pranced into Jean's office late one afternoon, after spending the day interviewing seamstresses and shopkeepers in the bridal shop section of downtown Manhattan. "Jean, darling honey gumdrop, I found the ideal women to make our wedding clothes. They love our ideas and they can do it, the whole shebang!" She plopped down on a chair and spun round and round on it. "But you have to go there with me tomorrow morning to go over the details, or they won't have time to make the clothes."

"Wait, who are these women? Where did you find them? What, what–?" Jean ran out of breath.

"They are expert designers and seamstresses, and," she hooted, "they are a married lesbian couple." She spun around a few more times until Jean stopped the chair.

And so it began and went on and on. There were sketches to consider, fabrics to choose, accessories to find, fittings and more fittings, until finally, it was done.

The brides wore white tuxedos with satin lapels, lavender satin stripes on the pants, and lavender satin bow ties. They sported white felt fedoras accented by lilac satin bands; Bobbie carried sprays of lilac with a white rose, and Jean's lilacs had a sweetheart rose. They were a gorgeous sight to behold, especially with their arms full of fragrant flowers. The eight lesbians–of–honor wore purple leather pants and dress shirts with perfectly square-knotted lavender satin ties, tailored lilac–flowered shirts with dark purple leather vests, and sneakers covered in sequins.

Bach and Sondheim was played for the ceremony at the Loeb Boathouse in Central Park, performed by The Tiger Lillies, a hot band that played every kind of music perfectly. The lesbians–of–honor came down the aisle hand–in–hand, followed by the four parents, two by two and hand–in–hand, and then the brides, arms entwined, scattering rose petals as they went. Christine, the minister, and her spouse took turns with the readings, while the brides said their vows facing the assembly. Linda, as requested by the brides, sang Voi che sapete, a love song from Mozart's opera, The Marriage of Figaro. Bobbie and Jean had met at a performance of the opera, when by some magic, they found themselves sitting next to each other at the Met.

After the mothers toasted the brides, the four locked arms and gave each other's daughters a glass of wine to sip from, then all four women stomped on the glasses, which they had wrapped in napkins to break in honor of breaking DOMA. Linda then sang "Why Do I Love You? Why Do You Love Me?" With everyone joining in, it was a fun ceremony, yet solemn and filled with love.

The dinner was at the Plaza Hotel in one of the private dining rooms, and the menu offered options for vegan, vegetarian, kosher, plus salt, sugar, fat, and gluten-restricted diets. There was a beautifully seasoned gazpacho filled with every imaginable vegetable; sushi and sashimi with brown rice; fish, vegetables, and tofu; a variety of gluten free and regular pastas and sauces; many vegetables baked, sautéed, and steamed; casseroles of tofu, mushrooms, ginger, garlic, spices; seafood entrees; as well as Southern-fried chicken, with gravy mashed potatoes, black-eyed peas, okra, collard greens, to please Jean's relatives up from Georgia. After the feast, the, parents, siblings, families and friends of the brides danced the night away.

Sara and Linda played their roles with respect and tenderness, happy for their friends, still unsure of their own desires. Sara was sure she could plan their wedding with the ideas she had been imagining for years. Bobbie and Jean's wedding seemed such a proper event. Sara knew she could come up with something complex and original—if she could ever get Linda to the altar.

Linda kept an approving smile on her face, but her thoughts were elsewhere. *These women are just emulating what straight people do*, she thought. Really, it seemed so conventional. No one would get her to do any of the stuff Jean and Bobbie had. And the clothes they were all wearing— really!! *No way, but yet, it was kind of sweet and fun, okay for them, but*, she thought, *not her style*. What was the matter with her? She felt so unsentimental, so confused. After all, two good friends who loved each other for years had gotten married. Did it matter what they wore, or that they were both women? No, it only mattered that there was love, devotion, a few tax advantages, and the vow to be together as woman and woman, spouses for as long as they lived. Linda admitted to herself that she understood, but she simply didn't feel marriage. Or could she? Was it possible she could?

Linda was very quiet on the way home. Sara listened to her favorite CDs as they drove to the apartment. Ella Fitzgerald was singing love songs—I'm in the Mood for Love, My Funny Valentine, Why Do I Love You—it sounded like Ella Fitzgerald was in the car with them. They did not speak; Ella's love songs spoke for them. *There's a reason for so many love songs*, Linda thought as she drove and listened to the music. *There's a reason for all this angst about marriage equality and these LGBTQ weddings, and it's not just about money, or the IRS, or the courts. I know damn well what the reason is!* "It's love, it's love, well who would'a thought it," she began singing at the top of her lungs. Linda was having a revelation, a breakthrough, a quantum leap into what, she did not know for sure, but it was the start of something very big, maybe even an epiphany.

They brought the beautiful leftover wedding flowers into the apartment and put them in vases with filtered water and flower food. They sat on the sofa without taking off their fancy clothes, as if they didn't want the moment to pass.

Linda went to the kitchen and came back with two glasses of diet Snapple.

"What's this for?" asked Sara.

"A toast," replied Linda, "a toast to love, for love is the answer, the purpose, the only reason I want to ask you this question," and she got down on her knee.

"I love you, my darling Sara, and here is the question." She raised her glass and clinked it gently to Sara's. "I have loved, adored, and admired you, been furious with you and loved making up with you, for all the years I've known you."

"And the question is?" teased Sara.

"Will you marry me, Sara Walter, and be my love forever?"

Sara cried, "yes, yes, yes," then asked, "are you sure, Linda O'Hara? You're not going to change your mind tomorrow, are you?"

Linda struggled to get up but her knees had locked. "I can't do it, I'm stuck."

For a moment, Sara thought Linda was backing out, but then she realized her sweetheart just couldn't stand up.

Laughing with relief, Sara used her arms to hoist Linda to her feet. "Well, are you sure?" Sara asked.

"I'm sure I love you. The proposal is absolutely for sure." They kissed, clicked glasses, and drank their Snapple. "When I saw how happy Bobbie and Jean were to be married, how much closer marriage brought them together, I was so moved, I rethought…" Linda seemed unable to continue for a few moments. She swallowed hard and went on. "I thought just being engaged would take care of everything, but I was wrong. I've seen the light, and it's all about love. Our engagement is over. A promise does not come true until it happens, so I'm ready to marry you Sara, love of my life, if you'll have me?"

Her question was answered in bed.

The wedding planning started in the morning. Sara was full of ideas, possibilities, and questions, all of which she ran by Linda every few minutes.

The best idea came a few days later. Sara came bursting into Linda's home office. She plopped herself down on top of the desk, crumpling papers and knocking things over.

"Linda, listen to this. You are going to be sixty-four in six weeks, so we're going to get married on your birthday. It will be spring, flowers will be everywhere, we'll have a chuppah covered with blooming blossoms of every hue and variety, we'll have a klezmer band, aaaand," here she paused dramatically, arms outstretched as if she was conducting a symphony orchestra, "our lesbian rabbi, Sharon, promised me she'd do the ceremony."

"But I'm not Jewish," Linda said, almost apologetically.

"No matter," said Sara waving the words aside, "Jewish weddings are so much more fun. Jean isn't Jewish either, and look how much she loved their wedding. Don't worry, no problemo."

Linda tried to get a word in here and there, but there was no stopping Sara. Sara knew what she wanted; she knew Linda would say yes to everything she planned, within reason (or maybe not), and Linda finally gave up, just listening and smiling, nodding her head as Sara went on and on.

"And it will be all flowers everywhere and music, and the food will be a mishmash of ethnicities, mostly Jewish, and there will be excellent wine and champagne, and everyone will get presents, and they will have to make a donation to a charity we decide on, and, and… " Sara ran out of words and breath, much to Linda's relief.

Six weeks later, on a gorgeous early summer day, at Linda and Sara's house on Peconic Bay, the setting was picture perfect. Three white tents were set up at just the right angles for the best water and garden views and a wooden dance floor with the band set up in the corner. There was a shaded long table loaded with hummus, tabbouleh, olives, raw veggies, eggplant caviar, Irish cold meats, chopped liver, gefilte fish, herring in cream sauce; a bar in the corner of another tent, the setting was even more picture perfect.

Wearing white jeans, white tank tops, and rainbow-flowered leis around their necks, the brides danced out the front door, through the grass, to the rainbow–flower–covered arch of the chuppah. "The Krazy Klezmer" band played, while everyone sang the lyrics from the Beatles *When I'm Sixty–four* printed on the programs: *When I get older, losing my hair, many years from now. Will you still be sending me a valentine, birthday greetings, bottle of wine?* Sara and Linda pranced down the aisle, throwing flowers, ropes of beads, and candy bars to everyone, from decorated baskets. When they were in place, their guests rose to encircle them, still singing, until the rabbi raised her hands.

It was a touching ceremony, with poetry that Linda and Sara had written for one another, some friends reading words they had created for the occasion, and Rabbi Sharon bestowing the appropriate Hebrew and Gaelic blessings. Bobbie and Jean, who appointed themselves the official flower girls, had made a long rope of hydrangea and squash flowers, into which they entwined Sara and Linda at the chuppah, then joined and danced around them when the ceremony was over.

Singing the Mazal Tov song, they arrived at the front of the main tent, where the dance floor waited for the fun to begin. The klezmer music started again and everyone embraced for the hora. Sara and Linda were raised up high on chairs and propelled around and around. It was very freilach, truly joyful. When the band started blasting Irish music, the O'Hara family paraded onto the dance floor and began knee–high step dancing, everyone screamed with delight. The group had rehearsed this with the musicians and practiced until it was perfect.

The appetizer table had been consumed with gusto and cleared for the challah, cut by the fathers and blessed by the mothers, one in Hebrew, the other in pure Gaelic—both had been practiced all week. The dinner was a mix of Jewish and Irish food: Long Island duck, corned beef and cabbage (though the Irish family unabashedly preferred the matzoh ball soup), soda bread, and sweetbreads and mushroom sauté in pastry cups. The wedding/birthday cake was decorated with flowers and part of the music score of "When I'm Sixty-four" in rainbow icing. There were flowers on the tables, circling the lawn, on the stairs, at the windows—absolutely everywhere.

What a wedding! Irish/Jewish/LGBTQ, gay and straight—what could be better!

Sara twisted the wedding ring on her finger around and around. Linda came to hold her, and Bobbie and Jean joined them. Four women: two couples, married to each other. Imagine.

Toys

A bag of good pot was stuck inside the raw chicken's cavity. They had packed Scrabble, Monopoly, and plenty of books. A cassette player and lots of music tapes—dance, opera, jazz, country, were in a carry–on with other odds and ends, including Annie's toys. She had put in a major collection of all sorts of dildos and vibrators: doubleheaders, ticklers, big ones, small ones—you name it, she had it.

"You can't take all that stuff," her girlfriend Jo said. "There's no room in that bag for all that stuff, and who knows if they open everything to check." She was a nervous wreck about Annie's toys. It was 1980, before x-ray machines and terrorist hijackings, and Annie felt sure her "pals," as she called them, would be okay.

"Okay, I'll just take a few things, necessities," she teased, and repacked her favorites in a zippered canvas tote bag.

A group of six lesbians went to Vieques, Puerto Rico, two times every winter: Annie and Jo, Beth and Phyllis—master chef and bartender—Martha and Lynn—doctor and lawyer, filled the small plane for eight, including the pilots. They flew from San Juan to their little island, loaded down with food and wine to have in their house on a mango farm overlooking the sea. Annie and Jo, architects, had bought the house together and renovated it beautifully.

There was only one small market on the island, a telephone booth, and a combination restaurant/bar/dancehall, so they had to bring all the necessities with them. Fish and seafood were plentiful, along with eggs and an occasional chicken. When customs wanted to know why they were bringing in a chicken when Vieques had plenty, they replied, "We all keep kosher."

They had made friends with an elderly local artist who grew vegetables on a small patch; that she was willing to sell to them when her crop was good. The women were prepared for everything culinary: they took turns cooking exotic seafood meals, and devoured mangoes until they got stomachaches.

They greedily ate their own cooking, no matter what each cook came up with, including sea turtle steaks, with which Beth had created many dishes. (This was before they knew the creatures were endangered.) Once in a while they ate in the one island restaurant and danced with the locals, who were almost too friendly.

They had a wonderful time snorkeling, boating, swimming, and sunbathing every day. It was an era long before sunblock, so they used tanning creams and oils with abandon, all browning perfectly, except for Jo, who turned red and blistered.

Across from Annie and Jo's house, which called Lesbos Lark was the nearby island of Culebra, the site of a U.S. military base. They could hear the guns firing during the Navy and Marine training sessions, but most of the time it was peaceful. The beaches were empty and private, the sand pristine, the Caribbean calm, a brilliant turquoise jewel.

On Saturdays, they managed to get radio broadcasts from the Metropolitan Opera, which they listened to under beach grape trees, drinking tropical drinks they had concocted like the Vieques Velvet Victim, made with vodka, vanilla, and vegetables. There was a special magic in hearing the sound of Joan Sutherland's sparkling soprano singing Norma, decorating the velvety, incoming murmur of the waves.

After two weeks of paradise, they were heading back home. Having flown on the little plane to San Juan, they were ready at American Airlines to put their baggage through to New York. The airport was filled with large families with many bags and packages. Babies were crying in a jarring variety of pitches, and children ran around crashing into people with abandon.

The women were settling down for a long wait on the customs line, but before they could get organized, Lynn came running up.

"They're opening bags and looking through everything, even handbags. Who knows why—drugs, probably."

"Make sure your stuff is okay," Jo warned. "Good thing there's no weed left," she said in a self-congratulating voice. "And there are no police dogs," she boasted, as if she had arranged it personally.

"Annie," said Lynn's girlfriend Martha, "I'll just die if they see your toys. You've got to get rid of them."

"All of them?" asked Annie, holding her hand over her heart.

"Absolutely all," insisted Martha. Beth and Phyllis shook their heads violently in agreement, while Jo was covering her laughter with coughs.

"All," added Lynn, echoed by Martha.

"What should I do with them?" Annie moaned. "They're good. And expensive." She was crestfallen. "They're practically new," she said, "can't I hide them somewhere?"

"No, get rid of all of it, now!" came the insistent order from Jo. "And hurry, we have to get on line."

Jo took a place with her friends on the line, moving her head in disapproval. "I told her not to bring those things, but she never listens." Then she smiled.

Annie looked around the airport and saw the room marked Damas, took her canvas bag inside, and looked for a garbage pail. The only one she saw was already stuffed full. She moved into one of the cubicles and saw the receptacle for used sanitary supplies. She checked all four—full. She went back to the hallway between the "Damas" and "Hombres" rooms. Outside the men's room was a trash bin, partly empty. She looked around, and then stuffed her canvas bag with the open top, into the space. The zipper had broken when she tried to close it. Some of the toys would not stay covered in the bag, especially the double dildo (which, sadly, had never been used.) It had been her favorite "show and tell" object. She stuffed it down as much as it would go. Now the pail was full, and she had a hard time getting the cover on until she sat on it. *Luckily*, she thought, *no men had come in.* She hoped no one would try to open it until after they had taken off. When Annie looked back before leaving, it looked like a penis was sticking out of the can. She raced back to her friends, breathing hard.

An announcement had been made that their flight was delayed, possibly for an hour. The six women found seats. "And they never even opened the bag," Annie said aloud without intending to. Jo poked her with a sharp elbow.

"Look, see over there," Jo hissed, "by the door where the men's room is."

"Oh shit," moaned Beth. Phyllis laughed nervously.

At the desk were several airport security men passing around the canvas bag filled with Annie's toys. Trying to shield their activity, they held one by one up turning them this way and that, then realizing they could be seen, emptied the bag on the floor, hiding the contents. They laughed.

The only words Annie recognized were mira, mira, look. *Oh god,* she thought, *they'll figure it out and we'll be in hot salsa.* Jo slumped in her seat. Lynn was biting her nails. The friends buried their heads in their books.

"They know, these guys know. We'll all be busted," whined Lynn.

"For what?" Annie asked.

"Indecent exposure," Jo said.

Annie looked up and saw one of the men standing across the aisle from her. His dark brown eyes met hers. How did he know? He must have seen her putting the bag in the pail. *This is it, we're cooked,* she thought. The man smiled broadly at her. Grinning at all of them, he made a lavish thumbs-up gesture, and strutted away.

The Geriatric Girl's Gym

The sign read: THE GERIATRIC GIRLS' GYM: Grandmas Welcome. It made Valiante giggle, and then laugh when she saw the SLOW sign (watch out for our women with walkers), as she drove into the village of Far Moreover.

"That settles it," Valiante said to Hiddigeigei, the little blue hippo sitting on her dashboard she had gotten from Zoe, her last girlfriend, who had taken off with another woman and broken her heart. "That sign is almost as oxymoronic as my name. I'm not so sure how valiant I am at this point in my life."

She drove past the real estate office, Slickton Dream Homes, she was dealing with. "No matter what this house looks like, if I can afford it," she told Hiddigeigei, "I'm going to buy it, fix it up, and live here. I just know this place will be perfect for me."

Actually, the house wasn't in as bad shape as she thought it would be, based on the low asking price. It was something between a cottage and a shack, and had a certain amount of *je ne sais* whatever. And if you drove fast enough, it was only ten minutes from a beach.

"Isn't it adorable, Ms. Valenti? Charming, I just love it, and you can do so much with it," the enthusiastic real estate woman said, almost bouncing off the ground in spite of her generous body, miraculously balanced on towering spiked heels.

"The name is Valiante (which she spelled out slowly), pronounced valiant, Valiante Strongwoman, Ms. Slickton."

Valiante began to walk the grounds, stopping now and then to peer into the windows. The agent slowed down, waddling after her and commenting as they went.

"In the winter, when the leaves are off, if you lean all the way to the left and squint, sometimes you get a water view of the marsh. There are ducks and swans occasionally, but you have to walk over to the water to see them." She stopped and patted her heart. "There's a great blue heron, who winters over and fishes in the marsh." She finally seemed to have caught her breath and ability to speak. "And you can get to the beach in no time." Ms Slickton waved her hand in all four directions.

"Really," said Valiante dryly. "Do you think we can see the inside?" She headed for the front door and turned the knob. The door seemed locked but opened with a slight push. *Cozy, that's the word, cozy,* she thought as she cast an eye over the sitting room, which had a wood stove in the corner and displayed a broken–down chair in the middle of the floor. There were some surprisingly nice wood planks on the floor, and a good amount of light coming through the grimy windows. This property had obviously not been staged for potential buyers. Good, thought Valiante, someone wants a quick sale.

There were two rooms probably meant to be bedrooms, and another small room that faced a stand of cedar and juniper trees in the backyard. A bare kitchen with only a sink, of sorts (no appliances to be seen), and a bathroom with a rusty showerhead, a floor drain, and the bottom part of a toilet completed this "adorable, sweet cottage," as Ms. Real Estate called it. Needs work, needs lots of work, Valiante thought, and turned to find the agent almost on top of her back. Ms. Slickton had nothing to say.

"What is the real price?" Valiante took a notepad from her shoulder bag.

"Well, the owner died and left the cottage to his plumber, and the plumber said I should get the most I can for it." She smiled a question.

"I'll give him $24,132 cash," and Valiante walked out the door to her car. She turned as she was opening the door, "By the way, Ms. Slickton, where is Near Moreover?"

Seven weeks later, Valiante took a surveying look around her new home. Ms. Slickton had recommended two women contractors who laughed when Valiante asked how long it would take to get permits. "We don't do permits here," they said, "and anyway, we own the hardware–lumber–tile–anything and everything you need supply company." After a big breath, she said "And we, Nanci and Drew, she said, pointing to Drew, are the fastest workers in Far Moreover." They had no trouble with the plans that Valiante herself had drawn. If the customer wanted "cozy with character," that's what it would be, exactly how she wanted it—and that's what Valiante got.

The walls were hung with work by women artists, most of them her friends: a mixture of abstract expressionist paintings, seascapes, and impressionistic watercolors. The nude sculptures of women were obviously derivative of Brancusi, although done by her favorite sculptor, a woman she had known since college. A variety of photographs, mostly of waterfalls, adorned the walls of the bathroom, which now had a tub and shower, a fast-flushing toilet, a sink with faucets that emptied into a graceful bowl, with a mirrored medicine chest hanging over it, and lots of shelves for towels and other necessities, like soap—a putto lying head on hand, stretched out to make the soap dish, and other toiletries. The furnishings were an eclectic hodgepodge of styles and periods, but somehow satisfying and comforting. There were rugs scattered hither and thither, from different parts of the world yet making some strange sense to Valiante, and just the way she wanted it. A second bathroom had been placed where a small back porch had been, contemporary in design with tiles of naked women in water scenes: Leda and her swan on a lake, a brown beauty washing her long black hair under a waterfall, and a Godiva–like figure, without her horse, drinking from a spouting fountain. An open shower, with no walls or doors but a well–placed drain, was cool and inviting. Best of all was the kitchen, where everything was new, shiny, and filled with professional appliances ready for Valiante's expert cooking. She was almost content.

It was early spring and she was ready for Far Moreover, on her way to find out if it was ready for her. She draped a shawl around her shoulders, opened the front door, and stepped outside onto her newly landscaped half acre. Nothing much was happening yet, but there was greenery, thanks to the trees wearing a hint of leaves, mulch where crocuses and daffodils were just starting to poke through, and some bushes here and there with names she wasn't sure about.

The high point of her day was approaching with a visit to the Geriatric Girls' Gym, from her "Must Do Today" agenda. She retrieved her bag from inside the house, fished out her car keys, and was on her way.

The first hand she shook upon arrival was that of a trim woman of a certain age, Japanese, with a short cut of absolutely white hair, wearing black shorts and a black T–shirt with GGG on it in large purple letters.

"You must be Ms. Strongwoman. Welcome to the GGG. I'm Sunshine, but please call me Sunni." She grinned a big toothy smile. "Can you pronounce your first name for me, I didn't quite get it on the phone." A bigger smile, ear to ear actually, followed.

Valiante was again spelled out slowly. "It's pronounced valiant," she instructed.

"Oh, how unusual, may I call you Val? I imagine everyone does."

"No, no one does. It's not my name," Valiante said, not smiling.

Sunni bowed her head in acquiescence. "What can I do for you, Ms. Strongwoman? Valiante, that is. Strongwoman is the perfect name for a GG–Gymer. How did you come by it?" Sunni was speaking faster than her mouth could handle the words, and she finally stopped when she tripped over her tongue. She was having a hard time charming this woman.

"My parents died and left it to me. Can I see the gym and equipment now, please?"

"Of course, but first there are a few details, if you don't mind," and Sunni took a form from a folder. "Just fill this out: address, phones, email, age, and primary care physician who can tell us if you have any restrictions or other information regarding your ability for exercise." Valiante felt Sunni looking at her carefully, as if what she saw would allow her to ask the next question. Sunni saw a very tall, quite stunning woman, with one half of her head of auburn hair cropped or possibly even shaved, and the other half partly covering her elegant, fine features. Prominent cheekbones supported brilliant green eyes that stared back at her, never seeming to blink. Sunni pulled herself to her full 5'4", tried to finger her short white hair behind her ears and asked the question. "Are you retired? You really don't look old enough. We are geriatric girls here, after all," she almost simpered.

"Why, do you have age restrictions?" Valiante was getting peevish. "I am forty-five, is that too young or too old?"

"No problem," Sunni answered, and then asked if Valiante was single. "You see, our gym is for women only. By members' request, mornings are reserved for single girls, and the afternoon sessions for married or coupled women, who can invite men friends and such."

Valiante said she was unattached, and for a moment thought of Zoe. She asked if she could have a tour before they proceeded. Sunni saw that the applicant was getting irritated with the delay, and quickly agreed to take Valiante around the gym before she filled out the forms, and so the two women began their exploration.

Classical music was playing inside, a Haydn allegro movement. The colors were mauve and dusty rose, and the equipment was almost completely occupied by mature women of all shapes, colors, and sizes. The women on the bikes were chatting quietly; those on the treadmills were reading; others were pulling, pushing, and pounding punching bags. There were Stairmasters, shuttles, weights, balls, elastic bands, and other equipment Valiante had never seen before. Another separate space had tables and chairs, water, a juice station, and a power–smoothie counter. A display of various gym accessories that were for sale, and GGG T–shirts in many colors were at another counter. These women of Far Moreover could be very proud of their gym. It was GGGGreat. Valiante chuckled silently.

Everything was pink in this gym, except for the equipment, Sunni pointed out, the color as one of the virtues of the establishment with pride: She listed the bathrooms with fast flush toilets and bidets, dressing rooms, lockless lockers, showers, and neatly shelved toiletries with pride.

"Are the morning members all from Far Moreover? When you refer to them as single, what does that mean?" Valiante knew she was being very inquisitive, but she wanted to know.

"Oh, the girls are all local, lots of them live in comfortable trailers in a retirement community started by two of them, Ardora and Marvel. They used to teach at the same school. Most of them never married, some are divorced, a few are widows—Honey and Canary maybe. I can't remember all that gossip. We're a mixed bunch of bags," Sunni said, mixing her metaphors without care. "We don't talk about stuff like that. We respect privacy...sometimes." Sunni rolled her eyes.

"Anyway, they'll answer your questions, if you have any, and be prepared, they'll want to know all about you." Sunni headed back toward her reception counter.

When Valiante asked when she could start, Sunni said after she filled out and returned the forms, and once her doctor gave details about her health and permission for her to join. She would have to make a two months' payment in advance and sign up for a year. Valiante took out her checkbook. She was ready, willing, and able. This was fertile territory for her project, if she could use such language, and she made short shrift of the questionnaire and wrote out the significant payment with pleasure. She would fax her doctor for the required details. Far Moreover GGGers, here I come.

"Leave the rest to us, Valiante, we will have this done in no time, and I'll call you as soon as the Geriatric Girls' Gym is yours." Sunni took the check and gave a quick look at the forms. "What does this say, here at 'employment?' I can't quite read it."

"Retired, it says retired."

"But you are so young to be retired. What did you do?"

For the first time during her gym visit, Valiante smiled sweetly. "I am a sex therapist."

This was met by a gasp from Sunni. "For lesbians." Another smile from Valiante, even sweeter. Sunni sat down hard on a nearby bench. "Actually, for older lesbians," continued Valiante, and sat down next to her.

A few days passed, then the weekend, with no word from the gym. Valiante waited patiently; she worked in her garden, put time in at her computer, and took long walks. The weather was gorgeous. "Spring has sprung, the bird is on the wung," came to mind. Dorothy Parker, Ogden Nash, she mused.

Valiante's ex, Zoe, now her close friend, was visiting for the weekend. Valiante knew Zoe could not quite remember why they had broken up—Valiante knew it had nothing to do with her work and availability—it was Zoe's own messing around with someone else, Valiante reminded her. Oh yes, Zoe agreed, that was it, but that was over. They couldn't really separate completely, so it seemed close friendship was the best option. Valiante still suffered from broken–heart syndrome, which was why she had moved to Far Moreover; why she had her gestalt moment to research and write the book when she saw the GGGym sign; why she had settled for friendship in place of love. She'd vowed never to suffer from heartbreak again, and that was final, absolutely.

The women were in Valiante's kitchen, wearing the GGG aprons Sunni had given Valiante when she had left the gym. Valiante's apron was almost covering her shorts. Zoe's was over her underwear, She had on a thong—somewhat disconcerting to Valiante. Was the damned woman being seductive? Valiante wondered, and her jaw tightened. No way.

This weekend they'd cooked fabulous vegetarian meals while they talked and reminisced. A local vegetable stand had opened and was selling beautiful asparagus, so the women had them for breakfast, lunch, and dinner: asparagus omelet in the morning; midday asparagus au gratin with a gluten–free multigrain bread Valiante had baked; and in the evening, steamed asparagus, sesame Brussels sprouts, with red and green peppers stuffed with white beans and brown rice, and zucchini doused in no gluten herbed bread crumbs.

Zoe leaned back contentedly in one of the living room club chairs that not only swiveled, but rocked easily, and surveyed the comfortable room. "My pee smells from all that asparagus," she said.

"Mine too." Valiante swiveled toward Zoe. "So how do you like my little village?"

"I love it. I'm coming for a visit maybe one weekend a month, if that's okay with you, oh ravishing ex-lover."

"I'll be here with arms full of veggies, if you bring the wine." Valiante stood and topped off their glasses with the lovely Sancerre Zoe had brought. She threw a large shawl over Zoe's legs, draped over the arm of the chair. "Shameless hussy," Valiante hissed. Zoe gave her the finger in response.

"How did they come up with a name like Far Whatever, do you suppose?" Zoe asked. "It's really strange."

"I think some early settlers from England wanted to name the place with something connected to where they came from, and Far Moreover fit the bill, you know, like Far Rockaway in New York." Valiante pulled the hassock near her chair close and put her feet up. Valiante liked to get her long legs off the ground any chance she could. *Good thing at least I am wearing real underpants and shorts,* she thought. But why the hell was she so obsessed with underwear, or was it what was under the underwear? Hell, she was glad Zoe was here with her—she missed her when she was not.

Zoe peeled a navel orange and handed a segment to Valiante. "Makes no sense, the name Over Farmore, I mean it's like your name, Ms. V, a name that's so hard to live up to, oh love of my life. Whatever were your parents thinking?" They laughed and shared more of the orange. Valiante was used to her friend's teasing.

"Well, what are you going to do here, honeypot, do they need a sex therapist this far from a city?" Valiante poured more wine into their glasses. Zoe sipped hers. The taste of orange with the Sancerre was delicious.

"I am going to start my new life by working out at the GGG every morning, starting tomorrow." Valiante went back to her chair and spun around clockwise a few times. "And then, I'm going to write a really sexy book about the GGG'ers."

"Remind me Prince Valiant, what in the goddess's name is a GGG, the Golly Gorgeous Gang?" Zoe spun counter–clockwise in her chair.

"You are looking at the newest almost–member of the Geriatric Girls' Gym, managed by Ms. Sunshine, who also makes delicious, nutritious GGG smoothies. And if you're a good girl, I'll buy you a GGG T–shirt of your very own, which will stand as your passport to Far Moreover. And you can keep the apron."

Zoe spun off her chair, fell, and started to hiccup. She always got the hiccups when she laughed too hard.

Valiante showed up at the gym at 7:00 AM sharp Monday morning, and greeted Sunni politely at the front counter. Her mood was much improved after the fine weekend.

"Did you get the medical report from my doctor? She told me she'd fax it to you on Friday. Here are all the other things you asked for. I'm ready to start, rarin' to go." She was in high gear and began walking into the exercise room without waiting for Sunni to respond. She looked around the room. It was empty. Valiante shrugged, strode toward the bikes, adjusted the height on a large one, and levitated up to the seat.

The manager followed, looked up at her and said timidly, "We don't usually start until 8:00 AM. Seven is a bit early for the women. I was in early this morning to get things ready. I usually come in early on Mondays. When the ladies come, before we get started we sing a song or read something as a warmup."

"My goodness," Valiante crooned, "do you do God Bless America, and the Pledge of Allegiance or 'Rock Around the Clock' or what?" *Watch the sarcasm, girl,* she thought to herself, *you're starting off on the wrong quip.*

"We have a committee that decides and makes the choices. It's very stimulating and a good way to start the workouts." Sunni's ivory skin reddened slightly.

Valiante started pedaling fast as Sunni backed off thinking that she'd better remember that the newest member was a sex therapist, and who knew what strange habits the woman might have. Valiante thought maybe she should visit Sunni's father's restaurant, The Sue-She Far Moreover Delec–Table De–Light. Yes, that's what she would do, when she had the time to do so.

Valiante felt good, strong, and ready for the GGGers when they arrived. She had brought her unread issues of *Opera News* to read as she walked the treadmill and pedaled the bike to nowhere. Valiante had decided to start with the latest one she'd received from the Metropolitan Opera Guild, and planned to go backwards until she would get to the first issue she had received but not read. She always looked at the covers, but never had time to read them. Or maybe she would start at this one with Renee Fleming on the cover, and alternate it with the oldest one, with Luciano Pavarotti on the cover. *Wouldn't that be great fun,* she thought. Was she losing her mind? The magazine plan was ridiculous, so were her other plans. Nevertheless, she would go with them. Everything she was doing since she broke up with Zoe was a little crazy, like moving to Far Moreover for example, or like the idea for her book. She pedaled faster, imagining she was Dorothy escaping the wicked witch on her own bicycle. *Time would tell,* she thought, *or else she'd just have to get a new clock.*

She pedaled until 8:00 AM without even noticing that GGGers were arriving in small groups, taking places around the room and doing some stretches. When Sunni walked in they stopped and waited. Sunni said, "Good morning, darling GGGers," and got a "Good morning, Sunni honey," in return.

Someone sang a pitch, and the women began to sing "You Are My Sunshine" in eleven- part-harmony, one to a part. Valiante did not join in. She refrained from putting her fingers in her ears.

Sunni smiled her big smile. "Girls," she said sweetly, "would you form a circle? We have a new member starting with us today, so we'll do our GGGGreeting." She took Valiante by the hand and led her to the center of the circle. "Everybody, this is Valiante Strongwoman. Let's begin. I'll start." She joined the circle, and began clapping and singing, "Hello dear Valiante, yes indeed, yes indeed, yes indeed, my name is Sunni, yes indeed, yes indeed my darling."

Each clapping woman joined the circle, taking her turn to greet the newcomer, and introduced herself by name. A caramel brown-skinned woman, taller by an inch than Valiante, stepped out of the circle and gave her a major hug. "My name is Vita, yes indeed," she wiggled her hips and raised her eyebrows as she sang her 'yes indeeds' in a deep, husky alto, and met Valiante's eyes for a long moment before moving back into the circle. Valiante stood transfixed. Yes, indeed, she would know this tall, black Walküre with a crown of hair so red it was almost a sunset; this goddess, younger than all the other GG's; she, Valiante, would know this Vita.

One by one they sang their greeting, sang their names, and what names they had: Vita, Dolly, Ardora, Chastity, Izzy, Honey, Bella, Marvel, Canary, Joy, Lucide, and Sunni. Valiante's name was a good addition—she was thirteen, her lucky number. But how would she remember all the other names? Ah hah, she noticed, they all wore nametags.

Valiante headed for one of the treadmills. Sunni approached, holding out a GGG tag with her name inscribed. "Here you are, Valiante, this makes it official." Valiante tried hard to look grateful and dignified, appreciative, as though a great honor was being bestowed upon her. Actually, she was having fun; she felt like a five-year-old. Sunni held out the nametag. "May I?"

"Of course," Valiante answered, "but watch out for my breast, I'm quite attached to it." Giggles from Ms. Sunshine. She felt Sunni's surreptitious little poke at her left boob as the manager carefully pinned the tag over it and not into it.

"My goodness, Valiante, you don't seem to be wearing a bra. Heavens, how can you exercise with no bra?"

"No problem, why should I?" Valiante replied. "My bosom stands up for itself perfectly well. Would you like to see?" More giggles. Face red, Sunni retreated.

Valiante unfurled her *Opera News*, set the machine for speed 4.0, and pressed Quick Start. Her plan for the GGG was going to take some careful thought but she'd figure it out. She was off to a good start, at least on the treadmill.

"My dear child," came a high, thin voice from the left, "you are going much too fast, you're going to win the race." This was followed by a series of quick little snorts, meant to be mirth. Valiante turned to face a woman on the adjoining treadmill going at a moderate pace, which you might call slow and not be wrong. She had a pert, pretty face, topped with a lot of shiny, jet–black curls that bobbed up and down as she walked. Her smile showed absolutely perfect white dentures, parenthesized by a pair of deep dimples in her cheeks.

Valiante read her neighbor's name card and waved. "Oh hi, Dolly, would you like me to slow down? I aim to please."

"Heavens, you actually remember my name," She became so flustered, she completely forgot about the nametag she was wearing. "I am impressed. Is that a trick you have, remembering names? Or is it because of your profession?"

"No trick at all," changing the wave to point at the name card, as Dolly reddened with embarrassment.

"I forgot I was wearing it, I forget things these days." Dolly straightened the card.

"So what do you know about my profession, Dolly, and how do you know it?" Valiante made sure to be pleasant and not confrontational. She slowed her pace and smiled.

"Oh, Sunni told us you were a psychotherapist when we met Saturday morning at The GGG Breakfast Club. We're all so excited and," she paused to breathe, "well, intrigued, I guess."

"Is that all, she didn't tell you any more?" Valiante's plan didn't allow for any further information for everyone at this time. But it was possible that Sunni had told all.

Dolly nodded. "I'm taking a Psych 101 course at the Far Moreover Community College, Retired Women's Department of Creative Aging, and I know that therapists aren't allowed to say anything about what they shouldn't talk about. Right?"

"It's true, we don't reveal privileged information; we have to protect our clients." Valiante shut the treadmill down and hopped off. "See you later, Dolly. Nice talking with you."

"Will we see you at the smoothie juice station? We all meet there at our break to raise our blood sugar in case it drops from too much exercise." Dolly carefully descended in order to be on the same level with Valiante, but her 5'2" made it impossible to meet the eyes of the much taller woman. She got back up to stand on the treadmill, adding some needed inches.

Valiante bent a bit at the knees to shorten herself. "I only drink water at the gym, but I'll say hello." She bowed with a flourish, and went off to try the weights. *Well,* she thought, *Dolly seemed a friendly sort, cute as a doll. Would she fit into the scheme, this little woman who was the essence of straight?*

By the end of her hour–and–a–half workout, she discovered that all the GGGs knew where she lived, what, and with whom she had renovated her cottage, and that she was a retired therapist. They did not know anything more, thanks to Sunni's discretion. Valiante had left them with a lot to talk about and much to find out about, but the object of their curiosity was not ready to reveal anything more. They would have to wait.

Valiante's gardens were coming to life as spring progressed. Daffodils, iris, and tulips provided color, while the cherry tree blossomed along with the flowering plum. She went to the gym most mornings, unless she had to leave the village for one reason or other. A visit to a doctor or lawyer, lunch or dinner with a city friend—there was always something to take her from Far Moreover. She was happy to go, but happier to come home. This Saturday, she had invited the dozen Geriatric Girls to her cottage for lawn games and lunch. They all eagerly accepted, curious to see exactly where and how Valiante lived. Zoe would not be coming till Sunday; she had taken Monday off from her job at the LGBTQ information desk at the Main Library, and would stay for both days.

The day came bright and sunny, and everyone arrived early. A croquet game was set up on one side of the lawn, badminton on the other. There were pitchers of lemonade and cut up vegetables set on tables, but the ladies wanted to see the house first and examine things up close. They were all so curious that Valiante expected them to take out magnifying glasses for closer scrutiny.

Once inside, the GGGymers examined the furnishings with compliments. Vita seemed only to be interested in Valiante's books that lined the walls in nearly every room. She moved slowly from shelf to shelf reading all the titles, and spent the most time at the shelf that held only women poets.

Audre Lorde's work interested her most and she lingered, reading while seated in a nearby chair. Valiante stopped at her side, and handed her a volume by Jewelle Gomez. "Take a look at these, Vita, especially Flamingoes and Bears, it's pure delight. And I have a good collection of the work of Vita Sackville West, if you're interested." Vita nodded and grasped Valiante's hand in assent.

The paintings and sculptures of nudes in the living room and bedrooms got the most attention from the other women, with some heavy whispering among them. The king–size bed in the master bedroom got a few knowing looks, and a gorgeous realistic painting of two women in bed, called The Lovers, much like the Corbet painting, aroused conversation. The textbooks on sex therapy and LGBTQ issues made things buzz.

Once outside again, Valiante saw the lemonade attacked, and was not pleased to see her guests head for the chairs and lounges instead of the games. The women arranged themselves in a horseshoe with the refreshments at the open end. Ardora, a curvaceous green-eyed blonde with a face lifted up from her sharp jawline, asked Valiante if it was all right to ask her a few questions, and then, despite a warning look from Sunni, and without waiting for an answer, went right ahead and asked. "Are you or have you ever been married Valiante?"

"Not really," was the reply. "Some close encounters, but too much trouble," was added.

"What kind of therapy did you practice?" came from Dolly.

Valiante wondered why it had taken so long to ask that question. "Sex therapy," she said.

It got really quiet until Chastity piped up with "What is that?" sounding like a three-year- old being naughty.

"It's therapy to help people with their sex problems, like impotence, premature ejaculation, penile dysfunction, frigidity, inability to experience orgasm, and many other issues."

It was very quiet, except for a soft breeze rustling the new leaves on the trees, a few birds singing, and some slurping of lemonade.

"I have a question for you, Sunni. Who owns the Geriatric Girls Gym—do you know?" Valiante was met with silence.

Finally Sunni replied, speaking very softly, "It's a secret, but if you all promise not to tell..." Everyone waited, and after a long pause while she examined her nails, Sunni spoke. "It's my father, Kyo Takashimaya. You will remember please that this is secret and you have promised."

"Bella asked, "But why is it a secret? Is it something illegal?"

Sunni bit her lip, and then explained, "My father is a very proud man. He did not want me to tell people that I was the owner's daughter, and that was how I had my job as manager. Also, he did not know what the word geriatric meant, and he was worried about it. I had to explain it. He only knows about his restaurant, and making sashimi and sushi, not a geriatric gym." Sunni squirmed and bent her head to look at the grass. "And he is having a tax issue, just a checkup examination," she said, making it sound like a medical condition.

"Not to worry, Sunni, we won't tell. Let's all have dinner at the restaurant someday soon." Valiante suggested. "Let's eat there as a group once a month, so Mr. Takashimaya can get to know us and feel comfortable with his daughter's friends at the gym. Everyone agreed, and Sunni smiled with appreciation. "Games anyone? Questions? More lemonade?" Valiante raised a pitcher. No takers.

Chastity again: "By the way, Valiante, what is LGBTQ? That's not a word, is it?"

"Lesbian, Gay, Bisexual, Transgender, Queer." Valiante had a much-needed swallow of lemonade, her answer had been quite a mouthful. "And I think you might like to know that I only treated lesbians, queers, or transpeople. Does that shock you?" The women filled the silence with murmurs of denial, or nervous little coughs. Lucide and Bella stood, which was a signal for all the others to do the same. "Any more questions. No? Okay, I'm around and available if you do. Lunch will be on the porch in an hour and twenty minutes," Valiante cheerfully announced. "Ready for some fun first?" she asked, pointing to the badminton court.

Some of the women went to the games area, but most stood around in small groups and talked. Canary and Dolly hit the shuttlecocks over the net with their rackets halfheartedly, but not really engaged in a game. After a while, they took off for a walk. Sunni stared into space and bit daintily at a cuticle. She smiled gratefully at Bella, who came to sit beside her.

Their host started to walk to the house when Isolda, called Izzy, one of the younger women, probably about fifty, sidled up to her and asked Valiante, without preamble, "How do you know if you're a lesbian, if you never went to bed with a woman?"

"That's a big question, Izzy, and I don't think I can give you an answer with so much going on around us. We need some privacy, don't you think?" Izzy looked lost, shoulders drooping, head down.

"Tell you what," Valiante spoke with some energy, "you can come and talk with me—not therapy, no money, just a talk to see if we can figure it out. Would you like to do that?"

Izzy brightened up immediately and stepped up jauntily to the plate. They made a date to have tea the next week.

Lunch was served at the big oblong table on the dining porch. Valiante had made a beautiful cold lobster salad and home–baked knotted rolls. When they were finished with that course, Marvel cleared her throat, squared her shoulders, and said, "I've been thinking." She paused and thought for a minute, then began again. "We've been talking about your occupation as a therapist, and we're all curious and have questions." Valiante put her cutlery down and faced the handsome woman eye to eye. Marvel wore her hair clipped very close to her scalp in a crew cut. She certainly fit the "butch" image. Valiante nodded and waited. "Remember that years ago, groups of women used to get together and just talk about their lives and problems?" Valiante nodded again. "Well, we wondered if you would be interested in our getting together once a week or so, and just talk, nothing formal, just talk, like women used to do?" "Oh, you mean MR groups, I think they used to call them," piped up Honey, one of the older women whom everyone seemed to take care of. Marvel smiled kindly at her.

"I think you mean CR, consciousness-raising groups," Marvel gently corrected.

"Yes, isn't that what I meant to say?" Honey joined in the laughter at her question, and opened her eyes flirtatiously while pursing her lips playfully at Marvel.

Vita came around to her chair and hugged her, almost lifting the small woman off her feet. "Exactly, sweet Honey," and stopped at Valiante's chair. "I think that's a great idea, valiant woman. This group is so bonded, yet we never talk about personal things, issues, problems. It would be a treat to exercise our tongues, instead of just our bodies."

"Really!" Canary pretended to fan herself with her napkin. "What are you saying, Vita?" and stood, knocking her chair over, stretched her arms wide, and sang "Ta da!"

Vita picked up the chair and sat Canary in it, shook her finger and said, "Behave yourself, woman. Canary's just showing off," Vita explained. More laughing, but somewhat uneasy, Valiante thought.

Valiante looked around the table. This was definitely the next step. It was happening fast, but seemed to be a natural progression. She was very pleased that the women seemed so eager to form a CR group that would offer an opportunity to talk about anything that was on their minds, to become closer in a different way than they were at the GGG. *Good,* she thought, *very good indeed.*

"I need to think about this...see if it is ethical for me to form such a group. After all, you could sit around and talk casually without me present. I've told you, as a sex therapist, I helped lesbians and other women with their special problems—broken love affairs, family issues, stuff like that. This may not be what you have in mind."

"But that was group therapy, wasn't it, Valiante?" asked Lucide. "My sister did that, but that was real therapy. We're talking about a friends' group, not a patients' group—but a consciousness raising group, to learn more about ourselves, right?" She turned to ask everyone.

"That's right, Lucide, and we know this, Valiante," Dolly interjected, "you've been very straightforward. Oh dear, is 'straight' a wrong word?" Valiante laughed. Maybe these women were more informed than she realized. "Besides, we might have sex problems that we never talk about, and other secrets that trouble us, that we'd like to share, or get advice about." Dolly added, her cheeks reddening.

"I will give this some serious thought. No payment will be involved. This would not be therapy, but hopefully, it would be helpful for you all. I'll just think about whether we could just have informal discussion meetings, similar to your breakfast club—maybe instead of your breakfast club—to talk about whatever you wished, but not a coffee klatch just to be social. Give me some time and I'll let you know. Oh, one thing more, you've probably noticed that I make notes in the little book I always have with me. Research, habit, is that okay with you?" No one objected. She held the book up. "I have a few questions, okay?" Everyone nodded.

"First, have any of you been married?" Honey, Canary, Bella and Ardora raised their hands. "How many are widows?" Honey and Canary's hands went up. "How many divorced?" Bella and Ardora whooped their assent. "Can I keep going?" Valiante asked. Unanimous yes.

"How many of you have always been single?" Marvel's hand was the first up, followed by Izzy, Sunni, Dolly, and Lucide, in close pursuit.

Vita spoke out in her rich voice, "You ain't reached my category yet, girl, so you better keep going." Valiante blew her a kiss and raised her own hand to join the single women. Chastity and Joy remained with their hands in their laps.

"Let's see, how can I ask this, how many of you have been engaged or had a serious relationship with a man, but didn't marry him?" Joy began to cry. Chastity had a coughing fit.

"I was engaged to my boyfriend, we were getting married when he was back from Vietnam, and he never came back. And I never got married." Joy wiped her eyes. Ardora used a clean tissue to wipe the mascara the tears had streaked and Joy gave her a grateful smile. "That was a long time ago."

Chastity stood, tall and voluptuous, "Can you imagine being cursed with a name like mine? Well here's how I dealt with it, I slept with everyone I wanted to, man, woman or anything in between. Chastity, my ass!" She sat down. Everyone cheered.

Valiante was astonished, blown away by the honesty of the women, but she was not done yet. There were Marvel and Vita left.

Marvel lit a cigarette, the only one she allowed herself for the day, and said in an almost inaudible voice, "I'm a lesbian, have been all my life. Mostly, 'I'm So Lucky To Be Me'. She sang the first line of a Leonard Bernstein piece from On The Town and put her cigarette out in her cup.

"Cool," said Vita. There were murmurs of assent around the table. "And I ain't talking," Vita proclaimed. "I'll let you know when I know, and tell you how it works out." And with that she stood up and left the table. Valiante set her little black book aside.

The lunch ended on a lighter note with much jollity and innuendo, and a few naughty jokes. Sex was in the air; after all, it was spring and love was in bloom. Valiante made entries in her notebook about her planned book, Every Woman is a Lesbian: No Matter Her Age, Race, or Religion. *I don't like that title,* Valiante thought, *I'll have to make some changes. Does anything ever go according to plan?* As a careful researcher with several books under her belt, she knew the answer to that question.

A month had passed and Zoe was back for another weekend with Valiante, this time bringing her new girlfriend, Ginger. "Well this is a record for you, Valiante cupcake. As far as I can tell, there is not now, nor has there been a new lover in that mammoth bed of yours since you moved to Far Moreover. What's the matter with you?"

"I'm a retired woman. I exhaust myself at the GGG six days a week. I'm too old and too weak for a lover." Valiante tried to look pathetic.

"Yeah, sure," Zoe smirked, "tell me another tall tale, hot stuff." Valiante ignored her and went on. "My mother says I can't do those nasty things any more. And, there are no eligible dykes in Far Moreover, none that I can cozy up to. Besides, I'm doing volunteer work here with my 'Let's Talk It Under' group, and outlining my book. Who needs sex?" Valiante exclaimed with open arms and a raucous whoop.

Ginger leapt into Valiante's arms, "I've got a great gal for you to meet. Whaddaya say?"

Zoe answered for her friend, "Yes."

Valiante shook her head no. Ginger shrugged and pulled Zoe to her feet. "Let's dance."

"There's no music," Zoe whined, and then began to move slowly, bending her body to Ginger's, holding her close as a CD Valiante put on spun out the notes to "I'll be Loving You."

Valiante sat and watched the women dance. She thought of the many times she and Zoe danced, had made love. Stop it. She reprimanded herself. Be happy for Zoe. *Nothing like a new romance,* she thought, and took a small toke on the joint she held in her thumb and forefinger. *What's the use of getting high and hot,* she thought, *when I'm here—all by myself, alone,* quoting an old song from the forties. She inhaled deeply and held it for a long time.

This damned plan is spitting in my face, she thought, *my own issues are getting in the way. All I wanted to do is find a little town, and I did; find a group of mature straight women who were tight, close, did everything together—the GGG was perfect—infiltrate and convert them.* Valiante was now talking out loud: "I did not intend any religious or spiritual stuff except for what came from friendship and then love. I meant to prove that deep down, and with all their nerve endings in the right places, women are or can be lesbians."

Realizing she was almost as loud as the music, she continued her thoughts to herself. *Then I'll write a book about it, a sizzling hot book. Shit, what is wrong with me?* Valiante asks herself and thinks she's the one who's miserable. *Vita the African Queen is in her way. She's just not thinking right. She's distracting me. Zoe and Ginger are upsetting her and she's getting really annoyed with herself. High, where are you? Feels pretty low to me. Okay, be valiant, Valiante, do something.* She must have said the last sentence out very loud because Zoe and Ginger stopped dancing and stared at her. Valiante waved and blew them a kiss.

Valiante took her cell phone from her pocket, looked up the Vs in its listing, saw the only names were Valiante and Vita. *This is wrong, only two Vs, no Valerie, no Violet, no Vagina. Uh oh, she had to stop thinking this way.* After a minute she reopened, hit the name, and invited Vita to dinner tomorrow. She checked for dietary concerns, no problems and set the time. *Change of plan, again,* Valiante smiled. *After all, we live in deeds, not words,* says the old adage.

The three women spent the next morning shopping and planning the dinner. First there would be butternut squash soup; followed by gluten–free linguine topped by assorted vegetables in a light yogurt, creamy tomato sauce, with sautéed mixed mushrooms decorating the top. A salad of assorted Asian greens and beans with blood orange pieces and sesame dressing; plus a gluten–free pastry they could all eat, a surprise made by Ginger.

"You devil, Valiante, I should have known you had something up your sleeve. There is no town or community safe from your lechery," Zoe said as she continued to expertly cut up vegetables.

"Zoe, this is research. Vita is one of the gymers, and I need to get to know her better. She's different from the other women: younger, smarter, more sophisticated, more complex."

"Are we going to meet the other eleven women one by one, as we come out? I mean, come here to Far Moreover?"

Ginger asked coyly. "That'll take eleven more months of research for all."

"Oh stop it, you two. This is a serious project I'm working on. I don't need you being cute. And I expect you to behave when Vita is here. Discretion is in order."

"Does Vita know that you're a lesbian?" Zoe cut her finger and cursed.

"She checked out every book in my collection, so she'd have to be a fool not to know, and besides, they all know because I told them."

"I don't believe you, Dr. Valiante Strongwoman, lesbian therapist supreme."

Valiante shrugged, "That's your problem, Zoe. And, Vita's the only African-American in the GGs, certainly the only one with red hair. I thought you'd like to know that."

"All the better, the group was sounding awfully homogeneous, but I still don't believe you," Zoe added as a non sequitur. "Valiante ignored her ex's comment, and added, "Did I forget to mention that Sunni is Japanese-American? Her father owns the best Asian restaurant in town."

"How many others are there?" Ginger asked, as she washed the blood off the knife, and some of the vegetables Zoe had cut along with her finger. She leered at Zoe with her best vampire imitation.

"None." Valiante made the sign of the cross at the would-be bloodsucker.

"Let's get back to Vita. What if she thinks that you have all those books on the subject because you specialize in treating lesbians, not because you are one?" Zoe thumbed her nose at

Valiante. "That is, if you still are one—a lesbian, I mean, not a vampire."

Ginger put on the band–aid Valiante provided, and kissed Zoe's cut finger. "Awwwlllll bedda, baby."

Zoe raised an eyebrow and pulled her finger back.

"If she doesn't know, she's sure gonna find out tonight," Zoe said, pretended to be a silent film villain and twirling a make–believe mustache. "Ginger and I gonna be our 'nat–u–ral woman' selves."

Valiante tried to not think about what she was feeling. Was it jealousy? What was this thing called love, anyway? She had broken up with Zoe because Zoe was having an affair, so how could she be jealous of Ginger and her ex now? Ginger flirted with everyone, she was hard to figure out. Made no sense to Valiante. Maybe she should see a good therapist. "But I am a good therapist." She finished setting the table.

Vita arrived at 7:05 with a basket full of portulaca in assorted bright colors, tomatoes from her greenhouse she apologized for, but saying they were pretty good anyway, and baby bok choy. "I'm a vegetarian, but I didn't remember if I told you. I didn't want you to do anything especially for me. I'll just eat what I can. And thanks so much for inviting me."

Introductions were accomplished, wine was poured, a Dvorak string quartet CD was softly playing. On the coffee table sat a platter of mixed olives and feta cheese, and a bowl of sliced raw carrots, peppers, radishes, fennel and seedless cucumbers. It was very quiet in the room. The women listened to the music, ate, drank, and exchanged pleasantries. Finally, Vita stood herself up and pulled her tight jeans loose around her crotch. "These are quite close–fitting and they get caught in my parts." Everyone laughed. She remained standing. "Okay, I'm going to ask you straight out, are you all lesbians, or dykes, or queers, or whatever you want to call yourselves?" She waited.

It didn't take but a breath and all three voices said in unison, "Yes."

"You betcha, honey," from Zoe.

"And I'm her current babe, sorta," offered Ginger.

"And what about you, Dr. Valiante? Did you say yes also?"

"Guilty as charged, as you know, Ms. Vita," Valiante answered, catching Zoe's eye and looking away quickly. "Well, now that that's settled, let's have dinner," she continued, "out on the porch. Absolutely vegetarian and organic, cooked by, the three mustbequeer!" Zoe waved her cap with a flourish, and they curtsied low in return.

Dinner was delicious; everyone laughed at anything anyone said; Ginger and Zoe were shameless, smooching, and silly. When Ginger's dessert arrived, the women howled with delight. It was called Ladyfingers Surprise, and it was no mere trifle. It came in a huge bowl filled with kiwi, grapes, peaches, pears, apricots, cherries, lady apples, assorted nuts, and topped with yogurt custard. Surrounding the fruit and custard, which formed in the shape of a vagina, were ladyfingers caressing the best spots. It was a gorgeous work of art.

"Can we really eat this?" asked Vita.

"Way to go, sweetheart," directed Zoe, grinning at Ginger. And they did, every last morsel, with much suggestiveness and innuendo. Shameless, as promised.

When they were having coffee in the living room, it got quiet again, really quiet. There was no music, no laughter, no questions, until Vita turned to Valiante and asked, "What are you up to, Valiante? Why are you in Far Moreover, at the Gym? Is this some kind of game?"

"No, it is not a game, and it's not anything hurtful or harmful. I'm doing research for a book I have in mind, and this village, the gym, those women are perfect subjects for me to write about." Valiante offered her hand to Vita, who accepted it carefully, as a kind of peace offering.

"What kind of book, Valiante? Is it a novel, a text, a memoir, what?" Vita retrieved her hand.

"I'm not sure, it was going to be a textbook for college Women Studies programs, then it changed to a memoir, and now I don't know what it will be, but I think it might be titled Every Woman is a Lesbian...I have to see how things go." Valiante stood to pour coffee for everyone and stopped in front of Vita. "I promise that as soon as it gets clearer for me, I'll share it with you. I promise." She put a warm and intimate tone on the last offer of information.

Vita grudgingly shook her head, then shrugged her shoulders, but with a smile said, "Good thing I love a mystery, girl," assuaged for the moment.

Ginger stood and twirled, "Let's dance, sweeties. We've got to work off that dessert." She put on a CD of forties swing music and reached for Zoe while Vita pulled Valiante to her feet. Halfway through, they changed partners, breaking in like their parents used to do at parties, then the foursome made a pretense of square dancing, which had no relationship to the music on the recording. Vita and Ginger stayed, dancing closely together. When "Feels Like I'm Falling In Love" came on the player, the two couples kept dancing as if they were conjoined.

Valiante was stymied; she needed to do some more research with the Geriatric Girls so she could make a serious start with background material. She decided to join the group during break time at the juice and smoothie station, to take over the conversation and steer it away from gossip so they could talk about personal matters, like love and sex. Did they talk about their husbands, boyfriends, lovers; what about children and grandchildren; how did they spend their time away from the gym, and with whom; what were their plans for the future? This would take time—well, she had time. Where should she begin? She'd bait the hook and throw out the line. She commandeered a treadmill, set the speed to five, and away she raced.

They were an even dozen today, and it took time for them to get their drinks. Valiante raised the glass of carrot–celery–pomegranate juice she had opted for instead of water, and looked hopefully at the women while avoiding meeting Vita's eyes. "I thought, now that we know each other better, that we could start having some girl talk."

"Yes," Honey offered hopefully, "like a CR group."

"If that meets with everyone's approval, that would be great, but let's set a time limit so we don't lose out on our exercise. We'll save the leftovers for our "Let's Talk It Under" time." Valiante was obviously pleased. Was this was going to be easier than she thought?

"What should we talk about, ourselves?" Ardora asked. "Like problems or other personal things?"

At this point Sunni came for her daily ginseng honey lemon iced tea, which was ready for her at the counter, thanks to Izzy, whose turn it was this week to make the drinks.

"Can I join the circle, women? What are you talking about?"

"We're going to spend our half hour break talking about ourselves, Dolly said knowingly, "as well as with our other Talk group. You can be part of it, Sunni, right GGs?" Everyone nodded or spoke affirmatively. "To get in touch with our consciousnesses," Bella inserted, "it'll be good for us." Ardora and Marvel clicked their glasses, then turned to their neighbors and did the same with them.

"I have a suggestion on how to start," Vita interjected. "We should go around the circle, starting with the women to my left: Honey, Bella, Ardora and Marvel, and continuing with Joy, Canary, and Lucide, ending with Dolly, Chastity, Izzy, and me."

"What about Sunni?" asked Bella, in her most maternal voice.

"And Sunni, of course. That makes an even dozen," Vita said triumphantly, as if she had created a tray of cupcakes.

"No, we're a 'bakers' dozen,' thirteen." Lucide clarified. Vita nodded her approval.

"Will there be time for bathroom?" Canary asked, plaintively. "I have to pee every twenty-two minutes. Valiante nodded reassuringly, while Vita put her arms around Canary.

Valiante watched this with interest, time for her to intervene before it turns into Vita's show, she decided. "We'd better have some time limits, or we'll be here all day, and the afternoon women won't like that, Valiante pointed out." She waved her hands in a circle to include each of the women. "Let's get going now! We'll stop at 12:40, that will be a half hour, and we'll continue next time. She clapped, and laughing, said "Then it's back to the torture room for the last hour." Valiante knew this plan would not work at the gym, she just wanted to get things going. "Who'd like to begin?"

She was surprised to see Joy's hand go up first. The woman had hardly spoken to her at all. Valiante nodded encouragingly at her, who at this moment seemed misnamed. Valainte had never even seen Joy smile.

"My name is Joy, and I'm miserable," and the woman began to sob. The GGGers alongside Joy moved to embrace her; the other women in the circle offered comforting words.

Valiante immediately rose, went to the woman and put her arms around her and whispered something gently into Joy's ear, and turned to the group: "I think it would be better if we arranged to have our talk group meet Mondays, once a week at my house, at 4:00 PM for about ninety minutes, with tea and talk, starting today. Is that cool with everyone? I know this is a quick decision, but I think we can agree that the gym is the place to get our bodies in shape, and my house will be where we can get our bobbleheads steady." They readily agreed, bobbling their heads and high–fiving one another. Valiante was relieved the transition had worked so well.

Honey said, "I baked cookies before I came to gym this morning: egg, gluten, sugar, peanut, salt, dairy, and fat free. It was an experiment, so they might be taste–free, should I bring them?"

"Why not," Canary tweeted in a singsong voice, "we GGGers are the taste–y cookies."

Valiante walked to a bike, mounted, and sat. *The plan changes and moves again,* she thought, *but the way I hoped it would.* Except for Joy's outburst, it was hard to get the GGs to be serious, and there was not much exercise happening either. She started to pedal slowly, and then, with a burst of energy, sped away.

As arranged, Izzy arrived promptly at 2:00 to get an answer to her earlier question: "How do you know if you're a lesbian, if you never went to bed with a woman?"

Valiante had turned one of the two bedrooms into a guest room, which also served as her study. Bookshelves covered one wall, a desk lined another, along with a couch that opened to a bed when needed. There were some small Indian rugs scattered around the room in the blues and greens of the furniture, which emulated the sky and grass that showed through the window looking out on the garden. Pillows the colors of the garden flowers made the room bright and cheerful. Art displayed a variety of flowers on whatever wall space was available, and an assortment of purple and red tulips and freesia sat in a ceramic vase on the small round brass tray that served as a coffee table.

She offered one of the two club chairs to Izzy, and sat nearby on the other. Izzy's feet could barely reach the floor—she was a tiny woman, but her posture was almost haughty, and she gained in attitude what she didn't have in size. Her fingers moved her dark hair behind her ears, and she shook her bangs into place. She offered a bright, open smile, and Valiante realized that Izzy was very beautiful. Two small bottles of Poland Spring water and glasses took up the remaining space on the tray table. Sunshine touched the water and made it sparkle, and the room was alive with good vibes.

"Do you remember what I asked you?" Izzy questioned, not meeting Valiante's eyes.

Valiante answered the question with a question of her own. "What makes you think you might be a lesbian even though you've never made love with a woman, Izzy?" After a deep breath, as if to fill her lungs with courage, Izzy managed to look at Valiante. After a gentle sigh, she began to speak, hesitated, and making a mighty effort to organize her thoughts, began again.

"Well, I had a very strange experience that I never had before, I mean, I just am very, well, I just don't know what happened, oh shit, this is ridiculous, I think I'll–" and she stood up as if to leave.

Valiante smiled benignly, and pulled her legs up to the edge of her chair. "Izzy, there is nothing you can tell me that would shock or upset me. You can't tell me anything I haven't heard before. This is between us, not to go any farther than this room, it's absolutely between you and me. You can trust me."

Izzy sat, rummaged in her canvas bag, brought out her own plastic bottle of water—or what Valiante assumed was water—opened it, and drank half. She stood again and walked to the window, her back to Valiante. "Well, okay, here goes. You won't laugh will you?" Without waiting for an answer, she continued. "Here's what happened. Some of us, the GGs, were on a trip, to, well it doesn't matter where, but we shared beds, six of us in three rooms. Queen size beds, so they were big, and we didn't have to touch. I'm not telling you who I had to share a bed with, so don't ask." She stopped and drank from her bottle she was holding close to her breast.

"I'm just listening, Izzy, no questions asked."

"So, well, um, she fell asleep. I just couldn't, and then it was weird, I mean nothing was touching, I wasn't touching anything—I mean I wasn't touching any part of myself. My hands were outside the covers, I swear." Her words were coming faster and faster as if she couldn't wait to get to the finish line. "And I was on my side of the bed. Honest." More water, the bottle was almost empty. What would Izzy do when there was no more whatever it was to drink, and the story wasn't over, Valiante wondered.

"Anyway," Izzy held her breath, exhaled, and stammered, her words stumbling out. "Anyway. I had, you know, this is really crazy, well, I had an orgasm, all by itself, without any encouragement from me." She turned, sat down, and put the bottle to her lips, but it was empty. Valiante reached over and took one of the bottles of water from her side table and handed it to Izzy.

"Lucky lady, I know lots of women who'd be thrilled to have your talent." Valiante took her bottle and toasted Izzy. "But why do you think you might be a lesbian? One orgasm does not make that so."

Izzy, calmer now that she had revealed her secret, met Valiante's gaze. "I've always had crushes on girls in school, women where I worked, and this one at the gym. I mean I can't take my eyes off her, but I have to make it seem that I barely notice her. For goddess' sake, I'm fifty-two-years old, this is crazy."

"I think it's marvelous, too marvelous for words." Valiante leaned and took Izzy's hand for a moment and squeezed. "Enjoy it, reach out and hold it, come alive, come."

Izzy looked at Valiante with eyes wide with wonder, was this woman nuts?

"So what, Izzy, maybe you're a lesbian, maybe you're a woman who's in love with a woman, maybe you're ready for love? Why not a lesbian? A lesbian by any other name would still be a woman. And you are a woman, and what a woman. I think you are great."

"So what should I do? What should I say? What?" Izzy jumped up and stood before Valiante. "I don't know what I can do."

"Invite her for dinner; find a trip the two of you can take; play tennis, go to the opera, be best friends and see where you can get to from there. I bet she has the hots for you too."

When Izzy asked Valiante if they could talk privately again, they made a date. A happier Izzy started for her nearby home to think things over, she said, before the get–together later. "I'll be back," she waved gaily to Valiante, as she practically skipped to her car.

The GGGers were due in an hour for their Geriatric Girls' Gabtime Group. Valiante went to the kitchen to lay out cups, saucers, napkins, and boil lots of water. *Things were moving along very nicely,* she thought, *and now it would be telling time.*

They arrived in a small bus for twelve that belonged to the gym. As promised, Honey came with cookies, Lucide brought a bowl of grapes, Bella came armed with a knife and a platter of cheese, and Chastity brought crackers. Dolly had a flat of pink impatiens, ready to go in the ground. Valiante was overwhelmed. "You can't do this every time you come here. It's too generous."

"Nonsense, we'll do as we like. We always do," boasted Vita, "let's sit outside," She brought small folding beach chairs from the bus. Ardora and Joy went into the house to do the tea prep, and in five minutes, everything was ready.

Joy said, "Okay, I want to start where I left off this morning."

"You go girl," encouraged Ardora, handing her a box of tissues. The women arranged themselves comfortably around the table that held the snacks and tea. They turned to look at Joy, and smiled at her in support. Valiante sat in the circle, making herself an equal part of the group. Everyone was quiet, except for the sound of chewing. The cookies would have done better with a hacksaw.

Joy sat up straight in her chair, tossed her long, straight, silvery–blonde hair in place, and said, "I'm not really miserable, I'm just not happy. Well, that's not always the case either; I'm happy when I'm with you all at the gym; I'm happy when…" and she stopped talking. It was as if she could think of no other time when she was happy. Everyone sipped and waited. They had given up on the cookies.

Valiante poured more tea and passed the kettle, and asked, "What do you think would make you happy? Can you remember times in the past when you were very happy? Tell us, if you can."

"The best time in my life was when I had a boyfriend. Then he went to Vietnam and got killed, and that was the end of happy. I'm still sad, and I'm lonely. No one to dress up for, put makeup on for, cook for, go to the movies with, be happy with."

"What about us, Joy, you say you're happy at the gym, because you're with us, right?" Ardora lifted her chin with the question.

"Yes, that's right," chimed in some of the women.

Joy stretched out her legs and looked around the circle. "Yes, but it's not the same. I love you all, but I'm not in love with you. Well maybe, I mean, you know what I mean, don't you?" Her question ended with an intense look at Ardora.

"What's the difference?" Bella's somewhat strident voice, tinged with a Brooklyn accent, rang out as she extended her hands. Her cropped pepper and salt hair moved with her head, which she was nodding in answer to her own question. "Love, in love, it's all the same, love is love," sounding more like her ancestors as she spoke.

"Love is love," repeated Sunni, "even in Japan."

"And even in Israel," Bella gave Sunni a hug, "especially in Israel."

Honey was squirming in her seat, not seeming comfortable with the conversation. "I love my dog," she said, "I love my sister and brother and their children. I never had any children I mean, but I don't know anything about romantic love. I can't even go to the movies anymore, the people are all doing sex on the screen. As the oldest woman in this room, I'm proud to say I'm a virgin."

Marvel applauded. "That's really cool, Honeybun. But don't you think you might have missed out on something special, something great? There must be something to it, this sex thing." At this she stood, put her hands on her hips, spread her legs, and sang, "Birds do it, bees do it, even educated fleas do it, let's do it, let's fall in love." At that, she pulled Honey up into her arms and added, "I'm hot for you, Honey darlin', you're the bees knees, the cat's meow, you're in all my dreams, little Honeypot. Whaddya say, let's fall in love."

Everyone clapped and whistled and Canary shouted, "Yes, yes! Let's all do it, let's fall in love." No one knew if she was serious or just having fun. Valiante thought it was a little bit of both. *What a beginning,* she thought, *I'm going to have to be careful to not let this go too fast, to get out of hand.* She did not want a broken hearts club.

The women fell on the cheese and crackers, the grapes disappeared and the tea was ignored. When Lucide brought out a bottle of wine, an opener, plastic cups, and Bella said l'chaim, everyone cheered and thus ended the first Geriatric Girls Gabtime Group. Vita and Valiante thumbed up at each other.

The weeks passed into the summer. The Gabtime Group usually met twice a week, becoming more open and revealing more each time. The women seemed to be getting closer as well, making plans as couples for museums, theater, and longer trips. The GGGers now knew that Valiante was gathering material for her book about women's groups—no names—and they were quite pleased about being part of her project, though they didn't know the book's title. With their permission, Valiante recorded parts of Gabbers (as they called themselves) meetings, and they were used to seeing Valiante make frequent jottings in her ever present notebook.

Zoe and Ginger now came for weekends every other week, and Vita usually joined them to make a foursome. Ginger was a charmer, and they all enjoyed being with one another more and more, but Valiante had to prepare herself for Ginger and Zoe each time they came. What is wrong with me? she scolded herself, I love both those women, they are my dearest friends. When they spent two weeks' vacation with Valiante, they came to the GGGym almost every day. It seemed Far Moreover was becoming Close Moreover for them.

Things were changing at the gym. The women were pairing off into what seemed like steady "best friend" couples. As the weeks went by, there was hand–holding and lots of longing looks. Valiante made a chart, she thought the coupling worked this way:

Marvel and Honey; Ardora and Joy;
Bella and Sunni; Izzy and Chastity;
Canary and Dolly; Lucide and Carmen

Carmen was the new woman from Cuba Lucide had met in her writing workshop and brought to the Gym. Diversity was thus enhanced. The group was quite fond of her, especially now that Carmen was teaching them to dance the tango and samba. And wonder of wonders, Joy seemed happy, she smiled most of the time. No one could figure out what was happening with Vita and Valiante. They seemed close, constantly exchanging confidences, but nothing that looked like the real thing.

Izzy had come to talk with Valiante several times, revealing that the object of her ardor was Chastity. "How can I have had the big L for a girl named Chastity. Isn't that silly?"

"No," Valiante answered. "What's in a name? A rose is a rose…did you tell her how you feel?" Izzy shook her head no. "Well, you're together all the time; I saw you hugging at the water fountain. You might be happily surprised if you told her."Time marched on and Izzy stopped asking for private time, lost weight, glowed. Valiante had lots of notes to write in her little black book.

The heat of August was hard to bear. The gym had closed for the entire month. Instead, the GGGers met three times a week at different houses, wherever there was air conditioning. This meeting of the Geriatric Girls Gabtime Group was taking place on the beach. Every couple brought an umbrella, beach chairs, and cold drinks. Valiante provided a picnic of cut and peeled melons, a medley of sliced fruits, Greek yogurt, deviled eggs, all kept icily cold in her large ice chest. Zoe and Ginger had come down from the city to escape the heat, and helped Valiante carry the load from the car. The beach they had chosen was completely private, with not another person to be seen.

When they were settled into a colorful circle of umbrellas and chairs, Chastity stood with arms outstretched, facing Valiante. "We are gathered today, to make an announcement: GGGers, with the help of the Gabbers—as you probably have already deciphered, dearest Valiante—this auspicious group has evolved. We have coupled off (first as best friends), and then having fallen passionately in love with love and each other, are really partners." The couples kissed, pranced in the sand, and then came to embrace Valiante. "We don't know exactly how you did it, but you helped make it happen. You changed our lives. Thank you." Chastity plopped down next to Izzy and took her in her arms.

Canary and Dolly emerged from their swim, dripping from head to toe. They each picked up a towel and dried the other. When they realized that everyone was watching, they wrapped up in the towels and sat down. "What did we interrupt?" Dolly asked.

"Chastity was thanking Valiante for changing our lives." Lucide explained.

Valiante picked up where Lucide had left off. "No my dears, you made it happen. You changed your lives. I only provided the opportunity, the possibilities. I made a space and you filled it." Valiante took a deviled egg from the ice chest, raised it, and toasted the women, "You are the best subjects I've ever experienced. You are the goodest eggs I've ever known. I love you, each and every one of you." And she popped the deviled egg into her mouth in one fell swoop. Everyone ululated.

Lucide and Carmen began passing plates of food and bug lotion. The afternoon breeze had come up and the waves of heat diminished. A few of the women napped in their chairs. Except for the waves and the shore birds, it was quiet, until the sound of castanets playing a Spanish rhythm clicked and joined in to create a trio with the birds and waves. Ginger rose and began to dance in the sand, bending and swirling in ment

sensuous movement, Carmen's castanets urging her on. Carmen stood and joined Ginger in the dance, the wooden discs in the Cuban woman's agile fingers providing all the music the two women needed. When they collapsed with exhaustion into each other's arms, the sun was beginning to set in a band of color that bathed all the Geriatric Girls' faces in a rosy, youthful glow. Valiante put her notebook back in her bag and marveled at the scene. She had a book: All Women Can Be Lesbians If They Really Try, Valiante's latest title, but probably not her last.

That evening, Ginger, Zoe, Valiante, and Vita sat on the porch having gin and tonics before dinner. "That was quite a day," Zoe commented. "Amazing. Do you have enough material for your book?" she asked Valiante.

"I've got everything I need, I just have to put it together." Valiante clicked her glass with Zoe's, then with the others.'

"Well, what's missing?" Vita questioned. "Did you achieve the hypothesis you started out with, whatever that really was?"

"And what kind of book is it now, a memoir, or what?" Zoe questioned.

"I bet it's a thriller novel," Ginger teased.

Valiante raised her eyebrows. "Maybe, Ginger girl, it's almost finished, but there's an important piece missing. I'll tie up a few loose ends, then I think it's on the way." Valiante waited. Time passed quietly. Drinks were sipped.

"Yes," said Ginger. "There is something more." She went to Vita and pulled her from her chair. "We've already told Zoe, so now we're telling you. Vita and I fell in love the first moment we laid eyes on each other. We belong together. We two are the women we've been searching for all our lives. My flirting—all of that stuff was just for fun."

"Wait a damn minute, what about you and Zoe?" Valiante asked Ginger. "Someone's got a broken heart here." She looked long at her former lover. "This just doesn't feel right."

"Oh, you mean the game we were playing, my little pop tart?" Zoe teased

"What game, Medussssssa?" Valiante hissed, and stood up to face both Ginger and Zoe.

"That was just a game Zoe and I were playing!" Ginger rose and did a little bump and grind into Valiante's belly. "To get you jealous, so you'd remember how much you love her." She ended with one more, but lower–placed grind. "We let Vita into the scheme after a while. Did it work?"

"Brava," saluted Valiante, "I think you did that very well—the game, I mean. However, I don't know if I should kill you or kiss you. She decided on the latter, to everyone's delight."

Vita moved to Valiante, "It was obvious to me from the very beginning that you and Zoe were still in love, have always been in love. You needed to play for a while, to be adventuresome, but it was always Valiante and Zoe, and that's how it should be." She raised her glass to Ginger, "Finding you was the treasure I never expected. It was love at first sight: corny, but true." Ginger clicked her glass with Vita's, knocking it out of her hand, much to her own amusement.

Valiante held out her arms and Zoe piled into them, as Ginger and Vita watched like proud mothers. The couples were coupled. It seemed that life was just a bowl of cherries.

After dinner of a mammoth salad with everything imaginable from the refrigerator—greens, yellows and reds, plus dried cranberries and roasted walnuts—they sat on the screened porch Valiante had added onto the house, watching Venus and the full moon flirting in the sky. "It's too hot to dance, but not to make love," was Ginger's pronouncement.

"Not yet," admonished Valiante. "I want to tell you about my book. It's titled The Geriatric Girls and the Therapist. I wanted to write about a group of unattached older women, who lived and socialized together in a safe space, in a far off community. My theory was that if placed in the right environment, with the possibility of open communication, with me on hand to make sure nothing harmful was happening, the inevitable would happen."

"And what was that, the inevitable?" Zoe asked, knowing the answer.

Valiante laughed and reached for her lover's hand. "That they would form close friendships, and eventually fall in love. And that's just what happened."

"In lust, also, I would hope." Ginger got up and twirled, then sat in Vita's lap.

"I imagine so," Valiante replied. "These were almost all 'straight women,' and what amazed me was how unlikely some of the couples were, unexpectedly so; how quickly it all happened; how brave the women are. They identify themselves as a new kind of woman, the Later Lady Lesbians, or the LaLaLes." She finished her drink and added, "I have disguised the place and the women to protect their privacy, added a few sex scenes...I think the novel will be serious fun! And, I have a publisher, Spinsters' Glue."

"Yay," the quartet shouted, and they made a hugging circle.

"So what does this all prove?" Vita asked in her most professorial voice.

"That, under the right circumstances, all women can be, or are lesbians—at least that's what happens in my novel," Valiante answered with a villain's leer.

"I like that plenty, Valiante. Makes good sense to me. Now let's go to bed," urged Ginger, pulling Vita out of her chair.

"And prove that all's well that ends in bed," proclaimed Valiante to Zoe. *She* would have the last word this time.

A Matter Of Taste

It is a really quiet morning until Tessa's scream cuts through the stillness like a seagull's screech, "Oh my god, oh my god, oh my fucking god," her pitch rising with every phrase.

I set *The New York Times* aside, down another swallow of tea and walk to the stairs.

"What's going on, Tessa," I call up, hoping I can stay downstairs and get back to my paper ASAP. Fat chance, if she's calling on a deity she has no belief in.

We live in an 1895 Victorian house on Heron Island off the East End of Long Island, New York, an island off an island off an island. It is usually very private except for noisy shore birds, deer that stare at us with wondering eyes, and other four–leggers: possum, squirrels, raccoons, and a variety of rats and mice. No cars, no loud music, no kids, nothing except Tessa's howls this morning.

When she starts braying "police, police," I take a deep breath and start for the third floor, resigned to my fate.

Three lesbian couples, good friends, rent the house, each couple on one of its three floors. Each of our apartments includes a bedroom, living room, full bathroom with laundry, and a small kitchen on each of the top two floors. Tessa and

Isabel are on the top, Carla and Mika in the middle, Dana and I on the bottom—the main floor—which includes a larger kitchen and dining room, where we can all cook and eat together if we choose.

When I reach the top of the stairs, I see Tessa sitting on a pile of underwear in her laundry area, crying and dramatically muttering "pervert" over and over. I kneel down and put my arms around her.

"What happened, girlfriend, what's the matter?" I get a tissue and wipe her eyes carefully, hoping her contacts are out.

Outside, the gulls seem to echo her earlier cries as they swoop back and forth looking for breakfast. I feel a pang thinking of my tea getting cold downstairs. It is a perfect late June day, a soft morning with sun and a breeze that wafts a subtle floral scent through the windows, thanks to Dana's prolific gardening skills.

Tessa looks at me, eyes red and still brimming over, speaking in shuddering gasps.

"We have to call the police, Ronnie. It was a pervert, a goddamned fucking pervert." The tears spill over again.

For a moment I am scared she has been raped or attacked. "Tessa," I say in my sternest lecturer's voice, "what is it? Has someone hurt you? You have to tell me now, right now, or I can't help."

She stares at me with deer eyes for a long minute, reaches into the pile, and holds up a pair of pale pink underpants.

"Look, Ronnie, see? No crotch. The crotch is cut—crotches are cut out of all of them. Every fucking one!" She holds out handfuls of crotchless panties to illustrate her words.

I stare, holding back a laugh at the ludicrous sight, and hide a smile behind my hands.

"I was going to do a laundry," she continues, "these were all on the floor like this, the hamper open. It has to be some pervert who got into the house, who must know we're dykes. Who knows what he'll do next? We have to call the cops, Ronnie!" The last word ends like a siren in a long wailing eeeee. At this fortuitous moment the other women come back from their morning run. I breathe a sigh of relief. It is conference time.

"Is breakfast ready?" Dana asks with a wide grin that changes to a question mark when she looks at my face. I have brought Tessa down to remove her from the upstairs scene. She has panties in each hand, which she throws on the living room floor and plops down next to them.

They all stare at Tessa as the laughing gull on the porch rail does its thing. The laughter is infectious and we join in until Tessa starts crying again.

"Contessa, sweetheart," Isabel joins her honey on the floor, "what happened, what's going on?"

Without warning, an unexpected loud clap of thunder shakes the house, followed by a flash of lightning that illuminates the sudden dark. Our power has failed. There is not enough light indoors, so we do some candles and sit around the coffee table. As if to match Tessa's tears, torrents of staccato rain come pouring down. *What a morning,* I think.

Dana pours tea for everyone, and I tell about the de-crotched underwear. Carla and Mika say in unison, "We have to call the cops, now." Isabel starts upstairs to retrieve the rest of the violated panties—the evidence.

The house phones are not working so we call the police with Isabel's cell phone. The officer answering the phone of Heron Island's miniscule force wants to know what the problem is. I stammer "someone weird has been in the house."

"So this is a robbery?"

"No."

"So what's the problem? Do you need an ambulance?" He is getting a bit annoyed.

"No, nobody's hurt. We'll show the officer the evidence when he gets here."

"Okay, miss. Someone will be there when someone can get there. The whole island is without power now, so you'll have to be patient."

I thank him.

While waiting, we fold the victims with their missing crotches face up, and discuss what we plan to say.

"Maybe it will be a policewoman," I say hopefully.

"Oh, Veronica," Dana shakes her head, using my full name, "you'll never learn. That would be too good to be true. It'll be some cop who will make a dirty joke out of the whole thing."

Why does she always call me Veronica when she lectures me? But of course she's right. Two hours later, the power returns, and a middle–aged police officer appears, complete with his notebook and a lacquered comb–over, and identifies himself as Albin Pitkowski. Officer Pitkowski looks at the panties with barely hidden distaste and separates them with his nightstick, not deigning to touch such offending items.

"You say there's no sign of anyone breaking in—no windows broken, no door damage or anything like that?"

"Well, Officer Pa-kowski," Mika says, "we don't lock anything unless we're all going to be away, then we just lock the front door."

"It's Pitkowski," the cop corrects, "When did you find these?" He points with his nightstick, first at the evidence and then at us.

Without waiting for an answer, his questions continue rapid fire. "Did any of you hear any noise during the night? Did your dog bark? Anything unusual?"

"We don't have a dog, except there's Figaro, our neighbor's dog. We sometimes take care of when she's away." Mika responds.

"But he wasn't here last night," Carla adds.

"How do you know this happened last night? When was the last time you were in the laundry hamper to get the clothes out?"

Tessa can't remember. All she can do is hold on to Isabel and shake her head. Pitkowski checks us all out. We are sitting as couples, close together, maybe too close. He shuts his book and stands to his full five-foot-five over us. We move even closer together.

"Uh," he clears his throat. "Uh, are you all, you know, uh, are you couples or something?" His face reddens and he opens his book again.

Nobody answers. "Listen," he begins again, "If this is some kind of joke, it ain't funny. Something weird is going on here." He slams his book shut.

"Officer Pit-kow-ski, this is no joke," I say firmly, carefully breaking his name into three syllables. "Obviously, some perverted person gained entry to our home and cut out the crotches of all the underwear in the upstairs laundry hamper. He could be dangerous. Are there any known sex offenders living on the island?"

"No, miss, we don't have any people like that on Heron Island," he proclaims proudly. "Unless you girls are, you know...and someone is mad about that and is trying to...teach you a lesson, or get you to move, or something, you know. We're all normal people living here." He writes something in his book.

"Officer, we are six normal women—three lesbian couples—and we have the right to have this deplorable situation investigated. What do you plan to do about this problem?" My honey, Dana, puts it right on the line.

"Uh, I'll bring this information to the Captain, and let you know."

"Let us know what?" Tessa demands with new courage.

"You know, let you–tell–uh, what we're going to do. Meanwhile, you could lock your doors and windows maybe." He puts his notebook in his back pocket, shifts his gun off his hip, and walks out the door.

I turn to my girlfriends. "Don't we feel safe now, ladies?"

Two days pass and we hear nothing from the police. It's been very quiet in the house. We are working: Dana is at the piano, playing her endless scales; Carla is refining lesson plans for summer-school teaching; Mika is sewing from new patterns; Isabel is writing an article for Ms; and Tessa is constantly checking doors and windows to make sure they are locked. I set up my camera for some outdoor work.

The fans are going constantly, moving the warm, stale air around without achieving much relief. "We've got to open some windows," Dana pleads, "I'm suffocating." She opens the window nearest the piano and smiles triumphantly at me as I come through the front door.

Tessa, with some sixth sense, comes flying down the stairs like a comet. "What are you doing, Dana? You know the windows have to stay closed and locked!" She starts for the offender, which I'm not sure is the window or Dana.

"Don't be crazy, Tessa, I'm right here. I promise I'll close and lock it when I'm finished practicing, so cool it." She starts playing again.

An unusually noisy motorboat goes by outside, disturbing a stately great blue heron fishing patiently in nearby water. The roar of the engine covers most of Tessa's retort, but the words "not" and "crazy" are audible.

I can see this augurs no good. Tempers are getting frazzled, work is not getting done, Tessa is acting weirder and weirder every hour that goes by.

"Okay, my dears," I say in my sweetest, most rational voice. "I'm going to pick up the mail and visit the police station to see what's happening. Do we need anything in the store?"

"Could you stop at the post office first and then come home before you go to the police?" Mika asks. "I'm expecting some new patterns today and I can't continue my work without them," she explains. I smile my agreement.

The little post office is crowded with islanders picking up their mail, this being the big social event of the day when greetings, news, and gossip get exchanged. I have brought our usual big canvas bag to handle the packages and other mail, and am stuffing it while I say my good mornings to everyone. The responses to my pleasantries are rather cool; somewhat stiff, off. Puzzled, I wave and leave with my heavy bag.

I wait until I get home to separate the mail for each of us, first giving Mika her package. *The Heron Islander Times*, our local newspaper drops from the bag, and the front page headline screams at me: "Intruder Enters Island Home, Destroys Women's Underwear."

I am stunned, speechless. My girlfriends, all gathered downstairs for their mail, stare at the page I hold up as if they don't know how to read. Tessa starts to cry.

> A police report filed on Monday gives few details offered by six women, describing themselves as three couples, renting Sappho House on Love Lane.
> One of the women showed Officer Albin Pitkowski several pairs of underpants with the private parts cut out. She said she had found all the underwear, out of the laundry hamper on the floor, in that condition.
> The women were concerned that a "pervert" had gained entry to the house, whose doors and windows were not locked, and carried out this malicious attack.
> The case is being investigated. We will continue to report on this strange crime as it develops.

"Now what do we do?" I ask as I suck the custard filling out of a chocolate-topped doughnut from the box left over from breakfast.

"Let's go kayaking," the ever-practical Mika pipes up.

I surreptitiously take another goodie, which Dana promptly takes out of my hand.

"Get your camera, piggie." She orders, tweaking my nose. "Come on girls, we're going to pack a picnic, no doughnuts allowed."

"I'll start getting the boats ready. Three doubles okay?" Carla heads for the door without any delay.

"You too, crotchless wonder," says Isabel pulling Tessa away from an open window. "You're coming with us. You are off duty."

An hour later, our lunches are packed, the kayaks are loaded, and we're lathered in sunblock and rarin' to go.

Our sextet is almost out the door when the phone rings.

"Don't answer it," I yell.

We've been getting some really nasty calls these past few days, hang-ups, heavy breathing ornamented with some really imaginative language suggesting what the caller would like us to do to him, or what he could treat us to, and scariest of all, threats about what will happen to us "dirty dykes" if we don't get off their island.

Tessa picks up the phone, listens for a minute, and starts to cry.

"Shit," Isabel growls, and grabs it away from Tessa. "Who is this? Oh, Mom, sorry, but Tessa's a little upset. You know about the 'maniac' on the island? How do you know?" She is quiet as she listens, her face reddening to an alarming hue.

"It's in the *The New York Times*?" She plops down on a nearby chair. "I'll call you back, Mom. Don't worry. No, don't come. We're fine." As soon as she hangs up, the phone rings again. We stare at it dumbly and let it ring.

"Now what do we do?" I ask, reaching for the doughnuts.

There are reporters parked in our driveway and all along the road. We have taken the house phones off their hooks and silenced our cell phones. We have pulled the shades down and closed the curtains. I have eaten all the doughnuts.

"There's a police car out front," whispers Tessa, who has been watching through the curtain at the front window. "I think it's the Captain, and Officer What's His Name." She takes a shaky breath. "They're coming up the walk."

Carla opens the door and lets the men in. "Good afternoon, officers. Welcome to the circus."

Mika uncurls her lanky six-foot self from the chair, puts her needlework down, and points her thimbled finger at the Captain. "Can't you get rid of the clowns hanging around outside? We're prisoners in here."

I point my camera at the police and before I can speak, Officer What's-His-Name places a sheaf of colored papers on a table and grabs the camera out of my hands. "No pictures, lady," he commands.

"I was just trying to say that I need to get out and do some work. I am a nature photographer. I don't take photos of cops or men." I take my camera out of his hand and pick up the flyers. "What are these?" I ask as I glance at them. "Where did you get these disgusting things?"

Dana takes them from me and shows them to Isabel. "Yuck," they say in unison. "Nasty and stupid. Look, they spell genitals with a j," Isabel points to a purple page, then realizes Pitkowski has turned the same color.

"Let's sit down and talk this over," the Captain commands in a tight, high-pitched voice.

I toss the flyers into the umbrella stand and lead the way to the living room.

"So what's all this with the reporters?" he waves his hands at the windows. "You girls looking for publicity? You got a plan? Or are you just troublemakers?" He leans back in one of the straight-backed dining room chairs Isabel brought in for them and falls over backwards. His underling rushes to pick him up. We try really hard not to laugh.

Dana, with her long red hair covering most of her face, succeeds in an effort to hide her grin. She puts all of her hundred-and-five pounds in front of the now-upright Captain, and lifts her chin menacingly. "You are supposed to be here to protect us, not to insult and belittle." All the women stop breathing.

"We had nothing to do with the reporters. We are expecting you to find the cutter-up of our–" she pauses dramatically, "underwear."

Carla fills the silence with her most authoritative schoolteacher voice. "Surely you know that the intrusive article in *The Heron Islander Times* got picked up by the A.P. and for lack of anything better to print, it went into *The New York Times*."

"We need protection," Tessa says, her voice strengthened with newfound courage. "What are you going to do about this? Or perhaps we should talk to the reporters and tell them that instead of finding the perpetrator, you are harassing us."

The cops, who have been standing since the chair mishap, look at one another grimly, and walk towards the front door." I will make a statement to the reporters," the Captain turns and says, his voice somewhat squeaky.

"And just what do you plan to say?" I demand, my voice an octave lower than his.

"Uh, I will tell them, uh, that we are investigating the situation, and will, uh, keep them informed." He nods his head in self-agreement.

"And what about those licentious, libidinous flyers I assume are plastered all over Heron Island? What will you do about them?" I snarl.

"Well, we're going to take them all down." He turns to his officer. "See to it, Pitkowski."

"And what about protection for us?" Tessa asks, eyebrows raised, waving her hand across the room in an inclusive arc.

"I'll post Officer Pitkowski here overnight."

Pitkowski pales, his purple face gradually fading to pink. "Yes sir, but—"

"No buts about it," the Captain interrupts and heads for the door, pushing Pitkowski, who seems lost, toward the coat closet.

"And the reporters?" we ask in unison, while Carla opens the front door with a flourish.

"I'll order them off," the Captain says, trying to sound like General MacArthur.

Much to our amazement, the reporters, sensing that there is not much news after the policemen exit, leave us in peace (we hope).

"So let's go kayaking for an hour. The boats are all ready and there is still some daylight," Mika says, ever hopeful.

"And Pitkowski, our mighty protector, won't be here until 8 PM. Let's go, women," I chime in.

As we assemble our stuff, lunch becoming dinner, jackets and bug spray handy, there's a little rap at the back door in the kitchen. Tessa peeks through the curtain and opens the door to Molly, our neighbor, with her brown Standard Poodle, Figaro. "Are they all gone?" she asks, barely audible. "What's happening? I read the article in the *Times*. What a mess."

"Which *Times*?" I ask, not really caring but not knowing what else to say.

"*New York Times*, what else? I don't have time for the local rag—it's just real estate and gossip."

Mika is playing with Figaro. The dog has his ball clenched tightly in his teeth, challenging her to pull it out without losing any fingers. Isabel waves a treat before him, and he drops the ball and leaps for the milk bone.

Carla is getting impatient. "We're just about to go for a kayak before it gets dark. We'll talk later, Molly."

On the water at last, it is sky blue with reflection, and still, with barely a ripple from our paddles. We glide along without speaking, paddling together in perfect union, and blowing kisses to the herons we pass along the way. A great blue, a small green, and perched on a limb, our favorite yellow-crowned night beauty. We are heading for an inlet sheltering a small private beach that seems to be our discovery. The sun is quite low casting a long shadow and a bit of warmth. The clouds are starting to change color as the sun lights them from below. It's just gorgeous. We're peaceful, happy for the first time since the crotch adventure. We pull the kayaks up on the beach, grunting with the effort, and line them up neatly.

"I'm starving," Tessa announces. "Let's eat."

"You must be feeling better, Contessa, if you're hungry," Isabel throws her a sandwich.

Famished, we sit on the sand devouring our dinner. Relief shines on our faces with the light of the lowering sun. When we have consumed every crumb, salad morsel, and cookie bit, we clean up and head for the boats.

"Let's go back before it gets dark," I urge.

Tessa groans. "I wish I never had to go back there."

"C'mon babe, this too shall end. We'll all laugh about it someday."

I take Tessa's hand and lead her to our boat.

Officer Pitkowski is sitting on the front porch steps. He stands when we approach. "You girls going in for the night?" he asks hopefully.

"Nope, we're changing into dry clothes and then visiting our friend next door. We'll be back later," Mika smiles, "we'll check in when we come back."

We barely get into the front hall when Tessa dissolves into tears.

"What's wrong now, Tessa?" Mika asks impatiently, then changes her tone and embraces Tessa. "Sorry. What is it?"

"Don't laugh at me, but all my underwear was in my hamper. I don't have a clean pair, and it's too late and too far to go shopping. And I can't wear panties without their crotches. It's indecent!" She hiccups a sob and then laughs with us at the image it evokes.

Mika purses her lips. "Okay, I'm going to solve this, uh, quandary. I'll cover Tessa's problem with a new red thong, still in its wrapping."

"What in heaven's name are you doing with a thong, woman?" Carla says, puzzled.

Dana butts in, not waiting for Carla's response. "I have a new package of three pairs of white cotton regular conservative panties that cover all the pertinent parts. They're yours, Tessa."

Tessa smiles her gratitude. "Well, that should solve the problem till I can get to a store in Southport. Thanks, darlings."

"But what about that thong? C'mon, tell," Carla teases.

"It was a Christmas present for you. Last Christmas, but I didn't give it to you," Mika answers shyly.

"Why not? Was there something wrong with it?"

"No, it's just that, well, it's, um, well I tried it on, and it was so, well, so sexy...I decided to keep it."

"But you just told Tessa that it was unworn, so is it or isn't it?" Carla giggled.

I decide an intervention is necessary before things get out of hand. "C'mon, let's get dressed and get over to Molly." No luck, Carla is waiting for an answer.

"Oh well, honey, here it is. I went to Victoria's Secret when I was in the city and bought another pair for you. I'm keeping the first pair." Mika blushes from her forehead down her neck. We are all fascinated. " Carla's face is a big question mark.

"Carla, don't be mad. I just thought...well, I thought we could wear them together sometime and fool around, like make believe or something. Just for fun." Mika puts her hands over her face.

"How cool is that, honey!" Carla grins and takes Mika's hands. "What a great idea, fun, oh yes." She puts her arms around Mika and dips her backward into a movie kiss. We all applaud.

Isabel strikes a directorial pose. "I know what—we'll all get thongs, different colors, and do a grand show all together! I'll direct."

"Never mind, this is getting to be too much fun," I scold. "Here's some advice, before you spend your money. I hear tell that thongs are uncomfortable and irritating, so give it up, girls, and go back to your respectable cotton undies. Now let's get going." Laughing happily, we make our way to our apartments to dress.

Molly is just finishing her dinner and piling her dishes in the sink. Dana hugs her, pushes her gently into a chair, and begins to wash the few dishes by hand. Molly smiles gratefully, and we all sit down around her.

"How are you feeling?" Mika asks. Molly, has been dealing with breast cancer for several months, and is tired from radiation and chemo. She's somewhere in her late forties, an art historian on sabbatical from Hamilton College. Worst of all, her sweetheart of twenty-four years died from a heart attack a year ago—the two women had lived on the island for less than two years. Molly and Figaro are each other's comfort and company. We take care of the dog when Molly has to get to her treatments or doctors; one of us always drives her there and back.

"You know, slash, burn, and poison, that's the way we lesbian witches do our magic until we can say 'all better'." Molly smiles bitterly. "How was your kayaking? It must have been beautiful out on the water." We murmur our agreement.

"Now what's this about some nutcase that got into your house and attacked your scanties?" Nobody answers.

"Is this for real? The story in the paper was ridiculous."

"Molly, it's not funny," Tessa interrupts. "Some weirdo got into the house, took the underpants out of my hamper, and cut all the crotches out of them. That's awful, not a joke." She takes her friend's hand and gently squeezes. "I'm scared, Molly, really scared."

My Dana stands and looks out the window. The moon is a bright circle and throws a beam of silver into the kitchen. "It's a lovely night, and good that the moon is full so there's plenty of light."

"That's when all the loonies come out, when the moon is full," Carla says. "We'd better go back. Officer Pitkowski must be getting nervous." We all giggle.

"Who the hell is Officer Pitkowski? This is beginning to sound like a combination of West Side Story and Fiddler on the Roof." As Molly questions, we explain.

"You have police protection? A cop on watch all night? That is the craziest thing I ever heard of." Molly stands and lets Figaro in the kitchen door, where he has been scratching for several minutes. "Good boy, Figaro. He's my protector," Molly says, rubbing his head and giving him a treat. "I'm too tired to walk him at night, so he walks himself. He always comes back home."

A few minutes later, we report in to our faithful Pitkowski, who has fallen asleep on a porch chair. "Any visitors? Vandals? Perverts?" I inquire politely.

"Huh?"

"A policeman's lot is not a happy one, happy one," I sing to him from The Pirates of Penzance. He glowers. I ask if he needs anything—food, water, alcohol, bathroom. He scowls. He does not like this assignment.

"I'll be downstairs inside the house all night, so just lock the back door. You can leave the bedroom windows open," he says, stumbling on the word bedroom, "and leave all the other windows closed." His police work done for the moment, he moves toward the living room.

Bedroom windows open, doors closed, goodnight hugs exchanged at each landing, we hope for sleep.

The phone starts ringing at 6:30 AM and Pitkowski answers. I am halfway down to the kitchen when he hands me the phone. "Some lady asking for Veronica, says she's your fairy godmother."

With a look that would terrify The Bride of Frankenstein, I take the phone. "Who the hell is this?" I ask in my most acid tone.

"Is this Veronica Woods?"

"And who might my fairy godmother be, if I had one?"

"Don't hang up, give me a minute first. I'm Dale Lowd from *The New York Times*. Are you Veronica?"

"I'm Ronnie, and you have one minute, so talk fast," I order.

"I'm writing about homophobia and the politics of being lesbian, and what's happening to you women is significant. Can I come and talk to you? I'm on your side—all of you. I'm in my car on the road near your house. No one else is here except one empty police car at the bottom of your driveway."

I know Lowd's work. She's a good writer, she's a feminist, she's cute. "Okay. But first I have to get rid of Our Hero The Cop asleep in the living room. When you see his car leave, park in the driveway."

I ring the ship's bell and bellow,"breakfast's on! Rise and shine, a guest is on the way. Coffee. Tea. Caffeine!" I ring the bell for another twenty seconds. First out is my ever-hungry Dana, and soon the others follow clamoring for coffee. I hand Pitkowski a container of coffee, with lid, milk and sugar added, and thank him for his vigilance. He mutters something unintelligible and leaves.

"Okay, my dears, Dale Lowd from *The New York Times* will be here in a couple of minutes. You know her strong writing on women's issues, and she's one smart dyke."

"Hot too," Mika adds.

"And just how do you know, my little cupcake?" Carla asks.

Smirks all around. Slurps too. "Any doughnuts," Dana asks looking in the fridge.

"I took a batch from the freezer. They're in the microwave. See if they're ready." I hear a knock at the front door and go to let Dale in.

"I smell coffee?" she holds her hand out for a cup and says "please," beseechingly.

"Doughnuts, too," I answer proudly.

We all pile comfortably onto the private back porch and wait for Dale, who seems entirely comfortable in spite of our blatant curiosity to hear her speak. She takes a recorder from her bag. "Do you women mind if I use this?" We all smile in agreement and Tessa pours more coffee all around. Like the fox guarding the henhouse, I am in charge of the doughnuts.

It's a beautiful morning, the sun barely up, the cool breeze making the leaves of the fruit trees and red maples in the backyard dance sinuously. Wafting from the kitchen radio is the Early Music program. In the background is a recorder quartet playing Telemann. We sit quietly for a few minutes, munching happily, listening to the sweet music. Then we tell our story to Dale.

Two days later, Dale's regular Wednesday column appears on the Op-Ed page in *The New York Times*.

The Heron Island Story

I met the three lesbian couples last Sunday in the kitchen of their aptly named Sappho House. They are Dana, a concert pianist, and her partner Ronnie, a nature photographer; Mika, a fashion designer, and her partner Carla, a high school English teacher; Isabel, a journalist, and her partner Tessa, a graduate student majoring in art. An article in *The Heron Islander Times* reported: "Intruder Enters Island Home and Destroys Women's Underwear." *The New York Times* ran this news in last

Sunday's Long Island section, and intrigued, I came out to the island to interview the women, (as my readers know,) not the first time I've come out. This is what I learned from my new friends: folks at the local post office stopped speaking to them. They received threatening phone calls. Police officers on the case could hardly make eye contact with them, or find time to investigate the case and after one night of protection, they seemed to lose interest. Except for their neighbor next door, no one answers their greetings. Soon the phone calls, letters, emails, and posted flyers flooded the byways, airways, highways. Stuff like: "Lesbians Leave: We don't want you here." "Aren't you ashamed? Does your mother know?" And others that can't be printed here. The Tea Party's words look really sweet compared to this toxic clique's language.

The women immediately shared the messages with the police, who said "These are just pranks. If you're scared, leave the island" was the advice of the police to the women.

We don't know who committed the original underwear caper, but the assault on these six lesbian women is teaching us that our work is not done. The issues—same sex marriage, gays adopting and having children, bullying gay students in schools, families banishing lesbian and gay relatives, neighbors boycotting and threatening gays and lesbians, laws against homosexuality—still need to be addressed.

What can you do? Finance supportive organizations, politicians, clergy, publications, human beings. The Center in Greenwich Village will provide a list.

Come out, come out, wherever you are! Show the world we are every-where: in your shops, your schools, your temples, churches, mosques, hospitals—the world. We are the performers you love, the playwrights, the composers, the writers, the judges, the police, the lawyers, the doctors, the nurses, the military.

We are your sisters, your brothers, your children.

We are everywhere. Come in and say hello.

We are next door at Molly's house enjoying the Indian dinner we brought. She loves the breads, the curry, the spices, and we are encouraging her to eat. Dale is here, and it feels like she has always been part of our group. She is staying with Molly in her spare room (they say) for a few days. Dale is gathering material for a follow-up article on homophobia *The New York Times Magazine* wants.

Dale's article last month has made quite an impact on the island. We are getting responses to our greetings, even smiles. Letters to the editor of both *Times* newspapers have been a mixed bag, but that is expected, we decide. The climate has certainly improved here, and friends tell us there have been panel discussions and meetings about the article. We have been asked to speak or attend at several, and we accepted. Issues around bullying, homophobia, and education have intensified with new energy at the LGBTQ Center

"Young people are really smitten with this," Isabel says, balancing a forkful of rice on it's way to her mouth. "Oops," she laughs as it falls in her lap.

"I think it's terrific—not your rice on the floor, Izzy, but the activism developing around the issues," I turn and high-five Dale. "New groups forming, people joining established ones, petitions on our issues being circulated, and funds are pouring in to help, a dollar at a time." Dale grins and applauds us.

"It's like a return to the good old sixties," Mika adds.

"How's the next article going?" Molly seems enthusiastic, eating more than she has for days. Having Dale around seems stimulating, and her energy level is higher. She is happy, smiling a lot. Dale is good medicine.

"Well, I'm going to go back to the city in a couple of days and talk to some of the organizers at the Center." Dale grins at her host. "I need some more interviews with the women activists for the mag. I've got almost all I need from you gals." She glimpses our crestfallen faces. "But I'll be back. You couldn't keep me away," she says, taking Molly's hand.

We gather the dishes, pack up the leftovers, and load the dishwasher. Tessa and I serve up Indian kulfi and pass the bowls around.

"What's that coming down the stairs, a herd of horses?" Dana asks.

"It's only Figaro," Molly says, reaching for her dessert.

Spoons are busy in all the bowls. For once, we are not talking. Figaro bounds happily into the kitchen.

The dog has a pair of purple panties in his mouth. They are crotchless. He has done a neat job of removing his favorite part.

"Those are mine!" Dale shouts, choking on her ice cream.

"That fucking dog is the pervert!" She throws herself on the floor and embraces Figaro. We join her. Tessa laughs so hard she cries.

"What should we tell the cops?" I ask.

"Absolutely nothing. Let's hope they've forgotten the whole thing," Molly says.

"I think this dog deserves a medal for what he started," and I wrestle the underwear from Figaro, substituting my bowl of ice cream. "Here you are, Figaro, a reward for your political acuity." The dog smiles and begins some serious lapping.

Mara's Piano Lessons

Mara could not imagine that she could love another piano teacher the way she loved her first one, her sweet Bea. After three years of study with her, Bea left to have a baby. Mara was disconsolate. Bea assured she would do fine with the replacement she was suggesting, and she and Mara's mother set the plans in motion. Mara was thirteen, too young to have much say in the matter, but too old, she thought, to be told what she must do. Broken-hearted, the young student submitted.

Flora arrived for the first lesson early, carrying a heavy briefcase and needing to use the bathroom. She had traveled from Queens to Mara's home in Brooklyn. The teacher was a plain and somewhat unkempt woman. Her brown hair was twisted into a bun on her neck. She wore sensible shoes, a brown tweed skirt with a green cotton blouse, and a tan sweater.

Mara's heart sank. Bea was so beautiful and young and gentle. Flora looked plain and serious. What would Mara do? What could she do?

The new piano teacher sat on the chair next to the piano bench and patted it inviting Mara to sit. The girl had been standing next to the piano, stiff as a tree trunk.

"Sit," Flora said softly. Her voice was creamy, nice. "Would you like to play something for me? Bea says you play the Scarlatti sonatas beautifully."

Mara sat and played; she didn't want to let Bea down. Her hands trembled at first, but then the music caught her and she was into it.

"You are gifted and very expressive," Flora said when she had finished. Mara smiled shyly, pleased with the compliment. Maybe this change wouldn't be so bad.

"Let me tell you about myself," Flora continued. "I don't know what Bea has told you, so forgive me if I repeat anything."

Her voice really was like singing a song, not like teaching, Mara thought, and folded her hands in her lap.

"Bea and I both graduated as music majors from Queens College three years ago. Mara, I know you've sung for her husband, Lester—he thinks your voice is very promising. Anyway, I now study piano with a renowned pianist, but my primary instrument is the viola. I've finished my master's degree in Music Education so I can teach at a New York City public high school. I love teaching. It's what I want to do most of all. I'm waiting for an appointment as a string teacher at Weston High School in Manhattan, but I plan to teach piano privately to a few students. I hope you will want to be one of them."

Flora opened her briefcase, took out two books, and placed them on the music stand. "Okay, let's get started and see if we're a fit." She smiled and their eyes met—Flora's were so blue. Mara liked blue eyes best of all colors. *Flora wasn't so plain,* she thought. *And she wasn't really old at all.*

The books did not look easy. One was a collection of technique exercises, the other a theory book. Later, towards the end of the lesson, a book of Schumann pieces came out of the teacher's case. Robert Schumann was Flora's favorite composer. Mara had never before played any of his music. The pieces seemed difficult, challenging, and she liked that.

It was mid–September when they started the lessons; by Halloween, Mara was smitten with Flora. She practiced for hours every day, even Saturdays and Sundays, so she would have a very good lesson every Friday. Flora came to Brooklyn once a week, teaching two other girls in the building. Mara's was her last lesson of the day, so she could always gave her extra time. Sometimes she stayed for dinner with the family— Mara's mother would not let her go back to Queens without something to eat. Student and teacher would walk to the train station together, talking about music for fifteen magical minutes.

When she thought her star student was ready, Flora took her to play for David, her own piano teacher, a concert pianist and composer. Mara prepared a Mozart Fantasia, a Beethoven Rondo, and a really difficult Kabalevsky piece for him. Her hands shook so much that David suggested they play all the major scales together until she felt safe. He kept changing the rhythms as they went which she could follow easily. Mara changed the accents, which David then ornamented as an extra challenge. It was fun, and they laughed their way through the major and relative minor scales; then Mara played her pieces brilliantly.

David was a tiny man, slight, with a large head, and somewhat wild, thick, dark hair. He had the most sonorous speaking voice she had ever heard. Mara was barely able to follow what he was saying, it was so rich in quotes and names and references, all offered in David's cultured and brilliant voice. Beautifully enunciated, the likes of which had never before been encountered by the Brooklyn girl. She was immediately fascinated.

David's response to her playing was serious, he said she had played nicely, with musicality and intelligence. He asked if she would also sing for him. Flora had told him her student had a good voice.

He opened a volume of Schubert *lieder* and said, "Pick one."

Mara had been studying voice every week with Rosea Walter for a year at the 92nd Street Y Music School, and a second weekly lesson at the Henry Street Settlement—she had full scholarships at both schools. She looked through the Schubert volume David had asked her to choose from. She had a modest repertoire, which included some Schubert. She picked Du bist die Ruh and sang with all her heart and soul. When she finished, there was complete silence. She sat and looked down at her hands.

David turned to her with tears in his eyes, took her hands in his and thanked her. The awkward, self-conscious fourteen–year-old-girl, who towered over him, turned to face him and meekly asked if her singing was satisfactory, if it was really okay.

"You have a talent," he said, "a beautiful voice that will grow more beautiful as you get older. I will help you. Flora will help you. I will talk to Madame Walter about you." He smiled a warm, open smile, and held her hands again. Mara could tell he liked her singing more than her piano playing.

Mara began practicing piano and voice four hours daily. No one was allowed in the living room while she worked on her music. One Saturday a month, she took the train to the Upper West Side to play and sing for David before her lesson with Madame Walter. He played the piano accompaniments for the songs and arias she was studying, and she was thrilled to be treated as a professional. He would always tell Mara how important it was for every singer to study piano in order to be a fine musician, and to be able to play the difficult piano accompaniments for the repertoire she learned.

One of Mara's two weekly voice lessons with Madame Walter was on Saturdays, with an accompanist, at Madame's studio. She always had performances to prepare for—on New York City's public radio Station WNYC—as well as vocal concerts at the Y, Carnegie Recital Hall, and the Henry Street Settlement Music School, which invited her back often.

By this time, Mara was passionately in love with Flora. Her sixteen-year-old adolescent hormones boiled whenever she thought about her beloved piano teacher, and she did think about her all through her practicing: what Flora said, when Flora smiled, how to play the phrase, how she listened—always Flora. At times, the girl could barely sit still. Mara was so restless during her playing she was jumping out of her skin. She agonized over what might be wrong with her.

One day, while practicing a Schumann piano piece, Mara was overcome with restlessness. The girl could barely sit on the bench, let alone play. All she could think of was Flora, Flora, Flora.

Without knowing why, Mara got up and went into the large closet in a corner of the living room and quietly closed the door. With Flora's face in mind, she put her hands inside her underwear and began to touch herself. In time for a whole note of music, she had an orgasm. It was thrilling, calming. She felt this as she felt a climax in music. Mara left the closet, sat quietly at the piano and began to play with confidence and care.

Years later, Mara recalled that closet as a lifesaver. *Without it,* she thought, *she could not have become the passionate musician and woman she now knew herself to be.*

After Flora's death, Mara, now a grown woman and a concert soprano of some renown, told David the story of the closet. He roared with delight. "Oh, if Flora ever knew, she would have died." He smiled somewhat ruefully and embraced Mara. "I loved her too, you know," David whispered gently, smiling in agreement with himself, "best not to have ever told her." Did David mean about the closet, Mara wondered, or that he loved Flora? She hugged David and returned his smile. "I never told Flora about the closet," Mara spoke softly, "but I told her I loved her."

The Songs Of Miriam

I The Student

Bianca D'Amico fell in love with the professor of her first music class, on her first day of college, January 12, 1949. She was just 16 years old and this was the beginning of her new life. Early on, she knew the professor was the woman of her dreams. She was tall, not as tall as Bianca who was almost six feet, but tall enough to make eye contact with her without looking up too far. Professor Miriam Garland wore her brown hair coiled around her head and pinned on top. Her hazel eyes were warm and welcoming, and she smiled almost fondly at Bianca who sat in the front row near the windows. The young woman scrutinized her professor carefully, taking in every detail of her clothing: the tweed skirt of brown and gray, the gray shirt and brown cardigan sweater that gave the slim woman a neat and casually tailored look. *But best of all,* thought Bianca, *were her brown tasseled loafers with flat heels.* Bianca would buy exactly the same pair later that day. That might be a problem, though, as she wore size ten AA shoes.

Bianca did not resemble her professor in the slightest—she wore her dark hair in a pixie cut—her large, dark eyes framed by abundant dark eyebrows. Her teeth had been straightened after years of wearing braces, and her shy smile disarmingly sweet. The teenaged girl carried her long, thin body with a giraffe–like stride, which drew attention from the women's basketball coach when she saw Bianca walking across the campus.

By the time the first forty minutes of the class had gone by, as the urgent, percussive rhythmic thrusts of Bela Bartok's Quartet No. 5 filled the room, Bianca had become hopelessly smitten. Although she had been in love with her piano teacher since she was nine years old, this was different. This was real grownup love. Miriam—the professor asked to be called Miriam—talked about music in a way Bianca had never experienced before. Miriam talked about being a composer, a performer, a listener. She talked about Bartok and her relationship to his music on a spiritual and sensual level, about the urgency of his rhythmic repetitiveness, and about his use of folk material. Bianca had rarely heard music described in such complex, detailed ways.

At the end of that first class, Bianca carefully made her way up to the phonograph where Miriam was removing the Bartok recording.

"Thank you, Professor Garland." Bianca still was not sure about calling her Miriam, although she thought of her as Miriam. "I never heard Bartok's music before. It's so wonderful."

Miriam returned the formality, and looked at the tall girl appraisingly. "How did it make you feel, Miss D'Amico?"

"Nervous," Bianca replied, "excited."

"Splendid. That's how it makes me feel also." Miriam closed the equipment closet and locked it.

Miriam knew that Bianca D'Amico—the young, tall girl who took all the music courses she taught, and studied her

songs—had a crush on her. It was really very sweet; the child
had even started to dress like her. She had noticed the new
brown loafers on the second day of classes. Bianca was a joy to
work with. Talented and bright, she was like a sponge
absorbing everything she could take in. Miriam became quite
fond of this student and eventually acted as mentor and guide
through her music studies. She was impressed by the sweet
lyric sound of the young soprano. Yes, Bianca could certainly
sing her songs.

Over the remaining semesters, Bianca took every course
Professor Miriam offered: Sight-singing and Harmony, Theory
and Composition, Orchestration, and spent many hours
meeting with her mentor in her small, plant-laden office. She
had found the same shoes Miriam wore in a shoe store
specializing in large sizes, had begun to walk like she did, and
even dressed like Miriam. Bianca began to speak in the same
soft, measured tones as Miriam, gradually replacing her own
New York accent with a more cultured-sounding voice. She
tried to resemble her teacher in every way she could. But most
importantly, she learned about music in so many new ways—
how to listen to it, how to write it, how to sing it, how to love
it.

Music classes with Miriam were pure joy. Melody,
rhythm, dynamics, and expression came to life through the
music her professor used as examples: the early, pure
straightforward music of Vivaldi and Telemann; the complex,
dissonant compositions of twentieth century composers Alban
Berg, Prokofiev, Shostakovich, Copland, Bernstein, and of
course, her favorite, Bartok. She played recordings of her own

compositions as well—Bianca loved when Miriam played her own music on the classroom grand piano.

"Yes," Miriam assured the class after they'd heard her music, "there are many women composers. I am not the only one."

Bianca was inspired by the music and wondered if she would ever be able to sing Miriam's songs. One day, she waited until the other students left at the end of class. "Professor Miriam, I want to sing your music. I think I could because it would be, I mean might be good–I mean, right for my voice." She tripped over her words, "I mean, I'd like to try and work on them with my voice teacher."

"I would be very pleased if you could do that, Bianca. Come to my office tomorrow at noon, and we'll go through some music and choose some songs that might be good for you."

Bianca worked on a range of vocal music to build her repertoire. Her lyric soprano was growing with some dramatic spinto quality, and she was gaining confidence as a singer.

Bianca learned the delicate beauty and imagery of the French Impressionist composers Debussy, Ravel, and Fauré. She marveled at the poetry they used, and brought songs to her voice teacher so that maybe someday she could sing them for Miriam. She also became intimate with song literature, the *lieder* of Schubert, Wolf, Richard Strauss, Robert Schumann, (she still did not yet know the beautiful music of his wife, Clara), Mahler, (nor did she know the strong music of his wife, Alma). The contemporary and avant-garde songs of the late twentieth century composers, including Miriam, fascinated and challenged her.

As a composer, Miriam Garland was known for her unique twelve-tone compositions. She wrote intellectual music but was always conscious of the plight of the poor, the disadvantaged, and the abused in the texts she chose for songs. She wrote several pieces for full orchestra, but the bulk of her work was chamber music. Her string quartets, piano trios, and woodwind ensembles were greatly respected and admired by other musicians. They were occasionally performed in major concert halls, but like all women composers, she rarely received her share of opportunities in the real world of music. She would frequently state that she was not a woman composer but a composer who happened to be a woman. Years later, the Women in Music Movement honored and championed her.

"I think I'm ready, I might be ready to sing some of your songs I've been working on with my voice teacher, would that be okay?" Bianca was talking too fast, in run–on sentences, amazed at her audacity. In fact, Bianca had been working on the songs almost every day, both her voice teacher and coach/accompanist providing the support the young singer needed to learn the difficult pieces, which she had done in three weeks.

"How about right now? I have 30 minutes before my next class," Miriam pointed at the piano, invitingly. "Do you have the music with you?"

Bianca handed three pieces to her with a shy smile.

"Do you need a warm up?" Miriam asked.

"I'm always warmed up," Bianca replied, blushing at her bold words, and without pause, Miriam began to play the first song. When Bianca had sung all three, Miriam swiveled on her piano stool and applauded loudly.

"That was lovely, Bianca, expressive, intelligent, and with a rich beautiful timbre."

"Thank you, Professor Miriam," Bianca turned to the nearest chair and practically fell onto it. She had performed with all the vocal ability she had, and felt exhilarated and exhausted at the same time.

"I have a good idea," Miriam said, standing to her full height, "I will be offering two classes on contemporary vocal music, and it would help me a lot if you could sing these pieces in each class. Would you?" Bianca was breathless with pleasure. She would sing Miriam Garland for an audience. "Thank you, thank you, she exhaled."

With the mentoring of her teachers—voice, piano, and Miriam—all genres and styles of music became familiar to Bianca. Her voice grew and matured with her, and she became a gifted performer with music her best friend.

II *The Professor*

Miriam Garland was in love. She had finally gotten over her failed second marriage and was now deeply enamored of Foster Ellsworth, a professor in the Political Science Department at the college. He was absolutely brilliant, the most brilliant man she had ever known. He was a dozen years older than Miriam, but that didn't matter. They were a perfect pair, Miriam would say. Even their politics matched—in fact he leaned more left than she. When Miriam discovered that Foster was a scholar of Hebrew, although he had been raised

Episcopalian, she was pleased that they shared this additional connection; Miriam had grown up in an Orthodox Jewish family. He was such a dear man; a small man, but very tall in spirit. He called her Mitzie. No one had ever called her anything but Miriam. She loved being called Mitzie.

It did not take long for Miriam to become seriously involved with Foster, and they were living together by the time Bianca entered her sophomore year. At this time, Foster became one of the professors fired from their CUNY College, after being blacklisted and named a communist by Senator Joseph McCarthy's investigative committee. Miriam became the couple's sole breadwinner. They decided that Foster would continue writing his book on labor politics, hoping to publish under a pseudonym. They divided her small Central Park West apartment so that each had a separate work–space, her piano and music in one section, and his desk facing the park in the other. His books were shelved in the next room with their sofa bed, expandable dining table, and tiny galley kitchen. Nevertheless, they had room to host dinner parties for six and frequently did.

One evening, after everyone had left, Foster, who was washing the dishes, turned to Mitzie, who was drying, and with soap-filled hands enclosed her face, knelt on one knee, and joined his bubbly hands beseechingly in prayer mode.

"Let's get married tomorrow, Mitzie darling. I spoke to Virgil, and he said he would do it."

Miriam dropped the plate in her hands. "Who's Virgil?"

"My friend, Judge Catalano, remember? He and his lover John came for drinks a few months ago."

"What about a license and the blood test, all that stuff?" she stuttered, and bent to pick up the broken pieces of plate, the soap still dripping from her chin, creating a bubbly beard.

"No problem. You just have to sign when Virgil comes tomorrow. John and Bianca will be our witnesses. It's all set: champagne, dinner at the Café des Artistes, a *fait accompli*, 4 PM tomorrow, wear your best."

It was a lovely wedding. The leaves were almost in full autumn color, and the late afternoon light brightened them to a palette that formed a gorgeous backdrop for the couple encircled by Virgil, John, and Bianca, facing the view. Each one held a luscious white spider mum. Miriam and Foster wore what they had been wearing the day they met: she, a colorful Mexican shirt and dirndl skirt; he, a dashiki and Deva drawstring pants. A recording of love songs composed by Miriam played softly in the background. After Foster had stomped on a jelly glass wrapped in a napkin, a Jewish wedding custom, Bianca sang his favorite song, *Ayelet Hashakhar* (Morning Star by Leah Goldberg) from *Songs of Childhood: on Hebrew Texts*, Miriam Garland, composer, translated by Foster Ellsworth. Miriam played piano, Foster turned pages.

> *What do the fawns do in the night?*
> *They close their eyes, their big eyes,*
> *They cross their legs, their light legs,*
> *They fall asleep at night.*
> *Who watches over their dreams, sweet dreams?*
> *The white moon from afar looks into the garden,*

Into the playground,
and says to the owl and the jackel:
Hush and sleep!
What do the fawns dream in the night?
They dream that elephants,
big elephants come and play marbles with them.
And who do you think is winning? The fawns!
Who wakes them in the dawn from their sleep?
Not the elephant, and not the ape,
and not the jackel.
Not the hare and not the rooster,
and not the rabbit.
But like a fawn the morning star wakes them
in the morning from their sleep.

Foster was hunting for a publisher for his nearly completed book. During this time, Miriam composed several song cycles set with the passionate poetry of contemporary women writers. They were with the poetry of Naomi Replansky, Grace Paley, and Jewelle Gomez. Another included a new cycle for Bianca—the love poems of Neruda—and some small instrumental works which were mostly performed by newly founded groups, such as The Congress of Women in Music, and the International Alliance for Women in Music.

Meanwhile, Bianca completed her bachelor and master's degrees with honors, and while working on her doctorate, she was singing wherever and whenever she could, Miriam's compositions were always included in her repertoire. The time passed quickly, the years filled with work successfully completed by the three friends.

When Bianca finished her Ph.D. which had been on "Politics in the Works of the American Composer Miriam Garland," Miriam had accepted a full professorship at another university and no longer had to hide her marriage to Foster.

Miriam and Foster attended Bianca's doctoral recital like proud parents. This important concert was given at Carnegie's Recital Hall to a sold out audience. She sang music she had chosen as much for the poetry as for the music: songs on the borderline of Romantic and Modern music; French songs of Ravel and Fauré with the sensuous poetry of Baudelaire, Verlaine, and Rimbaud; romantic German *lieder* of Richard Strauss, and Gustav Mahler; and two Mozart *arias* from Cosi fan tutte, the opera that makes fun of men, women, and love, with glorious music. She sang works in four languages across an array of genres: impressionistic French, romantic German, dramatic Italian opera, contemporary English. Most dear to her heart was the poignant, somewhat atonal, though melody–filled, contemporary music of the powerful Garland/Neruda songs, as well as several more of Miriam's songs that showed the equal attention the composer paid to both poetry and music.

Music reviewers received promotional publicity for the concert, which did not mean they would attend, but as this was a premiere performance of Miriam Garland's "Love Songs of Neruda," and because Miriam was a respected composer in spite of her gender, an unexpected number of music critics from major newspapers and magazines attended. When Bianca acknowledged Miriam, after singing her songs, the composer stood to the enthusiastic applause of the audience.

"What does it feel like, dear Bianca, to sing songs like Miriam's?" Foster asked after the concert in the green room.

"It feels like being so in love that only my singing voice can express my feelings. It is physical: I am the instrument. And emotional. I must use my whole body, my whole mind, my whole self. And the songs sing."

Foster took her in his arms for a fatherly hug.

Bianca met Miriam and Foster in their apartment the next morning for breakfast and reviews.

"I don't want to hear any of them if they're bad," Bianca almost whispered in her day-after-concert voice.

Foster harrumphed and ruffled a newspaper. "Okay, ladies, listen to this," and he read a short, but complimentary review from the *The New York Herald Tribune*.

"'Bianca D'Amico immediately demonstrated an instinctive understanding for this repertory with scrupulous musicianship.'"

"And listen to this from *The New York Times* review:

'D'Amico's musical sensitivity and emotional honesty was convincing...with a capability of vocal flamboyance...her English enunciation was a model...'"

"Mitzie, sweetheart, this is marvelous." Foster waved the paper like a flag over his head.

"'The young soprano is to be congratulated for including the songs of Miriam Garland, a recognized and award-winning American composer...'"

The women met Foster's reading at first with silence, then burst out with whoops and hugs and ended up pulling Foster from his chair, the three dancing around in a wild circle.

"What else do they say about the music?" Miriam asked when they had collapsed into their seats.

"And the singing?" Bianca sang out in high soprano notes.

"Wait, let me catch my breath," Foster pleaded, then found his place in the paper, adjusted his glasses with a flourish, and read on.

"'Miss Garland's setting of 'Five Love Poems of Neruda' is a masterpiece, her music matching the sensuous gorgeous tone of the poetry, while creating an effective wide-ranging vocal line, which gave Miss D'Amico the opportunity to sing with her lovely soprano voice, achieving power above the staff when necessary.'"

"A triumph, for my Mitzie-composer divina; for Bianca, my daughter-in-love diva suprema." The *bravas* rang out from the joyful trio.

Miriam was not surprised that Bianca had become a first class musician and a fine soprano: she had attended Juilliard, which awarded only certificates, not degrees. At the same time, she had studied for her Bachelor of Arts and Master's in Music at a City University of New York college, majoring in Vocal Performance and Music Education (in case she did not become a world–famous soprano,) she would explain when asked. Bianca had worked with fine vocal teachers and coaches at Juilliard, and had also become an accomplished pianist. All this took place under Miriam's watchful eye and guidance. Those discerning eyes were now brimming with tears. This was why she taught, Miriam knew—this made it all worthwhile.

III The Singer

Bianca D'Amico had a fine career as a recitalist, and as professor of music at her alma mater where she was happily teaching at the same college where she had first studied with Miriam. She, Foster, and Miriam enjoyed the irony of the situation: all three were now teaching at where Foster had been blacklisted and fired, and from where Miriam had resigned a year later in support of Foster. He had completed his book, Labor Pains and Political Birth, under his own name, the school rehiring him and awarding him a full professorship. The book was a veritable tome, receiving fine reviews and small sales.

The three spent many hours in the little apartment laughing and gossiping about faculty and school affairs, as well as Bianca's affairs. Bianca was enjoying her grownup, sensual life, and had brought each new girlfriend to meet Miriam and Foster.

When Ruth, Bianca's current girlfriend, whom she had met at a conference, rang the bell and was invited in by Foster, it turned out that Ruth was really anxious to meet Dr. Garland, whose music she adored. Ruth and Bianca had been strongly attracted to one another when they first met, and now, a few weeks later, Bianca thought it was time Ruth met Foster and Miriam. Ruth was a string player, and a composer. She had played Miriam's string quartets with the Sappho Quartet. Bianca was not Ruth's primary romantic interest when she arrived, but that changed as the evening progressed when love became part of passion.

Bianca had explained to Foster that her "flame," as she called Ruth, warranted the sobriquet. "It has to be a really hot romance to be my 'flame,' and Ruth is it." Miriam blew a kiss to Bianca in approval. She knew what it was to have a flame of her own.

Bianca had called Miriam soon after she and Ruth had returned home from the conference.

"I'm on fire, Miriam, you've got to meet her."

"Bring her for tea, lover girl, and Foster and I will take your temperature," Miriam teased.

"No, this is no 'ember,' this is serious. Dinner, if you please. I'll bring it from Dean & DeLuca, you won't have to do a thing."

When Bianca had first met Ruth—a short, athletic, boyish, redheaded violist and composer of avant-garde electronic music—they were irresistibly drawn to one another, both physically and intellectually. Their affair began the night they met, and the sex was hot and hungry.

The night Bianca brought Ruth to Foster and Miriam was special, fraught with excitement and curiosity about this woman who had captivated their Bianca. Ruth's arms were filled with daffodils, while Bianca was carrying two shopping bags filled to the top. Bianca dropped the bags on the kitchen counter and made the introductions. By the time dinner was halfway finished, Foster proclaimed "TaDa, Bianca's flame is burning as red as your hair, Ruth," and Bianca explained what that meant to Ruth.

They were now a quartet—Miriam and Foster were charmed by Ruth—and Bianca was a happy woman.

"Ruth was no ember—plenty of heat there," Miriam said to Foster when the women had left. The relationship remained at a fever pitch for a year before it cooled down little by little with the passing months.

Bianca had known since childhood that she loved women and was not interested "that way" in boys, and later, men. An only child, her parents long dead, Bianca knew she was safe with Miriam and Foster. They had been supportive and accepting of Bianca's choices, and the young women were always welcomed for tea, although it was possible, if not probable that they would not appear again. Bianca was having fun waiting for Ms. Right to come along. Miriam worried about Bianca not finding Ms. Right amongst her plethora of girlfriends.

"Some of these days," Miriam warned, quoting Sophie Tucker's signature song, "Ms. D'Amico, you're going to get your heart broken, and you'll be singing the blues."

Bianca enjoyed teaching where she had first studied with Miriam and fallen in love with her, a love that had changed from young adoration to a grown woman's respect and devotion, which Miriam and Bianca shared for one another. Bianca was also deeply involved in singing her chosen repertoire of works by women in concerts. Successful performances, in lieu of publishing, were required for receiving tenure by the college. Bianca's professional career was enhanced as well.

In the early 1970s, after singing traditional and contemporary music by male composers, Bianca was inspired by Miriam's songs to research the vocal music of women composers. With the help of musicologists emerging from the newly formed women in music movement, and the surge of feminism helping this course of action, there was serious interest in and support for her work.

Now, as the '70s progressed, Bianca was singing mostly music by women composers, living and dead. She made several recordings of the works of women composers and sang their compositions all over the world. Bianca wanted to have women's music heard by as many people in as many places as possible, and her reputation grew as she became recognized for this expertise.

Music and women, composers and otherwise, were Bianca's passion, but there was one unfilled need that had not been satisfied. For years, Bianca had thought about becoming a mother; she wanted a child to love and care for. She wondered about a variety of ways to achieve this without the participation of a man. When she spoke of this desire to women she dated, it scared them away. Bianca and Ruth had only been together for a year, and Bianca decided it was not a good idea to talk about her maternal desires, that discussion would have to wait. She was still too bewitched by her flame; too enthralled by Ruth to jeopardize losing her by raising the subject.

The couple did not live together, but had their own apartments in Greenwich Village a few blocks from each other. The two women needed separate spaces to practice and satisfy their highly individualistic music needs. Ruth had one of her bedrooms converted into an electronic habitat, complete with a huge Moog synthesizer and other equipment for her compositions. Sometimes the music, or rather the noise, was overpowering.

Bianca's living room was her studio, with a Yamaha concert grand, and many shelves filled with music. Reel-to-reel tape recorders, speakers, and other equipment occupied a large part of the room. The walls were hung with memorabilia of her performances and paintings done by her women artist friends.

When they were not performing, Ruth and Bianca spent weekends and holidays together. They socialized with each other's friends and tried to take short trips, in order to spend time away from their work. They did special things as a couple; attending theater, concerts, opera, and movies was their favorite way to relax.

The two women also tried to spend some much needed time apart. Neither had any desire to live together. How could they? Bianca couldn't stand much of the electronic music Ruth produced, and Ruth would go mad if she had to listen to Bianca's vocal warm-ups.

The passion and urgency of their early days had abated, and now Bianca and Ruth had been in a comfortable relationship for almost two years. They were celebrating Women's International Day with a gathering of lesbians they knew. Two couples had brought their children, which Bianca correctly assumed were from previous straight marriages.

"Do you ever wish you had a child?" Bianca asked Ruth when they were alone. Bianca looked directly into the emerald green eyes of her lover, feeling brave after two martinis.

"I never think about kids," Ruth shrugged. "I don't think I have any maternal instinct... but I like cats."

"I've always wanted a child, a daughter." Bianca started on her third drink. "I have no siblings, or cousins or relatives, maybe that's why I want one, I mean, want to have one."

"Give birth to one—really? How?" Ruth looked at Bianca with curiosity. Ruth was sure this was not what she would ever want. This was new territory—lesbian couples having children were not then part of homosexual culture.

Bianca set down her drink; she had run out of courage and changed the subject. "Have you figured out the new computer yet?"

Bianca still wanted to be a mother. She had thoroughly researched artificial insemination and sperm banks, which seemed successful methods for single women, and for married couples having conception problems. Why wouldn't it work for a lesbian who wanted a child? When she and Ruth had been together for almost three years, she broached the possibility again.

"I'm not sure if this is what I want," was Ruth's careful response. "I know I couldn't live with a child," she added, "but I wouldn't stand in your way."

You're the oldest of five siblings, did you like having them?" Bianca asked. "My mother had them, Bianca, darling, and if I ever have to change another diaper in my life, I'll enter a convent."

Bianca got the message, but still she felt it was now or never. She had discussed this thoroughly with Miriam and Foster, and they had urged her to be honest and say what she needed to say.

"I am going ahead with my plan for insemination. You don't have to be involved. You know it only takes one to tango." Neither of them laughed. Bianca forged ahead.

"I will take complete responsibility for my child in every way," Bianca assured Ruth. "You'll have no financial or emotional involvement—there will be no requirements from you other than what you choose to offer. I'll have a live–in baby nurse and a nursery for my daughter. I just hope you'll like her."

"How do you know it will be a girl?"

"I just know." And that was the end of the conversation.

Bianca persevered, choosing all the right characteristics she hoped for in a donor: creativity, musical ability, health, good looks, intelligence, and whatever other desirable traits she could think of. The process was exhausting and lonely for a single woman, but with the help of the caring nursing staff, in a reasonable amount of time and for an unreasonable amount of money, Bianca had her daughter, named for the composer Clara Schumann.

Ruth broke up with Bianca when Clara was ten months old. She had been uncomfortable and unsure of her role in the new family Bianca had created. Ruth began seeing other women and in a short time fell in love with someone else. The breakup had happened so fast that Bianca could hardly fathom it. She became briefly unraveled by the split, but was so enchanted with her little girl that after a short time she felt almost relieved to be free. Bianca felt she needed no one else, and devoted herself entirely to Clara. Bianca thought herself to be the only single lesbian mother in the world. She knew there must be others, somewhere, but she did not know them or where they were. No matter—she had Clara, Miriam and Foster—that was all the family she needed.

The first time Bianca brought her baby to meet Miriam and to ask her and Foster to be godparents, Miriam lifted the infant from Bianca's arms and sang a lullaby she had composed for Clara. The text was from an interned child's poem written in Terezin, the Czech concentration camp. Translated from the Czech, the poem was about a little yellow butterfly longing to be free. It turns into a yellow star and floats up to the sky. The baby looked up at Miriam and listened to the song as though she understood it. She smiled at her godmother and Bianca joined Miriam as she sang the song again. Clara cooed.

Oh, Miriam, thought Bianca, how I do love you.

"You certainly cannot earn enough performing only the work of women composers and teaching," Miriam said to Bianca. Bianca's teaching job paid a good part of the bills for her and Clara, although the costs of childcare and school loomed large. They were walking through the park on an idyllic day, wheeling Clara in her stroller. The baby sat propped up and shook her rattle, smiling at it, and putting it in her mouth. She had dark hair that fell in little ringlets and large brown eyes, framed by long dark lashes. She looked very much like Bianca. A pretty child, she smiled and made happy sounds.

"There's a simple solution, dear." Miriam said, "You must sing repertoire of all genres and composers. This you have been well trained to do. You can always include contemporary repertoire and your preferred works by women in your programs."

And so Bianca performed as Miriam had advised, in concert halls all over the United States, Canada, Mexico, Asia and Europe, at conferences, and on TV and radio.

At the college, she made her way up the academic ladder, from Assistant to Associate, and eventually to Full Professor, which provided a salary and benefits that her concerts augmented perfectly. Bianca was now a concert singer, a professor, and best of all to her, a mother.

IV The Composer

Bianca consulted with Miriam and Foster in her search to find other poetry written in concentration camps for which Miriam could compose a song cycle. The four texts they found were also by children of Terezin. Foster translated the poems for Bianca so she would know what the texts were about before trying to sing them in Czech, their original language. They were titled in Hebrew at Foster's insistence. One was about a bird in a nest with three eggs with a golden baby in each, another about an angry cat, the third of a morning star and sleeping fawns, and the last about a seesaw.

> **Nad Nãd (SeeSaw)**
> *Up and down and down and up!*
> *What's up high? What's below?*
> *Only me and only you,*
> *Like two weights on a scale.*
> *Now to the ground, now to the sky.*

Foster's knowledge of languages was enormously helpful to Bianca. When the songs were ready musically, he taught her to pronounce whatever the difficult language, and to understand the children's hopes and dreams in their poems. Bianca's new recording, Songs by American Women Composers, included a Native American, an African American, a Jewish American, and others who used texts to address social issues and progressive political themes. Love, grief, illness, and pain were included themes along with racial problems and struggles of minorities. Foster did the translations into English and Hebrew from the Czech, as well as extensive program notes. Miriam was the pianist; a percussionist and a South American wood flute player were additional instrumentalists. It was a unique recording, of which both Miriam and Bianca were extremely proud.

Bianca, like many other musicians, felt that Miriam's best works were her songs and song cycles. Although she composed beautiful pieces using Shakespeare's sonnets and poetry of Herrick, her genius poured out with songs like "Hiroshima," for soprano, violin, cello, and clarinet, words sung in English and Japanese.

> *Who saw the silent butterfly?*
> *Sun the powdered spectrum of its August wings?*
> *Who saw this spirit enter on a scented breeze*
> *to touch the laurel bough,*
> *to touch the laurel bough?*
> *None saw at all.*
> *Eyes that were not glazed with fire*
> *shed sorrow down for tragedy: Hiroshima.*

Bianca loved singing Miriam's Mixco, a song for piano and voice, the poem of Asturias sung in Spanish and English. The colors of the words in both languages gave the singer every opportunity to vocally express the poetry. She could whisper, she could reach for the stars, she could hiss like a snake. What more could a singer wish for?

> *A whisper of heartbeats comes from their hands*
> *that stroke the wind like two oars,*
> *and their feet leave footprints like little soles*
> *in the dust of the road.*
> *The stars that you see in Mixco remain in Mixco,*
> *for the Indians catch them for their baskets*
> *that they fill with chickens.*
> *And the big white flow'rs of the golden izote.*
> *Serenely, serenely live the Indians,*
> *more serenely than we do.*
> *And when they descend from Mixco*
> *all that you hear is the panting*
> *that hisses on their lips like a silken serpent.*

Bianca D'Amico once more recorded "Ayelet Hashakhar," the songs, as part of a splendid new recording: Miriam Garland: A Retrospective of her Music.

One day, Foster actually danced into a rehearsal in Miriam's studio with copies of the recording in one hand, his other hand filled with mail.

"Here we are, my Mitzie, our Clara and her Momma, hot off the press." On the cover was a stunning photo of Miriam in the studio, seated at her piano with books, music, and plants in the background.

"Okay, okay," said Miriam, embarrassed, waving the cover away, "let's just play the damned thing."

"Not yet, my darling." Foster waved an envelope in front of Miriam's face. "Here's something from the National Academy of Arts and Letters. Open, please."

Little Clara clapped her hands, which she had just learned to do, laughing because everyone was excited, and she was, too.

Bianca had to open the letter because Miriam's hands were too shaky. She handed it to her, took off Miriam's music glasses and replaced them with the necessary reading glasses. "I'm too nervous to read it. You, Foster," and Miriam passed it to him.

It was an announcement that Professor Miriam Garland, Ph.D. had been elected to the prestigious National Academy of Arts and Letters, the second woman composer ever to receive this honor. The first, in 1908, was Julia Ward Howe, the composer of "The Battle Hymn of the Republic."

Miriam took Clara from her highchair and bounced her up and down. "Do you hear that, my little strudel? Your Godmama is a big strudel now."

Later that evening, after Clara had been settled in at home with her au pair, Foster, Miriam, and Bianca had dinner at their favorite restaurant, the Café des Artistes, where they always celebrated their triumphs and disasters, no matter which. Bianca and Foster loved the murals of playful naked women and nymphs that adorned the walls. They celebrated being together and loving one another; they celebrated Clara;

they celebrated Miriam's election to the Academy; they celebrated the new recordings of Bianca and Miriam, and that their recordings were actually selling and being played; they celebrated Foster's book; and most of all, they celebrated one another. This time it was all music to their ears—for the composer and the singer—the composer who happened to be a woman and a wife; and the singer, a lesbian and a mother.

V *Foster*

Foster was Miriam's great love; Miriam was Foster's. It was as simple as that. Although retired from teaching they continued their lives' work. Miriam composed less at the piano because her bad back would not allow her to sit for hours. Foster, now in his early nineties, wrote an occasional book review, an article for a journal, a letter to the editor at *The New York Times*, *The Nation*, or *The New Yorker*.

Foster struggled with his deteriorating health, and the energy it took to keep Miriam from knowing how difficult it was. He grew very successful at keeping pain from showing on his face and in his eyes. His greatest joy was when Clara, now a student at Sarah Lawrence College, would visit with him. She would bring him "forbidden" pastries, which they would collude to devour. She was a creative writing major and would bring her latest poetry to read to him. Foster was the only father she had known, and it never occurred to her that he was an old man. The same was true for Miriam. Her Foster was not old. She was his Mitzie, and he was her lover.

One morning, Miriam woke, startled by something she could not recognize. She looked at Foster lying next to her. He seemed to be sleeping and she wondered why he was sleeping so late—he was always up hours before her. She stared and stared at him, and saw that the cover was not moving like it should. Was he breathing? She asked. "Foster, are you breathing?" No answer. "Foster, my love, are you dead? Foster?"

VI *The Women*

Bianca is sitting in the room that has been transformed with all the trappings of a hospital; special bed, trays of medicines and supplies, a couple of chairs for visitors, and one for Joya, the health care aide who leaves the room when there are guests to make tea for the visitors. Joya is a black woman who comes from Jamaica, where she was a licensed registered nurse, a surgeon's assistant at the biggest and best hospital. She watches over Miriam, taking care of her with expertise, and daughterly love. Miriam's bed is where Foster's desk used to be, so she can see Central Park; Joya's bed is a few steps from Miriam's.

Foster had died eight years before Miriam became ill with dementia, and she's mostly bedridden. Bianca visits her several times a week. Some days, especially when Clara is with her, Miriam recognizes them. Today is not one of those days. Bianca has brought poetry of Adrienne Rich for Miriam. She reads the beginning excerpt from "I Dream I'm the Death of Orpheus."

> *I am walking rapidly through striations*
> *of light and dark thrown under an arcade.*
> *I am a woman in the prime of life,*
> *with certain powers*
> *and those powers severely limited*
> *by authorities whose faces I rarely see.*
> *I am a woman in the prime of life...*

Miriam smiles.

Bianca brings different poetry each visit. When Clara comes, she often brings her own poetry to read aloud. It seems that Miriam loves when her strudel girl is there, she doesn't really need to understand the words.

On a day when Clara is there alone, Miriam knows her. Clara reads Audre Lorde's poem, Woman.

> *I dream of a place between your breasts*
> *to build my house like a haven*
> *where I plant crops*
> *in your body*
> *an endless harvest*
> *where the commonest rock*
> *is moonstone and ebony opal*
> *giving milk to all of my hungers*
> *and your night comes down upon me*
> *like a nurturing rain.*

Today, Bianca is reading to her when Miriam interrupts. "Oh look," she says, pointing to the window, "Here comes Foster." Bianca stands to see. "He's coming," says Miriam joyfully. Bianca sits, not sure what is happening. Joya smiles and puts her finger to her lips for silence. Miriam seems lit with an inner light, alive, happy. Bianca feels uneasy, almost frightened, but she continues reading.

Miriam's bed is raised and she is propped up on pillows. She is looking at the ceiling. Bianca stops reading.

"What are you looking at?" Bianca asks.

Miriam smiles her wonderful wide smile, one that rarely comes these days. "It's Foster, he's flying around the room." She waves. "He's always with me except when he goes to the park. It's so lovely. We just talk and talk. He says he is going to take me with him." She settles further back into her pillows and sighs deeply.

Bianca gives up trying to read. Joy offers Miriam some cool weak tea to sip, and Bianca leaves with a promise to come back the next day. "Good," says Miriam. "We might be here." And she giggles behind her hand, and mischievously looks at Bianca. *Miriam has a secret*, Bianca thinks.

Bianca is hoping that Clara will come with her tomorrow. What were those lines of Clara's poetry she read to Miriam the other day? Prophetic words?

> *the day you left I lifted 3/each,*
> *smooth and hard;*
> *iceland, tofu, goat's milk;*
> *cookie, mother's kind.*
> *I need gone.*

When Bianca calls early the next morning, Joy answers. "She's gone, Bianca. I didn't want to wake you too early. Miriam's gone."

"Good for my darling Miriam," Bianca answers. "She's safe. She left with Foster last night."

The poem, "the day you left" is by Mikael Berg

A Match Made In Heaven

Carlos

The first time Constance heard Carlos sing was at his audition at the college where she was head of the Voice Department. He sang Ravel, Debussy, and Fauré so ravishingly that the little hairs on her arms stood up and she felt goose bumps on her scalp. He was a tenor from Panama, a beautiful young man with café au lait skin and shiny black hair that formed a curly cap on his head. He was unanimously accepted into the master's program in vocal performance and given a scholarship from the Brooklyn College Conservatory of Music. Carlos chose to study with one of the two male voice teachers on the faculty, also a tenor, but he took the weekly voice studio class with Constance. At the first session, she cried when he sang Morgen, her favorite Richard Strauss *lieder*. Being moved to tears had never before happened to her in class.

After Carlos had been at the college for a year, Constance began coaching him for his degree recital. He seemed distracted, and when she spoke with his other teachers, she was told he was not doing well. He was not turning in papers and often missed classes.

She did not like the way he looked. He had paled and his eyes looked puffy and tired. After a coaching session, she invited him to dinner at a local restaurant.

"Can you tell me what is wrong, Carlos? Are you ill? I know something isn't right and I'm concerned." Constance felt uncomfortable questioning him, but they had a warm, easy relationship and she hoped he wouldn't be annoyed.

His dark eyes became inky and veiled, and he looked down at his cup of coffee. He turned his hands sideways, palms almost up. "I'm okay, just tired."

Constance had been teaching at the college since 1965—almost twenty-three years. She knew when a student wasn't being honest with her. "Bullshit," she said. "What's going on?" Then, she knew. She was sure she knew.

Students seemed to know everything about the music faculty—who was straight, who was gay, who drank, and who was having an affair with whom. The gossip mill was strong, and usually right. They all seemed to know she was gay. Faith, Constance's lover, had her music frequently performed at the college, as well as in other concert halls, and they were often together in public. Constance knew that Carlos was gay—he often brought his current lover to the studio class, but they had just never really talked about it.

Constance leaned over and took his hands in hers. They were hot, and his palms moist. "Carlos, don't be angry with me. Tell me to shut up if you want to, but I am going to ask this anyway. I'm asking because I care about you very much. You are the only student who makes me cry every damned studio class." They both started to laugh, hers ending with a sigh, his with a cough.

"Carlos, did you get tested? Are you positive?" She sat there, immobilized by her audacity. How could she? Constance thought. Was she crazy? After staring at her for a long, intense moment, Carlos put his head down on the table and cried quietly, shoulders heaving. Constance moved to sit beside him, put her arm across his back, and cried with him.

Carlos had no health insurance; the school did not provide any for part–time graduate students. Constance took him to a specialist in infectious diseases, and Carlos received the best medical care available, which she paid for.

When Carlos did sing his degree recital, it was an extraordinary musical event. He sang arias, zarzuela, French and German art songs, and a group of gorgeous classical Spanish songs, worthy of Victoria de los Angeles, the reigning Spanish soprano. It was the most accomplished student performance ever done at the college, completely professional and thrilling, and they were both happy beyond measure with the concert. Carlos received his degree with honors, as well as several large monetary awards from the Voice Department and the college.

After Carlos graduated, they became even closer friends. Constance often invited him to operas and concerts. He visited her New England home many times, usually with a current lover. They had lunch or dinner, sometimes met for tea or drinks, and now and then went to parties together—Carlos loved parties.

He sang tenor roles successfully with small opera companies. His acting was convincing and further enhanced by his singing. Carlos became a permanent member of a well-known contemporary vocal ensemble that did *avant garde* material, including modern dance, for which he had trained early in his career. Carlos was remarkable. His career grew steadily, and he was being noticed and praised by reviewers. His health was fairly stable, helped by new medications and quality care. He almost earned enough money singing to support himself, but worked nights as a legal proofreader in order to receive hard-to-get health insurance, imperative for his condition. After several years, Carlos had advanced to AIDS, but it was still under control.

Constance retired and moved full-time to her country home, where she lived with Faith. Carlos visited them often, and Constance was usually in New York City twice a month. He had no contact with his family in Panama. An only son, with five younger sisters, he had been abandoned by his parents years before when he had come out to them. Carlos had no idea where his sisters were, nor they, where he was. Constance was the closest person to a mother or sister that he had.

By 2001, Carlos grew sicker. His medications were changed frequently and never seemed to work for any length of time. As new drugs were developed, they were added to his regimen, but his hopes were dashed soon after they were tried. He developed severe diabetes, circulatory problems, skin lesions, and a liver ailment. Within the year, he had stopped working, and he applied for disability payments.

Constance and Faith helped him financially as much as they could. She thought his voice was still lovely, but as he got frailer his singing weakened. He had to leave the ensemble—dancing and singing were impossible. He had been hospitalized several times and was forced to refuse offers of opera roles. He was worried that his illness would become known, and he could no longer work nights. At least on Medicaid and SSI disability, he was able to get free medical care, medicines, and pay the rent for his modest studio apartment.

As Carlos approached his fortieth birthday, he had gotten very thin and joked about his new, gorgeous body. "Made in the USA by AIDS," he'd quip. "I'll be all right. I just have to get the meds right. I just have to be able to keep food down. I just have to get my appetite back. Then I'll get stronger." Carlos tried to reassure Constance, to reassure himself.

Carlos had faithful friends, some former lovers, mostly from the music world. James, his, current lover of two years, was a faithful caregiver and companion. They were deeply in love, regardless of AIDS, and completely devoted to one another. And there was always Constance, his teacher, his aptly named, devoted, loving friend. All were there with him, through those difficult months, following the schedules carefully crafted by James.

Carlos was never alone. Friends and neighbors brought delicacies he might eat despite his lack of appetite, filled the apartment with flowers, and played CDs of his favorite music.

"I'll be fine, you'll see, don't worry." Carlos promised them all, but then spent hours listing the music he wanted played at his memorial celebration, as he named it. Included were favorite recordings he had made, singing his French and German repertoire. "I'm no fool," he mocked, "where there's an audience, I sing."

RuthAnne

Constance met RuthAnne at the Metropolitan opera in the early 1980s. They each came alone and had subscription seats next to one another in the Dress Circle. The two talked as if they had known each other for a long time, easily exchanging personal details about themselves. Constance revealed her lesbian identity, and RuthAnne, with a regretful smile, that she was a straight woman. They trusted one another, and a warm friendship developed quickly. RuthAnne, the older woman, drove down regularly from Vermont, where she lived alone in a stone house near an old cemetery. The house had lovely gardens, thanks to RuthAnne's skills as a gardener. It was set on a hill that overlooked a dairy farm, whose inhabitants provided frequent mooing for company. The cemetery was blissfully quiet.

RuthAnne also had a studio apartment in New York City where she stayed when she came in for the opera, a concert, or to see her city friends and eat fabulous dinners. She was a psychologist, still practicing in Vermont, with three passions in her life: music, travel, and food. She had never married, but was the paramour of a mysterious man," a Boston Brahmin, married of course," she confided to her seatmate and new friend. She and her lover had been together for many years, in spite of his wife and four children. They were best friends, she told Constance, assuring her that she would never do anything to hurt his marriage.

He would fly his own plane up to Vermont, or visit her in the city, as often as possible. They occasionally met in Europe when RuthAnne was traveling, as she did every year, to visit opera houses in England, Italy, France, and Germany, wherever she was in pursuit of an opera performance for which she was passionate. It happened several times through the years that they could meet in a foreign city and enjoy what music and food it offered. He seemed to have an unending supply of money, though not time, but neither ever complained.

"I'm grateful his snobby mother wouldn't let us marry when we were single, years ago," RuthAnne revealed during the intermission at a performance of Der Rosenkavalier. "It seems I just didn't have the right family connections." She smiled mischievously. "This way his wife has his four children, and I have him." She seemed quite smug about the arrangement.

As time went by, the two women grew to be even closer friends. Constance shared her priority opera ticket arrangement with RuthAnne, and together they carefully chose which operas they attended. They had dinner together before each performance, at an equally carefully chosen restaurant, their passion for interesting and excellently prepared food an important part of their friendship. Occasionally, Constance's lover Faith would be with them if the opera was contemporary, or its composer interested her. Faith was in the throes of composing an opera based on "The Yellow Wallpaper," although she bemoaned the fact that works by women composers were rarely, if ever performed, and had no assurance that hers would be. Constance mostly cared about the singing, while RuthAnne just loved all of opera. The friends traveled together to music festivals and performances in Europe and the states. Faith frequently traveled with them, and the three women always attended concerts where Faith's music was being performed, or when Constance was singing, no matter the venue.

Constance and RuthAnne often skied together, wherever the snow was good. RuthAnne, now over seventy-five, was proud of her Senior Skier pass, accepted at any place she and Constance chose to ski. Faith was afraid of heights and never went near the slopes. The three friends also went to the Marlboro Chamber Music Festival in Vermont for a week every summer. Music, food, skiing, and friendship forged the beautiful trio.

RuthAnne developed a passion for early music and began playing the recorder again, Faith providing her with lessons and ensemble playing with trios, quartets, and anything up to orchestras. RuthAnne was delighted with being able to make music on her own, as she had when she was young.

Constance and Faith eventually met Bradley, RuthAnne's mystery man. He had invited the women to a Greenwich Village club for dinner and to hear his favorite pop singer, Susannah McCorkle. They never saw him again, as six months later Bradley was dead from a virulent form of leukemia. His death left RuthAnne heartbroken.

RuthAnne had two Burmese cats, sisters named Pansy and Violet, who were her adorable companions. When Violet had two kittens, RuthAnne kept one named Rosie, and presented the other to Faith and Constance. He was a little male Burmese with a knotted tail, promptly named Cherubino for the adolescent boy in Mozart's Le Nozze di Figaro. Now the three women shared a cat family, as well as their other loves. Without Bradley, RuthAnne needed her friends, music, food, travel, and cats more than ever. She felt very fortunate to have them all.

Carlos and RuthAnne

Carlos and RuthAnne died the same Sunday night. Constance had called his apartment on Monday morning to talk to James and to see how Carlos was. He had just come back from the hospital two days before. The machine picked up. She said, "It's Constance. I want to come today to be with Carlos. I need to see him. Please call me ba–" The phone was picked up before she could finish. It was his James.

"Carlos died late last night. It was very peaceful. He just slipped away."

Constance couldn't breathe. She tried to take a breath, to talk. Nothing came out. Finally, "Wait, wait, give me a minute. What did you say?"

"I'm sorry, Constance. He died. Carlos died. I was going to call you," James said, but she didn't believe that—he wanted to keep Carlos's death for himself for a little while. She understood.

"I want to help. Let me know what you want me to do." She didn't know what else to say, to ask, to think.

"I'll let you know what the arrangements are." He was weeping and could not speak, he could only sob. He hung up. Constance went out to the front of the house to look at the bay. It was late April. The daffodils were up, some yellow tulips as well, and the weeping cherry was just beginning to bloom.

Faith and Constance had many beautiful trees, to which Faith had given silly names and Carlos had thought were very funny. That day he had laughed and laughed when Faith had hugged "Betty Boop," the flowering plum; his laughter went on until it turned to tears. Later, Constance had found him sitting up against the tree with Cherubino in his lap, and with that memory Constance's tears flowed. Carlos was gone.

An hour later, a phone call brought news of RuthAnne's death. It had happened late Sunday night, the neighbor said—the house had caught fire. The fire department thought it had probably started in the fireplace, maybe a hot ember had jumped out and set fire to the rug or the club chair RuthAnne sat in to be close to the fire. She always forgot to set the screen up. She forgot a lot of things these days. She shouldn't have been living alone.

Constance had spoken to RuthAnne on Saturday to remind her to put the opera on the radio. It was their arrangement that Constance would call her every Saturday afternoon when the Met opera would be on, to remind RuthAnne to press the radio On button when the opera was to start. RuthAnne could not bear to miss the Saturday afternoon broadcast of the opera, no matter which opera was being played. She couldn't remember to turn the radio on without the phone call. This week it was Parsifal, RuthAnne's favorite.

The firemen found RuthAnne's body near what was left of the front door, Rosie dead in her arms. They both were severely burned. Violet and Pansy had probably died upstairs in Ruth Anne's bed. There was nothing left. Everything had burned.

Somewhere, there was a tenor with a gorgeous voice singing *Una furtiva lagrima*, one of the most beautiful tenor arias ever written. RuthAnne was drawn to the sound. She floated towards it, amazed that there was opera in this awesome entity. She had expected choral music, sung only by angels. The sound was getting closer. *What a bella voce*, she thought. Do you say that for a male voice? Oh well, never mind, those things didn't matter anymore. One of the advantages of being dead, she supposed. She reached the singer just as the aria was ending.

Perched on a cloud was a handsome, light brown-skinned man with curly black hair and luminous dark eyes, smiling at her, his teeth gleaming. She clapped her hands and he bowed.

"That was fantastic," she bubbled. "I loved it."

"Would you like to hear something else?" he asked.

"I adore *Che gelida manina*, you know, from Boheme," she gushed.

"Sure," he grinned, "I know them all. And you know what's fabulous, I'm always in good voice. In heavenly voice, as a matter of fact," and they both giggled happily.

After he sang the aria, she said, "I'm RuthAnne, from Vermont, and these beauties are Pansy, Rosie, and Violet. We all love opera."

"I'm Carlos, from New York, but born in Panama. I'm a tenor and I think I know you."

RuthAnne stopped and thought for a moment. "Oh my heavens you do, you do know Constance. She is, she was a professor of voice. She talked about her student Carlos all the time." Although Carlos and RuthAnne had never met, they felt as though they were old friends. He hugged her and smiled a big smile. What beautiful white teeth, Constance admired silently and thought I guess we still can brush our teeth here. Carlos picked up Pansy, then took RuthAnne's hand and shook it gently, saying "How do you do?" and bowed.

"Constance is my teacher, my beloved friend. Do I know Constance? I'm her Carlos. And you're RuthAnne, her opera friend, the psychologist. We were supposed to meet a hundred times." He picked up Violet and Rosie and hugged them all to his chest, and began to sing *Celeste Aida*.

When the last note ended, she handed him the red rose that had appeared in her hand. He bowed again more deeply and acknowledged the vast applause, which seemed to come from all around them. RuthAnne, who had never sung a note in her life—at least not in front of anyone—began to sing the soprano part from the first act love duet in *Madama Butterfly*. Carlos joined her, wearing the uniform of Lieutenant Pinkerton, and their voices rang throughout heaven.

Finale

Down below on solid ground, Constance and Faith shared a bottle of champagne and toasted RuthAnne and Carlos. "Do you think they could be together someplace making beautiful music? Constance mused.

"That's a lovely thought," answered Faith.

A breeze came up from somewhere, smelling sweetly like a red rose, rustling the branches of the weeping pussy willow.

"Hush, Faith," Constance whispered. "Listen, hear that heavenly singing."

The Story of Rachel

A Novella

Chapter One

When I saw Rachel in a dismal New Jersey State institution, she was wearing a bleached out, flower print cotton housedress buttoned unevenly down the front, and no bra. Her dull brown hair hung limply on sloping shoulders, and her features seemed swollen and loose. She wasn't the pretty 22–year–old woman she had been just a few months before, well groomed with lovely features. She sat on a folding chair in the visitor's room. Dozens of the same chairs were scattered about. The windows were grimy, casting a gray scrim over the light that filtered through them. Whatever they had medicated Rachel with had turned her into a slack–faced zombie. She didn't know me, her cousin Cara, and did not reply when I asked her how she was.

In fact, she never uttered a sound, nor did her face show any expression while I was there. I left soon after arriving. That was 48 years ago.

Rachel married my cousin Rob in 1948, three years after the end of the Second World War. Their escape from the Holocaust left them part of the multitude of survivors who struggled to live normal lives. Rachel had given birth to a baby girl, Leah, seven months after the wedding. The infant was adorable, like a doll, with big round blue eyes framed with darker lashes, a blonde curly halo of hair, and a pink and white complexion that seemed too perfect to be real. Leah was amazingly responsive, smiling when she was smiled at, and cooing when she was spoken to. When she was 12 weeks old, Rachel tried to smother her.

During the first months of her marriage, Rachel was very quiet, speaking only when she was spoken to, and rarely smiling. She looked introspective, and if I had known more, I might have suspected she was listening to voices no one else could hear. Her pregnancy, in the beginning, seemed uneventful, and all I knew was that she seemed apprehensive, but I had no idea why. My Aunt Marya, Rob's mother had been against the marriage and advised her son to take more time to get to know Rachel better. But when she learned that Rachel was expecting a baby, she backed off and helped with the wedding. She was determined to be both mother and father to Rachel, whose parents were dead. My short, round little barrel aunt, in her somewhat bossy way, gave Rob and Rachel a really nice American wedding, as she often told me. Everyone seemed to have had a good time, I thought, except the bride, but that was because, as my aunt explained, Rachel was a little bit pregnant.

As time moved on, Rachel's pregnancy became troublesome. She lost weight instead of gaining. It worried the obstetrician, my aunt told me, when she went with her daughter–in–law for her checkups. Rachel's morning sickness was more like all–day nausea, and she only ate oatmeal and toast. Rob seemed totally unconcerned about his wife's condition; in fact, he seemed much more concerned about his thinning hair than he was about Rachel. He never asked what the doctor said after the visits. He said stupid things like, "This baby better be a boy, because I don't like girls much." I just laughed at him derisively and said I'd report him to the Women's Society of America, if such a group existed.

Rachel, in spite of being pregnant, seemed to shrink, as though she had taken a bite of Alice's mushroom. She'd glance at her husband disdainfully when he made his misogynist statements, and then she would look away quickly before he could notice. Rachel almost seemed afraid of Rob. She would not sit or stand near him, but would always stay far away so they could not touch.

The baby was born three weeks early after a protracted labor that resulted in a C-section delivery. It took almost eight weeks for Rachel to recover from the surgery, and she still walked with leaden feet, and could not, or would not lift Leah. Rob turned the care of his wife and daughter over to his mother, who had moved in with them temporarily. I thought he was being totally awful and told him so.

"How can you be so mean, Rob?" I asked during a visit. "Your mother is doing everything for Rachel and Leah, and you are being a total ingrate. You don't seem to care about Rachel or your baby."

"I didn't want to have a daughter, I told all of you that. I wanted a son," he said coldly.

I shuddered in disbelief at his crassness. What was the matter with Rob, the man I had once looked up to—the fun guy who made me laugh—who introduced me to art museums and foreign movies? Where was my cousin, my friend? I guess I had just been a silly teenager who didn't know anything about men.

"Don't you know, you jackass, that it's the male that determines the gender of the child, not the mother?" I shook my finger in his face. "It's you that made your daughter, and Leah is a wonderful baby. You should be proud and happy." I stormed out of the room.

When Rachel had recovered enough to take care of her baby herself, Aunt Marya moved back to her own apartment in Brooklyn. I visited Rachel often, usually bringing my aunt with me. Rachel was attentive to the baby, but she cared for Leah in a robot-like way, never talking to her or showing her any affection. Rob and his mother didn't seem to notice, but I did, and it confused me. All my aunt said was that the baby was very clean and well–diapered. Rob said nothing. Something was very wrong, but I did not know what it was. Then, when Leah was almost three months old, Rachel tried to smother her baby with a blanket.

"They told me to do it," Rachel kept repeating, "they told me to do it." Rachel was hospitalized, and began undergoing treatment for a schizophrenic break.

Rob, his mother, and I were sitting at his kitchen table. The room was fairly large, and painted yellow, with a canvas wall covering in a cheerful pattern of assorted china teakettles. The windows, which overlooked a courtyard garden, were curtained with yellow percale. It was a pleasant room, homier to sit in than the living room. I was holding three-month-old Leah, giving her a bottle that she was slurping happily.

"What shall I do?" Rob pleaded. I almost felt sorry for him. He was just miserable, and seemed on the verge of tears, probably for himself. The cheerful yellow room was not doing much for him.

"They say the shock treatments will help. It will calm her down and she'll be herself again," he said.

My aunt was once again living with her son and granddaughter, taking care of them both. She showered the baby with affection and tender care, and cooked Rob's favorite dishes, Jewish–style German food from his childhood, dishes not at all to my taste. The food was fatty and heavy, with unfamiliar names, not like the food I'd grown up eating. My mother served fish, vegetables, and salad. Her delicious lamb stew, beef stew, or cabbage rolls were also on the menu now and then. During the war years, meats were rationed, but my mother believed too much meat was not healthy, and would not have served it often in any case. Mom was ahead of her time.

"Rachel is not normal, Cara, I knew it from the beginning, I knew something was wrong, maybe the war." My aunt spoke softly, not wanting to upset Leah. "I warned Rob not to marry her, to wait, but he wouldn't listen to me."

She turned to her son and said, "You should do whatever the doctors say, Robbie dear." Aunt Marya took Leah from me, kissed the baby and held her close.

"I tried to help Rachel," my aunt said. "I could see she was troubled, but I could never get close to her, she never let me into her heart."

"Maybe the treatments will work, Rob," I said, hopefully. "You can't just leave her the way she is. You have to let them try to help her."

I wanted to be an adult, but I was still young, and I really didn't know what I was talking about, which my parents did not hesitate to tell me. I knew Aunt Marya was telling my father about the problems Rob was having, and I hoped my dad could help, but I did not know how. My mother was completely occupied with taking care of my two sisters, who were five and seven years old. I knew better than to try and discuss other problems with her. She had her hands very full.

I was a 16–year–old college student majoring in violin performance at the Curtis Institute of Music, studying with a renowned violinist, and also pursuing an undergraduate degree in Music at Temple University in Philadelphia. My best friend, Rosa, was a violist who also studied with my teacher. She and I shared a small dorm room and practiced at Curtis. I told her about Rachel and Rob, but although she was a little older than I, we both were absolutely ignorant about mental illness, and most worldly things as well.

I had been a little jealous when Rob and Rachel had married. I'd had a secret crush on him when I was 13 years old, but knew that a relationship with a first cousin was a no–no. He was seven years older than I, but treated me like an equal. In spite of my adolescent romantic feelings for him, something about Rob put me on my guard. He came too close, wanted to know private, personal things. He never touched me, but still, although I cared for him, he made me nervous. I was relieved when those feelings for him evaporated completely, and were replaced by a devotion to my violin teacher, and my special feelings for Rosa, who was a far better choice for me to love. I was horrified and sad about what was happening to Rob and Rachel. I wanted to say and do the right thing. I wanted a miracle to happen. I wanted everything to be all right.

After the shock treatments, Rachel came home. She was even quieter and more distant than before. Aunt Marya continued to stay with them. "To keep an eye," she said. After several weeks, they tried leaving Rachel alone with Leah, who was now 8 months old, and had become the apple of her father's eye. Leah was irresistible, her father had become totally devoted to his little girl, and we all found it impossible not to adore her. She had the most delicious giggle and was playful, clapping hands and playing peek–a–boo, and waving bye–bye even if no one was going anywhere. It was hard to leave her unsupervised with her mother. The doctors had said that if Rachel took her medicines, it would be fine, but Aunt Marya and I both worried.

One night, when Rob came home from his jewelry design studio, he found Rachel and an empty crib. His mother had gone out with a friend.

"Where's the baby? Where's Leah?" he screamed. Rachel just stared at him, unresponsive and frozen. He searched their first floor apartment frantically without success, and looked up and down the hallways of the small four-story building they lived in. When he thought he heard crying from the basement, he ran down the stairs and found the sobbing baby behind a garbage pail. She had three layers of mismatched clothing on, and three diapers which were completely filled and soaked. Rachel had put clean ones over the dirty ones, instead of changing them. He had no idea how long she had been there, but the baby did not seem physically harmed. When he went upstairs, he did not allow Rachel near Leah.

After he gave Leah a quick bath, and put a dry diaper and clean pajamas on her, he gave his daughter a warmed bottle of formula. She drank it eagerly. After two minutes in her crib, she was fast asleep. While not taking his eyes off Rachel, Rob phoned the emergency number of her psychiatrist who arranged for an ambulance to pick Rachel up and return his patient to the psychiatric hospital.

Rob followed the advice of several specialists and agreed to a frontal lobotomy for his wife. The doctors claimed the surgery was not dangerous or painful. They urged him to allow the operation, but did not tell him that a vital part of the brain would be removed and would leave the patient with a vacant mind and no affect or personality. They assured him it would make her peaceful and quiescent, and do her no harm. It was the latest treatment for schizophrenia and was being used more and more, they told him. Perhaps he was convinced by the information that there would be no payment necessary, as Rachel was part of a trial.

I tried to convince Rob to consult with other doctors before the surgery. Aunt Marya drank endless cups of tea, and just sat and listened. "This is a public hospital, Rob, and it's part of a trial, an experiment. Maybe a specialist, an expert in Rachel's illness, would have a different opinion." I tried to reason with him. He was determined to go ahead, and it seemed we could not stop him from agreeing to the procedure.

"Who should I listen to, a musician or doctors in big hospitals like New Jersey State and Bellevue? When I want advice, I'll ask for it," he said and stormed away, slamming the door.

The surgery left Rachel completely uncommunicative and blank. The violence was gone, but she was lost. She never came home from the institution. She never saw her baby again.

Rob took a larger apartment for his mother, himself, and little Leah. He hired a woman to come in five days a week to help his mother. They were a family, my family also. I visited the hospital whenever I could, often bringing Rachel the shoes, underwear, and dresses my aunt gave me for her, but many of the things disappeared, never to be found. The hospital laundry was a maw that swallowed them up, like a clothing-eating monster.

Time moved heavily, yet quickly, as seasons passed and Leah grew. Rob never visited his wife. He seemed totally disinterested in her welfare. He started going out with other women, and eventually divorced Rachel in Juarez, Mexico, which offered easy, inexpensive divorces that were not as difficult to obtain as American divorces. Many lawyers specialized in divorces with set, formulaic processes whereby men and women could sue for divorce using the legal code that was accepted in Mexico. A quick flight to Texas, then a connecting flight that brought only one of each couple, (only husband or wife was needed) to Juarez. The applicants for divorce would go for a morning of sightseeing with their lawyer's clerk, then on to visit a shabby courtroom where they swore to the truth of the divorce papers. These were usually suits for incompatibility, and the divorces were always granted. There were mostly women on these flights, and they always had champagne together in the airport bar before they left Dallas for their home cities, pledging eternal friendships, exchanging heartbreaking farewells, and then never seeing each other again.

I talked to my cousin Rob about seeing Rachel, helping with her care by providing small things like decent soap, shampoo, and deodorant, different from the cheap, strong toiletries provided by the institution, which irritated Rachel's allergic skin. His mother urged him to pay for more attractive clothing for Leah's mother, sure that they would improve her condition. He was quite annoyed with us and said we should bring Rachel those things if we cared about her so much, and I did so in my monthly visits.

"Rachel is the mother of your child, Rob, doesn't that mean anything to you?"

"I didn't escape from Hitler with my family to take care of a crazy woman. That's what we have state mental hospitals for. All they want is for me to give money for her care," he slammed his fist on the table and said with clenched teeth, "and they won't get a penny from me. We're divorced and I don't have to."

I wondered what had become of the cousin I had been so crazy about years ago, whose child I loved as if she were my own.

I thought about how 12–year–old Rachel had escaped the Nazis through the help of Kindertransport, of how she had to leave her parents in Germany and go with her 14 year-old cousin Barbara, and other Jewish children, to a stranger's home in England. She and Barbara had remained in England throughout the war, without ever again hearing from their parents. How Rachel's mother and father must have wept, holding onto her, their beloved child, as long as possible, until she was taken from their arms and put on the train to go wherever she and her cousin would be placed. Not until the war was over, only then did she learn that her family had all been killed in Auschwitz.

The Hebrew Immigrant Aid Society, HIAS, was a Jewish refugee organization that placed children with relatives in America. HIAS arranged for Rachel and Barbara both to be taken in by a relative who lived in Brooklyn, New York.

Rob, with his parents and siblings, had been rescued from Hitler through the Herculean efforts of my father, who had arranged for his sister Marya and her family to come to America from Germany. I remembered my father bringing me, and my mother, to the pier where the three-stacked Queen Mary arrived on July 4, 1938. My mom wore a blue linen suit with a white blouse and red scarf in honor of the Fourth. My aunt enveloped us in her ample arms, and although she did not speak a word of English, she communicated her love and gratitude clearly. She, her children and husband, had just barely escaped being sent to a concentration camp and certain death. My parents had provided them with a good home, and the children with good educations. My dad was able to save at least part of his family from the ultimate horror of that horrendous war. His two other sisters and their families in Poland were imprisoned in the camps, and did not survive.

Unfortunately, both my parents had recently died from cancer, within three years of each other, and my diminished immediate family consisted only of my two younger sisters.

Chapter Two

Rob and Rachel met at a Holocaust survivor's group, the same one where her cousin Barbara had met her husband. It was a pleasant place on Ocean Parkway in Brooklyn, where rescued young women and men who'd escaped concentration camps, and others who had survived the camps, met Saturday nights to exchange stories, have drinks, and dance to recorded music. Sometimes singers performed music from the home countries of the members. At other times there were lectures, films, and other presentations, but mostly, these were young people who wanted to meet other young people from similar backgrounds, anxious for love and the possibility of a serious relationship. Rachel was there because she was lonely, although she didn't want to go to the Club alone. Barbara rode with her on the bus and waited until she went in.

Rob was there because he wanted a wife. On her first night at the Survivor's Social Group, Rob spotted Rachel and began a one-way conversation. He was a slight, almost handsome, attractive man, who spoke German, Yiddish, and English well, which made Rachel feel comfortable and safe. And, as she told her cousin later, he was polite to her, like her father was to women.

Rachel was a pretty young woman, very shy, and completely inexperienced with men. She was flattered by Rob's attention, and they saw each other almost every night. The relationship quickly moved to romance, and then, in a short time, to intimacy, Rachel confessed to me in tears one evening when we were alone.

"He made me do it, he said it was what all people did when they were in love." It seemed to me that was practically rape, even though Rob had rushed her into an engagement. When Rachel's unplanned pregnancy forced them into quick marriage, Rob told me that he had deliberately chosen not to use protection to achieve that end.

"It is imperative that Jews marry and have children as quickly as possible," he lectured me, "in order to counteract the debacle of the Holocaust, when so many of them have been murdered." I wondered why pregnancy had to precede marriage.

Between 1955 and 1960, Rob remarried twice, each failure lasting less than two years. I barely got to know the women, but I had a sense something was strangely amiss. I'd get a hint now and then that sex was the reason, that it was more than just not satisfactory, it was sick. But the women would not say anything definite, at least not to me. What really mystified me was my cousin's ability to attract women. He had been a fairly good-looking young man, but he was not aging well. He sported a comb-over that did not cover his baldness successfully. He was slender, but had very poor posture, so that he appeared to be looking for something on the ground. Mostly, I was amazed and somewhat disgusted by the garish socks Rob always wore with his conservative black-laced oxford shoes. The socks were brightly colored, with geometric designs, and had gold or silver thread woven through them, making his feet glitter. I thought it a ridiculously vulgar and silly way for a grown man to dress. His wives told me they found him "cute," but his cuteness seemed to wear off rapidly.

Between marriages, Rob's mother lived with him and her granddaughter, to whom she was completely devoted. Leah was very attached to her Grandma Marya, whom she depended on for constancy and maternal love. She never formed an attachment to any of her father's wives. Still a young girl, Leah was honest and not afraid to tell me how she felt. She would say, "You are my fairy godmother and I can tell you anything." I would wave my magic wand and say, "Of course, your majesty."

"I just want to live with my Grandma and Dad, and not with those women he brings home. They just yell and scream a lot and it scares me." I responded with a big hug. It was all I could think of to do. There were no words of comfort.

I was at the beginning of my concert career, playing in a string quartet with Rosa and two other women from the Curtis Conservatory of Music. We were starting to get some good reviews in local papers, and our agent encouraged us to take every offer she could get for us. During a rare break after a Canadian tour, I went to see Leah, her father, and my aunt. The subject of Rob's marriages came up when I asked about his most recent one. My aunt smiled her encouragement at my questioning. Leah did not wait to hear his answer, but excused herself to do homework.

"I'm trying to find the right mother for my little girl," Rob said, which is what his answer was each time he was asked about his wives, "but it's not my fault, they always make trouble." His wives always left him, he would tell us, they were the reason the marriages failed. But the small contact I had with his wives, their hints about Rob's offensive sexual demands and behavior convinced me that something was seriously wrong with his predilections in lovemaking. Even in his reading material, which he would leave lying around, revealed something was weird. Books and magazines with sadistic themes, such as whipping and bondage, were his preferred reading fare. Torture seemed his favorite topic, I could see from the top pages of junk that he read. I could not go farther than the covers. What was wrong with him? How could he leave that stuff around for his mother and daughter to see?

When I asked Marya if she ever saw his reading material, she answered, "I just throw that garbage away so Leah won't see it." I worried, but did nothing, said nothing.

"I found out she had epilepsy," he explained angrily, after his second divorce. "She would have fits. She wouldn't sleep in the same bed with me."

"Don't talk like that, Robbie," my aunt admonished. "It's not right to say those things. She was a nice girl," she said, trying to calm him.

"She wasn't right for Leah," was the excuse for breaking up with his third wife. "She never read to her, or took her places, or bought her things," Rob complained. "And she didn't smell nice." He grimaced with disgust. I thought of his socks.

Rob had become an expert in the quickie Mexican divorce, and knew how to avoid paying alimony. His wives were glad to be rid of him and out of the marriages, and they did not complain, take legal action, or ask for anything.

When Leah was eight, Rob took her and his mother to live in Arizona. He had built an impressive reputation in the jewelry business with his own designed and handmade pieces. The Phoenix area, with its wealthy retired population, was an ideal setting for him to establish a beautiful studio and showroom.

The string quartet I played with was doing well, and I had a successful career with my musical partners. Rosa was also my true-life partner, and we made music, as well as our personal lives, together. I visited Leah as often as I could during the next two years. She seemed happy to be with her father and grandmother, and still had no curiosity about her mother, the mystery person who was never mentioned. I spoke with Leah every week, and I felt hopeful that this good life would continue for her and my aunt.

But my hopes were dashed. When Leah was ten, Rob married for the fourth time. His latest wife was mean and vicious, according to my aunt, who was getting older and less patient with the upheaval in her son's life.

"If I want all this drama," she told him, "I can go to the opera." Aunt Marya left her son's home and moved nearby to a small, tidy house of her own, after Rob promised Leah could stay with her Grandma as much as she wanted. Leah was with her as often as possible, and finally moved into her grandmother's home permanently.

Leah was a quiet and very private girl, with few close friends, except for her cats, to whom she was devoted. The older she got, the more beautiful she became, with expressive blue eyes and long blonde hair that she wore in a braid that shimmered down her back. Leah was as delicate and elegant looking as a noblewoman from the fifteenth century. Her features and posture were like those of a young woman in a Botticelli painting, with a sweet profile, long neck, and modest bosom.

An artistic and creative child, Leah spent hours every day crafting art. She made watercolors, sculptures, and jewelry for her grandmother, Rosa and me. These beautifully made gifts decorated our homes and selves. Leah loved to go to her father's studio and watch him create jewelry. He would let her fashion arrangements of gemstones into necklaces and bracelets, which she particularly loved doing. Then he would use some of her designs to make actual pieces, which she found extremely satisfying. He created a shelf in his studio called, "Leah's Bijoux," which usually attracted his clients' attention, and occasional purchases. His daughter put her earnings in a savings account her grandmother helped her open. I thought it did wonders for her self-esteem.

Living with her grandmother and finding ways to be alone with her father saved her from being with his current wife, who was truly a shrike. I was sure this marriage would not last much longer, and I was right. When I next saw Rob, he would not discuss the subject of this fierce woman who evidently did not react well to his attentions, or so I gleaned from the scratches on his face. His socks still glittered, but his eyes did not. They seemed lifeless and defeated.

Chapter Three

I only saw Rachel a few times during these years. She was in state institutions in New York and New Jersey, uncommunicative and not interested in what I had brought her or what I had to say. I visited her less and less and eventually stopped. Then, group homes replaced the large institutions, and patients were moved frequently for no apparent reason. I finally managed to find the group home Rachel was in and it was absolutely ghastly. It was overcrowded, with too many patients in each small room. It smelled awful, the kitchen was not clean, and the people in charge were dreadful. I hoped I would not be going back there again, if I could help it. It had been easier to follow Rachel's moves from hospital to hospital, but the record–keeping in the group homes was slovenly and inaccurate, and if a move was interstate, the patient would often be difficult to locate. The era of computers was not yet established, and social workers were overwhelmed by huge caseloads and paperwork.

I asked Rob if he knew where Rachel was. He said he didn't know and didn't care. My career was growing and the hours of practice and rehearsal were overwhelming, so I had a good rationale for not continuing any search for her. I think Rob just wanted to make sure he wouldn't be financially responsible for Rachel in any way. I occasionally called the place where I'd found her to ask her current location, and was usually told someone would get back to me. They almost never did, or if I heard from someone, the information turned out to be incorrect or outdated. The rules and regulations for how long a client could stay in each group home were wearisome and ridiculous; the State was responsible for patients. Social Security and Medicaid were liable as well. And families were relieved of financial obligations. I gave up, but couldn't give up feeling guilty.

When Leah, soon approaching her teens, finally asked her father about her mother, Rob told her that her mother had died when she was a baby. When she asked why, her father said her mother had been very ill and died of pneumonia. She had no reason to disbelieve him, and I did not have the courage to tell her the truth. How could I tell this child that Rachel was mentally ill, and that we had—that I had—abandoned her mother? It was easier to let the lie tell the story, to keep Rachel dead. But it got harder to keep up the lie as Leah grew up. She wanted details.

"Cara, I want to ask you something." I knew it would be a question about her mother.

"Did you know my mother?" I told her the truth. I told her Rachel was sweet and beautiful. Each time there were more questions.

"Did you see her before she died?" I told her the truth, partly. I said I did.

"What was she really like?" I described the wedding and told her how happy Rachel had been. Every word was an exaggeration or a lie.

"Do you have pictures of my mother?"

"I think your Grandma has the wedding pictures. Ask her."

I hoped that was the last question, but no, there were more. This was hard.

"What sickness did she die from?" she asked slyly, checking up on her father. This was a new Leah, a teenager. I could feel her distrust. I was defeated.

"Ask your father, Leah," I said, playing it safe. "I don't really remember." The truth was, by that time, I wasn't sure if Rachel was alive or dead.

Chapter Four

Rosa and I were living in Manhattan on the Upper West Side, surrounded by what seemed like every string player in the world. We had been together since our years at Curtis, and had grown up together from teenagers into women. She was a fine violist, and I was, as my honey said, "a pretty hot fiddler."

We often played concerts as a duo, in addition to being part of our chamber string quartet which performed all over the world. In summers we taught and performed at Marlboro, and in Santa Fe, at their Chamber Music Festivals. Music filled our lives—when we weren't performing, we were practicing—and when we didn't dare to practice any later, due to the neighbors pounding, we were in bed, making love, and, after all these years of practice, we were pretty good at pleasing each other.

We were really happy with our own lives, when Rob and 16 year–old Leah moved back to New York and were living in Brooklyn. Her Grandma Marya had chosen to live in a retirement home in Sun City, Arizona, where she had many good friends. Now that Leah was 16, she did not need her grandmother to take care of her. At the age of 75, Aunt Marya was finally free to lead her own life.

Rosa and Leah were great friends, and together they fixed up our guest room so that Leah could stay with us when she visited, which she did often when we were in town. Leah was in a wonderful high school that specialized in art and music, and she was happily designing and making her jewelry.

The reason Rob had returned to New York, much to our amazement and incredulity, was to yes!yes!marry again! This time to Willa, a woman he had met through a dating group, and someone Leah liked a lot. It was his fifth marriage, and–yes–it soon ended, much to Leah's, Rosa's, and my disappointment. I also liked Willa and wanted to warn her in some way not to marry Rob, but it happened before I could say anything. She was also a jewelry designer and admired Rob's work, which seemed to be why she married him. She was very fond of Leah, and Rosa and I felt that was the other reason.

"I was lonely," Willa confessed to me soon after she had left him. "New York can be a really solitary place for a woman who is single." I was filled with warmth as I thought of the long love affair with my Rosa, who I lived and worked with, and with whom my life was filled.

"You know, Cara," Willa confessed, "I'm well into my forties, too late for children. I wanted a husband, but I guess Rob was the wrong one." I wanted to tell her how lucky she was to be out of the relationship, but she interrupted me before I could speak.

"I have to tell you this, just so you don't think I'm a bad woman," she went on. "He's just too weird, Cara, I mean really weird. I'm talking about sex, he's just not normal, he's into S & M and stuff like that. I just couldn't take it. He scared

me to death. I had to get away from him. I can't look at him."
She picked up her dinner napkin and twisted it into a garrote.
Once again, I was overcome with guilt. I should have told her
what I knew about Rob, I should have.

Rob, as usual, had to tell me his details of this latest failed
marriage. "Violent," he told me, "the woman was absolutely
violent." I was repelled—he was telling me about Willa, his
most recent wife—a kind and gentle woman whom I liked so
much, as we all did, who had left in terror of him. Now, he
was telling me the same things he had said about his fourth
wife, and maybe his third. I forget. It seemed he always told
the same story. It was their fault, they were mean, every
woman was mean to him. "She threw things at me." He
shuddered convincingly. "I was really scared of her. Besides,
she hated sex. She said I was a pervert. What a bitch." I
thought sadly of Willa, wife number five, a good woman, and
that awful marriage.

I did not want to hear another word. I was disgusted with
his marital exploits for a very long time, and I barely listened,
but with an unsympathetic ear. Several of his wives had hinted
of his sexual peccadillos, and I now had a better
understanding of his marital disasters. I remembered my
caution with him when I was still a teenager, how I felt uneasy
about letting him get too close in spite of my schoolgirl
yearnings for him. Had his fascination with Nazi
concentration camp tortures, which he read about frequently,
affected him so strongly? His passion for bondage, whips, and
rape, according to his latest wife, was horrifying, and yet he
created gorgeous jewelry and carvings. I had no answers, only
questions.

I could not imagine anyone staying married to my cousin. The women left the marriage quickly, and never asked for any support. I wondered how much his disgusting demands might have driven poor Rachel over the edge. These were secrets I never breathed a word of to anyone, except for my Rosa. I was ashamed of my teenage feelings for Rob and felt sullied by them, but my sweetheart wiped them away with stories of her own inappropriate teenage crushes.

Rosa and I were more than happy that we could see Leah often, and talk. She wanted to confide in us, to ask for our advice, happy to have us for family, for friends. We were completely willing to be there for her, and we loved her without reservation. Leah often said it was like she had two mothers. Leah was the child Rosa and I never had. After all, she had been in my life since she was born.

Leah's grandmother was in regular contact with her, visiting New York frequently. She often stayed with us, saying, "Nothing like a big Manhattan West Side apartment for plenty of room, just like in Europe." She was understandably fed up with Rob. His frequent marriages, and the suspicions she had about his sexual antics, made her very uncomfortable with her own son. But Leah was precious to her, and she kept a sharp watch on her granddaughter's life.

Chapter Five

Leah was having problems in her junior year at high school. Her tumultuous home life had finally taken its toll. She was living with her father full–time after Willa, stepmother number five, had moved out. Rob loved his daughter, although he was not affectionate or demonstrative. Was he afraid to be too close to his 15–year–old daughter? I had no clues, only suspicion and distrust of my cousin. Leah was growing up to be a lovely young woman with fine features, a clear, fair complexion, and the same blue eyes, but darker blonde hair than when she was younger. Her infectious giggle had disappeared. She was too quiet now.

During a visit to New York, my aunt Marya told me she thought Leah was gripped by depression and could not handle her schoolwork.

"She just sits in her room listening to music, and stares out of the window for hours. She hardly eats or sleeps."

"Does she have friends?" I asked. "When she's here with us, she seems just fine."

"Her cats are her friends. The phone doesn't ring like a teenager's should. She doesn't go out except with me, or her father. I'm so worried about her, I think I should move back here to be with her."

I hugged my sweet aunt Marya who had always been special in my life, from the day she got off the Queen Mary and embraced and kissed me as if she'd known me all my life.

"Don't worry," I assured her, "she's not like her mother. Leah will be all right." Was that the truth? I deeply hoped so, but I, too, was worried after my aunt's description of Leah's behavior. "Rosa and I will talk with her when she next visits with us," I promised.

As usual, during her stay with us, Leah asked about her mother. "Where are the pictures of my mother?" she asked. The only one she had ever seen was her parents' wedding photo. "Where is Rachel buried?" This was one of those rare times when Leah referred to her mother by name. Not knowing where her mother was, or if her mother was alive, I had no answer, but deep in my heart, I knew I had not tried hard enough to find Rachel. I was afraid of what I might find, what I would have to do, what would happen to Leah. The image of a lost Rachel, her humanity stolen, her identity destroyed, haunted me.

Leah wanted to find and visit her mother's grave. She questioned her father, her grandmother. She nagged me and begged for help. All I could do was urge Rob to get her to a psychotherapist.

When I advised, "Rob, you could talk to a psychologist, tell about Rachel, her illness, the lobotomy, about Leah, and see what the doctor says,"

Rob answered, "No way," and that was that. But after several weeks and more urging from me, he became concerned about his daughter's depression, and took her to a psychotherapist, Dr. Clare Gelb, whom Rosa had researched and recommended. Dr. Gelb specialized in working with adolescents. At last, I thought, help is on the way.

Rob had two sessions alone with the therapist, followed by several more for Leah. After a meeting with her father and the psychologist, at the next session, Leah was told everything about her mother's mental illness and treatment. She was angry at the deception, and saddened by the revelation, but Leah was determined to trace and find her mother. After much searching, Dr. Gelb, who was devoted to Leah's cause, found Rachel alive and living in a group home in Queens, New York.

Rachel's doctor at The Golden Years Home warned Dr. Gelb that Rachel was mostly unresponsive. "She probably wouldn't know her daughter, even if Leah came to visit, "the doctor further warned.

Rob was very much against Leah going to see her mother, and seemed frightened at the prospect. He was most likely worried they would demand money from him for Rachel's care.

"Dad said I would only upset her if I saw her. That it would be a very painful experience for her and for me. That it would serve no purpose either for me or for my mother. I might even cause her harm," Leah's voice trembled. "I don't know what to do," she said tearfully.

"What does Dr. Gelb think you should do?" I asked.

"Dr. Clare, that's what I call her, says it's up to me to decide," Leah said "But I'm so mixed up." She was crying hard now. "My doctor thinks I could wait a while, that I don't have to see her right away, that I can take my time, and we can talk about it in more sessions."

"When you're ready, if you want me to go with you, I will," I offered.

"It's too scary now," she told me. "I don't think I can see her. I'm not going to see her. What for?" she wailed. "Why did everyone lie to me? She's my mother and they all lied to me. You too, Cara, you and Dad and Grandma, you all lied to me."

All I could do was say how sorry I was.

"I'll work it out with Dr. Clare, and I'll see my mother when I am ready. I'm going to Brooklyn with my Dad. I have exams tomorrow." And she went with Rob without a backward look at me, and for the first time she left without a goodbye kiss.

Chapter Six

Leah finished high school and went to a local community college where she studied jewelry design. Her creations were interesting and lovely, designed and crafted from silver and natural gems. She was sculptural in her approach to jewelry, and many high-end shops were attracted to her work. She felt closer to her father, learning to do what he loved to do, she told me, and wanting to be able to do what he did so well. She graduated in two years, and when her beloved Grandma Marya died soon after, she was devastated, as I was to lose my precious aunt. Her grandmother had been the only real mother Leah had known. After a few miserable weeks, she told her father she planned to see her mother. "I want to see her, Dad, I want to see my mother, no matter what."

All Rob said was, "We'll see, Leah sweetie, let's give it a little more time."

"I don't need your permission, Dad, and you don't have to come with me." Leah stiffened her back with resolve. "Cara and Rosa will go with me. I'll be alright."

Leah was having dinner with us at our apartment, when she said she wanted to see Rachel as soon as possible. "I hope you both will go with me." Rosa was getting ready to leave for a friend's concert in Alice Tully Hall, but she stopped to hug Leah and whisper, "Count me in, baby." Rob had refused to join her when Leah asked him, and she understood. She was not angry with her father; she was just determined to see her mother. I nodded my agreement and sealed it with a kiss.

Rob, who had not been invited for dinner, was coming to pick Leah up and bring her back to his apartment. I was happy that Rosa would not be here when Rob arrived. He was not a favorite of hers. As planned, he came at nine and I offered him a cup of coffee, which he accepted, along with a pastry.

I could see the determination in Leah's face as we sat at the table. She took her father's hand and said, "Dad, listen, please. I know you are not coming with me, you told me you couldn't. It's okay. But I think we know where my mother is and I am going to see her. Rosa and Cara are coming with me. I'm asking you to understand. Will you?"

"It's too late, Leah," her father said. "She's gone. She died a year ago. I didn't want to upset you so I didn't tell you. I wanted you to finish school. I'm sorry, sweetheart." Leah sat stunned, not moving, not saying a word. Rob stood and went to retrieve his coat. When he returned, Leah stood in front of her father, blocking his way.

Is this true, I asked myself, why didn't he tell me? How did he know this? I just did not trust him. Neither did Leah. She shook her head and said, "I don't believe you, Dad. It's not true." She stopped to catch her breath. "I am sick of your lying to me about my mother." Rob said nothing. "You, and you too, Cara, and even Grandma Marya lied and lied to me for years and I'm not allowing it any more. I have a right to know the truth, whatever it is, about my own mother." I felt like I was being swallowed in a sinkhole. But Rob and I could say nothing. Leah was right, and when I could, I said so.

"I'll never lie to you again, Leah, I promise. We'll find out the truth about your mother." When I tried to hug Leah, she shook me away. "We'll do what we have to do, if she's alive, we'll find her. No more lies," I promised. My sweet Leah thanked me, and moved out of her father's way.

We contacted Leah's therapist, and she advised that we visit Rachel's last known residence to get some answers. When Leah and I went to the last group home where her mother had been, we spoke to the director who begrudgingly gave us some information. "Rachel had been hospitalized for pneumonia," he informed us, and sheepishly added, "There is no record of what become of her after that." Leah told him, in a tone that belied her youth, that his lack of information was completely unacceptable, and turning to the door, added that she would be in touch with her lawyer. With a raised hand, Mr. Director got busy, and after much shuffling of papers and with downcast eyes avoiding ours, he told us to which hospital Rachel had been sent.

The hospital people had no real answers either. Leah pressed for more information from the administration office. I was impressed with her mature handling of the situation, and proud when she made it clear we would not leave until we were told where her mother was now. The fire in Leah's eyes was incendiary. She meant business.

The most information she could get was sparse. It seemed Rachel had been taken from the hospital by ambulance to one of the many rehabilitation centers in Queens. The hospital had no record of which one, and unbelievable as it seemed, it was up to the ambulance drivers to find a facility that would accept another patient.

Leah had reached the end of her endurance for this charade. "This is my mother you've lost, my own mother. How can this be? How could this happen? A person cannot just disappear."

The hospital administrator, who joined us when he heard Leah's passionate voice, tried to calm her. "Ms. Baum, it was during the Christmas holiday, there was a major snowstorm, and we were in a crisis situation and unable to reach any local relatives." This sounded so lame I almost laughed. They did not know any more than that, he tried to assure us, but his twitching grimace, meant to be a smile, achieved the opposite effect. The ambulance company they used was out of business, and the hospital personnel could find no record of Rachel Baum anywhere after she had left. It seems the woman had ceased to exist. He was truly sorry, he would try to help, and please be assured, they would stay in touch with Leah.

This was too much to bear. We had reached a stone wall with no doors in or out. Leah and I did not know what else we could do, and left. We decided we would call every facility in Queens to see if we could find Rachel. And if that did not work, we would hire a detective to search for her. We even tried to see if she was buried in Potter's field. But our efforts were all fruitless.

The detective we had hired suggested that she might have used a different name; been sent to another part of New York; that the nursing homes, rehabilitation centers, and senior residences were filled with many such nameless or wrongly named patients. It would be very expensive, very difficult to track Rachel down; and there was no guarantee she could be found. The picture was so negative and seemed so hopeless, we put the search on hold and went on with our lives.

Leah found a good job designing and selling jewelry on Madison Avenue in Manhattan, and left Brooklyn to live on her own in a tiny apartment nearby, on the Upper East Side, independent, but lonely.

We saw each other, usually for dinner, whenever Rosa and I were in New York City, in between concert tours. Rob was traveling with a variety of girl friends a good deal of the time, and I think the three of us gratefully gave him and his life's navigations a wide berth.

Chapter Seven

Soon after, I got a phone call from a man named Maximillian, who told me we were related. My grandmother and his grandfather were sister and brother. He had grown up in Argentina and was trying to make contact and explore family he'd heard about from his parents. I had only heard tidbits when I was younger about those relatives who lived in South America. They had immigrated there when other countries, including the United States, had turned them away as they tried to escape from Hitler and his murderous policies.

"I am making a family genealogy. It will include the Argentine, American, Canadian, and European families, and everyone in your family that you know of and don't know of," he informed me in a heavily accented voice. "There is going to be a family reunion in Florida in a few months, for as many relatives I can find. Do you want to go to this?" I refused the invitation, but agreed to answer his questions to the best of my ability, about myself, and my family. He was endlessly inquisitive and could not seem to get enough information no matter how much I said in our too–long phone conversations. He asked about the family circle organization my father had founded after his youngest brother Arnold had died in 1936. He wanted to know all about everyone and everything.

"Tell me about your grandmother, who was my aunt," he asked.

"She was formidable," I answered. "She died when I was a kid."

"Well, what did she look like, what did she do? Did you like her, was she nice to you?" He pressed his questions one after the other.

"Max," (Maximillian was too big a mouthful I had decided,) "I don't really remember her, except that she was always reading and didn't want to be disturbed when she had a book in her hands. She scared me, I kept my distance."

"That's good, tell me more," he urged.

"She had a big bosom, I thought she would smother me once."

"What happened," Max persisted. He was absolutely insatiable, so I resigned myself to his questioning.

"My dad wanted to take a photo of me and his mother, and he kept urging me to get closer to my grandmother. Really, I didn't want to, but the next minute she swept me into her arms and held me so close I almost couldn't breathe. That's how I knew about her bosom." I laughed at the memory and Max chuckled. "I still have that picture. It's sweet."

"So you did like her, Cara, didn't you?"

"I liked that she read so much, just the way I did, and still do." I paused. "And I liked all the jewelry she wore, gold chains, pearls, and a fancy watch on a fob with diamonds, always pinned to her clothes." I surprised myself with how much I could remember, as I waited for the next question.

"Tell me about the family circle your father started," he said, as he charged ahead with his endless inquiry. "Tell me about Arnold?"

"But Maximillian," I whined, separating the four syllables of his long name, "I don't know much about those relatives." My life as a student and musician kept me apart from the family my father had sought out, or at least that was my rationale. My Dad, while he lived, never stopped searching, investigating, and tracking down every possible relative, embracing them into his beloved family circle.

The truth was, my lifestyle was private to me, and even my parents and younger sisters did not know at that time that I was a lesbian. During the years Max was asking about, I felt uncomfortable with relatives I had no relationship with, and I barely had any contact with them. Aunt Marya and my cousin Rob were my closest family, other than my sisters. They all knew Rosa and liked her, as did my parents, when they were alive. When they met Rosa, they met my "best friend." Of course Rosa and I eventually came out to them gently, when the moment was right. I was so happy that my parents knew and loved Rosa before their deaths, as did my sisters, Aunt Marya, and Leah. Rob seemed grateful to us for the loving relationship we had with his daughter.

"Tell me more about Arnold and your father," Max poked. He never gave up, so I did, eventually.

"I do know that Arnold was Dad's youngest brother. He died after a tooth extraction when I was a little girl. I wouldn't go to a dentist for some time after that. My father was very upset, not about me not going to the dentist, but about his brother. That's all I remember."

"What else did your father say?" Max pushed. I pulled up a memory of a conversation with my dad at one of our oyster-eating contest dinners, which he always won. He could eat three-dozen Blue Points at a sitting.

"Well, Max, when I asked my father why he was so relentless in his search for relatives, he answered my question, his voice breaking every few words.

"We have lost so many relatives to Hitler and his camps, I must find the ones who are left. I lost my sisters, their husbands and children in that terrible war—cousins, uncles, aunts, so many with whom I share blood and history—it is my duty to find whoever is left." Dad wiped his red-rimmed eyes and continued, "I saved my sister Marya and her husband and children, but they weren't enough, there were so many others." I could hear Max crying softly at the other end of the line.

"Max, I had never seen my father cry. I just sat there motionless, in front of him, moved to deep respect." Max was now silent. I said to him quietly, "At that moment, I loved my Dad as I never had before."

"Your father was a wise man," Max said. "Thank you, Cara. Now I know my uncle."

Other than my immediate family, whom I saw infrequently, except for holidays and special events, I had not been involved with cousins who seemed to be scattered everywhere. I simply had no interest in them. This Maximillian person seemed intent on digging up every relative, just as my father had been. In fact, Max had found the family cemetery plot with its Reunited Cousins in Memory of

Arnold name chiseled into the stone arched entrance. The family had bought the gravesite so they could all be buried together, no diaspora after death for them. Max had unending questions about the occupants.

"I don't know where my grandparents lived in Hartford. I don't know where they're buried. I don't know, I can't remember, I've got no time for this," I moaned. I needed to practice, to clean my kitchen, to watch the news. Go away, I thought.

Max persisted. He phoned or wrote every day. He asked me to fill out questionnaires and information sheets, which I did reluctantly, but as well as I could. Max went to the family cemetery plot on Long Island to collect names from the tombstones. He went to Hartford looking for my grandparents' home and graves. The man was obsessed. He was driving me crazy.

Rosa and I were preparing a major program of music by women composers for our next tour, and we were researching and practicing many hours a day. There was no room in my head to think of information for this persistent Max person. I had to turn him over to some other relatives.

"Max, I have a great idea," I told him. "Come to Rosa's July 10th birthday party at our Long Island house next week." He started to accept before I could tell him the details. I went on anyway. "My sisters and their families will be there making it a sort of family gathering." I had put Max in touch with my much younger sisters early on, and they had spoken with him at length, as they later complained to me.

Max kept repeating like a mantra, "I'll be there, I'll come," even as I kept talking. It made me laugh, and he joined me with an unexpectedly deep guffaw.

I had done this party almost every year since Rosa and I were together. Not having children of my own, this was a way of keeping in touch with my nieces and nephews.

Rosa and I had, in addition to our apartment in Manhattan, a beach house on Long Island's North shore that was party perfect, and where, best of all, there were excellent caterers.

"I'll invite a couple of cousins who live not too far from us, and you can interview everyone to your heart's content."

Max accepted again. For him, using the computer for his investigations was not enough. He said he loved meeting relatives and talking with them in person. Actually, I was looking forward to meeting him. He was such an oddball.

Saturday, there was a large tent set up facing the Sound and thankfully, a cool breeze had just come up. There were 24 family members here. I was amazed at how our little family had grown. I had a nice feeling of pride and pleasure as I saw the children settling in to watch the magician I had hired for the occasion.

Max arrived early. He was dressed in a seersucker suit that was way too big for him. He looked really cute and very boyish wearing a bow tie and a vest over his long–sleeved starched white shirt, but he must have been roasting on this bright and hot July day. Max had more books, papers, and photos with him than we needed or wanted to see. He was taking pictures furiously. He was asking questions tirelessly.

He was everywhere, a small, scurrying man constantly underfoot. He looked like a tango dancer with black hair slicked back from his forehead with gel. Actually, I thought he was adorable. FI was getting fond of my cousin Max. He was really charming and bright. I'd never known anyone quite like him.

My middle sister, Gigi, was somewhat annoyed. "Who invited him?" she asked angrily. "Honestly, Cara, we didn't need to have total strangers here at our special gathering." Uh–oh, I thought, me big sister, bad again, well, nothing new.

My youngest sister Felicity, thought Max was fabulous, as I did. "How great that you have him and the other cousins here," she praised. I smiled gratefully, as did Rosa. We knew our Gigi would come around, just as she always did.

Within the next months, Maximillian found my grandparents' graves, the name of the ship they came on from England, medical records showing the causes of their deaths, and copies of their passports, including the photos. I recognized my grandma, the generous bosom well in evidence, even in the typically poor pictures from long ago. Max also told us about our grandmother's secret second husband, a total surprise to us all.

"That must be the man we always saw leaving the house as we arrived for a visit to Grandma. He'd look at us and smile, and then would be gone."

"Why would he do that?" my sisters asked in unison. They often spoke in tandem, as they were only a year apart in age.

"I guess Grandma didn't want us to know she had married again," I mused. "She must have been ashamed." Another family secret, I thought.

I was mostly thrilled with Max's discoveries. I had told him all I knew about Aunt Marya, Rob, and Rachel, and I had given him Leah's phone number. I suppose I should have worried about his finding out how neglectful I'd been to Rachel, as he did tend to moralize at times. But come what may, I thought, I was not going to be apprehensive. Go Maximillian, go, I urged.

Heaven knew what he thought about me and Rosa, but I'm not sure he even got that we were a couple. He was single, so Rosa decided he was probably gay. She thought everyone who was not married, was. My Rosa, is a Rosa, is a....

I put it all out of my mind as best as I could, and examined the documentation of all his findings, and some wonderful family photos taken at the Florida reunion. The pictures of the huge family gathering came with lists of names, how they were related to us, and where they lived. There were more copies of death certificates of my grandparents, and the hospital reports. He'd also found their wills, and I was touched to find my grandmother had left me her gold fob watch with the crescent moon of diamonds. Where was it? I was amazed and moved by his zeal and accomplishment. I was overwhelmed by his intensity. I shoved my guilt about Rachel in a drawer in my mind, closed it, and concentrated on my music.

Chapter Eight

More than a year later, I was surprised by a call from Leah, whom I hadn't seen since I'd been at her second wedding, although we spoke often. Her first marriage was a sad story. At that time, her jewelry making was very successful, she said she was dating a "sweet guy," and had good friends. She seemed to be in good shape then, but when she told me she and the sweet guy had eloped, I was shocked. This brief first marriage had been hastily arranged when she found out she was pregnant with twins. Her boyfriend was a young man she had met in Brooklyn in a jewelry–making class. Neither of them had ever had a relationship other than casual dating; sex was a new experience for them. He was a devout Catholic, a principled person who was struggling with his attraction to men. He had confessed this to Leah, and they had tried to have a satisfying sexual relationship. The young couple loved each other, but the relationship was hopeless. Their lovemaking attempts only convinced him more than ever that he was gay. When Leah became pregnant after their first real intercourse effort, perhaps due to his fumbling with a condom, he insisted that they get married so he could "do the right thing." Shortly after the twin girls were born, their father was killed in a car accident. Leah was devastated and heartbroken that he would never know his children, or they their father. Leah missed her grandma Marya, who would have come to help with the babies, as she had done for Leah when she was a baby. Leah had named one of the girls Mara, and the other, CaraRose.

Rosa and I helped financially as best as we could. Leah needed us now more than ever, and as we were the two grand-godmothers, we were with her as much as possible. Leah continued her jewelry–making business, which she did in her home, and was successful with her career and with motherhood. Rosa and I were so proud of her courage and determination to be a strong single mother.

Rob had been strangely angry with Leah when she became pregnant. He had the temerity to say to me, "Like mother, like daughter." I told him he was a perfect shit, and I was ashamed of him. He did help his daughter financially after her husband died, but continued on his mission to seduce as many women as he could and marry whoever said yes. He was not the ideal grandfather, to say the least, but CaraRose and Mara had Leah, Rosa, and me, and we doted on them.

Leah and her second husband, Dan, lived in Phoenix with their large family, which included his and her children from their first marriages, her twins, his three, and their daughter Jamie, with whom she had been pregnant at their wedding.

This time, things were different, but better. She and Dan were "madly in love," she told me, and had decided not to use any contraceptives, and if she got pregnant, they would get married.

"We were having so much fun, and such good sex, it became a game with us," she confided to me in a phone call, "and that's how we knew we were perfect for each other." Dan was a fine man with whom she had gone to school in Arizona. Back together in Arizona, they seemed blissfully happy, which was lots more than I could ever say about her father and his wives.

Her father came to her second wedding with a slinky blonde woman who was wearing makeup on top of makeup, a dog collar around her neck, and black leather bracelets and anklets with prongs of metal sticking up threateningly. She wore leather pants that seemed to be her skin, and a see–through tank top decorated with black sequins covering her nipples. She was quite a sight, and Rosa and I couldn't believe our eyes. Rob wore his sequined socks to match. Her name was Jane. I suppose he was Tarzan.

Leah and I had a big laugh remembering the pair, and then went on with our weekly phone conversation.

"Do you know someone named Maximillian?" she asked timidly. "I think you told him how to get in touch with me." I said I did and had, and that he was our cousin. "He came to Phoenix to speak to me and some other relatives, to get information for his work on our family history," she said, and was silent. I waited. I was ready for what was coming.

Leah finally went on, her voice stronger now. "He was so nice. Maximillian told me about your big party for Rosa on Long Island that he went to. He really likes you a lot, Cara, he liked the whole family, except for one of your sisters," she added.

"Hmmmm," I responded carefully, and left the subject.

"I told him everything I could. I didn't have lots of answers for him, but he was nice and we had a good talk together. He told me he had located your grandparents' graves, and lots of other things about them. And he asked me if there was anything he could do for me."

"Those are your great-grandparents, he was talking about," I added, then carefully asked, "Did you ask him to do anything for you?"

"I asked him if he could find out where my mother was buried, and something about the last years of her life. He said he would try. What do you think?"

"If anyone can do it, he will," I answered, and the drawer of Rachel guilt opened wide.

Two months later, the second call came from Leah on the subject of Rachel. She was breathless with excitement. "Maximillian says he's found her. She's alive. Can you believe it? I'm so excited, my own mother, I'm so happy, Cara. I knew Dad lied to me. I told you so. Why did he, how could he?"

I did not, could not answer her. But she went on like an express train making no stops.

"She's in a residence for, you know, disturbed people, in Far Rockaway, wherever that is. Maximillian even went to see her. I've spoken with Vera Block, her social worker. She tells me my mother remembers me. How could a schizophrenic with a frontal lobotomy remember her child after all these years? She only saw me as a baby. She calls me Leah Joan." I had forgotten that Leah had a middle name. "That's me, I am Leah Joan," her laughter ended in a sob. "I'm going to see her next week. Can you come with me, please Cara, please darling

Cara, and Rosa to the," she paused, then went on, "home? To see my mother?"

At that moment I was sixteen again, and Leah a baby, my baby. I hugged the phone trying to get closer to Leah, and pulled myself together to respond. "Of course, sweetheart, of course I will, and Rosa too."

I immediately got in touch with Mrs. Block and made the arrangements. I was completely engaged with this drama, elated but apprehensive. I suppose I never really wondered if Rachel was still alive. In my gut, I knew she was not dead. I certainly did not do much to find her, and I never believed anything Rob told Leah about her mother. I knew better. Didn't I imagine that Rachel and Leah would somehow meet someday, didn't I see the scene of them embracing one another, mother and daughter? Why did I never do anything to make it happen? What was I afraid of? Why? Was cowardice my only answer, or did I want Leah for my own?

Chapter Nine

Far Rockaway was a marvel. It was teeming with African and Caribbean-Americans, Latin-Americans, and ultra-orthodox Jews. The Jewish men had curled sideburns—peyis and beards, and the Jewish women wore sheitels—wigs. There were lots of children everywhere. The streets were filled with all kinds of Haitian herb shops, and religious Jewish schools and stores to buy menorah lamps, tallis prayer shawls, and beches, the silver wine cups for blessings. The Golden Years Center was one of several institutional buildings on the block.

Leah and her husband Dan were standing on a corner, trying to get across a street with no traffic lights and unending rows of cars lined up bumper to bumper, horns blaring warnings. Dan was a very tall, probably 6'6". He was a handsome man, whose Irish good looks were noticeable, probably because of his height, even in this hodgepodge of humanity we were surrounded by. Rosa and Max had decided not to come, thinking that too many people, all at one time, would not be good. Mrs. Block had agreed.

"Hello Leah darlin'," I chirped cheerfully. "Hi Dan, it's been a long time, almost a year at least," I babbled, looking up at his smiling face, then bending down to embrace his petite wife. I had been completely involved with my own life, teaching, performing, and traveling with my honey. Dan and Leah had slipped a little from my existence, except for our phone calls and emails. We stood there awkwardly, feeling like aliens among so many strangers, then hugging and kissing more warmly a second time. Dan shepherded us across the street, holding up a hand to stop the traffic. Much to my surprise, it did. We crossed and stood on the crowded street staring at one another. We were not sure what to do next.

"I'm ready," Leah announced, after squaring her shoulders and exhaling noisily. "Let's go find my mother." We followed her into the shabby brick building, took the elevator to the third floor, and walked into the office. "We'd like to see Vera Block, Rachel Baum's social worker. She's expecting us." I took Leah's hand.

Mrs. Block was a very large woman with dyed black hair that she wore wild and curly. At first I thought it was a wig, like the religious Jewish women wore, but it really was her hair. She welcomed us with a pleasant smile, explained that Rachel was across the street at Happy Hours, the adult day care program where she spent every day. Mrs. Block would take us there.

"Now don't expect too much, dear," she said in a somewhat unctuous tone, as she took Leah's arm, "your mother is an old, sick lady, and she gets mixed up. She probably won't know who you are, so don't be disappointed."

Leah turned to find Dan and took his hand, without saying a word to the woman.

"And Rachel is hard to understand, her words get funny, but she's harmless." I saw Leah's grip tighten on her husband's hand, but she didn't respond. I felt nothing but admiration for her self–control, and love for her, my Leah.

Mrs. Block walked us through the traffic without concern, without raising a hand, just marching in front of the cars like a general leading troops.

After a long wait in the lounge at Happy Hours, Mrs. Block led Leah's mother to where we sat. Rachel was a tiny woman in a gray coat with gray hair and a gray complexion. I thought she looked frightened and worried at the same time. She bore no resemblance at all to the pretty young woman I had once known.

Leah released my hand and Dan's and stood to meet her mother. She spoke to her in a warm and gentle voice. "It's me, it's Leah Joan. I'm here." She held out her hand.

The little gray woman took Leah's hand in hers and looked up at her with searching eyes. She smiled a sweet toothless smile that had a child's careful but trusting look.

"I always knew you would come. I was waiting for you a long time," Rachel said quietly, in a childlike voice. Her speech was unclear and halting, as though she was searching for the right words. The two women sat down on a red vinyl couch, still holding hands. Leah's face was shining with tears. Her mother sat motionless, waiting. Dan and I stood back to give them space.

Happy Hours was a dismal place. I saw no windows, which accounted for the lack of any fresh air. The room we were in smelled of dryness, of age. The noise was a cacophony of shrill, complaining voices, and things being dropped or perhaps thrown. Here and there was the sound of shuffling. Everyone shuffled as they came and went.

I could hardly breathe. My heart was beating so fast that I thought it would jump right out of my chest. I knew my ears were hot, beet red. I could feel them pulsating, like they always did when my blood pressure went sky high. I watched and waited, as though this was an event I had waited for all my life. This was happening, I thought, at last, it was really happening.

"Thank you, Max," I whispered to myself. "Where are you, Rob? You should be here," I mouthed silently. I remembered their wedding, the frightened young woman in her white gown with a tiara slightly askew on her hair, walking down the aisle, tripping on the carpet for a moment and clutching my father's arm for balance. I was already at the altar when she approached, I saw the tears glistening under her veil, and I thought she was crying because her parents were not there, alive, to see her married. Now I know they were not tears of happiness, but of fear.

"What shall I call you?" Leah asked gently. "Do you want me to call you Rachel, or Mother, or Mom?" Dan and I stood a bit closer, marveling at the soft sweetness Leah had for her mother, this woman who needed her daughter's love and care, who could not be a mother to her daughter, and never had been.

"Call me MaMa. That's what I call my mother." Rachel smiled her sad, sweet, closed–lips smile again. We moved forward to join them and Leah introduced us.

"This is Dan, my husband, and this is my cousin Cara."

"Oh, Cara from Brooklyn," Rachel greeted me, with an open, toothless grin.

"Yes, Cara from Brooklyn. How are you, Rachel?" I asked hoarsely, choking on the words, for lack of anything better to say. I was amazed that she seemed to remember me.

"Okay, I'm okay. This is Leah Joan. She is not a baby anymore."

I swallowed hard and choked back my tears. Oh Rachel, where have you been? Where have I been? All these lost years.

Eventually, we made our way to the Starlight Diner for lunch. Rachel carried a worn black fake leather bag that seemed to be filled with packs of cigarettes. She took one out, and Dan lit it for her. She inhaled deeply and coughed. Leah asked what she would like for lunch. We were not sure Rachel could read the menu. Without hesitation, Rachel asked for a shrimp cocktail, of all things. Where had she learned about that unlikely dish? Certainly not in the group home where she was living. She ate a shrimp with her fingers, gumming it quickly.

"Why don't you wear your teeth, MaMa?" Leah asked, like a daughter who knew all her mother's foibles.

"Because they hurt me," Rachel replied, frantically shoving another shrimp into her mouth. This one got caught in her throat, but she managed to cough it up. Worried at her frantic attack on food, I thought I might have to do the Heimlich maneuver before this lunch was over. Mrs. Block had warned that Rachel ate too quickly and frequently choked on her food. I was ready for anything and was too watchful to eat my grilled cheese sandwich. Rachel took half of my sandwich and tasted it, putting aside the remaining shrimp, finished my grilled cheese happily. Leah watched over her mother carefully, their mother-daughter roles reversed, Leah now the caretaker of this elderly woman.

Back at the Golden Years Center, we looked at photographs Leah and I had brought, and some sent by Maximillian from other family members.

"That's me," Rachel said, pointing at the bride in the wedding picture. "And that's Marya and Evvy and Ed," accurately naming my aunt and cousins. "You're not in this picture, Leah Joan."

"That's because I wasn't born yet," Leah explained. "This is the picture taken at your wedding. Do you know who this man is?" Leah asked, pointing at her father.

"Oh sure, that's José Morales. We had seventeen children. But he went away," she said unconcernedly. She remembered everyone, even a cousin from Canada. She remembered everyone except the man she had married. She had done away with him completely, replaced Rob with a make-believe man who could do her no harm, who had just given her made–up babies to make up for the real baby she had lost. Who could blame her?

Rachel was obviously tired, but her expression was triumphant. Leah was drained of energy and emotion. She leaned on her husband, and he supported her as she said goodbye to her mother.

Rachel accepted the hug from Leah, and turned from the kiss, which she was not ready for.

"You come back, Leah Joan. Please." She seemed quite rational.

"I'll be here, MaMa. Yes, I will."

Rachel smiled and this time leaned forward to kiss her daughter. Now she was ready, her Leah Joan was back.

Chapter Ten

We met Maximillian for dinner at a favorite restaurant in Manhattan, where Rosa and I often ate. She was an ardent vegan, and I a gluten-free vegetarian. Max was kosher. This time Rosa decided to come along. She said it was to be with everyone, but I think she couldn't resist the food. The Very Veggie was small and quiet, filled with greenery, walls covered with work by neighborhood artists, with quiet classical music playing.

Max came armed with more photos, documents, and a large binder in which he had organized all the material concerning our family that he had found so far. It was, as young people would say, awesome. When I could interrupt Max's beginning speech—before he had started his entire recitation—before we all sat down—before I could greet everyone—and before we could even look at the menus—Rosa explained what all the dishes were made of and how they tasted. At last we were able to order beverages and food. Rosa rolled her eyes at me, smiled and dug into a roll made from fava and garbanzo bean flour.

Max began to speak again, from exactly where he had left off, to fill in the details about Rachel's parents, her brother, and how she and her cousin had been rescued.

We listened attentively to him tell the terrible tale as he knew it, although I had learned some of the details from Rachel's cousin Barbara, when I had met her years ago. Max spoke about the terrible time Rachel's family had endured in the camps, how her parents had finally died in Auschwitz, part of the six million murdered. Leah crumpled into her husband's arms, and stuffed her fingers into her ears so she wouldn't hear. After a minute, she sat up, clasped her hands, and bravely paid attention. I had never seen her react with so much melodrama, but she had been through such a range of emotions this day, I thought it was a good thing.

Rachel's younger brother and cousins were sent to work camps, where they had been shot and killed when trying to escape. Her cousin's parents were cruelly split up and sent to other camps where older Jews ended up in the ovens, all part of those who had perished. Max kept repeating the phrase, all part of the six million Jews, after each sentence, like a mantra, making his recitation a terrible rondo. His extensive research had provided him, with amazing accuracy, details about the family members, augmented by conferring with the Holocaust Museums in Washington, D.C., and in Israel.

"It is important that we know how our families spent their last days, so we can honor and respect their dignity," Max said, with his head and hands held high. "And we must remember and tell the story over and over to new generations, so it can never happen again, never again." He wiped his eyes with his napkin.

Leah reached for his hand. "Thank you, cousin Maximillian."

Max had a very different story to tell about his and his family's escape from certain annihilation to Argentina. He had not been torn from his parent's arms, like so many other children. He traveled a circuitous route with his family, and, with the money and jewelry they had safely hidden among their possessions, they had found safe haven.

"I am compelled to tell this saga of our escape from Germany, again and again," he spoke gravely. As he began to speak, we all sat stiffly in place, unable to eat or drink, while he began to recite his story with every detail.

Rosa sat, stunned, and reached for my hand, which she held on to tightly. My sweetheart, sensitive and practical as usual, and concerned about Leah, tried to lighten the atmosphere, and, in her gentle voice, said, "This is very hard for all of you, I know, but why don't we just try the soup while it's still hot, or my friend, the chef, his feelings will be very hurt. We can have privacy to talk more in Cara's and my apartment that's just around the corner. I baked some pastries to have with tea or coffee," and then she blew to cool the spoon of soup and swallowed.

"Pastries fit for every special food restriction, I'm sure," I added, squeezing Rosa's hand in gratitude. Everyone warmed to the suggestion, and slowly began to eat. Max did not continue the conversation, nodded, and began to hungrily spoon his vegetable soup. We all followed his lead, grateful for the delicious food, and, I hoped, for our good fortune in having it. Conversation at the table was about Leah's children, and the eagerly anticipated meeting with their grandmother at the Golden Years, a more joyful subject.

In our apartment, with tea and Rosa's array of assorted rugelach, we waited for Maximillian to tell what was probably the most important happening in his life, that drove him to find every possible family member he could, to find every survivor and every survivor's children. He reminded me of my father. They even looked alike. We listened to his amazing story and marveled at his courage.

HIAS, the same organization that had found a home for Rachel and Barbara, and many displaced Jewish emigrees, had placed Max and his parents with friends in Argentina, who had wisely left Germany earlier. The long time friends were eager to give Max's family a safe home. This was very different from Susan, the reluctant relative, whom HIAS had found in Brooklyn for Rachel and Barbara to live with. Understandably, Susan was unsure and worried about the responsibility when she accepted the two young girls, but eventually grew to love them.

Max was sad when he told us how he, only ten years old, and his beloved parents, had left behind most of their friends and almost all of their belongings. "But think how lucky we were to have our lives," he declared.

"Imagine," I said, "this little boy, traveling far to people he'd never met, who spoke a language he had never heard. They must have been very wonderful people to have given our Max and his parents a welcoming home."

Max smiled when he spoke about the kind and caring foster family who had been friends of his mother as long as he could remember, exchanging letters written in German, their common language. The women had been schoolmates in Germany, and one of them moved with her husband and children to Argentina, when the National Socialist Party in Germany had begun to rise. Although they were not Jews, they did not like what was happening in their country and left.

Max's family opened an antiques and jewelry business, bought a home, and had a comfortable life. Eventually, Max managed the fine arts department of the business, and was very successful with paintings and sculpture in the gallery he ran, thanks to the good education in the arts his family had provided. But he yearned to get to America and find the relatives his parents spoke of. His parents still mourned for who and what they had left behind, and spoke of them often.

"One day," Max remembered, "I asked my mother what her name was before she got married. She had to think for a moment and then smiled with the memory as she said, "Weber, yes, Maxie, my name when I was born was Frieda Weber." Once he had awakened her memory, she told her son, "And my brother Alfred Weber lives in Mexico City. Is that far from here, from Argentina?" Her knowledge of geography was painfully sparse, and she had to learn from her young son.

"That's all I needed," Max said, "and my research began in earnest. I was off and away, and here I am, with family."

The conversation turned to Rachel, and we talked about her life when she first came to America with her cousin Barbara. I told what little I could, and Max added details from his research. Of course, he knew more than I did about Rachel's early days in New York.

We knew Rachel and her cousin Barbara gratefully lived with Susan, the distant cousin of Rachel's mother, whom HIAS had found in Brooklyn. This young woman had given them a home until they could be on their own. The arrangement had turned out quite well: the girls had gotten along well with the cousin. Susan's parents had died within six months of each other when she was 18, and she had left her home in New Jersey to attend Brooklyn College and start her life in a new place. She had a comfortable one bedroom apartment near the school, and the insurance money her parents had left her took care of her expenses. HIAS, and other organizations which raised money to help the refugees, contributed monthly towards Rachel and Barbara's support, which was helpful to Susan. 22 years old, after graduating from Brooklyn College, Susan had an interesting job in Administration at the college. With the funding she received for the girls, they managed. When Rachel and Barbara finished high school, they were ready to find jobs and be independent. Susan urged Barbara to visit The Single Survivors' Club where Barbara met, and, in a matter of months, married her husband. Rachel met Rob at the Club the first time she went there, with an even quicker outcome.

Susan had urged Rachel to marry Rob, most likely because she needed Rachel's bedroom. Her baby had been born recently, and Rachel felt pressure to leave the household where there was a newborn baby and an impatient husband who clearly wanted her gone.

Sadly, Rachel's cousins Barbara and Susan, with whom she had first lived, had no further contact with Rachel after they were told about her mental illness. Maximillian offered to put Leah in touch with them if she wished. She told him she would think about it, but never raised the issue again. Leah had no interest in seeing the two women, her mother's only relatives, who had abandoned her when Rachel needed them most.

After the family left, when Rosa and I were clearing the living room and kitchen, I turned and said, "The hell with this, it can wait until tomorrow. Let's go to bed."

Rosa turned to me after wrapping the leftover pastries. "I love you, Cara mia," and kissed me, hard. "What a family, what a story, you ought to write a book."

"No way," I said firmly. "I'm too old."

"Me, too," said Rosa.

Truth is, we were well on our way to senior-hood.

Chapter Eleven

Leah was so exhausted she probably fell asleep as soon as her head touched the pillow. I knew this day had been more than exciting: it had been almost unbearable, a mixture of joy and sadness that was painful for us all. When I passed their room, the door slightly open, I heard whimpering and sighs from Leah as she slept. I knew Dan would soothe her with what Leah had called butterflies since she was a little girl. He would gently stroke her back with light swirling touches, as Aunt Marya and I had done, which usually calmed her. She was not a good sleeper and frequently had nightmares. After a while, she seemed to sleep quietly, and I returned to my bed.

I was awakened by heartbreaking cries from the guest room and rushed out to see what was wrong, with Rosa closely following. Leah was sitting up, wild-eyed, in bed with Dan holding her.

"It was a dream, sweetheart, just a dream," he soothed.

"No, I was there, it was real," and she sobbed and shook in his arms.

I did what I had been told to do when she was little—I asked her to tell us what she remembered of her dream. She was quiet for a few minutes and then began to speak in a shaky voice.

I am on a long line behind muttie and popa and brudder it is cold and I do not have my coat or shoes anymore

Leah shivered in her blanket.

where am I who are all these people I start to cry muttie turns and says sha mein kind mein shayne tochter wein nicht a man in a brown uniform is yelling at them his mouth enormous and filled with pointed yellow teeth I am very frightened and I am shaking so hard I can hardly stand what is happening to us now everyone is weeping soundlessly everyone is afraid my brother is sick and he can't stop coughing the man shouts at him and pulls him off the line and puts him on another one my muttie screams and papa goes to get my brother the terrible man hits my papa with his whip muttie screams and screams and screams my screams get stuck in my throat then muttie and and papa and brudder are all on the other line and maximillian comes and holds me and covers my mouth gently and I call for muttie and papa and brudder they are gone where have they gone there is a big hole and people are in it they have no clothes on they are crying and reaching their hands out for help but there is no one to help them get out of the big hole begging for something

Leah turned and looked at each of us, imploring, asking for something we do not have to give.

I see my mother and father and brother reaching out asking me to get them out of the hole and I try to go to them to get them out but maximillian says nein nein nein

"Nein nein nein," Leah said in a dry voice, "I never could help them, I never did, never did." I gave her the cup of chamomile tea Rosa had gone to the kitchen to make, and Leah whispered, "thank you."

When Leah, Dan, Rosa, Max and I visited Rachel the next day, I tried speaking German with her. She was still fluent in her original language and was amused at my efforts, covering her toothless smile with her hand. It was difficult to understand her in any language because she would not wear her teeth. Leah again tried to encourage her mother to wear them, but she adamantly refused. I suggested to Max that we investigate dental possibilities for Rachel. Maybe it was possible to arrange for her to have false teeth that would not hurt.

Thankfully, lunch had become simpler, grilled cheese and coffee for everyone at the corner deli. Rachel decided she wanted to eat what we were all having, a grilled cheese sandwich with bacon. When Rachel chose to add the bacon, it became her favorite sandwich. It was a lot safer than shrimp cocktail.

"Do you get bacon for breakfast, Rachel?" I asked, curious as to why she wanted bacon in her sandwich.

"Oh no, no bacon there. But José Morales used to make it for me every morning. And for all our children, too." Her eyes misted over at the memory.

Leah, Dan, Max and I visited Rachel every day for the week Leah was in town. Max and I did not go for the last day so Leah would have time alone with Rachel. We felt secure about doing that because Dan watched over her, a clichéd tower of strength. After they returned to Phoenix, Max and I decided we would see Rachel separately, each rotating every six weeks or so. Leah, Dan, and perhaps two of Leah's children would be back in the summer to meet their grandmother, but that was a big maybe.

"Do you think I should try to move my mother to a place in Phoenix so it would be easier to see her, and she would have a whole family to visit on a regular basis?" Leah asked me at the airport.

"Of course, that would be so much easier for you, and she would adapt eventually," I reassured, not at all sure of myself. "As long as she has you and her cigarettes, she'll probably be fine." Leah looked worried. "Why don't you start looking around in your area, find a few possibilities. Send her pictures of nice facilities. Talk to her about it in your weekly phone calls. Get her used to the idea." I pulled suggestions out of thin air, not having any expertise or experience, but offering advice anyhow. Leah seemed comforted.

Chapter Twelve

Rachel was now at least 78 years old. She had chronic bronchitis, heart and lung disease, diabetes and Hepatitis C, which she had probably gotten in a hospital from transfusions, a doctor said. She seemed afraid of men and kept them at a distance. She had been young and pretty when she was first institutionalized, before the surgery. Her daughter strongly resembled the young Rachel. Who knew what horrors had happened in all those years Rachel had spent in mental hospitals and group homes? She bought three packs of cigarettes a day with the money from her disability allowance, plus what Leah and I gave her, and shared the tobacco bounty with her friends on the smoking balcony at Golden Years. She smoked a fair amount herself, taking quick little puffs in rapid succession, lips pursed around the cigarette, barely inhaling, but enough to further damage her already damaged lungs. This did her chronic cough no good, but the staff did not force her to give up smoking, and the doctor who saw the patients weekly did not seem to care. She poured as much sugar as was available in the sugar bowl into her coffee, unless stopped. She drank many cups of the easily available coffee throughout the day. In spite of her diabetes, the doctor did not forbid the

Lucille Field

sugar. Sometimes, if you could understand her toothless speech, she made sense. Other times, she babbled on and on.

"Just change the subject," said Ms. Block, "and she'll stop." I did, and she did.

Rachel's life at the Golden Years Center was fairly simple. She woke up in her room, got toileted and dressed, ate a breakfast of cereal, bread, hard–boiled egg, and black coffee that she sweetened generously. She took the coffee to the smoking deck, then smoked two cigarettes, and drank more coffee. The patients sat in the TV room staring at whatever the staff had turned on, and waited until it was time to go across the street to the Happy Hours Day Care, where there'd be more TV, coffee, and cigarettes. Sometimes the art therapist came in, and they'd make things like potholders, for what purpose I had no idea. For lunch, there were peanut butter sandwiches, sometimes with grape jelly, with soda to wash it down.

For the afternoon there was more of the same, and then back across the street to Golden Years to wait for dinner. Many sat on the floor in the hallways—the patients seldom spoke to one another—but sometimes squabbles and fights broke out, which the caretakers quickly squashed. No one seemed curious about the occasional visitor who might appear mainly on weekends. The group home did not have the fevered atmosphere of the institutions where I had visited Rachel years ago. There, screaming, raging, and bizarre behaviors were usual. The patients in Golden Years were lifeless, probably all their spirit had been medicated away, and without pleasure except for their cigarettes.

- 332 -

Here is what Rachel was clear about, what she knew for certain: she has a daughter whose name is Leah Joan. Leah Joan is not a baby any more. Leah Joan is pretty. She is waiting for Leah Joan to come back. She is Leah Joan's mother.

Chapter Thirteen

Iam going to see Rachel today. It has been many months since Leah, I, and the others were here that first time. Leah has a job, and she and Dan do not have much money for travel. Their house is full of children, including a couple of grands, who need them to be home. Rachel is deteriorating gradually from the woman Leah and I first saw, the woman who recognized people in the pictures we showed her, who knew her daughter, and me, Cara from Brooklyn. Time is not treating this old woman kindly, but then, it never has.

I dread going to The Golden Years Center, but I try to visit every six weeks, if I can. Golden Years indeed! It takes me more than a couple of hours to get to Far Rockaway, and the charm of the neighborhood has long since worn off. It is shabbier and dirtier with each visit, and I find the crowds of people oppressive. I have to struggle to find a parking place, and I'm never sure that the car will be where I leave it. It is better when Rosa comes with me, but usually I dissuade her from doing so. I wonder if this will be a day when Rachel is lucid enough to let me take her to lunch, or if all she wants are three cartons of cigarettes and for me to go away. Whatever, I mutter to myself.

She is wearing the flowered cotton dress I brought her last visit. Her hair is neatly combed, and her face is shining and rosy. What a surprise.

"You look very pretty today, Rachel. I like your colorful dress." She loves flowered dresses. At this compliment, she spins around and almost falls. I catch her and hug her very carefully. She still doesn't always like to be touched.

"It's my birthday," she mumbles. It sounds like, "Ish I burdy." Rachel has a birthday every time I visit because she wants a present. Why not? Actually, I've lost track of her exact age, but she must be over 80 by this time. What does it matter? I'm not so young myself any more.

"Would you like to go out to lunch for your birthday? "

She nods and pulls at my sleeve. "Prezin?" Leah asks hopefully.

"What present would you like?" I ask, knowing full well what she will answer.

"Shigret," she says with a sly look.

"Okay. But first we'll have lunch."

She pulls me toward her room on the first floor to get her coat. Even if the weather is warm, she has to wear her coat. We walk down the hallway past the chairs lined up against the wall where residents are waiting to be called into the dining room, men and women muttering, arguing, staring at nothing, two women pulling at a doll. "That's my baby," one says. The other one just pulls at the bedraggled doll. A very thin, tall man is dealing an invisible deck of cards, his legs jiggling to some soundless rhythm. Rachel has a little room to herself now. I give the manager some extra money, so he will let her keep it for as long as possible. He explains this to anyone who asks by saying that Rachel coughs so badly during the night, no one can sleep in the same room with her. So far so good, at least it's something I can do for this woman I care about. I tell him I'm taking Rachel out to lunch.

Rachel wants to show me what Leah has sent to her. As usual, there are greeting cards all over the room. I read the notes to her and she nods her head with satisfaction. Leah sends the cards regularly, calls her mother every Sunday, and visits once a year, twice if possible. She does the best she can. Dan had a severe heart attack and is not well enough to work. Rosa and I help them financially. Bringing Rachel to Arizona now seems impossible.

The luncheonette on the other corner is now Rachel's favorite place to eat. She won't go to the deli anymore, because she thinks they laugh at her. Actually, the people at the deli never do, they are quite kind to the customers who come from the local institutions. Rachel is one of many from the group homes in the area, and they are good customers. They seldom cause any trouble, and the owner warns his employees to be kind to them. But there is no point telling this to Rachel, as her paranoia rules the day.

Rachel has a new favorite lunch now—a grilled cheese sandwich without bacon, a scoop of chicken salad on iceberg lettuce, and a heavily creamed and sweetened cup of coffee. I cut the lettuce up for her, but she only eats the chicken salad. She chews, after a fashion, noisily and too fast, with me handing her napkins to wipe her mouth. She won't wear her newly acquired false teeth. I'm always afraid she'll choke because she coughs and chews at the same time. I only put down two sugars for her, but she goes to another table to take all its packages. I stop her at six. When lunch is safely over, I'm relieved.

I walk slowly while Rachel scurries to the store that sells the cigarettes she smokes. They are called Ezy Smokes, the cheapest ones available, but the brand she insists on. I buy three cartons, she takes one, and I give the other two to the manager to keep for her when she runs out.

Well, why not, it's her birthday, and I don't know when I'll be back. When we sit in the garden where smoking is allowed at her residence, she chain-smokes until I tell her I have to go. I bring her to her room, and she lets me kiss her goodbye on the cheek today. I check in with the manager to report that Rachel is back, and leave my contribution and the cartons in a desk drawer, as is our arrangement.

Tonight I will phone Leah and report on my visit. She is always grateful to hear good news about her mother. When I call, Leah sounds upset and tense.

"Dan has developed additional heart complications," she tells me, "so we won't be able to come to New York." After a long pause, she continues. "I don't know when I'll be able to see my mother again." She has never brought her twin daughters to see Rachel, even though I'd be able to get tickets with my mileage rewards. I think she feels it would upset the girls to see their grandmother. I suppose now it will never happen.

"Oh, Leah, I'm really sorry about Dan. But keep sending the cards and calling when you can. It makes your mother happy. And I'll try to get there when I can," I say reassuringly, but I'm not happy about this added responsibility.

I call Max to tell him the news.

Chapter Fourteen

Max tells me his own news. "I'm in love," he practically sings. "I'm in love, I'm in love, I'm in love with a wonderful girl," he sings.

"I believe you, Maxie dear," I try to be happy. "Tell me about her."

"She's a distant cousin, I found her when I was searching the French part of the family. Her name is Michelle, she's gorgeous, she is Parisian and Jewish. *C'est bonne, n'est-ce pas?*" Now he's crowing.

"Paris, France?" I ask weakly.

"Of course, where else could Paris be," he states emphatically.

"Paris, Texas," I say hopefully. No dice, la belle France it is.

"Now I'm on my own with Rachel," I tell Rosa later at dinner. "What shall I do?" I ask.

"Easy," answers my darling, "now we go on our big eight-week tour, and we'll worry about it when we're back. After having the biggest success of our career, perhaps our last big tour, considering our ages," she says, pouring herself another glass of wine. "Let's play this one by ear and see what happens." I hold my glass out and she fills it, as she fills me with her love.

I call Leah and tell her about our tour plans. I tell her about Maximillian. I again offer to send her money for plane fare if she wants to visit her mother, but she can't leave Dan. She will call her mother every week. She is so sorry she can't do more than call. Her children need her to help with their young children, who all live with her and Dan. I have almost forgotten that Leah is a grandmother. I promise that Rosa and I will visit when we are finished touring, and I hear her say "thank you" through her tears. I feel sad for Leah, I know she is having a hard time. I feel sadder for Rachel, she is losing her Leah Joan again.

When Rosa and I are giving a concert in San Francisco, we make a side trip to visit Leah and Dan. Dan is not well, he seems to have trouble breathing, and he is not the robust man he was when last we saw him. He has had several heart surgeries, wears a pacemaker, and spends most of his time in his recliner chair. Leah is upset because once again, she cannot locate her mother.

I have been on tour with Rosa for weeks, and Max is in Paris with Michelle, planning their wedding. Neither of us has been to see Rachel in almost two months. The manager Leah always speaks to is not working at the home any more, and the new one can't help her. He never met Rachel and has no file on her. "She must have been moved to another group home, and her file would have gone with her," he tells Leah.

Leah is frantic because she thinks that her mother has died and the home did not let her know. Max can't help. Rob is nowhere to be found, not that he would be any help. I'm not much use either. Leah doesn't want to upset Dan. "What should I do, I don't know what to do," she cries like a child.

"We will be back in New York in a week, and I will go to the home and see what I can find out," I tell Leah. "Rachel can't have died, they'd have to let you know," I assure her. "I promise you I will find out where she is." I promise what I cannot be sure of, but it seems to calm Leah.

Chapter Fifteen

Rosa and I are back home after our very successful tour. With great reviews and the sound of applause still in my ears, I get to work on my promise to Leah. I drive out to Far Rockaway to speak with the personnel who know me and had taken care of Rachel. I discover that she was hospitalized for a variety of serious ailments and did not return to Golden Years. The office staff said they could not reach me because my answering machine said I was out of town. They did not leave a message, and they did not try to call Leah because it was long distance. The management said they could call a local number but not an out-of-town number. All anyone could say was that Rachel was no longer there; she might still be in a hospital or another home; and the records had no information about any additional relatives to inform. This was unbelievable, because Leah usually called about her mother every week, but had missed a few weeks when Dan was again hospitalized. And when she finally did call, she was told her mother was no longer at Golden Years. It was like being on a combination of a crazy carousel and an out-of-control roller coaster.

When I go back to the group home in a few days, this time with Rosa who insists that "we'll get to the bottom of this," as she says in that firm voice I know so well, the manager is still totally inept. I can't believe this is happening again, but Rosa keeps me grounded. At first I think maybe Rachel really has died, which makes me feel that familiar mixture of grief, guilt, and relief. Then I am furious. How can they treat people this way? I rage at the new manager. Rosa, sweetly smiling, convinces him to make some calls, and he finally gets information from the hospital where Rachel had been taken, which he actually tracked down. They direct us to the nursing home in Rockaway for mentally ill patients where Rachel has been sent as Mrs. Morales, wrong name, lost records. I immediately call Leah with the news and tell her Rosa and I are like Holmes and Watson. She laughs lightly.

At the nursing home, the head nurse—her title, not my bad joke—tells me Rachel is completely confused and disoriented. She will not know you, Nurse Rachett (my attempt at levity) says, "Poor creature is really out of her mind." Her words. "We did not get records for Mrs. Morales, if that's who she is," the nurse informs us, and I believe her. This has been a total screw-up. Rosa and I ask to see Rachel Baum, using her correct name, hoping that will help. When we do see her, Rachel does not know me, nor do I know her, not anymore. She has shrunken to the size of an eight-year-old child. She is almost bald, and is dried– up and yellow. She does not ask for Leah Joan. She is a blank page and cannot speak. Back to square one.

Chapter Sixteen

Ido not visit Rachel for the two years she is at the nursing home, which is really a horrible psycho ward I can't bring myself to visit. The ranting and raving, the smell of urine and feces, the bizarre behaviors have all returned to the front of my memory, and I don't like it there, after I had tried so hard to push those memories back. Rachel's room for six women includes what seem to be several with obsessive-compulsive illness. One bangs her head four times against the wall, then stands and turns four times in each direction, and bangs her head again. It is relentless. Another woman tears a hair from her head and carefully lays it on her pillow, then tears another, continuing the activity over and over. Another screams the Old Mother Hubbard nursery rhyme over and over, moving her arms as if doing calisthenics. Rachel sits on her bed, not uttering a sound, just rocking.

The two times I was there, I thought I'd go mad. Now, somehow, I just can't seem to find the time, and being of "a certain age," I haven't the energy any more. Truthfully, I don't want to see Rachel "out of her mind," or those other pathetic women, either.

Max goes to see Rachel every few months, when he has to be in New York to meet with the editor of the American travel magazine he writes for in France. He tells Leah her mother is very confused, but peaceful. When I call the home, I am told Rachel is okay. Leah does not visit, but calls the facility and asks to speak to her mother. When the nurse puts Rachel on the phone, Leah is usually met with dead air as she tries to engage Rachel. Leah tries to talk to her mother every time she calls, but Rachel is unintelligible, and does not know herself or her daughter. Leah is burdened with work, grandchildren, and a very ill husband. The three of us—Max, Leah, and I, call to find out how Rachel is in three–week shifts, one of us each week. The contact gets more difficult as time passes, the calls more infrequent. Rockaway seems farther and farther away.

I send Leah an open round-trip air ticket from Phoenix to New York and tell her when we will be in New York. She wants desperately to come and see her mother. Dan is stable for the moment and encourages her to go.

"I think MaMa will know me when she sees me, Cara. I think she is waiting for me to come, just like she did for all those years." I don't say anything in response to that idea. I just tell her I will be here when she comes, if it's during the dates I have sent her, telling her when we will be in New York. Rosa and I will be waiting.

Chapter Seventeen

Leah, Rosa, and I are going to Pilgrim State Hospital on Long Island to see Rachel in the latest facility where she has been placed. The institution has opened one of its smaller buildings for severely ill mental patients, although the main ones are still closed, as they have been for many years. We call Max to tell him we are going to visit Rachel. He insists on being with us, and before we can say anything more, he buys his air ticket, and rents a limo to pick us all up at the airport so we can comfortably travel to the hospital. He will fly into JFK from Paris and join us at about the same time Leah arrives from Phoenix. He is so generous, we all benefit from his largesse. Darling man, who must tell us how perfectly wonderfully married he and Michelle are, and as often as he can. We are happy for him.

"I feel responsible for Leah and Rachel," Max tells us as we wait for Leah's plane to debark. "I am part of this situation. I found Rachel. But right now it's like standing in line waiting for something awful to happen. I have to be with you."

I want to tell him we are not in a concentration camp waiting to be chosen for work or for death. But he is a Holocaust survivor without having been in a camp, so perhaps he is always waiting for something terrible. Instead I say,

"Maxie, you have a wife and her grandchild that you love. You should be home with them. But we are so happy you are here."

"The limo is waiting outside. Is your car parked at the airport?"

"Yes, we're fine. It's wonderful that you are with us, Maxie dear," I repeat. With Max, you have to say everything at least twice, just as he does. "It means a lot to me, Rosa, and Leah." He bows like the gentleman he is. As soon as Leah arrives, we make our way to the limo, which is huge and luxurious.

During the drive, I think back to those many years ago when I first went to see Rachel in the New Jersey State Institution. She was 22–years old, young and pretty, and very ill. I was terribly sad for her, for Rob, and their baby Leah. A circle, things always happen in circles, it seems.

We have a hard time finding Rachel's room, but eventually a young Spanish man pushing a food cart takes us to the desk where a nurse gives us permission and directions to find Rachel. Leah's thin body starts to tremble, and then to shake from top to bottom. Her brown hair has wiry gray streaks, which seem to be standing on end, her skin is as white as a cloud, and her eyes seem pained and unfocused. We sit her down on the first chair we see, because her legs are barely holding her up. Leah is not the eager young woman she was those many years ago, the first time she met her mother, when she was full of high hopes and courage.

"I'm so scared, Cara. I'm scared of what I'll see, what she'll be."

"Shall I go in first, to see how things are?" Max quietly offers.

"No, just give me a minute to get calm," Leah says, taking deep breaths.

"I think we can go in together, slowly, without talking," I say, trying to offer Leah courage. We give her a paper cup of water, and after a few more breaths, Leah says she's ready to go in. Max takes her arm, and Rosa and I walk behind them into the room in pairs, Rosa holding my hand.

The institutional green room has two beds, both empty, and a large chair in the corner, near the window, which looks out on nature's greenery that somehow clashes with the green paint on the walls. A tiny figure in a blue–striped, cotton hospital gown is tightly curled up in the chair. She does not turn when we come in. When we get closer, we see that Rachel is in "soft restraints,"as they are called in hospital jargon, which tie her into the chair. She can turn her head if she wants to, but does not move when we walk almost into the room. Leah goes near and takes her hand. Rachel still does not look up to see whose hand has hers. Max pulls up a chair for Leah, and Rosa gently pulls me back toward the door.

"Let's just leave them alone, to see if…" and her voice trails away when she hears Rachel's racking cough. We stop at the door.

Max sits on the bed behind Leah and recoils at the sound of the terrible coughing. Leah does not move a muscle, she has stopped shaking, and does not take her eyes off her mother. Finally, she whispers, "It's Leah Joan, MaMa, I'm here, MaMa dearest." Rachel seems not to hear her.

We wait in our places, Max on the bed, Rosa and me by the door, Leah now on her knees alongside her mother, all of us watching, waiting. Leah leans forward and in a little louder voice repeats, "It's Leah Joan, MaMa, I'm right here, MaMa darling."

Did I see Rachel lift her head a little, the question in my mind?

"Did you see that, Cara, Rosa? I saw MaMa move her head a bit. Did you, Max?" Leah asks us all. Rosa smiles, tilts her head and barely nods yes, as Max and I do as well.

Leah turns and smiles at us, grateful for our confirmation. She speaks to her mother, saying the same things several times. Each time Rachel responds a little more. Finally she raises her tiny eyes that are barely open, to look at her daughter.

"Leah Joan," the old woman says in a barely audible voice. "Leah Joan, Leah Joan."

"Yes, MaMa, it's me, I'm here with you, MaMa." Leah unties her mother's bindings and enfolds her in her arms. The two stay that way for a long time, not speaking, not moving. We are silently weeping.

Rachel moves her lips, trying to say something. Leah holds her closer. Finally we hear, "Leah Joan, good," then Rachel falls asleep. A nurse and an orderly come in when we hit the call button. They pick Rachel up like a child and put her into bed, Leah tucks her in. We follow the nurse outside to the corridor.

"She'll sleep for a long time now. She won't eat or drink, but we'll try to give her something when she wakes."

"Did my mother say Leah Joan 'good' or 'goodbye'?" Leah asks. None of us knows the answer. It could have been either so we don't respond except with hugs and soft touches.

"Maybe Rachel meant to say both," I say. "She did know you were there with her, and that was good." Leah returns to the bed and gently kisses her mother goodbye.

Leah is worried about her husband. He does not sound right, she tells us, when she phones later that day. She calls the hospital again to ask about her mother and is told by the nurse caring for Rachel that she is in a semi-coma, and probably will not wake for a long time. If ever, I think, or do I hope? Rachel's exit line was exactly right, goodbye, *addio, l'historia e finito*, the end.

Leah decides to go home and we arrange for an overnight flight. She and Max will go to the airport together. Her small travel bag is with her, she has kept it at the ready ever since she arrived. Leah came to say goodbye to her mother, and now she is going home to Dan.

"I think my mother said goodbye to me. I think she knew I had to leave."

It is time for Leah to leave. There are no more words. I hear my inner voice as it keeps up its monologue. We hug and kiss, and I make my silent farewell to this edifice of misery. When at last, we are dropped at our own car by Max's limo, Rosa and I feel that odd mixture of relief and sadness.

A few weeks later, Dan calls to tell me that Rachel is dead. "Pilgrim State called Leah to give her the sad news," Dan says in a tired voice. "Rachel is in a funeral home, and someone in the family has to identify the body. Can you do this for Leah?"

I am flooded with guilt and relief to hear about Rachel. A circle of misery and grief for the child who survived the Holocaust, only to become a deranged woman, one of the living dead until the last years of her life, when she knew her Leah Joan.

"Of course I will, Dan," I promise, and shudder.

I call Rob, who now lives in Israel—still failing miserably at love—while obsessively avoiding making support payments to his former wives, or allowing them any access to his money, or providing for his first wife. His current paramour is an Israeli woman who speaks no English. Rob speaks no Hebrew, and so they are getting along quite well. Leah has forgiven him for his duplicity, convinced that he lied for her own good, as he has assured her many times. I instruct him to call her, and he says he will, and thanks me for calling.

Leah is a fine, strong woman, this child of survivors, loved by her family, caring devotedly for her husband. Despite my reluctance, when I speak to her, I promise I will arrange for the cremation and have the ashes sent to her. She will not have to come to New York to identify Rachel. I owe Rachel, and Leah, this much, but mostly, I love Leah, and want to do what I can for her.

Chapter Eighteen

The funeral chapel calls Friday morning to say that the body of Rachel Baum is ready for me to identify. I am still queasy, and try to see if I can worm my way out of it. "Why do I have to identify her? Hasn't the hospital done that? Or the nursing home, or...why me?"

"Because you are the only family member available, and her daughter said you would. She cannot, her husband is ill, and she will not leave him. She has faxed her permission for you to identify the body. Can you come today?"

This is serious. I can't find a way out. I'm it, but I answer, "No, absolutely not today."

"When can you come? It has to be soon. We can't do the cremation until the body is identified." He gives me the address in Rockville Center.

Damn, I don't want to do this. This is not how I want to say goodbye to Rachel. "I'll come Sunday morning at eleven, on my way to Manhattan to hear a concert." I bite my lip. I'll be fortified if Rosa is waiting for me in the car.

We pull into the parking lot of the funeral home at 10:45 AM. Rosa has put a small jar filled with Johnny Walker Black Label Scotch, and a container of lavender hand lotion on the front seat.

"I'll be out of there in a flash," I say out loud, to give myself courage.

"Are you sure you don't want me to come in with you?" Rosa asks, hoping I'll say no to her offer, but asking anyway.

"No, I mean yes, sweetheart, I'll be okay," I answer bravely.

"Go do it, tiger," she raises her fist triumphantly, and leans over to kiss me. "We'll be waiting," and she raises the Scotch up high.

I close the car door, almost smashing my finger, make sure I'm buttoned and zipped properly, take a deep breath and hold it for twenty seconds, an old trick for steadying myself. At 11:00 AM sharp, I push open the heavy glass doors and walk into Bloomberg Memorial Chapel.

The funeral director is waiting for me. A card on his lapel identifies him as George Weisman. He is wearing a black suit, a grey tie, and a solemn face. We shake hands. "I'm sorry for your loss," he intones. I wipe my hands on my jacket and mumble thanks. I look around the large lobby. It is filled with the overwhelming scent of the white lilies that are everywhere.

In my purple suit, pink blouse, and red loafers, I am the only color in the room. Mr. Weisman surveys me from top to bottom and back. He seems to be shocked. He recovers and tries to take my elbow to lead me further inside. I shake him off, square my shoulders, and take the lead to where another black suit stands inviting me through an open door.

I follow Thomas Kelly, as his lapel card names him—which puzzles me, such an unlikely name in this place—into a large chapel-like room. I stop after taking two steps in. The body is at the far end of the room in a coffin, which I wonder about for a moment. Does the coffin get cremated as well, I wonder? It is mostly covered with a blue velvet spread that has a gold Star of David embroidered on it. I hold my breath. I feel nauseated. No, Cara, I tell myself sternly. Don't.

Another black suit appears from behind the heavy blue draperies, and George walks down to the front, while Thomas stands beside me, in case I should collapse with grief, I suppose. The two black suits stand rigidly in their places alongside the body, and begin to slowly, reverently pull down the velvet cover. I shut my eyes tightly before I can see any more of that ominously descending cloth and what lies beneath.

"That's she, that's Rachel Baum," or should I have said that's her? Silly woman, I chastise myself. I turn imperiously, open my eyes, and leave the room, heading for the exit and Rosa. I can almost taste the Scotch.

"Just a moment, Cara, you have to sign some papers. Please come to the office."

"I hope this won't take very long, Mr. Weisman," I emphasize the Mr. to show I'm not pleased about his using my first name, "I'm on my way to a concert," but I know I have no choice. This time I follow him, my legs feeling like cement blocks. There is a tall pile of forms marked with yellow stickers on his desk, indicating where I have to sign the never–ending pile of papers. George pulls up a chair for me and hands me a pen from a desk drawer. In a pathetic show of control, I ignore his offer and open my bag for my own Pilot extra fine point. He checks to see that it's black or blue ink, making sure that I'm not trying to use a pen with ink that matches my shoes, I suppose.

I sign and sign while George hangs over my shoulder to make sure I'm doing it right. I don't like either him, or his pungent, funereal aftershave, so close to me. My signature gets messier and messier as I keep writing. It's a good thing I don't have to perform today, because my hand is throbbing with pain from signing what seems like a hundred papers.

There is also a bill for $5,727.00 for all the funeral expenses, which includes the costs for a coffin, and "preparation of the body," neither of which will ever be seen by anyone except closed eyes me, and the black suits. What a surprise. Again, I wonder why it includes special charges for a coffin and body that will be cremated, but I am too tired to question it and too anxious to get out of there. I write a check and ask that they send a copy of the bill marked paid in full, to Leah. Good that I had my bounce-proof checkbook with me. Thank you Morgan Stanley. Finally I arrange for Rachel's ashes to be sent to Leah in a "travel urn" by special delivery, and pay $1,818 for all this also, which along with the other bill is my final act of goodwill for Rachel. The guilt drawer is finally closed.

I race out to the car, where Rosa is outside leaning against the door looking worried, but I throw my arms around her and hug with all my strength. I wipe my hands with a Wet One, use the lavender lotion, and watch Rosa open the promised Scotch with eager anticipation of the treat to come.

"Just take a little sip, *Cara mia*, then I will take you to a beautiful spot where we will enjoy what's left." She takes the jar from me after I have a taste of the magic brew.

Rosa drives to a nearby park with a stunning view of water and gardens. There are swans swimming serenely, and when I see a black one, my favorite, I think of the lovely violin solo I have played many times in many places, in the aria written by Menotti "The Black Swan," from the opera, The Medium. I take it in with an appreciative sigh, and allow my body to relax. My darling takes two glasses from the storage space in the car and pours an equal share of scotch into each one. I raise mine in a toast. Rosa joins me.

"Rachel, I wish you peace at last." Rosa clinks her glass with mine. I down a big swallow. This is peaceful, this is right. Rachel is finally in a better place, better for everyone. Rosa and I finish our drinks after we toast, "to us." I think it is the best drink I have ever had. I play a favorite CD of Lotte Lehmann singing Strauss and Wagner *lieder*. Gorgeous. Rosa moves closer, I sing along with my shaky soprano voice. Good thing I'm a violinist. "Violin and cello, what a perfect pair," I murmur to the swans.

I am so grateful Rosa is with me. How lucky I am to have had her for so many decades, my perfect person, sweetheart of my life. I place my hand over hers for a moment, and then move it to her cheek. She smiles and speaks my name.

"Cara, my Cara."

"Rosa, my flower." We sip our drinks and Rosa pours the rest as we watch the swans. "Isolde and Tristan," I name them and we both giggle.

"Rosa," I say somewhat tentatively, "Rosa, let's go to Europe, to Italy, to France, to wherever we wander. Not to do concerts, but to have a car and go where we choose, for as long as we like, to do as we please." I look at her with a question mark.

"That's a fine idea. When shall we leave?"

"Soon as we can," I say, no question now.

Rosa nods and kisses the tip of my nose, then my lips. It's a nice kiss. It's soft but sexy. It promises a good time.

"Yes," I say, "how good it is to be alive."

"And to be in love," my Rosa adds, as she starts the car. "Let's go, we've got lots to do, but first, off to the concert, then Europe."

"And the world. I'm ready," I say, and click my seat belt on. And I am *really* ready.

Photo by Jon Nussbaum

Meet The Author

Lucille Field is Professor Emerita of Music, Brooklyn College of the City University of New York. She is a soprano who has performed worldwide, and is especially known for singing the works of women composers, one of whom is Patsy Rogers, her partner of 38 years. Professor Field is recorded by Cambria.

An 88 year–old, ardent lesbian feminist and passionate activist, Professor Field has written short stories for her own pleasure since childhood. Her book of 18 linked short stories, *On The Way To Wonderland*, was self–published with Lulu.com in 2009.

Lucille is the proud mother of Carol Elizabeth Goodman, who designed the covers for both *On The Way To Wonderland*, and for this second book, *I Want To Write Something Funny But I'm Too Sad*. She is also the doting grandmother of artist Leo Zackerly Walsh, and poet Mikael Berg.

Lucille and Patsy live on the North Fork of Long Island, New York. Their cats, Bella and Jasmina, left for cat–heaven this year, and the two women are anticipating adopting two who will choose them as their MommaCat.

February 2017
musicfield@optonline.net

CPSIA information can be obtained
at www.ICGtesting.com
Printed in the USA
FFOW03n0539290317
33983FF